FALL
OF THE
HORIZON

JESSICA J. AYALA

PRAISE FOR
FALL OF THE HORIZON

"*Fall of the Horizon* is what a fantasy reader's dreams are made of! Ayala has built an intricate world that's rich with history and fully immersive down to the last detail, complete with complex characters and a beautifully vulnerable romance."

Nicole Platania, author of *The Curse of Ophelia* series

"Hauntingly beautiful and devastatingly commanding, this heart-pounding romantasy is the first in what will be the next great high fantasy series! For fans of the morally gray love interest, this one will hit."

L.B. Divine, author of *The Prince of Snow* series

"Bursting with action, magic and sizzling romance, *Fall of the Horizon* is an epic tale sure to be adored by fantasy lovers. Ayala's starkly detailed world, rife with war and sinister dealings, is highlighted by a cast of fiercely determined characters and a wonderfully executed mystery. The ending is both satisfying and bound to leave readers longing for more."

Max Francis, author of the upcoming dark academia fantasy novel *Honor & Heresy*

"*Fall of the Horizon* brings the reader to a new world that feels like home from the first page: the incredible worldbuilding, the originality of the lore, the complexity of the characters and their stories . . . Ayala executes every aspect to perfection. An incredible first book for a very promising fantasy series."

Chiara Gala, author of *The Goddess and The Hawk* series

ALSO FROM
JESSICA J. AYALA

Of Fangs and Shadows

A NOTE TO THE READER

This book contains subject matter that might be difficult for readers such as graphic violence, emotional trauma, grief and loss, as well as sexually explicit content.

The fictional world of *The Dusk and Dawn* series is inspired by events, myths, and legends from various parts of the world. None is intended as a faithful representation of any one country or culture at any point in history.

To the women with weary souls, who carry their heartaches
through difficult battles and still blaze their own path.

THE TRUTH ABOUT MONSTERS

The truth is this,
every monster
you have met
or will ever meet,
was once a human being
with a soul
that was as soft
and light
as silk.

Someone stole
that silk from their soul
and turned them
into this.

So when you see
a monster next,
always remember this.
Do not fear
the thing before you.
Fear the thing
that created it
instead.

Nikita Gill

THE CONTINENT OF RIBERA

Realm of Elios

The High Realm, residence of the High King and the Council of Deities; new home to the archangels and deities who waged the War against the Primordials as well as to elves, shifters, and humans; member of the Aligned Realms

Realm of Ikarria

The draconic realm, residence of the ether-wielding elves as well as shifters and humans, once home to the dragons; independent from the Aligned Realms

Realm of Adrastea

The vampiric realm, original residence of the vampires; member of the Aligned Realms

Realm of Kairos

The realm of the sands, residence of the shifters, especially the jackals and the wraiths; member of the Aligned Realms

Realm of Valenzia

The guardian realm, sister kingdom to Damalis, charged to protect the Gates of Celestrea; destroyed during the War of the Skies; surviving citizens were either slaughtered by the High King or are now scattered about the Continent

Realm of Damalis

The guardian realm, sister kingdom to Valenzia, charged to protect the Gates of Celestrea; destroyed during the War; no record of surviving citizens

Realm of Celestrea

The ethereal realm, kingdom of the Primordials and original home of the deities and archangels; the Gates of Celestrea had allowed the gods to sustain the mortal world; the Gates were destroyed as a result of the War, removing any contact between the Primordials and the mortal world.

CELESTREA

◉ASHERAS

DRAGON'S
TEETH

IKARRIA

◉DAE ASARI

THE JADE SEA

THE CONTINENT OF
RIBERA

FALL

OF THE

HORIZON

PROLOGUE

Fourteen Years Ago
In the wake of the War of the Skies

The gods had lost.

Their ether, pure and abundant, had coursed from the Gates of Celestrea throughout the mortal world one last time. It had made this place. The ground that was now sodden with blood and the sky thick with ash.

It was said that the Primordials had grown careless, had abandoned the mortals they claimed to love. And so, the Continent began to decay with the hatred of its mortals. Crimes had risen, the wildlife and innocent taken advantage of.

A group of deities had advocated for more control of the Continent of Ribera to save the mortals, but the Primordials had paid them no heed. The lesser gods did the only thing they could: rebel.

They had emerged from the Gates of Celestrea with their deity armies, bringing their celestial dispute to mortality's door. It wasn't long before the Primordials pursued them. Horror followed the terrifying beasts as they clawed their way from the ethereal plane into Ribera. How the seas and skies trembled with their very presence.

Now the Gates had been destroyed, the Primordials somehow locked within.

A mystery that remained unsolved.

King Idris of Ikarria supposed it did not matter. He had fought the gods, rallied his forces to stand beside the deities as they revolted against their ethereal homeland. His kingdom was and always had been his priority and his soldiers knew it. Each of them had fought with the brutality of a dragon.

Evidence of Ikarria's victory in defending their realm was found in the blood that stained his gray armor. His white hair had fallen free from its leather band, now splayed in tangled knots over his chest, the ends dipped in red. Wounds decorated his dark skin.

And his heart—his heart now lay lifeless in the caravan. Her body had been wrapped in linen, armor and blades still clasped to her skin. Idris would never take them away from his warrior queen. Ikarria had lost their better ruler and his daughter had lost her mater, even if she didn't know it yet.

He wasn't sure how he was going to tell Daria. Pain radiated within his chest, along with the fires that claimed his soul. He wanted to rage, to cry, to fall.

The draconic king could do none of those things. Not yet.

Idris gazed at the wreckage before him, a town within the borders of Valenzia now made of flames and broken stone. Elios's forces had been scavenging for survivors of the guardian realms, seeking to punish them for fighting with the Primordials.

He understood the need for order, but he still found himself helping survivors of Valenzia escape the Elios soldiers. The few who had survived.

There had been word of a rising archangel leading the battles alongside the deities, one of the first mortals to raise a blade against the gods and succeed. Ironic as the archangels had also originated from Celestrea, created by the deities.

Idris exhaled a tongue of flame. "Search for anyone who still lives."

His soldiers filtered through the debris. They were primarily elemental elves, using their ether to either lower the flames or raise the broken buildings from the ground.

The king's armor clinked as he waded among the ashes and

corpses. Death surrounded him; it never failed to send a chill along his skin.

There was a hum in the air. It tickled his elven senses, causing his ether to shiver in delight.

Idris followed the call and stopped at the remains of a temple. The building still stood upright, even though parts of its walls had fallen. It was small, but he could tell the town had taken great care of this place of worship. The king stepped inside.

Statues of the Three Sun Gods stood at the end of the hall, their figures still in place despite the destruction.

Idris stared at the Primordials as he walked farther in. He had little regard for them. He had designed his destiny alone, without having to lean on the gods and goddesses. Prayers hadn't given him his crown and seat of power. He had *earned* them.

The ripple in the air Idris had been following stopped, and he heard the cries of a child.

The king saw her then. A little girl with slightly pointed ears was curled at the foot of Mikatán's statue, the Primordial of Death seeming to bow over her protectively.

She wiped the tears and dirt from her face, holding a knife in her trembling hand. Bright green eyes looked up at him, her teeth bared. "Don't come any closer."

Idris stopped. There were no major wounds that he could see on her person, but he was sure that she was experiencing more pain within. He slowly sat on his haunches.

"I mean you no harm," he said. "My name is Idris Calderón. I am the king of Ikarria. May I ask for your name?"

The elven child narrowed her eyes. "My mater told me that the king and queen of Ikarria were kind rulers. That your people are well taken care of."

She wouldn't give her name so freely and he respected that. Idris would've liked to acknowledge the compliment with a swell of pride, but he was more worried about the child's current state. "And where is your mater?"

The girl shrank back into the Primordial's grasp. "She's dead."

"Do you have another parent?"

"A pater. But I don't know who he is."

Idris raised his gaze to the red-gray sky through the broken ceiling. It wouldn't be long now. He would have to be quick if the girl was to be saved. "As a child of Valenzia you are not safe here. Though the War of the Skies has ended the danger is not gone. I have been helping others from your homeland find passage to safety and I want to offer you the same. Will you come with me?"

The child stared at him. He could see the wheels turning in her head. For someone so young, she was smart not to trust a stranger.

"You can keep your distance, if you like," he said. "And that little knife you have there."

She looked down at the weapon in her hand, then around the destroyed temple. "If you get too close, I'll hurt you."

Idris could only smile. "As you should."

The child followed him out of the temple. One of his soldiers appeared from the ashen mist, her long, plaited hair whipping the air as she yanked off her helmet.

"Anything to report?" Idris asked.

The soldier shook her head. "There is no one left. Our scouts say that the Elios army is a day's march away from here."

Her gaze landed on the child standing behind him. "Only her?"

Idris nodded. "Rally the others. We cannot linger."

The king of Ikarria made way to his caravan, when there was a distant sound of beating wings. He halted as he felt the archangel land several yards behind him. His heart quickened, his gloved fingers curling into fists. The elven king refused to cower.

"What are you doing, Idris?" The low voice rumbled through the weakening flames.

Rumors had also spread of the archangel's grit and valor. How he had supported the mortals' right to live of their own accord, flourish through their own ether, without having it feed the Primordials.

Idris had met the male when the archangel had requested Ikarria's support. The draconic king had been ready to order his forces to prepare for the imminent battle, but it was his queen who had advised against it. She wanted to declare neutrality to protect her people. He believed that Ikarria would suffer grave consequences if it did not join the fight, causing the mortal realms to see the draconic kingdom as a traitor, like the guardian realms. Eventually, his wife had been convinced.

Now the queen was dead, and he was ruined.

The Ikarrian king turned to the archangel, stepping in front of the child, who willingly fell into his shadow.

"Raziel," Idris said in welcome.

The archangel was young. His wine-red hair flowed to his shoulders, mussed from his flight. He wore Elios's gleaming white armor and, even though it was currently splattered with blood and gore, Raziel still shined like a star among the wreckage. His massive brown wings aimed to touch the hidden sun, his golden eyes fixated on the draconic king.

Raziel angled his head, trying to peek at the child hiding behind Idris. His nostrils flared, most likely smelling the elven girl, before a softness creased the corners of his gaze.

"Do you think I am here to harm her?"

"I received word that your soldiers were executing those of Valenzia and Damalis." It was all Idris said.

Raziel looked taken aback. "Only those who raised arms against us. The others we have taken to be relocated. In our new world, there will no longer be Valenzia and Damalis. The Gates have been destroyed so there is no more need for the guardian realms. We simply wish to prevent another war from happening."

Idris raised his chin. "Their lands have been demolished, it would take years for them to rebuild, never mind *fight* you. The deities made sure of that."

The archangel sighed. "I pity the sister realms. It was their blind loyalty to the Primordials that led to their downfall."

Idris had witnessed the gods battling the mortals they had once vowed to cherish. The world had cracked in hues of silver and blue. Thunderous cries from their beasts and undead. It had sickened him, reminded him of his own weak flesh and blood.

"I heard you are to be the new king of Elios," Idris said.

Raziel bowed his head. "High King, to be precise. The deities who supported us are forming their own Council, and they seek to place me on a throne that will oversee the Continent."

"It sounds like an honor."

The corners of the archangel's lips lifted. "You and I will speak again about the future of Ribera. I have plans for the mortal kingdoms who fought together. We will be the Aligned Realms, united and strong as one."

Idris wasn't sure how he felt about the proposition, given all that had happened. His wife had not wanted this battle, he had pushed her for it and now—

It was his fault. She had been killed because of his actions.

It should've been him.

Never again.

The ache in Idris's chest slowly squeezed the air from his lungs. And an anger, birthed by the flames of his draconic bloodline, took shape within him. He looked at the archangel, repulsed by anything that had to do with their new world. The king could hear his queen's voice now, urging him to tread carefully.

"I assume the Aligned Realms will have to swear fealty to you?" Idris asked.

Raziel surveyed him with an unreadable expression. "You are correct. Do you oppose this plan?"

Idris knew that his queen would consider it. She would be meticulous in evaluating every advantage and disadvantage to this idea. The draconic king looked around at the wreckage, the new High King at the head of it.

The anger within him growled, ready to unleash torrents of flame. He should never have joined the fight. Look what his ideals had brought him. What was most precious to him had been taken from him, a price he would suffer for the remainder of his days.

A voice, whether of his late wife's or his own, reminded him of his kingdom. Ikarria had always ruled on its own, stood strong from the love of its citizens and rulers. It was something his queen had always cherished. And though he had failed her, he would do everything in his power to protect the home she had held dear.

Idris decided to heed it. *Forgive me, my heart. I do not know what else to do.*

He bowed his head. "Ikarria has been an independent kingdom since the dawn of this Continent. I do not intend to change that."

There were sure to be some consequences for what he had and had not done. Raziel only nodded. "We will speak on that matter later. As of now, my concern is in regards to the Valenzian hiding behind you."

Idris hesitated. The archangel was bright and youthful, ready to take on any future discords that would inevitably rise. Perhaps it was what the mortal realms needed. A young mind with fresh ideas.

Despite all that, there was something that prompted Idris's decision. It may have been due to his frail, damaged heart still suffering from the loss of his wife. Or it may have been the unclear connection he'd felt when he'd stumbled on the little storm.

The draconic king inhaled slowly. "I'm afraid I cannot give her to you. I have decided to adopt her—she is now protected by Ikarrian law."

He could hear his soldiers murmuring. But there was not a single doubt in the seasoned warrior's heart.

Raziel blinked. Whatever he felt about the development, he did not show it. Wise. Perhaps, the archangel had the makings of a ruler after all.

"So be it." Raziel bowed, wings rustling. "I can't promise there won't be repercussions. In the eyes of the rising Council, it may be seen as an insult."

Idris squared his shoulders, his hand drifting behind him to urge the child farther away. "Come what may, I'll be prepared."

Raziel unfurled his wings, preparing to take to the sky. He stopped and glanced at the girl. "As I was flying, I felt something in the air. I thought—"

The archangel paused and inhaled again. He smiled as if to himself. "Never mind. I will see you again, King Idris."

Idris nodded. "Fly well . . . High King."

The archangel grinned, golden eyes aglow as he launched into the air. After the sound of flapping wings had disappeared, the crackle of dying flames rose again, together with the sound of the soldiers' boots walking away on sloshy dirt.

Idris turned to the child and bent to one knee. "I'm sorry for what I said without consulting you. You do not have to return with me. It is your—"

"He was who you were trying to protect me from."

He blinked to see the girl's green eyes sharp on him. Observing every feature on his battle-kissed face. "Yes."

"Did you mean it? Do you really mean to adopt me?"

"I do."

The child took a breath and nodded. "Take me with you. Wherever you go, I go."

Idris was surprised by the relief he felt. For some reason, he truly wanted to take her under his care. "By the ethereal skies, I will protect you with my every breath."

He went to stand, and the girl extended her small hand. "I had no pater, so I took my mater's family name. I am Zara . . . Santos."

Idris took her hand in his large one. "It is an honor, Zara. Let's go home."

Six months had passed since the day the elven king had gained a daughter. The newly proclaimed High King had sent a courier, baring a treaty drafted by the archangel himself. A result of Ikarria's unwillingness to pledge fealty to the High Throne and join the Aligned Realms. That parchment was now bunched in Idris's hand, the pale brown paper crinkling under his tight grip.

Idris knew this day would come. It was retribution.

Zara was bright, much like Daria. The two had bonded quickly, spending their days wandering the castle library or the Ikarrian forest. They would be venturing into the capital today, most likely for the street food and dances. He knew the guards he entrusted to watch over his children would ensure they stay away from the castle for the time being.

Soldiers straightened and bowed as Idris entered the fighting fields within the forest. He acknowledged his forces, his gray cloak drifting with the mountain wind.

A sense of dread told him the War may have ended, but the true battle had just begun.

Idris had saved Zara, only to fail her.

Hakim Salvador was where the king expected to find him, training the new soldiers. The *Dragonheart* had rightfully earned his title, his strength having surpassed even the capabilities of an elf. The human male's skill on the battlefield reminded every armed man and woman why he had been called such.

As a young prince, Idris had found the human beating a band of thieves down to a pulp. When the prince had discovered the male's opponents had been shifters, he had immediately sought to recruit him to Ikarria's forces.

His most trusted soldier was monitoring the newest warriors with a sharp eye. His large arms were folded as he stood along the tree line.

Hakim glanced his way, and the sight caused Idris to falter. There were dark circles beneath the man's eyes, the skin on his face leached of health. Idris despised himself for having to come to his general at such a time as this. For Hakim, too, was mourning the loss of a wife and his only child—a daughter.

They were both still suffering from the death of their loved ones. At the end of a working day, when the soldiers had retired for the night and his children had been put to sleep, he and Hakim would drink their sorrows away in his office. One could argue that the general was the draconic king's closest friend.

Idris's brow pinched. "Have you not slept?"

Hakim blinked as if processing his words. "It's been . . . a challenge."

"If you need, I can send a healer."

The human waved a hand. "That won't be necessary." He studied the king's face. "I know that look, Calderón. Something ails you."

The draconic king's lips thinned, holding up the treaty in his closed fist. "Raziel managed to find a way to appease the tension among the Council. A hunting season will be hosted in his honor. Every realm, including Ikarria, will send their guild of mercenaries to participate in the hunt as a pledge to remember the peace that was established the day the War of the Skies ended."

The fires of his ether threatened to swallow him and everything within range of the forest. "As Zara is protected by the adoption, they cannot take her away from me, but since she isn't of Ikarrian royal blood, she will become a mercenary. Every hunting season she will serve the High Throne alongside the Ikarrian guild." His voice broke.

Hakim searched his eyes, his expression reflecting the same anger that the elven king felt. "She is a child."

Idris gritted his teeth. "She is Valenzian. In the eyes of the royals, that is all they see. We have five years to prepare her for the first annual hunting season. To them, that is more than enough time."

His general shook his head, watching the soldiers spar. "It's been six months and I have yet to properly meet her, your daughter."

The king gave a soft smile. "She is still becoming accustomed to life here, I didn't want to overwhelm her. Nor you, for that matter. Duty hasn't stopped since we returned home."

Hakim made a sound of agreement in his throat. "What can I do?"

Idris finally met the *Dragonheart's* gaze. "I need you to rebuild the guild once more, to lead Ikarria's mercenaries. For her. You are the only one I trust."

Hakim Salvador considered his king's words. He glanced at the training ground, listening to the clamor of wooden swords and arrows piercing the air. "I have led your armies for as long as I can remember."

Idris nodded. "I will not force you. I couldn't and wouldn't do that to you."

"No." Hakim unhitched a dagger and cut the stitched Ikarrian symbol—a crescent sun with the face of a dragon—from his tunic. He offered it to the king. "What I mean to say is that I have spent most of my youth and adult years strengthening our kingdom's armies. And what an honor that has been. I have you to thank for that, giving a useless human such as myself an opportunity to prove myself."

The draconic king took the emblem, understanding where Hakim was heading with this. His trusted soldier and friend bowed his head. "I will forge stars as if they were made by the Suns."

Idris's sense of dread began to lift. There was no other he would rather place this responsibility on. Hakim would hone the mercenaries, craft them into warriors of steel and heart.

He also knew the *Dragonheart* would personally see to his daughter's training and safety. Take her under his wing and care for her.

Her future was sworn in blood, and he hoped she would become a force that caused crowns to fall. "Thank you, my friend." The king exhaled.

Hope was the only thing he could offer his daughter.

PART I

HEART OF A BROKEN MONSTER

ONE

Blood tracked Zara Santos's cheeks like tears, the red droplets rubies that glistened underneath the dying sunlight.

The thundering crowd didn't reach her elven ears. Neither did the smell of piss and alcohol. She was nothing but the heartbeat of pain, the endless throbbing at the corner of her eyes and mouth. A bruising that tainted her sun-kissed olive skin.

It was in these bleeding moments that a pleasant silence found her.

How far she had fallen.

How little she cared.

Zara's lips split into a wild grin as the world slowly returned to her. Her knuckles tightened around the collar of her opponent's tunic before she swung her fist. The throng of Ikarrians, elves, shifters, humans and the occasional vampire—both young and old—surrounded them into a makeshift ring. Many wore Ikarria's famous obsidian in the shape of squared earrings or arm cuffs. Their tunics were woven in colors of the bleeding sun or the deepest shade of the sea. Their roaring vibrated through the dirt beneath her boots.

Zara laughed, the sound cold and empty, as she ran the back of her hand across her mouth. She raised her fists as her opponent—the female, a common ring fighter three times Zara's size—rose from the ground and charged. Zara missed nothing and purposely slowed her footing. She followed the fighter's meaty punch and welcomed the pain that exploded across her jaw.

She fell onto her back. Her dark waist-length hair sprawled over the leaves, her gaze stuck on the burning orange sky. The ancient trees of the Ikarrian forest arched overhead, thick trunks and large branches wide enough to hold a small battalion of soldiers. Torchlights flickered, preparing to welcome the oncoming night.

The world blurred and her head began to feel heavy. *Ah*. She might've had too much to drink this evening. The fighter shouted with a victorious grin. Competition rekindled Zara's urge to draw blood as she pushed herself from the ground. Despite the alcohol burning through her body, she managed to fight through the mental haze.

Such willpower was the result of fourteen years of sword and combat training. A resolve that had been carved into her essence. Zara Santos had, after all, been honed and refined, by blade and by the mind, to become one of the most distinguished mercenaries of the realm.

There was no need to call upon the ether that ran through her veins. It would have made it too easy. Zara circled her opponent, ducking and lashing out with her fists.

No weapons were allowed in the Ikarrian ring fights. That was only part of the appeal. She liked to remember how it felt to break skin with her own hands. Her weapons were being used too much as of late.

The female fighter's attacks managed to graze Zara's sides and cheeks. She relished every sting. Zara lunged and dodged, striking fists and sweeping her powerful legs. As she broke skin and fractured bone, red misted across her eyes. The color thickened until the only thing she could see was the Summons that she had received this morning. The parchment had bunched between her battered knuckles and her teeth had almost ground into dust.

Cheers echoed with every stroke until her opponent finally fell unconscious at her feet.

Zara didn't bother to raise her hands in victory, didn't bother to prance and beam at those who bet on her to win. Her lungs burned and her skin tingled. Pain pulsated throughout her body. She got what she'd come for.

She extended her hand to the ring's manager, who dropped a sack of silver in her palm. Gods, they needed to pay the fighters more. She kept her gaze downward as she walked through the crowd. Like rippling water, they cleared a path for her, the air about them a mixture of awe and fear. Zara was used to it after all these years. They might not have known who she was, but they undoubtedly knew *what* she was.

"Santos."

Shit. That voice, so deep it was like the rolling thunder, usually meant she was in trouble. Zara lifted her gaze to the mountain of a male with too-broad shoulders. He was practically made of corded muscles. Even more impressive considering he was a human.

Hakim Salvador. Dark gray armor was melded to his large body, designs that resembled dragon scales etched around his hips, along his chest and shoulders. A black, hooded cloak billowed gently against his long legs. Whorls of ink decorated his dark skin, crawling up the column of his throat. Dreads were tied at the nape of his neck with a leather band, and bronze jewelry glinted along the round curve of his ears.

Zara offered a dry smile. "Hakim, you just missed it. I was amazing."

The head of the Ikarrian guild folded his powerful arms. "You're drunk."

"How dare you." She mocked offense only for her words to end in a stifled giggle, the sound still cold and empty. Hakim gave her a heavy look, most likely noticing the cuts and bruises on her face.

He sighed and jerked his chin. "Let's go. We have an assignment to prepare for."

The words plunged her into stark reality, temporarily sobering her thoughts. Zara grunted and followed Hakim into the dark path between the trees. The fighting ring was tucked within the forest, an unofficial establishment that was shut down during the day.

Ikarria's capital, Dae Asari, was a mere walking distance from the fighting ring. Its torchlights flickered like ember stars. She could faintly see the array of dark stone buildings that stretched along the green slopes of the hills that trailed to its highest summit. The obsidian castle sat at its peak, a myriad of large and small flat-roofed homes, businesses, and temples scattered at the fortress's feet.

The night markets would be at full force at this time, air ripe with the taste of cooked bell peppers and onions. String music would be skittering off the saltillo tiled paths and cobblestone roads. Zara knew people would be dancing and drinking at this hour, basking in the peace that followed a full day's labor from operating shops and trade to tending to the crops.

Hakim broke the thick silence between them. "Why must you continue this?"

Zara raised the small sack of silver. "What? I won."

He released a frustrated breath. "You get paid enough as part of the guild."

"I can have a hobby."

"You make a mockery of what it means to be a Horizon, and your *hobby* has been intensifying every year." Hakim didn't bother to hide his disappointment, and Zara couldn't fault him for that. No matter how much it stung. "You forget your oaths."

Zara tried to ignore the shame that burned her face at Hakim's words. She glanced down at her simple garb and brown leathers. She would need to change into the scaled armor of the Ikarrian guild.

To be titled a Horizon was an honor bestowed on all mercenaries who joined a guild. Before the War of the Skies—the civil war between the deities and the Primordials that occurred fourteen years ago—each realm formed its own guild of Horizons. However, the mercenaries had been united and upheld vows of loyalty to one another. Oaths were taken and bonds were forged. After the War, the new guilds were forced to sever ties to each other and pledge servitude only to their designated realms. Over time, they all became estranged.

Her eyes caught on the bracer wrapped around her left wrist. She clasped a hand over it, her stomach dropping.

Hakim missed nothing. His voice dropped to a whisper, gentle and kind. As he always tended to be with her. "I know it is because of the hunting season. But I worry about you—we all do."

She gave no reply, cursing herself for leaving the fresh decanter of wine at the fighters' tent. How she craved the raw burn and sweet tang of berries.

The hunting season. Another result of the War of the Skies. When the ashes of battle had finally withered to dust, a treaty had been enacted. The newly created High Throne in Elios called for all realms of Ribera to swear fealty. All kingdoms had bowed, except for Ikarria. After much debacle, the High King had enacted the hunting season for all realms to honor his rule by sending their guilds to cleanse Elios of its criminals. It became a reminder to the draconic realm that they couldn't be fully independent from the High Throne.

What rested beneath the leather bracer, imprinted on the skin of her wrist, was a symbol of her and the guild's duty to the High Throne. Though the others hadn't had to do what she had over the years . . .

Hakim's brow furrowed as they walked, his own brand hidden beneath his leathers. He knew exactly what she was thinking, but didn't voice it. Something she appreciated.

"Do not lose yourself, little warrior. You are not alone."

The words made her throat thicken. They threatened to soothe the pain that still ebbed throughout her limbs. Her elven body would heal quickly, but she wanted to relish in it as long as possible. Zara rolled her shoulders, the muscles at her biceps tightening.

She would prepare to meet with the Ikarrian guild and, once her weapons saw the light of the night, Hakim's words would mean little to nothing.

There was always a thrill to the hunt. Zara wished she could say otherwise, but that would be a lie.

Night had unfurled its star-speckled wings. Moonlight glinted off the form-fitting scales of Zara's dark gray armor, the black hem of her hood drifting lower over her brow. Tucked beneath the folds of her cloak, she was strapped to the teeth. Zara curled her fingers over a set of throwing daggers.

She stood on a massive branch of an ancient Ikarrian tree. Moss and chipped wood slid underneath her boots as she pressed her back against the trunk. The canopies of leaves covered her, hiding her from the eyes of the Fates. Or so she hoped.

Shadows moved amongst the trees around her. The guild's agile movements were so familiar to her senses that she didn't need to look to see where they were.

Her gaze fell to the marks below. Common marauders who had stolen valuable goods from the guild's employer, a . . . healer? The details of an assignment weren't something Zara cared to know. Truth be told, she wasn't even surprised that someone who devoted their profession to helping others would hire mercenaries. After spending the past nine years as a Horizon, she quickly learned that most mortals would resort to drastic measures to look out for themselves.

All that mattered was her mark and whether they needed to be brought back dead or alive. Dead was usually the answer.

A bird call fell from her lips, the sound low and fluttering. The darkness of the forest answered, echoing the same tune.

The marks began to quicken their pace, their hushed voices rippling with fear.

Zara's lips curved upward. The ether in her blood thrummed with excitement. Muscles in her legs clenched with anticipation.

The whistle of an arrow speared through the night air, piercing a marauder square in the back. Panic was unleashed. The marks shouted, raising their blades as the guild flew from the trees, weapons shining in the dark.

A snarl ripped through her teeth as she leapt off the branch. Power surged through her veins and up her legs, sending her flying into the air. The throwing daggers slipped from her fingers and found purchase in a mark, the three small blades landing with a *thwack, thwack, thwack.*

Zara landed and rolled to her feet and a pair of marks stumbled back at the sight of her. A wicked madness overtook her senses as she reached for the twin khopesh blades strapped to her back. She moved.

Rivers of blood soared through the columns of pale moonlight. Red sprayed the ferns. The muscles in her arms burned with every swing of the curved obsidian swords in her hands. Zara's marks screamed and screamed.

She felt herself sink into the abyss of her thoughts, where emotion was drowned and vulnerability stifled. As her heart blackened.

The mercenaries surrounding her danced within the havoc. Their cloaks and hoods obscured their faces, but she recognized their forms, how their bodies blended with the night. Gleaming swords, daggers, and bows.

The power in her veins hissed, and she twisted around to slash her blade across an approaching mark. His gut split open, the sickle-shape of the khopesh managing to rip through his fighting leathers. The marauder gasped out his last breaths and clutched at Zara's legs.

She cocked her head and waited for him to bleed out before the sound of snapping branches caught her attention. A marauder hurtled through the bushes, fleeing from the bloodbath. A chuckle hummed through her chest as she gave chase.

Starlight streamed through the canopies. The smell of damp wood engulfed the air with the welcomed cool bite of the mountain wind. The ether streaming through the very ground of the Continent seemed to pulsate under her feet. A breeze pushed through the strands of her brown hair tucked beneath the hood. It seemed to hiss at her to go, go, go.

Her teeth clenched with adrenaline as power ran through her legs. Soft tendrils of red mist curled around her body. The ether pulled her off the ground, light flaring in her wake as she landed on a thick branch, giving her speed, strength.

Zara flew between the trees in a flash of red. A shard of dawn light.

The mark disappeared from her line of sight. She paused, narrowing her eyes over the dense landscape. Her lips parted with a voice of battle and storm. "I know you're out there."

She scaled the branches, boots near silent as her senses called to the world around her. The damp bark and heady floral scents. Noisy nighthawks and bats. Spilled blood and guts. And there, amid the sights and smells, was the rustling of cloth and leather. And ragged breathing.

A savage smile stretched over her face. Zara stepped off the edge of the branch and fell into the shadows. She could hear the rattle of the mark's overworked lungs as if she were standing next to him. The rusted smell of blood wafted beneath her nose, but that could've been the red that already stained her face.

The mark could only watch as Zara stepped out of the wall of night and into the moonlight. He sucked in a breath, his face turning red with rage.

"I recognize you," he seethed. "I've seen you in the streets of Elios. You are not any Horizon. You are who they call the Rogue."

By the fucking Suns. That title was a blade dragged across a wound that never seemed to heal. It was pain that gritted her teeth, threw her into the fighting ring, and built within her the war cry she longed to release. Her blood simmered, and her lips twitched into a snarl. She spun the curved blades in her palms but said nothing.

The mark raised his sword. "It'll bring me joy to cut down the one who is most feared and hated in all realms."

Their weapons collided, clangs of metal reverberating between the trees, and he managed to thrust his blade toward her face. She moved to block him, the tip of his sword ripping the leather bracer on her wrist open. Zara sucked in a breath at the sight of the tattoo, a pair of wings with three suns at its center.

Something in Zara's chest cracked. She couldn't pull her gaze away from the fyrebrand.

The mark began to laugh. "*Oh.* The Rogue. The Horizon. The title matters not, does it? You are less free than me, mercenary."

Anger fogged her vision. Ether curled around her as it propelled her forward like a crack of lightning. The air snapped and popped as she appeared directly in front of the marauder, her blades now deep in his torso.

Hands clawed at the leathers on her chest. Red liquid gurgled between his lips. When Death finally found its mark, she yanked out her weapons. The man's remains dripped from the tip of the black steel, joining the blood that pooled underneath her boots.

Zara's chest moved heavily up and down. The sight of the fyrebrand had almost been strong enough to snap her resolve and send her into the depths of madness. For a moment, she had lost control. And it had nearly cost her.

Gods. Her pater and the guild would be furious if they found out. She couldn't help it. The mark's words rang through her head.

You are less free than me, mercenary.

It was true. Her fate had been bound in chains and bloodshed for as long as she could remember. If it weren't for her pater adopting her when he did, she would've been long dead or living under High King Raziel's roof in Elios. Though she supposed there would have been no difference between the two.

Every Horizon had been marked with the fyrebrand, an etherlaced tattoo that served its purpose only during the hunting season. At every kill, or every *assignment* the High King ordered, the fyrebrand would burn—signifying the end of their job, communicating it to the archangel and ruler who sat on the High Throne.

For being a Horizon was a lifetime privilege, while the hunting season was a fifty-year sentence. Only nine years of it had passed. As an elven woman who had reached her late twenties, her aging had begun to slow already, so she would still be youthful enough to continue wielding the blades in the name of the High King for many years to come and till the end of the sentence.

Zara tried not to think of how much time remained, but it was difficult to ignore. Ever since she had first started her work as a mercenary, she had been thrown into the yearly hunts for the High Throne.

A voice rose in her head. The fyrebrand tingled against her skin. No matter how hard she tried to change it, it always came in Raziel's voice.

Did you like it, hunter? When blood ran in the wake of your fancy blades?

She sheathed the khopesh over her back and quickly secured the bracer on her wrist, slamming her mental walls down on the voice.

"Fuck you," she seethed.

Zara searched the body for the contents of her assignment. It didn't stop the voice from slithering in the back of her mind.

The hunting season arrives. You've enjoyed this year of tranquility. It is time to pay your dues ... Rogue.

She wasn't sure what bothered her more, the fact that the mere mention of her unwanted title sent her blood boiling, or that the fyrebrand's voice had been haunting her thoughts for as long as she could remember.

Zara tugged the hood of her cloak over her face and stepped over the lifeless body at her feet. The mercenary returned to the folds of darkness.

Streaks of red in her wake.

TWO

The cool morning kissed the sweat on Zara's brow. Her loosely curled hair was plastered to her skin, her green eyes blazing under the flood of daylight. She watched the mercenary circling her. Axar Tallon's brilliant teeth flashed, sword winking in his hand as he twirled it.

Zara and the wolf shifter, who was a few years her senior—she being twenty-seven years of age—had trained and joined the Ikarrian guild together. Zara could recall all the days they'd spent grappling each other during sparring matches. Ever since they were young, they had been practically attached at the hip.

Axar wore brown training leathers which cut off around his arms. It did little to hide the array of tattoos that covered the entirety of his body. The lower half of his head was shorn while his hair was styled into multiple short braids, tied back with a band. Lean muscle carved his tawny skin and built his athletic frame.

Hakim bellowed from the sideline. "Since you like to fight in the ring so much, Santos, you will continue to train until you fall."

"Gods, you truly pissed him off," Axar muttered.

Zara grimaced. "Like you never have before."

He barked a laugh before charging her. She raised her twin blades, letting the strength of her arms run through the length of her weapons.

The sparring ground was nothing more than the main chamber of the mercenary temple of Ikarria. Though it was more of a ruin than a place of worship now. The flat-roofed building was hidden within the forest, about a mile from the Ikarrian capital. Sun-dusted pillars lined the temple's entrance, wildflowers and vines penetrated the cracked rock. The walls were carved into murals of feathered beasts and winged warriors.

In Zara's opinion, it was the jewel of the draconic realm.

There were many mercenary temples scattered throughout the Continent. Before the War of the Skies, they had been used as gathering places for the guilds who used to travel the realms for work. The Horizons had the freedom to stay and visit the other temples. Now the original sanctity had been botched by the ink that made the treaty. Mercenaries were to reside solely in their kingdom's temple, only to ever serve the needs of their rulers. Never to pledge loyalty— or even camaraderie—toward the other Horizons like before. Only the Elios temple was still being properly used as a meeting place for all the guilds—during the hunting season.

"Are you ready to yield?" Axar's bright smile flashed, distracting her thoughts.

Zara gave him a dark smile. "Not a chance, wolf."

She twisted herself free from his reach. Her lithe body danced between the columns of golden light. Behind her was the open wall of the temple, lined with more pillars. Beyond it, the forest and hills stretched as far as the eye could see. In the far distance loomed the Dragon's Teeth mountain range. Golden mist clung to the peaks and blended with the morning.

Zara's blade hissed as she slashed down toward Axar, but the shifter rolled out of her reach. His laugh belted throughout the chamber.

"Mind your footwork, Santos." Hakim's deep voice could have shaken the crumbling walls.

Another voice interjected. "You're sloppy, pup. Do not get comfortable solely because you are fighting someone you know."

Eshe Abara was sprawled on one of the settees in the chamber.

The archer of the guild had rich brown skin, the long strands of her dark hair tucked back with a deep red headwrap. Large silver hoops pierced her ears. Her gleaming alabaster bow was perched on the weaponry rack beside the sparring ground while the archer sunbathed, and her underlings sparred.

Zara spotted the glint of fangs as Eshe sipped from a chalice. Zara could only imagine what was inside the large cup fit enough for a vampire.

Eshe had originated from one of the nomad vampire clans. She had little to share about her past. The skilled warrior had found Axar when he was a pup. He had been abandoned within the dunes of Kairos and she raised him as her own. When the War ended, Eshe made the decision to move to Ikarria. She had met Hakim working as an ink artist trying to make ends meet and through him, she landed in the guild, Axar in tow.

The shifter growled in frustration, his eyes flashing a bright yellow. The eyes of a wolf. He rammed his shoulder against Zara and the air was punched from her lungs. She felt another force behind his touch, another presence that rumbled and howled. His inner wolf was ready to snap.

She grunted as she fell to the ground. The tip of a blade poised at her collarbone. Axar was breathing heavily, sweat dappling his light brown skin.

That obnoxious smile returned. "I win."

Zara rolled her eyes. "Fucking Suns."

Axar helped her up as she tried to avoid Hakim's burning stare. Tried and failed.

"Your power is getting stronger," he said. The compliment halted her. She eyed him warily and he gave her a dry look. "I am not mad at you, Santos."

She scoffed, smirking. "Not *anymore*. You haven't scolded me like that since that time Axar took me to a tavern when I turned eighteen."

Hakim ran a hand over his beard, covering his growing smile. "Tavern? I'm quite certain it was a *pleasure house*. Axar had no business taking someone as young as you to such an establishment."

Zara cackled at the memory. "I had begged Axar to take me. I was curious about their live shows." The elf shared a knowing look with the wolf shifter.

The head of the guild shook his head. "Regardless, today's training is a mere reprimand. I can tell your power is growing even through your sword fighting, so you need to be careful. Remember that no one, no citizen or soldier—including the other guilds and the High King himself—must know what you possess."

The ether stirred through her veins as if in response to Hakim's words. Both her pater and Hakim had advised that her power remain in secrecy. She wasn't sure why there was so much concern around it, the power Zara held was hardly anything worthwhile. It helped her appear from one location to the next in a short span of time and in a crackle of light. It was unlike the magnificent ether she'd seen in her kingdom.

"I still don't understand the reasoning behind keeping my power a secret. It doesn't seem to be at its full maturity yet, anyway."

"Ether made the realms, the very earth, the sky and everything in between. It affects the mortals living within it. The elves were gifted with the ability to control it in the form of the elements—fire, water, earth and wind. You, an elf, do not possess elemental ether, but the power of light. A power that is unknown to us. Do you see why that would be concerning?"

Zara rubbed the back of her neck. She'd heard this so many times over the years and yet, it still baffled her. Only she, the Ikarrian guild, and her pater and sister knew what coursed through her blood, though none of them knew what it would develop into, if anything more than what it was now. "Ikarria is heavily populated with my kind. I am but one woman with an ether that is but a fraction of what the others can do."

Hakim shook his head. "For you to hold this kind of power—to wield light—instead of wielding any of the elements, makes you an anomaly. Use it sparingly during mercenary hunts."

"I know," Zara said with a dismissive wave of her hand.

Her mentor made a disapproving sound. "It is for your safety.

We've been fortunate that High King Raziel is not aware of your unique ability."

Zara grimaced at the name of the archangel.

"Raziel assumes, just like everyone else, that it will mature into an elemental ether," she said.

Hakim gestured between her and Axar. "We can continue this conversation while you begin another match."

Zara took a step back. "I'd rather not—"

"It wasn't a suggestion, Horizon."

Axar scowled, shooting her a glare. "You *had* to ask more questions. Now he's going to lecture us *as* we fight."

"You will both battle Eshe."

Zara could've sworn there was a touch of amusement in Hakim's voice. The head of the Ikarrian guild was teasing them—and enjoying it. He was hardly any better than they were.

Eshe swung off the settee, replacing her chalice of blood with her favored weapon and sauntered toward them. Her bow seemed to smile from behind her shoulder.

"We're dead," Axar groaned.

Eshe tilted her head. Stray brown curls fell free from her headwrap. "Still scared of me, pup? I thought I had raised that fear out of you."

The wolf shifter grinned. "I know my limits, especially when I am against you, oh mighty teacher."

Before Zara could muster another thought, an arrow tore through the daylight and aimed toward them. Her arms moved of their own accord, muscle relying on memory, and she snapped the projectile in half before it could make impact.

Axar did not hesitate. He pivoted to the side and swept his blade in an arc. Eshe moved with the speed of a shadow, bringing her elbow across his face. Axar fell to the ground with a grunt.

Eshe rolled her shoulders. Those dark eyes landed on Zara. "Little warrior, I believe what Hakim is trying to say is that the High King has already been fixated on you for years. Raziel *created* the Rogue. He doesn't need another reason to keep his personal assassin close."

The vampire darted toward her, and Zara managed to swing her blades in time to drive Eshe back. Zara glanced behind the mercenary's shoulder, catching sight of Hakim.

His lips twisted in disgust. "The bastard is still bitter that Ikarria refused to swear allegiance and—"

"Yes, yes." Zara's grip tightened on her swords. She already knew where this was going. "It is because I am the adopted daughter of the male who dared defy him. That is why he made me the Rogue."

Hakim sighed. "Precisely. That is our theory at least."

Axar slowly helped himself to his feet. He winced as he touched the growing bruise on his cheek. Zara leapt back when Eshe sent another arrow toward her face. Her footing slid against the temple ground as she dodged it. "If you're quite done, Tallon, I'd appreciate some assistance."

Axar discarded his blade. His eyes turned bright yellow. "Enough of this."

Light flared from his limbs, drowning him in ether until a dark gray wolf emerged. The beast scraped the floor as he lunged for Eshe. She only smirked, twisting her body just enough to evade Axar's fangs. She tried to wrap an arm around his massive neck as the wolf prepared to buck. But the strength of a vampire more than matched that of a shifter.

Eshe dug her heels and slammed Axar into the ground. Zara sprinted past them and managed to graze the vampire with her khopesh. The tip of the black blade ripped through Eshe's ivory cloth and leathers, nicking the skin.

The vampire flashed her fangs. "Well done." She ducked into the sunlight and appeared before Zara in a blink of an eye. Zara gasped as Eshe's hand clutched her neck, pinning her against a pillar. The archer grinned. "But it wasn't enough."

Hakim folded his arms. "They lasted longer this time."

Ether flashed from across the temple as Axar shifted back into his human form. He was still sprawled on the floor and flung an arm across his eyes. "Both of you are so cruel. And I swear you're even holding back."

Eshe and Hakim shared a glance, smiles tugging at their lips.

When they didn't respond, Axar sighed. "I still think rebelling against the hunting season would only work in our favor. Or stay the same at least. All this talk of the High King and I don't see how his rule has benefited us."

Eshe released Zara from her hold. The sudden absence of the vampire's strength pinning Zara to the pillar caused her to stagger. The archer gripped her elbow, steadying her.

"I think you know the point we are reminding you of," Eshe said.

Zara offered the mercenary a tight smile. "To *not* reveal my ether."

Eshe mussed Zara's hair with her hand. "It is fine to question, little warrior. And know that we will always protect our own, despite what laws or rules say." The vampire swerved to where Axar lay. "And you, my pup, be careful when you speak of rebellion. There are those who believe the High Throne helped the mortal realm flourish without having to rely on the Primordials' mercy and wouldn't take kindly to this kind of talk."

Axar grunted. "I do not care about the rest of the Continent. I am speaking for *our* wellbeing. The guild alone. I don't believe our situation has improved since the Primordials disappeared."

At the mention of the gods, Zara dragged her gaze to the floor-to-ceiling statue that sat at the back of the chamber. It had a humanoid shape with a burly chest and thick legs. Its face was that of a skeleton and, on its head, was a headdress of sharpened daggers that resembled feathers. It bore a crescent-shaped breastplate and armor hung over its chest and shoulders, adorned with strings of bones and teeth. A wrap hung around its waist as the figure sat upon a throne. It faced the open wall, watching as the forests were bathed in the growing sunlight.

One of the Three Sun Gods. Mikatán, the Primordial of Death.

Axar's voice sliced through the brief silence. "The Primordials have forsaken us. It won't be long before the High Throne does so too."

Throughout the Continent of Ribera, every realm honored the Three Sun Gods: life, nature, and death. Each kingdom also worshiped a select group of Primordials, based on their culture and beliefs. There were many factions and civilizations within each realm that had their own patron gods.

For the mercenaries, it was Mikatán.

When the Horizons used to gather throughout the Continent, they would honor the god of death. Ikarria's guild still paid respects to their patron today, but she wasn't sure if the others did. Not since the War.

Zara had heard terrifying stories of the ethereal being. How he had unleashed the spirits of the dead to ravage the mortal lands during the War of the Skies.

The rebelling deities had removed the Primordials' connection to the mortal world by breaking the Gates of Celestrea, the original realm of the gods, as well as the archangels'. The deities had claimed the Primordials were selfish beings and were only using the mortal world as a life source—sucking and draining the mortal forms of ether that had evolved over the millennia for their own uses. The deities somehow won the War and created the Council that ruled from Elios beside the High Throne today.

Axar appeared beside her. He dug the steel point of his sword into the cracked stone ground and rested his hands above the pommel.

She jerked her chin toward the statue. "It is curious how one of the most powerful Primordials went to battle against the rebelling deities only for that immense power to be diminished by the fall of Celestrea. For the Continent to be ruled by a mere *archangel*."

He grunted in agreement. "It comes to show that power does not guarantee victory."

Deities were considered lesser gods, who had served and lived amongst the Primordials. Their hate toward Celestrea must have been great for them to wage war against the ethereal beings. The archangels had also originated from Celestrea. It was said that the first deities had created the winged race, thus they were the first mortal species to live in the ethereal world. It had been thousands of years since then, and now most of the archangels were born and raised in the mortal world.

It had taken years after the Gates were destroyed for the kingdom of Elios to begin taking down the temples that worshiped the

Primordials. The concept of having gods as patrons still existed, though Zara wasn't sure for how much longer that would last.

"In the end, the guilds were forced to satisfy the political demands of the Continent," Zara muttered. She cocked her head, feeling a sliver of bitterness seep into her veins. "We spill blood to serve. We spill blood to survive."

Axar exhaled through his nostrils. "There is little choice in the matter."

The ether-laced fyrebrand on Zara's skin seemed to hum, its presence growing heavy. She eyed the same imprint on Axar's own wrist and wondered if it haunted his thoughts like hers did. Zara had never told the guild of its voice, afraid of what it meant if it was happening only to her.

Hakim gazed at the statue of the Primordial. "Both of you have taken the oaths of the Horizon. It has been this way since the Age of the Primordials. I taught you the old tradition to remember the nobility of the first mercenaries."

The head of the guild looked to them, his dark eyes bright. Hakim desired for the guilds to be united once more. He had been a general of Ikarria's army, had led and won battles. A human who had earned the name *Dragonheart* and had served in the War of the Skies beside her pater, retiring from his position to rebuild the guild.

Hakim held their gazes. "We rise when the blade falls. We tread the path of silver and red."

The oath of the mercenaries echoed through the temple. The mountain-kissed air swept between the pillars, large leaves fluttering over the broken stone floor.

Mikatán's statue seemed to loom over them, as if listening to the old words.

Zara bowed her head, feeling the voices of her guild reverberate through her heart as the same words left her lips.

"We are the Horizon."

THREE

Ikarria's obsidian castle watched over its dark capital from the summit. Deep-red tiled rooftops trailed down the slopes of the hills. Massive ancient trees surrounded the wide roads, a river flowing at the foot of the peak.

Ikarrians painted the pathways in an array of reds and blues with their tunics. Their obsidian jewelry was dazzling upon their sun-kissed skin. Branches hung over the buildings, large leaves drifting in the air. Occasionally, horned deer and four-winged owls could be seen meandering about.

That was how Zara loved her home. A merge of wildlife and civilization.

The mercenary stepped through the castle doors. Her boots echoed on the dark marble, torches guiding her down limestone halls. She felt the weight of the daggers and knives hidden beneath the folds of her leathers. The soldiers and staff recognized her, saw the subtle glint of silver strapped to her body, and steered clear of her path.

Though she was a Horizon, others seemed to forget it. Word of the Rogue had traveled far, even to her own home.

Zara entered the private dining suite, the smell of vanilla and brewed tea greeting her senses. Daylight filtered through the glass windows, specks of dust fluttered through the beams. Three iron chandeliers hung from the ceiling, gently lit with candles. The walls were filled with paintings of Ikarria's forests and hills. Plates of cooked potatoes, eggs, and steamed chili peppers had been carefully set across the dining table.

Scrolls and tomes were sprawled about one end of the long table. The king of Ikarria was hunched over a book, flipping its pages.

Zara smiled, placing a hand on her hip. "Good morning, pater."

The elven ruler looked up and his eyes shined. "It's about time you arrived."

Idris Calderón was an older male, yet the hard-lined muscles of his battling years still thickened his torso and chest. His dark skin was decorated with tattoos from his left shoulder and along the left side of his face, curving just above his eyebrow, and his pointed ears were adorned with ear cuffs and piercings. Her pater's silver-white hair was braided into multiple strands, a half-knot tied atop his head while the rest trailed over his shoulders. The obsidian crown was nowhere to be seen.

Zara would never be able to thank the Suns enough that this was the male who had adopted her all those years ago. Ikarria was her home now but, by bloodline, Zara was Valenzian.

Valenzia and Damalis had been the guardian realms charged to protect the Gates of Celestrea, the home realm of the Primordials and deities. They had been the first of the mortal world to join the fight against the deities and Elios, and those who had suffered the most. In the wake of the War, Raziel had led massacres, ridding the Continent of what remained of the sister kingdoms. In the eyes of the mortal world, they were traitors.

King Idris of Ikarria had found her before Raziel's armies could.

Any survivors of Zara's homeland were scattered throughout the Continent, while all that remained of Damalis was bone and dust. There were no records as to what had happened to its citizens or their king—the *lost* king of Damalis. It was said, out of his family, none had survived—except for him. So many years had passed, and the Continent had simply stopped caring.

Her sister, a year younger than she, sat at Idris's side. Daria jumped from her seat. "Zara, you've joined us!"

Warmth melted something in Zara's chest. A faint smile touched her lips, and she swaggered inside to hug the heir to the Ikarrian throne. Her sister was an otherworldly beauty. Tall with long black hair and dark skin, eyes a shade of amber-brown. Zara and Daria may not be related by blood, but they were as close as any sisters could be.

"You don't have to make it sound like I am hardly ever here. I often join our family for weekend breakfast."

Daria rolled her eyes. "That is because you *are* hardly here. I always send an invitation to the mercenary temple just in case."

Zara had spent most of her childhood within the Ikarrian castle, though nowadays, all she saw and heard was the blood that stained her palms and the voice that haunted her waking thoughts. It had become harder and harder to return to the place of her youth.

While she served in the guild to appease the treaty with Elios, Daria Calderón was the true princess of Ikarria. She constantly drowned herself in academics, learning the histories of the Continent, to one day rule over her realm.

The king of Ikarria watched them, the same colored eyes warming. "My firelight and my storm."

Zara sat across from her sister, giving her pater a peck on the cheek. "What are you reading, pater? And since when have you discovered such a *strong* taste for reading?" Zara eyed the many books piled on the table.

Daria raised her hand. "I said the same thing."

Their pater chewed his food slowly, a measured look in his gaze. "It's nothing you need to concern yourself with."

Zara shared a puzzled look with her sister. "Do you have meetings with the advisors today?"

"Always," Idris replied. He shuffled the books to the side, clearing some room for her. "The advisors are concerned about the Summit."

It was hard to miss how the skin between her pater's brows pinched together, his jaw bracketed with tension. The Summit was a gathering of all the realms, except for Ikarria, who remained independent from the Alliance. It was a celebration held in Elios, an array of festivities to honor the leaders and royalty in one place, showcasing a new age of peace. A chance to discuss the progress between the kingdoms and how else they can expand business and support.

How truly beneficial were these meetings? Zara had yet to discover that answer.

Daria perked up from the seat on her pater's other side. "Why are they worried? The other kingdoms have all sworn fealty to Elios. Ikarria has never attended the Summit; it has never been our concern. We haven't caused any issues for Elios."

Idris lifted the kettle and poured Zara a cup of tea. The steam coiled in the air, twisting with the scent of vanilla and green leaves. He angled his head to Daria. "Firelight, what have your academics taught you? Everything that happens in the Continent is our concern."

Her sister briefly shut her eyes. "I'll rephrase. What exactly are the advisors so worried about?"

"Apparently, Adrastea's forces have been increasing within the streets of Elios. It seems the two realms have become more than mere allies. The advisors of Ikarria fear that the High Throne and Adrastea may be up to something."

Zara's attention swayed when her eyes landed on the cooked potatoes. She filled her plate and ate as she watched her sister shift uncomfortably in her seat. Daria was on her own.

Her sister stared at her own cup of tea. "What could the vampire realm possibly want that would require their armies to be in Elios? What do they hope to gain?"

Idris leaned back in his seat. "Let's make this a lesson, princess of Ikarria. Tell me your theories."

The excitement that lit Daria's face was hard to miss. Her slender fingers tapped the table, nails clinking against the utensils. "Adrastea and Kairos are part of the Alliance. Damalis and Valenzia were both destroyed during the War. There is still tension between the realms, but that doesn't compare to the High King's overprotectiveness over his own people. Elios's capital, Soleira, itself is divided between its inner and outer districts. It is possible that Raziel would like to show his strength, keep any opposition in line who may think to take advantage of Elios's vulnerabilities and unrest."

She paused. "That doesn't feel right, though. He doesn't need massive vampire armies to do that. Unless Adrastea's army's presence has something to do with the Council of Deities, who remain a mystery to me. I have yet to understand what their purpose in Elios is."

Zara's lips thinned at the thought of the High Realm. Her sister continued. "Elios and Adrastea are plotting something, then. We need to keep an eye on their doings . . . they are not our allies, but they are also not our enemies."

Her pater's voice was grave. "I agree. What is more concerning to me is the slowed harvest."

Both Zara and Daria perked up in their seats. Idris sighed. "Farmers from around the Elios region have reported that not nearly as much crop and fruit have grown this season. The acolytes have theorized that it is due to the dying ether of the Continent."

Zara's brow furrowed. "I've traveled across the Estrella Territories and Elios many times and this is the first that I'm hearing of it."

"That is because it is only now being noticed. Our Continent has always been ripe with ether, a power that replenishes the plants and trees, gives us rain and sunlight. The temple-goers have always believed there would be consequences after the Primordials were banished. As if the natural order would balance the scales. Of course these beliefs were dismissed but, if the farmers are saying that the very dirt is *weakening*, then that is not something we can afford to ignore."

They sat in silence, the king's words landing heavily between the sisters. The concept of the mortal realm's natural ether dying was terrifying. And baffling. Zara didn't think it was possible. These were all theories, and it was a problem beyond her capacity. Zara trusted that her pater would manage.

He looked at her then and reached for her hand. "I heard the Summons arrived. You will be off to Elios soon."

She felt the warmth from his palm and sought comfort in the touch. "We leave at week's end."

Daria leaned forward, her fingers digging into the wood of the table. "This is ridiculous, pater. We cannot send her and the guild there again. When will it be enough?"

Idris's eyes narrowed as sparks of flame ignited in his gaze. "I know. I have argued with the High Throne countless times. I am still seeking a way to mend the treaty."

The voice slithered in the back of her head. *Raziel's* voice. The fyrebrand wrapped around her, nuzzling the corners of her mind.

You must serve, so they can live.

Zara pulled away from her pater, shaking her head. "Do not worry about me."

Idris's gaze narrowed. "I have not given up, my storm."

Zara's throat bobbed. She wanted to fling her arms around her pater and let his words soothe her like they did when she was a young girl.

The words didn't come to her. It was easier this way. The blades had been forced into her hand, so that she and those she loved may live.

Death had crowned her, had somehow found a liking to her, tracing its red-dusted fingers around the jagged pieces of her soul.

Mercenary. Reaper. Monster.

A truth that gilded the thorns that already pierced her heart.

FOUR

Alcohol seeped between Zara's lips. A light burn blossomed in the center of her ribcage. She watched as the amber light of the torches bled together and the ground tilted on its axis. Her eyelashes fluttered, a hum escaping her.

The night markets were teeming with citizens tonight. Scents of peppers, chili, and corn curled from stalls with crimson and azure cloth. Banners made of colorful parchment had been strung across the streets. Sellers pulled their goods of pottery, meats and fish, tools, and trinkets under their tarps. Shoppers meandered through the market as musicians performed under the balmy air.

Zara drank in the sight. Tried to imprint the image in her head. At first light, the Ikarrian guild would travel through the kingdom's wild territory toward the border with Elios.

The week had passed too quickly. She had spent the remainder of her time training with the guild or in the castle library with her sister and pater.

Her fingers tightened around the decanter of wine as she stumbled from an alley, lips still swollen from her quick mingling with an elven soldier. Zara had had enough to drink that she didn't think twice of the decision. They had slipped to a dark corner between two buildings where she had guided him to sit on a stack of wooden boxes. Zara had unfastened his trousers enough to free his cock, pushing her hands against his chest as she rode him. The male's teeth had scraped the skin of her neck, holding her in place, their gasps and grunts echoing in the dark path. Anyone could've seen but she couldn't bring herself to care. The encounter had been satisfying enough.

Zara ambled through the night market, passing an array of shops and taverns. Her body thrummed with a wave of numbness. She pressed a finger to the corner of her eye. It was still sensitive from her earlier fight in the ring.

The door of a tavern opened, music and laughter blasting out onto the street. Zara had her gaze down and didn't sense someone stumbling into her path. She bumped against a hard chest and the familiar scent of pine had her looking up. Her lips spread into an easy smile.

"*Axar,*" she slurred.

The mercenary grinned brilliant teeth. "It seems you and I are both late."

Zara snorted, placing her fingers over her mouth. His lips danced with amusement as they leaned toward each other, responding in unison.

"Shit."

The ink on Axar's skin shifted with his flexing muscles. He braced a hand on his hip and made a disgusted look. "Gods, Zara. I can still smell whatever male was on you."

"Your wolf senses can be irritating."

He shrugged. "I can't help it."

Two females appeared from behind Axar, one human and the other elven, their hair mussed, painted lips smeared. They cast their doe-eyed looks to the shifter before disappearing into the night market. Zara leaned toward Axar and caught the delicate scents of rose and soap. Her senses were not as prominent as those of a wolf shifter, but they were enough.

She gaped. "I'm impressed that anyone would want to sleep with you."

Axar shoved at her shoulder with a playful smile before his hazel eyes narrowed. "I see that you visited the fighting rings again."

Zara blinked and looked away. "It's a good distraction."

He grunted. "I can understand that, Santos. But it's not sustainable. How many times must we have this conversation?"

She growled and raised her decanter at him. "Don't ruin my mood, Tallon."

He grabbed her drink and slid his arm around her shoulders. "Let's be off. The others are waiting."

They passed several stalls. Market sellers beckoned to passersby, raising their trinkets and pottery. An elderly woman dressed in white and red robes stood within a clearing, surrounded by others wearing similar attire. Their eyes were a milky white.

"Acolytes of the Primordials," Axar grumbled.

Zara nudged him. "I thought the acolytes were extinct by now."

When the Council and the High King had banished the Primordials from the mortal world by breaking the Gates of Celestrea, many of the Primordials' followers were executed. Some had managed to find refuge on more neutral ground, such as Ikarria. Though some of the Primordial temples still existed, Zara knew it was only a matter of time before the High King removed any trace of the gods.

"They are here!" The acolyte cried out, thrusting her hands into the air. "Prepare, o' lost stars. Prepare for the new world, the Three Sun Gods have returned!"

A small crowd was listening to the woman's preaching. Zara made it past the group when the woman slid her blank gaze to her.

"They feel the power that hides from them," she warned.

Zara felt the hairs on her neck rise. Axar grunted and pushed her to keep moving. "It's not the first time I heard that," he rumbled. "Rumor has it that there are ethereal beings wandering the lands wearing crowns of silver."

She twisted her lips. "Sounds like the words of fanatics."

"They are. There is no way the Primordials can ever return."

They approached an open-air tavern and Zara pushed through the iron-welded gates. The roses that weaved and crawled along its entrance pricked at her fingers. They headed up stairs made of deep blue and yellow tiles. Stars shimmered above as more of the paper banners fluttered gently across the tavern's center.

The rest of the guild were drinking and laughing in a corner loft. Hakim was hunched over with his elbows on his knees. Instead of the usual scaled armor, he wore dark fighting leathers fitted with a gray tunic. He said something that had Eshe rolling her eyes. Her curly hair was unbound, though she still wore her headscarf. Form-fitting trousers clung to her thin, muscled legs where she had a boot kicked up against a chair.

The pommels of the mercenaries' weapons peeked from their attire, catching the amber light of the torches. Always strapped to the teeth.

Zara noticed her sister among them, the sight tightening something in her chest. Growing up, Daria had often visited the Ikarrian temple and watched Axar and Zara train. She hadn't been allowed to practice the rigorous courses that they underwent, as it was reserved for those preparing to take their oaths, but the guild had welcomed her nonetheless. Zara didn't think the mercenaries would have behaved otherwise, as Hakim was close with the king of Ikarria—not including the fact that Daria was also their princess.

Zara had been raised by both the king of Ikarria and the guild; she had come to appreciate the support given to her from both sides.

The princess was the most protected individual in the room—probably in the whole realm.

Daria beamed at her. "Where have you been?"

Axar covered his laugh with a cough. Zara shrugged, waving the question away as she slid into the seat next to her. Her sister grabbed her hand and didn't let go as they talked most of the evening. It was their last night together. The bleak reminder loomed in the back of Zara's thoughts. She fought against it, refusing to let it ruin tonight.

As tradition, the guild always visited the local tavern the evening before they were to set off for the hunting season. They would drink and eat together, basking in each other's company. It was their farewell to the peace and genuine work they did for their home realm. After this night, their hands would be plunged into the bowels of Elios, ridding it of its tainted flesh, prisoners of their fyrebrands.

After the guild had passed another round of drinks, Zara looked to Eshe. "Do you have your tools?" she asked.

The vampire took a quick gulp of her rum and nodded. "I brought them, as you requested."

She slid out a leather bag and sidled closer to her. Zara perked up in her seat, watching the archer take out a needle and a small canister of black ink.

Daria went silent. Zara could feel her curiosity burning toward her. She ignored it as she rested her arms across the table. She had worn a body tight tunic that capped at her shoulders, exposing her tattooed forearms, so Eshe could access her skin more easily. Her skin was designed with a mural of skulls, suns, stars, and leaves.

Eshe cleaned the needle with a rag, the sharp sting of alcohol wafting in the air. "We are finishing the stem around your fyrebrand, yes?"

Zara nodded. Her voice came out more raspy than intended. "Please."

A twinge of desperation there.

The vampire leaned forward, silver-hooped rings jingling. Concentration pinched the corners of her eyes as she dipped the needle in the ink. Zara winced at the first prick. The sting soon melted into a soft, familiar burn.

Tattoos were customary among the Horizons, but it was not common for the mercenaries to attempt to *hide* the fyrebrand. The ether-laced ink was imbued with a power that prevented it from being covered with another tattoo. If a Horizon tried such an act, the fyrebrand would punish them.

Zara was not one to balk at a challenge. She hated the High King's ink on her skin and did all she could to blend the image with the other designs that Eshe had graciously drawn for her.

Daria propped a hand under her chin, those amber eyes on the tattoos. "When will you finally tell me what it's like for you during the hunting season?"

Zara stiffened. The others fell quiet, shifting in place.

Her sister was ever the curious one. Always daring to peek beyond the walls that Zara had carefully erected all these years. But Zara couldn't let her sister see the beast that she truly was.

"Drop it, Daria." She responded.

Her sister leaned forward. "I feel as though you've withheld a whole other side of you for years. I want to know what the High King demands of you, it is your life I worry for. I want to know if you're well—"

A dry laugh escaped Zara's lips. "If I am well? Gods, you sound more and more like pater." She glared at Daria. "If I wanted to tell you, I would. Leave it alone."

Her sister shrank back in her seat.

Zara felt a kernel of guilt but it was quickly muddled with something that twisted her gut. Daria lived her days within the castle and had only ventured to Dae Asari, sheltered from the cruelties of this world. Of course Zara was grateful for it, but there was a small part of her that . . . *envied* Daria's life. Gods. She hated the sickening sensation that curled in her stomach.

She couldn't bring herself to look at Hakim. She knew he was staring, and she heard Axar mumble something to Daria. Trying to reassure her, no doubt.

Mercifully, Eshe cleared her throat, leaning back and wiping a hand across her headscarf, "I'd say I outdid myself."

Zara gazed down at the finished tattooed piece. Leaves were etched along the border of the fyrebrand, small blossoms designed throughout the vines. The canvas on her forearm was complete, the insignia of Elios, three suns between a pair of wings, blending in with the inked images. She felt a burn behind her eyes. It was truly beautiful.

There was a subtle brush in the back of her head. *You can hide me all you want. You will never be rid of me.*

Zara's jaw ticced. *Shut up.*

Never.

"Do you remember the promise I made you, my storm?"

The Ikarrian king stood in the main chamber of the mercenary temple. It was rare for royalty to visit such ruins, but not for Idris. Zara knew he would be there to see her off. As he always had for every hunting season.

Dawn had risen, painting the walls in purple and red.

Idris seemed to smile, the action softening the intimidating tattoos that curved along the side of his face.

He opened a palm and flames sparked to life. The fiery tongues burned a bright red, lapping at the air. "Even though I raised you to be strong enough to defend yourself, I will *always* fight for you." Idris flicked his fingers. The fire twisted into the shape of a burning rose. "Never forget this, especially when completing High King Raziel's assignments. Do you hear me?"

Zara felt the weight of her khopesh blades at her back, the morning light on her face, and welcomed the scent of the distant jungles and woodlands filling her lungs.

Ikarria. Home.

"I understand, pater," she whispered.

The king embraced her. Zara tried to relax in his hold, to allow herself to be a child seeking the comfort of her pater.

As she had all those years ago. Before her first hunting season, it was easy for her to seek his guidance and support. Idris had always been there. From every nightmare and illness, every tear and laugh, every academic lesson and training—he had upkept the vow he made to her.

Then everything began to change when Zara returned from her first hunt. It was harder for her to lean on him. She couldn't look him in the eye as before. The realities of the treaty and her new fate began to weigh on her.

While it didn't take away the ache that had been digging into her soul all this time, she knew Idris was doing everything he could to help her.

Even if a small part of her was disappointed in him.

Zara wrapped her arms around him.

"I love you, daughter."

Then her pater spoke over her head. "Protect her."

The plea of a loving parent.

Hakim's voice rose from the distance. She hadn't realized he had stepped into the chamber. "With my life."

FIVE

The meeting hall within the stone chamber was silent, except for the *drip, drip, drip* of blood. Ronan's steel gaze slid to the shadow dealer before him, shoved to his knees with a bruised and broken face.

The archangel was aware of the other shadow dealers watching the spectacle. They held important positions within the Sombra Quarter, the organization of illegal markets he was the leader of, and he needed to garner their loyalty. They were, after all, sitting at *his* stone table.

He spoke to the male crumpled at his feet. "Do you know why you're here?"

The darkness within the stone chamber seemed to flare at the sound of the archangel's voice, but the shadow dealer spat a wad of blood and bared his teeth. "Fuck you."

Ronan Menodora had once been filled with light and love. The old flames of war had destroyed all that made him worthwhile, and from those ashes he had emerged . . . hollow.

He was nothing.

Feathered wings of midnight furled over his back as Ronan slowly tilted his head, his voice almost bored. "You were hired to kill me. You and your mysterious employer are in Elios's pocket, thus betraying the Sombra Quarter."

As expected, the shadow dealers around them lurched from their seats. Ronan fought a grin. They did not take kindly to betrayal. He understood that sentiment. How it bruised his heart and soul even to this day.

The traitor hissed. "High King Raziel has his eyes set on the Sombra Quarter. He wishes to destroy the illegal markets. You won't survive for much longer, *Menodora*."

Ronan suppressed the urge to roll his eyes. The threat was weak and hardly news to him. The High King of Elios had never been interested in the shadow markets—until recently. The Sombra Quarter's influence was expanding. Its growth was immeasurable, and it had extended across the realms of Ribera like water to the earth. It was distracting citizens, especially those of the lower class, from the legitimate trade the High Throne provided. The thought alone was a victory.

In truth, this was the third traitor Ronan and his soldiers had captured within the past six months. It was only this time that the archangel thought to make a show of it. The shadow dealers would learn what would happen if they crossed him. They were never to know the dire truth behind his dark smiles and vicious threats.

He needed them more than they needed him.

Ronan folded his powerful arms, black hair falling over his brow. "The Sombra Quarter is *my* domain. You forget that we are not just criminals selling fancy knives and glowing rocks." He bent to one knee. The dark fighting leathers on his body made him look like an assassin rather than the king of the shadow markets. "We offer aid to those the High Throne abandoned. You should know, you were one of them."

The male seethed. "The true purpose of the Sombra is nothing more than a sham dream. You aren't making a difference, archangel. The High King has more power than you ever will. It will be your end."

Ronan smoothened his expression and exhaled through his nostrils. "Poetic. Let's get to the point. I understand that you were merely following orders. Any information you gathered would ultimately reach the High King, but I know there are other parties involved. So, who did you report to?"

The traitor let out an exasperated laugh. "No one."

"Funny." Ronan flicked out a dagger, swiping a sharp line across the male's face. The traitor shouted, eyes burning with pain and hatred. *Even better.* "Rumor has it you have been seen wandering within the inner district. Now who in the damning Suns could you have visited?"

One of the shadow dealers hissed. "Imbecile."

The traitor's face paled. Ronan pressed the tip of the dagger under the male's chin. Forced him to meet his gray eyes. "I will do what I must to survive too."

He snatched the shadow dealer by the throat, forgoing his dagger. Ronan lifted the male off the ground as he slowly got to his feet. The traitor clawed at his arm, his eyes going wide and the skin of his neck purpling.

Ronan's fingers tightened. He curled his lips and spoke through clenched teeth. "You said that I wouldn't survive much longer. What makes you think I live now?"

The pressure of his grasp built until there was a *snap*. The male's body slipped from the archangel's loosened hold, falling with a deafening thud. Guards entered the hall to remove the body, a trail of blood streaking the limestone ground behind them.

Ronan turned to the other shadow dealers at the stone table. He placed his hands on the cool surface, showcasing the tattooed ink on his battered hands. Black wings arched behind him as he met every pair of eyes.

"Now," he finally said. "Where were we?"

The warmth of the torchlight within the chamber kissed the planes of his cheekbones, gilding his deeply sun-kissed olive skin. The shadow dealers shifted in their seats and Ronan bathed in their discomfort for another breath.

Illegal markets had existed long before him, but it was he who had grappled with the underworld and tamed it. He remembered having to build his reputation. Had challenged the old leaders of the illegal trade. There was only one way those altercations ended, but that was the cost he'd had to pay to be where he was today.

He had been expecting the bureaucratic burdens that came with leading the shadow markets—but *gods*, he hated these meetings.

A vampire twirled the cup of wine in her hand. "What an entertaining distraction." She was utterly relaxed, as if Ronan hadn't just killed a man just moments earlier. "You have my loyalty, archangel. I am, however, concerned with our business trades in the Estrella Territories. We haven't heard from our contacts in Huerta in a while."

Ronan sat at the head of the table. "How long ago did we send resources?"

"A month. They've been silent since."

He ran a hand over his jaw. "That is concerning. I will send my trusted commander to consult with our connections in Huerta, if you will use your forces to uncover who our fallen traitor had been in contact with from the inner district."

The vampire flashed a devious smile. "It is settled."

Only the flicker of flames responded. His gray eyes roamed across the table once more. "Anything else we need to discuss?"

When no one answered, Ronan dismissed them, every shadow dealer bowing to him as they left the meeting hall. As soon as he was alone, he sighed. His wings slackened against the stone seat.

Gods, the Fates must be mocking him. Never did he think he would be here, at the age of thirty-two and spearheading the growth of illegal trade to survive. Ronan's tattooed hand drummed the table. His eyes followed the light of the torches along the carved walls.

Images of large beasts with wings and feathers, warriors of bones and teeth charged the ivory stone. Whispers of ancient peoples who had once thrived within these caves. Ronan suspected the old nation and murals were from the Age of the Primordials, but who really knew.

The engravings reminded him of a place where palm trees swayed, and the smell of jasmine weaved through the salted air. It brought a sense of belonging—a yearning that tugged at something chained deep within him.

A force, faint and tired, trembled beneath his skin. It strained against the mental barriers, a bloodied palm with only enough strength to slide down an unseen wall.

His power. Locked and hidden away. Ronan felt it at times like rippling water. Its presence brushed its knuckles against the fabrics of his mind, but he always ignored it.

The archangel could no longer call out to the ethers of the Continent. Long ago he had been able to feel the tendrils of power that veined the ground and sky. Not anymore. That part of him died all those years ago.

The flames on the torches seemed to turn brighter, the sound of crackling and popping growing stronger. A blast of embers fluttered into the air and he flinched. He could've sworn he'd heard screaming.

It was in these moments when he met his retribution. Those tortured memories always hurtled back at him, their poisoned teeth ready to hurt him more than what had already been done.

Ronan left the meeting chamber, entering a narrow corridor. More torchlights. More fire. He kept his head bowed, ambling through the cave system that had belonged to a past civilization, until he finally reached the grand hall. The walls towered above him, made of stone and dust, darkness and age. There were no doors, only statues of skeletal warriors guarding the entrance.

He stopped at the threshold, gaze landing on the array of lights and adobe buildings before him. The Stone Orchard, hidden city, home to those of the Sombra Quarter and a refuge to many others. Among the hills of Elios, an entire civilization thrived within the massive caverns of a canyon. Enormous arches of old rock crossed over the secret city, exposing slivers of the night sky while still hiding it from view. A waterfall poured through the openings from above, flowing into the river that ran through the city. Some homes had been carved directly along the canyon's rocky walls, stone bridges acting as elevated pathways for the raised buildings.

Ronan had built this place from nothing, when he had cut down the old rulers of the Sombra Quarter. Desperation had made him more beast than archangel.

His black wings unfurled and he pushed off from the ground, dust exploding from where he stood.

The air sang to him as he dipped between the columns of

moonlight, following the path of the river. The soft dark strands of his hair fell back from his brow. A breath escaped his lips as he closed his eyes.

Ronan didn't know why he always came to this place, there had yet to be a night when he hadn't. He stood within a grove of trees that were made of stone and slid a palm over a smooth trunk. Silver light sifted between the carved branches. Shadows etched over the planes of his cheekbones and jaw. Another sacred place that had been here long before the Sombra Quarter arrived.

It had become his refuge. A twisted sanctuary for the forgotten, the lost, and the misfits.

The thought clamped hands around Ronan's chest and tightened. *This is enough, it must be.* Even the plea sounded unconvincing to himself. The Sombra Quarter was a temporary solution to a graver problem, but he could not ponder more on the topic. That was a matter for later.

Since he'd left the meeting chamber, the memories hadn't left him. They continued to shatter his world with every blink of his eyes.

The bloodshed. The screams. The fires.

And the chains.

"Ronan."

His breathing grew rapid. Lungs failing to fill with air.

The bloodshed. The screams. The fires. And the chains—

"*Ronan.*"

He blinked, sucking in a sharp breath. His gaze landed on a brawny archangel emerging from the dark. Dark plaited hair hung over the male's thick shoulder, dips and curves that carved his brown skin. Dove-gray wings, touched by the stars and moon, folded behind his back.

The male's dark eyes sharpened. "Where did you go, brother?"

There was no blood relation between Ronan and Orion Solterra, but that did not matter when their bond had been forged by the battlefield and heartache. Ronan turned his face away so his brother couldn't see how he shut his eyes, combating the remnants of those images. The horror that seeped into his bones.

"The past," Ronan whispered. "It is always there, waiting for me."

Orion was silent at first. His brother had known his struggles. Had been there when Ronan first experienced the flashbacks.

A constant silent war, one he felt he was losing every bleeding day.

"What do you need?" Orion asked gently.

Ronan shook his head, finally looking up. "You are back from patrol."

His brother watched him a moment, must've seen his need to deter his thoughts from the pains of his past. Orion's lips curved upward. "Did you miss me?"

Ronan chuckled, albeit a bit tiredly. "Always. I'm sorry I didn't bring flowers, I was a bit distracted."

Orion snorted at his dry tone. "How messy did you make it?"

He scoffed, though he tried to hide his recoil at the mention of the blood-stained event that had transpired earlier this evening. "Messy enough," he replied. "I did it in front of the leading shadow dealers."

Orion barked out a laugh. "Shit. I wish I had been there to witness that."

Ronan smirked. "You would've enjoyed it." His expression fell, tension bracketing his mouth. "Though I have grave news."

He clapped his brother's shoulder as they ambled deeper into the grove. Dust sparkled beneath their boots, twisting with the starlight. He informed Orion of what was discussed during the meeting.

His brother swore under his breath. "What if Huerta is terminating their partnership with us?"

Ronan frowned. "Unlikely. The Sombra Quarter brings them more profit than their own king. I hate to ask, but I am going to need you to come with me to visit the Estrella Territories and see what is happening with our silent tradesmen."

Orion nodded. "We can leave first thing in the morning." He gazed at the shards of the sky above. His wings looked more silver than gray under the light. "Ronan, we do not have the manpower nor the capacity to continue the way we have been. You've endured so much the past fourteen years and I know there are wounds you have not healed from yet—but the living are still here, *we* need you."

His brother sounded like he was considering his words. Fucking Stars, Ronan had a guess where this was going.

"You can't continue to ignore your calling," Orion said. "Are you sure you don't want to undo—"

"My *calling?*" Ronan bit out, harsher than he intended. "If I remember clearly, my so-called destiny is what caused all this. The choice I made is the very reason we are here, ensuring every day that the Sombra Quarter continues to thrive in order to provide and sustain ourselves and those who depend on us, who have nowhere else to go after what happened. We've had this conversation so many times, Orion. Don't you understand? I *failed.*"

His brother flinched and Ronan hated that he had caused such a reaction. He knew Orion meant well, expected nothing less from him.

Ronan was always reminded of his deepest failures. The past haunted him. It was relentless, fraying at the tired seams of his soul. It left him longing for something beyond the chains he had placed upon himself, but he would never seek it. A future without this heart-wrenching burden was not something he deserved.

Everything he did would be penance until he drew his last damning breath.

SIX

The ground cracked as the archangels landed. Ronan hauled himself to his feet, a plume of dirt rising with his wings. He ran a hand through his damp hair; sweat already beaded underneath the collar of his fighting leathers. Since they'd left the Stone Orchard, it had taken them two nights to fly through the Estrella Territories.

Ronan took one look at the city of Huerta and cursed under his breath. "What in the gods' name happened here?"

The once colorful buildings—walls of orange, yellow, and blue— were now broken, some of them completely destroyed. There were gaping holes in the walls and doors. Pieces of stone littered the dirt roads, and the white steps to the townhomes now painted in red.

Huerta, a place that was popular among common travelers and tradesmen, had been reduced to dust.

A relationship had long been established between the Sombra and the city's leaders, along with a steady flow of commerce and funds. From the looks of the destruction, Ronan was beginning to understand why they hadn't heard from their business partner.

Orion drew up beside him and shuddered. The archangel who had once led a battle under a red sky *shuddered*.

"Shit," he muttered.

Ronan tilted his head up and listened. The air was still, the paths were too quiet. Not even the wild animals had made their way through this place. His heart started to race as he caught a familiar coppery scent. "I smell nothing but blood."

"There are no bodies here," Orion observed.

Ronan scoured the city. Intriguing—there really were no bodies, nor any sign of them.

They passed the entrance of a home, the door barely clinging to its hinges. Ronan paused long enough to peek in. Tables and chairs were splintered into pieces. As soon as he stepped inside, his gaze landed on the red handprints that smeared the walls. The pounding of his heart went to his ears as he followed the streaked blood, not bothering to look down when the tip of his boot nudged a piece of shattered clay.

The violence that had occurred here, it cut open old wounds he thought were long healed. In an attempt to recollect himself, Ronan gestured to the disastrous scene. "Tell me, what do you see?"

Orion eyed the red-stained walls, the rotted food and waste littering the dining place. "Judging by how the flies have devoured what's left, whatever happened occurred some time ago."

"What else?" He asked.

"What is this, training like back when we were younglings?" Orion rumbled. Ronan's lips twitched at that. "The blood on the walls has dried. This family was attacked but there are no signs that they died. At least not here. They fought hard though." Orion paused. "Perhaps they were captured?"

Ronan made a sound. "I suspect the same thing."

Orion wandered back out to the city's center and called out to him. Ronan followed. "My turn to ask the questions, what do *you* see?"

His brother pointed at the ground, and it didn't take long before Ronan's eyes widened. "Footprints."

"What else?" Orion pressed.

Ronan's gaze followed the tracks that led out of the town and into the wilderness. "They left their city. They were attacked, but their prints—assuming it's the citizens of Huerta's—seem calm and collected."

Discomfort gnawed at Ronan's stomach. Who had attacked the city? Where had its residents gone?

Something in his body shifted. Within the seams of the realm, he heard a call.

It was neither a person nor a beast. A whisper, striking a chord in the air, tethering to Ronan's senses. Orion seemed oblivious to the sensation as the bulky archangel bent to lift pieces of a wall that blocked their path into a desolated building.

Ronan brushed past his brother and stepped inside. Debris cluttered everywhere in the space. There was hardly a roof left, allowing the light to shine on his dirtied path. A beam of wood had fallen across the expanse and pierced through the broken stone wall. He walked on, treading over the white dust and bloodied rocks.

He followed the hum in the air, held on to that line as it guided him.

"Ronan," Orion warned.

He stepped over the large beam and froze when he caught the sound of mewling and scratching. His fingers stretched out, ready to unsheathe whatever weapons he brought with him, despite the fact that it had been years since he'd actually raised a sword.

He trudged deeper through the wreckage, following the hum and—

The blood drained from his face. Ahead of him was another beam of wood and a large slab stone. Crushed underneath it was a human—a woman.

The lower half of her body was flattened beneath the debris. Her head of knotted hair swung side to side, hands clawing at the dirt. The tips of her fingers were stained with dark red, blunt fingernails ground to the bone. The woman's lower jaw hung awkwardly. She could not speak but another torn cry peeled from her broken mouth.

The human shouldn't even be *alive.*

Her eyes glowed a cerulean blue, the color glistening like gems. When the woman saw him, she went erratic, the sounds she made indistinguishable. More animal. Ronan unhitched a knife from his belt.

He slowly approached her. "What happened to you?"

The near-silent call hadn't stopped, urging his senses to move forward. The ether in his blood shifted. A beast raising its head from a long slumber. The sensation was enough to halt Ronan in his tracks. It had been so long since he had felt it.

There was a rumble. A heed of warning before his power fell quiet once more.

Ronan couldn't understand what had happened. Wasn't ready to dive into that long-forgotten part of himself. Suns Above, he was not prepared for any of this.

There was no second thought as he drove the short blade into the base of the woman's skull. The snap of bone caused the flashes of fire in his mind to roar at his face. Screams seared through his ears. And the pain of his breaking heart—Ronan grimaced, nearly dropping the dagger.

Orion missed nothing. "Easy," he breathed. "Easy."

Ronan listened to his brother's voice, using it as a tether to return to reality. The memories flickered to nothing but a shroud of mist. The pain dulled to a pulsating throb at his temples. He breathed through his nostrils.

Fight it, you bastard.

He slowly brought himself upright. The blade hung loosely in his grip. Ronan worked a swallow, managing the words from his throat. "Ether."

Orion stepped over the beam. "What?"

Ronan shoved the dagger back into his belt. A slight tremble to his fingers as he pointed to the lifeless woman, her vacant eyes now void of the glowing blue and back to a natural brown shade.

"That was the work of ether," Ronan rasped. "A malevolent form of it."

Orion's face blanched. Sweat plastered the black strands of hair to his thick neck. "You mean to say someone transformed this human into . . . whatever that was?"

Ronan shook his head. "No. Yes? Gods, I don't know. Whatever ether existed in that poor woman touched my own. I *felt* my power—only for a moment."

His brother's eyes gleamed with something a lot like hope. Ronan's stomach twisted.

"What do we do now?" Orion asked.

Ronan ran a hand through his hair. An entire city had been attacked, its residents gone. His mind whirled with questions and theories. Inevitably, his thoughts went back to the Sombra Quarter and the business it conducted with the Estrella Territories.

"We will tell the shadow dealers that the town was destroyed—by raiders, rebels or fucking pirates, I do not care. But we do not breathe a word of the ether we have just witnessed. Traitors have been found amongst our followers, we do not know who to trust. Whatever happened here may have taken place in the other settlements we trade with. I rather we save the Sombra Quarter's livelihood before the High Throne catches wind of this atrocity and closes all trade routes."

Orion's expression turned grim. "We must act quick then, it won't be long before Elios's forces get involved."

Ronan glanced down at the lifeless woman. Whether or not this had been a calculated or random attack, he couldn't afford it happening again.

The word that escaped his lips was ragged. "*Fuck.*"

SEVEN

With every step of Río's hooves, the more withdrawn Zara became. With every mile that distanced her from Ikarria, the colder she felt.

It was a shedding of skin, shifting from the woman she had been raised to be to the monster she truly was. The lack of her family's presence, as well as the loss of the Ikarrian ancient forest and mountain ranges, caused her to feel empty.

If anything, it gave her the strength to do what needed to be done for the hunting season, in order to secure the safety of those she loved. Emotion proved to be a weakness. Especially for the likes of her.

Zara ran a hand over her horse's deep yellow coat, her gaze landing on the guild. No, she wasn't entirely alone. Unlike her family at home, the guild were familiar with who she became in Soleira. What she *had* to become.

Río threw his head, flipping his black mane. Zara's nails ran over the faded lines and scratches along his neck. The sight was not uncommon for a retired warhorse, but her heart still panged for her beloved Río. He had been through so much.

A large dark gray wolf leapt from between the trees, landing beside her. Axar's voice echoed from behind the animal's closed lips. "*I did not sense any potential dangers within the area. Aside from the wild-life, we are alone."*

Hakim, who had been riding up front beside Eshe, waved a hand in dismissal. "The road to Elios from Ikarria is always an easy one."

The terrain toward the Continent's capital was filled with hills, woodland and rivers. There were no major cities or landmarks between the two regions, except for small farming and trading towns, which made for a seamless journey. They had left Dae Asari over a week ago, and they would reach Soleira within another three days' time.

"Surprisingly enough, I never grow tired of this road," Axar said. "It's quiet and peaceful."

Zara rolled her eyes. "You say this every time."

The wolf made a sound that was a mix between a growl and a whine. Axar stood as tall as the horses, though they were unbothered by the sight of his large fangs and glowing yellow eyes. Especially Río, who simply snorted and picked up his pace.

Axar's ears twitched. *"He still doesn't like me."*

Zara smirked. "He hasn't forgiven you for stealing his bushel of apples."

"That was ages ago, and I was only teasing him. I pray one day Río may let go of his grudge and forgive me." He whined, sending what looked to be a forlorn look toward Zara's horse.

She chuckled and tipped her head up. The warmth of the sky kissed her cheeks, a faint smell of rain in the air. Zara's thoughts wandered to the capital that awaited them. "I wonder how many assignments Raziel will give us."

Axar growled. *"The High King always has an endless list. Too many enemies to slaughter—it should be concerning. But so be it."*

"Charming."

He snorted. *"It is not as if you care what happens to the Continent either, Santos."*

The truth slipped through the air, sinking into her bones. The relationship between her and Axar was as such: brutal honesty. He knew the darker shades of her heart, as he bore the same. The Continent had done nothing for those like them.

Beams of sunlight poured through the trees. Large flowers the size of a man's torso were strewn about the forest ground. Vines curled around the trunks. The sound of creeks in the short distance.

Río bucked his head again. Zara's hands tightened around his reins. "What do you hear?"

Hakim pointed to a bush. "Look."

Blue orbs of flame popped up from the leaves. The light reflected from its surface.

No, not fire. Water.

Zara's jaw dropped as more floating spheres of water bounced from the branches. They bobbed over the shrubbery, nearing the mercenaries. In the span of a blink, the blue orbs morphed into humanoid shapes.

Hakim's voice was low. Almost reverent. "Chaneques. Elemental forces that guard the land. Loyal representatives to the Primordial of the Hunt and Harvest, Junya."

Eshe gently tugged on her horse's reins. "They never show themselves to mortals."

Zara couldn't tear her gaze away from the little elementals. "How do you know so much about them?"

Hakim extended a finger as a chaneque approached him. "I read about them in my youth. I've only had the pleasure of seeing them once, other than now. That was before I became general of Ikarria's armies; not long after that, I met your pater, the king."

Water flowed with the creature's movements as it grasped his finger with two small hands. It made a chittering sound and Hakim chuckled in response.

"Can you understand them?" Zara asked.

"No, but you can feel their energy. This one seems to be quite the jester."

Other water sprites were dancing around Axar's head. The wolf playfully nipped the air, pretending to chase them.

Something wet touched her cheek. Zara shot her head to the side, hand flying to the dagger at her thigh. Her eyes narrowed on the chaneque that lurched back in surprise.

"Do not touch me." She gritted her teeth.

The chaneque cocked its head. Water continued to shift and move over its figure, revealing a feminine face. Zara stilled as the sprite floated closer and extended a hand.

When she realized it was waiting for her, she slowly leaned forward till she felt the small press of its palm on her cheek. The chaneque chittered. The sound was low, full of lament, causing her heart to throb. The water sprite emanated . . . sadness.

The little elemental made the sound again as its little hand ran small circles against her skin. Zara felt like she understood what Hakim had meant about being able to feel their energy. Little rivers of sorrow pulsated from the creature. And deep, deep pain. The way it tilted its head, its little hand still rubbing her cheek, made Zara feel as if the chaneque was comforting *her*.

Zara's brows pulled forward as she watched the sprite. The words fell from her lips before she could stop herself. "I am fine."

Water trickled down her skin as the chaneque leaned forward and pressed its brow against hers. Zara closed her eyes for a moment and breathed before the elemental moved.

She could only stare as the creature slowly retreated to the forest, the slip of its palm leaving an empty feeling inside her.

It wasn't long before the rest of the chaneques disappeared as well. Axar tousled his mane. *"That was intriguing. The Primordials are cut off from our world, does that not have any effect on the chaneques?"*

Hakim spurred his horse forward, the guild following. "The Primordials are still connected to the ethereal beings in the mortal world despite the Gates having been destroyed. Nature will always find a way to connect with its origin. To restore its balance. I am sure the chaneques can still feel the wants of their goddess, even if they cannot communicate with her."

"It used to be said," Eshe murmured. "That sighting of a chaneque meant good fortune was on the horizon."

Zara doubted that would be true.

EIGHT

Soleira, the capital of Elios, never failed to send Zara into a pool of bitterness.

A full week's worth of travel. The guild had spent countless nights sleeping among the blades of grass and the wild blossoms that glowed like silver stars. Now, under the blinding Elios sun, nothing but white and marble stretched before them.

Pale ivory buildings stacked too close together filled the outer district, the roads narrow and less kempt. The inner districts, however, had towers of marble and luxurious villas. Houses were lined with copper and the roads were paved with cobblestone. Temples dedicated to the Primordials—that had managed to survive the slow purge of the High King and the Council—were scattered about the capital.

Zara's lips curled at the sight of the bronze-domed castle in the distance. Adjacent to it was the coliseum, where many royal games took place. Sun-kissed spires surrounded the magnificent structure, pinning the sky with its pale teeth.

A salted breeze swept through Zara's cloak, brushing through the tendrils of her brown hair. To the west, the ocean shimmered. Out of everything, *that* was the most welcome sight. Massive ships bobbed in the docks, masts stitched with the emblems of the various kingdoms.

The guild made its way through the capital's inner district. She ignored the stares, brushed away the whispers. The fear and hatred was practically tangible. Everyone knew what this time of the year meant. Soon the mercenaries of the realms would stalk their streets, dousing them in red.

But it was *their* High King who had decreed this life. *To protect the kingdom,* he claimed.

The guild dismounted at the entrance of the castle grounds, leaving their horses with the staff who had been waiting for them. Silver light exploded from Axar's wolf as he shifted into his human form. Zara squinted against the light, sliding her hand from Río's neck.

Hedges and gardens delicately wrapped around the property. Statues of armored archangels lined the main path to the doors of the fortress. Not a single depiction of a Primordial in sight.

Shadows flickered from above, catching Zara's eye. The winged race soared through the cool blue sky. A common sight nowadays, except for the new string of vampire soldiers from Adrastea patrolling the grounds.

One of their units strolled past them, their wine-red cloaks flapping in the breeze. Zara recalled the conversation between Daria and their pater. Adrastea's strengthening relationship with Elios was not something to ignore. She shared a look with Hakim. The wrinkle between his brows told her he was also concerned.

White pillars lined the entrance to the throne room as the guild walked in silence. Archangel soldiers pushed the bronze doors open. Zara rolled her shoulders, the gray scales of her armor shifting over her muscles. The comfortable weight of silver teeth strapped to her body stifled the unease that curled in her stomach.

One of the archangels twisted his lips in disgust. "Rogue trash," he sneered.

The fyrebrand seemed to laugh in her head. *Rogue. Rogue. Rogue. See, they do not appreciate the dirty work you do for them. How stained have your palms become in order for theirs to remain clean and unscathed? Show them what it means to be the Rogue.*

Red seeped through the corners of Zara's vision. A tremor in her veins. Shit. Zara inhaled, forcing the fury back. If she was to murder a soldier on the High Throne's doorstep—well, it certainly wouldn't do her any favors.

Though, she doubted Raziel would be offended by it. If anything, he might've enjoyed it. That was the type of male the High King was.

And she was his favorite.

Zara resorted to simply curling her lips into a wicked smile and gave the soldier a mocking salute. "At ease."

Axar couldn't help his cackle, the sound echoing against the pristine marble. He tugged on her arm to keep up the pace. She couldn't fight the smug smile that grew over her lips.

Eshe looked over her shoulder. A hint of humor touched her voice. "Gods, the soldier's face is beet red."

Zara squared her shoulders, refusing to glance back. "He was a coward."

Shame, the fyrebrand criticized. *I was hoping for some violence.*

Whatever victory she felt in that moment was quickly washed away as they entered the throne room. Reality struck her numb when she spotted the other mercenary guilds already gathered inside. As the years passed, the unease never waned. She was secretly grateful for the hood that hid her face, how it shielded her from the eyes of the other mercenary guilds.

White and wine-red cloaks, silver and bronze breastplates, the insignias—but Zara didn't have to face the other Horizons, the High Throne was all she saw. No. It was the male who sat upon it she couldn't look away from. Elios may have adored him, proclaimed him their hero, but he was something else entirely to her.

The creator of her darkness. The thief of her childhood. The author of her demise.

High King Raziel's gaze snapped to her, golden eyes tracking her every move. He lounged on a throne of white oak. The old wood was made into the shape of wings, veined with melted gold. His red hair fell past his shoulders, brushing sharp cheekbones that could cut glass, his brown wings splayed out against his seat.

An alabaster crown sat on his head, and he wore a brown leather breastplate over a deep blue tunic. The High King did not care much for extravagant things. Power was his only obsession.

Above, watching from the balconies, was the Council. A shroud of mist lingered where they stood. Zara couldn't see the faces of the new governing body of deities—the very deities who had rebelled against the Primordials they once served—but their presence brought a near-silent hum of energy to the room.

She wasn't fond of Raziel nor did she care for the Council, but Elios's people believed they were dedicated to the kingdom's future.

Zara lowered to one knee and bowed her head.

"Rise."

The voice never failed to chill her blood. The very same voice that came through her fyrebrand.

Zara kept her expression blank as she slowly lifted her gaze. A knowing smile seemed to curve over Raziel's lips. She clenched her jaw. Raziel's presence was so distracting that she hadn't noticed the archangel standing beside the throne. Long platinum blonde hair, wings white as snow. Erebus, the Hand of the High King, watched her with an unreadable expression.

The High King finally dragged his gaze across the throne room. "Under normal circumstances I would welcome you to another hunting season, though it seems this time it will be a little different."

The mercenaries shifted in place. Wings rustled and fingers tapped the pommels of blades. Zara slowly stepped back to join her guild, their presence providing a warmth that not even the sun could offer.

Raziel swung onto his feet, sauntering down the dais. "There has been a silent battle here among the streets of Elios. An enemy makes a mockery of the new world we are creating."

The new world. Zara would have laughed at that. Raziel and the Council had destroyed the mortal world's connection to the ethereal realm. They had tipped the scales. Ether was a natural force, essential to their lives and the Continent's, and it had been disrupted. Zara was not entirely sure what that would entail, but she was not naive enough to think that there wouldn't be consequences.

But what did she know? She was a mere mercenary, meant for killing, not ruling. The Aligned Realms seemed to believe in this new future without the Primordials. While the royals and politics executed their convictions, she would continue to serve.

"Every hunting season, I have assigned each guild a set of marks to hunt. And every year, the Horizons have cleansed our capital of traitors and criminals." Raziel's eyes glittered with dark hunger. "This season, you will all have one common enemy. Your mark is the Sombra Quarter."

Murmurs rippled through the congregation of mercenaries. The High King's wings flared, a subtle curl to his lips as he continued. "The Sombra Quarter is not a mystery to any of you. I want these illegal markets to be ground to dust, every shadow dealer and every supporter on a pike. My spies have done extensive work in exposing some of its members, so you may expect assignments to help lead your hunt. The Sombra Quarter's influence will end by your blades."

There was a wave of unease, a shifting of leather and steel, as the Horizons cast curious looks to one another.

Raziel's wings rose higher. "I understand your confusion. The hunting season has never focused on one enemy. As you all are aware, for your realms to prove their dedication to the current peace, every guild is obligated to serve the hunt for fifty years. To make things more interesting, I will cut the total sentence by half for the guild who slays the most shadow dealers. A gift from me to you."

The ground seemed to slip under Zara's feet as gasps and chatter echoed throughout the room. Disbelief as icy as winter winds swept through her. It couldn't be true. Their sentence to the High King could be reduced. Zara would take sixteen years over the current forty-one that remained.

This was an opportunity. A way to free herself and the guild from the clutches of the High Throne. Zara couldn't dwell on what happened in the past to her because of the High King, for she had the living to look after. The safety of her loved ones depended on how well she obeyed. And now, they had a chance to be free sooner than they thought.

Raziel's gaze landed on her again. She stilled, fingers tensed and prepared to reach for her blade, not that she could do such a thing.

The High King spread his arms. "As for the *Rogue* . . . ."

The throne room fell into a thick silence. Every pair of eyes fell on her, and she knew the guilds were not watching her in admiration. Her throat bobbed. *That fucking title.*

Raziel seemed to know how much attention it drew. He fed upon it. The Rogue was the representation of his power and influence. His creation.

He smiled. "My personal assassin will bring the ruler of the Sombra Quarter to their death. And as a member of the Ikarrian guild, she is still obligated to complete their hunts as well. If the Rogue meets *both* targets, only then will I consider halving her own sentence."

Another assignment. Another set of kills. Another burden. She had ended many lives during the hunting seasons. This would be no different. Her blades would be put to good use.

Raziel clapped his hands together. "Let us begin the igniting of the fyrebrands. Rogue, as is tradition, you may have the honor."

Zara's nails dug crescents into her palms. She was about to take a step when Hakim's hand wrapped around her arm. The simple act was enough to make her blood race—in fear for *him*. He had never held her back before, had never dared defy the King. She couldn't look her mentor's way to see his expression.

"Raziel's watching." Zara whispered.

"Something isn't right." Hakim's grasp only tightened, and something in her heart squeezed at that. At the genuine, undeniable love he had for her.

Eshe's murmur was soft and coaxing. "She will be fine, Hakim. Release her."

When he did—albeit reluctantly—Zara shifted through the crowd and stopped at the foot of the dais.

"How lovely it is to see you, Zara Santos." Raziel's voice grazed talons against her skin. It was enough for her to grind her teeth.

She raised her chin. The hood of her cloak still shadowed her features, but it didn't hide the sharpened look in her eyes. "Your Highness."

The High King kept his gaze on her as he rolled the sleeves of his tunic and extended his arm. On his wrist was the same tattoo that every Horizon had been forced to hold. For he had been the creator of the fyrebrands.

Zara unclasped her bracer and offered her arm. His hand slid over hers, icy to the touch. Raziel angled his head, golden eyes on her array of tattoos. "I see your designs are complete. They complement my mark."

She clenched her jaw, saying nothing. The High King kept his gaze lowered but she saw the smile that brushed his lips. "It doesn't change the fact that you serve me. And for that, I thank you. Your services ensure the success of our new world."

Ether flared from Raziel's tattoo and hers glowed in response. Tendrils of silver materialized in the air, cracking through it like a whip. The stark lines of power dug into her fyrebrand and a sharp hiss escaped her.

There it was. The final stroke of the High King claiming his dominance. Every kill the Horizon made during the hunt would be communicated to Raziel. Something that she and most of the mercenaries were not fond of.

It was a safety measure for the High King, for if a mercenary decided to abandon their commitment to the hunting season, then they'd be subjected to the Reckoning. A slow demise as the fyrebrand would inevitably torture the body and mind until its bearer went completely mad.

Zara refused to let the King see how much he affected her. It was a silent battle, a gnashing of teeth and thrashing of wings, as their connection was sealed.

Raziel slowly tilted his head to the side, his voice too low for anyone else to hear. "Do not forget your purpose, Rogue. Those you care for most will remain safe, so long as you honor the treaty. The Continent is our priority. Even above our own emotion."

A war raged inside her heart. The unseen chains around her neck tightened.

"As you will, High King. I serve you."

In the deep corners of her thoughts, the fyrebrand laughed.

NINE

Come sunset, the guilds made their way to the mercenary temple of Elios.

It was far from the capital, sitting on the green edges of the border with Ikarria—thank the gods. Zara wasn't sure if she would be able to live in the castle without wringing someone's neck.

The Elios ruin was not built like the one in Ikarria. It sat at the top of a narrow, rocky hill, the temple made up of three conjoined domed edifices at the top of it. Small waterfalls cascaded down the slopes from its base, where the stables were located, the guilds' mounts safely tucked away in there.

She walked down the familiar dining hall. Windows lined both walls, allowing light to splash onto long tables made of white oak. The floor was a dark green marble like the Jade Sea, a contrast to the bronze chandeliers that hung above.

The guilds gathered inside, the color of their cloaks representing each realm. Wine-red for Adrastea, white for Elios, and brown for the realm of Kairos. Zara was thankful for the black of Ikarria, it suited her more.

They all kept within their circles, sizing the others up. Except for a large elven male who broke away from the Adrastean group. The sides of his head were shaved, leaving a strip of plaited blond hair on top.

His large arms were spread out, a wide grin plastered on his face. "Hakim!"

The head of the Ikarrian guild brushed past her, meeting the male midway. Hakim clasped his arm. "Warrick, it's good to see you. How does the land of the bloodsworn fare you?"

The elf shrugged a massive shoulder. "You get used to the vampires, though I've missed you, old friend."

"As have I. You know I wish to see you and the other guilds more often. For us to connect as we did in the past."

Warrick inclined his head, smiling. "Ah. Your *dream*. It may have to stay that way for a bit longer, Hakim. I don't see these bastards wanting to bond anytime soon."

The elf chuckled as he spoke loudly and gestured to the guilds standing around them. Slowly, the mercenaries began to intermingle. Every year, Zara noticed how the more seasoned Horizons were more inclined to reunite with the other guilds than the younger ones. They had, after all, been unified once—before Zara's time, before the War divided them.

Zara peeked out of the arched windows. She slid the palms of her hands over the stone threshold as she stared at the ribbons of deep orange and purple; firebirds streaked the golden sky, their tails dipped in indigo.

She felt the hairs on her neck rise and glanced over her shoulder. An archangel watched from across the dining hall. Zara immediately recognized her as Tamaya. The head mercenary of the Elios guild was terrifyingly beautiful, with her long black hair and deep brown skin. A jagged scar ran down the left side of her cheek, giving her a permanently harsh look. Her red wings were folded tightly behind her back as she leaned against the wall.

Zara felt Axar approach her. His eyes followed hers. "Look at you, making friends."

She scowled at that. "Tamaya has always hated me."

"You're the Rogue." He gave her a sidelong glance. "And she is a Horizon of Elios. She *always* serves the High King, not just during the hunting season. And yet, he prefers you. Tamaya may see it as an insult."

Zara's gaze dropped, her heart sinking with it. There was no honor in being the Rogue. Maybe Tamaya knew this, but it still mattered little to her. Perhaps Tamaya somehow believed there was an advantage to being the High King's favorite. There wasn't. If only Zara could be rid of that title, be removed from Raziel's spotlight.

Axar nudged her shoulder. "What do you think of the assignment for the hunt?"

The thought of all the guilds battling for the same prize caused her lips to twist in disgust. "Raziel has never bargained with our freedom like this before, it is a bit unsettling."

"He must be desperate."

Zara leaned against the windowsill, kicking up the heel of her boot against the wall. "I didn't realize how influential the Sombra Quarter was becoming. The King hadn't been interested in them before."

The shifter shoved his body beside hers as he took his turn to gaze out the window. "Are you nervous about your task?"

Shadows flickered across Zara's expression. The dark depths of her soul opened wide like the maw of an unknown beast ready to drag her down to the void where she would abandon reason and emotion. That was where the Rogue would be waiting, with arms made of black mist that would wrap around her and suffocate what remained of her heart.

Zara was neither nervous nor afraid.

"No," she said. "The head of the Sombra Quarter will be like any other mark. I will hunt as I always do."

Her mercenary brother exhaled through his nostrils. "I thought you would say something like that."

Eventually, a yawn crawled up her throat, exhaustion sinking into her bones. Axar jerked his chin for her to follow, and she did. They ambled to the back foyer and into the hall that led to Ikarria's designated suite. A door at the end opened to a small living room with a roaring fireplace, cushioned seats arranged in the center. More corridors split into private chambers.

Axar mumbled a *goodnight* and disappeared. It was still the afternoon, but it had been a long day. Zara's body walked almost by its own accord. Her muscles remembered every wooden panel, every chipped stone on the walls.

In her room was a large four-post bed, white linen draped over its gray wood. The walls were stacked with dark brick. Shelves were filled with withered books and decorative vases and trinkets she'd placed there over the years—it had been pure luck that no one had touched her little collection.

Zara stripped off her armor and crawled under the sheets, the High King's assignment immediately invading her thoughts. She was familiar with the illegal organization. She suspected it would be a challenge to scour the underbelly of Soleira to find her mark, but she wouldn't shy away from it. Zara felt the tender flesh of her fyrebrand, an ache that reminded her of how little power she truly had.

When she awoke, it was almost night. The last of the sunset bled beyond the horizon as a faint curtain of stars began to fall. Zara heard a knock on the door, a single sound that pounded through the wood and echoed through her bones. She knew what the message meant.

After washing herself and donning her leathers once more, Zara padded out of the Ikarrian suite. The living room was dark and empty, the others must have retired to their rooms. She wrapped her hand around the iron door handle to the hall before a shadow caught her peripheral.

Hakim leaned against the threshold of the corridor arch that led to his and Eshe's rooms. His face was taut with tension. "He asked for you specifically."

The head of the guild had been the one to knock on her door. Zara nodded, unable to find her voice.

"This hunting season worries me," Hakim said.

She hesitated and forced herself to speak. "Why?"

Concern pulled at the lines around his mouth. "I don't know."

Zara wondered if that was why Hakim had halted her in the throne room. His intuition was gnawing at him. But there was nothing she could do, there were orders to heed.

So, she left the Ikarrian suite and made way to the ruin's strategy room. It sat at the upper level of one of the conjoined edifices. The domed ceiling was made of glass, allowing the night sky to bathe the marble floor in starlight. Bookshelves lined the walls while long tables filled the space. Scrolls were splayed about the dark wood surfaces, as well as trinkets and instruments to observe the moon and stars. Zara fiddled with the glass canisters of crystals, powders, and colored liquids as she passed.

The elf was familiar with the strategy room, but it never failed to kindle her curiosity. But she couldn't stop. She pushed the balcony doors open and the ocean breeze swept through her hair. From this view, the realm of Elios was a map of torchlights flickering in front of the sea.

Zara rested a hip against the doorframe. "I assume you have an assignment for me?"

The silver-haired archangel was standing along the edge of the balcony. The soft gray tunic melded to his hard body, the insignia of three suns within a pair of wings stitched on his lapel. His arms were folded, white wings tucked behind him.

Erebus, the Hand of the High King, smirked. "Couldn't it also be to say hello to an old friend?"

Zara chuckled. "Friend is a stretch."

He placed a hand over his chest. "You wound me."

A knowing smile touched her lips as she strode toward the archangel. Her hands slid up his chest, feeling his strong arms wrap around her. Erebus tugged her against him as he slanted his mouth over hers.

Her tongue swept against his, allowing herself to drown in the familiar touch. His lips were unhurried, as if he had been waiting for this since the last hunting season and would take his time reuniting with her.

The archangel was beautiful. His eyes were as blue as the sea. His silver hair ran past his shoulders. Erebus was the first ally she made in Elios. When she first started the hunting seasons, and as Raziel's interest in her grew, Erebus had been commanded to deliver tasks meant only for the Rogue. A forced companionship that had kindled into genuine friendship over the years, which somehow began to include casual sex.

She was the one who had initiated it.

Zara could feel his hard cock against her breeches. The last male she'd had sex with had been mediocre, but Erebus would make up for it. And gods, she needed the reprieve. He kissed a line down her throat, teeth scraping her skin. A whimper sounded in her throat as his fingers dug into her back. She was on the verge of falling to her knees to take him in her mouth.

But Erebus was *here*, which meant it was for something other than their usual escapades. The Hand of the High King was on duty. The thought was enough to snap her out of her lust.

Zara slowly peeled herself away from him. He did not fight it and watched her take several steps away.

"The assignment you are here for," she said, clearing her throat. "Is it for the Rogue?"

The light in Erebus's gaze deflated. "Not yet. This one is for your guild."

Zara flipped a dagger in her hand, twisting and twirling the thin blade between her fingers as Erebus unrolled a piece of parchment. As easy it was for them to get lost in their physical desires, it was even easier for them to stop as if nothing had happened at all.

It didn't bother her. It was not as if she had romantic feelings for the Hand of the High King. He was a means to an end, just as she was for him.

"The name of your mark is Cadoc. A vampire who was once one of the leading shadow dealers before he went legitimate. His leadership was driven out, and recently he started to feed the High King's spies information about the Sombra."

Zara didn't look up from her dagger. "Let me guess, Cadoc's usefulness is running short."

Erebus grunted. "He's been abusing his partnership with the High Throne. Thinks he can leverage his knowledge for more wealth and power. You and the guild are to find out what he knows by any means necessary."

Her lips twitched, fingers aching to curl around a weapon. She hated serving Raziel, but there was a part of her that relished the fight. She had become all too good at it.

Zara sheathed her dagger and took the roll of parchment. She sat on the balcony's stone railing, letting her legs sway over the edge. Her eyes went to the sky. The stars glimmered and winked within the growing darkness. Another breeze tousled her hair, and she caught the scent of grass and salt.

Erebus rested against the stone. His back was to the glittering capital, his eyes on her. "You know you can always talk to me. I know how the hunting season affects you."

Zara was tempted to scoff. "I have been raised as a mercenary. One would think I would have grown accustomed to all this, but the hunting season is not the way of the Horizon."

"That sounds like Hakim talking," he replied.

She shot him a look. The truth nearly clawed its way out of her. *I would like to know what it is to be* more.

Instead, she said, "You should understand how I feel, know what it's like to be wronged. To have your future taken from you."

Erebus was not one to share about his past, she did not know where he had been born and raised. It had taken several years before he had shared even a sliver about himself and, from what she had gathered, he had been let down by those he cared about, which somehow resulted in him working for Elios.

The Hand of the King had always been a mystery to her, but one she trusted. She didn't need to know every tendril of information about him to know that he had been there for her since she had first started as the Rogue. Although she was still curious.

His expression turned a shade darker. "Yes, but the difference between us is that I had nothing to lose. I clawed my way through disappointment and heartbreak, creating a future that satisfied my desires, and I only had myself to worry about. Be wary when you talk of change, it may bring the deepest pain."

Zara swallowed back the disappointment of her reality. She worked up the courage to ask, "Who were you before you became the Hand of the High King?"

A shadow of a smile touched Erebus's lips. "You are never going to stop asking, are you?"

She shrugged and rested her arm against his. "At least tell me *something*. If you do, then I will consider us friends."

Erebus chuckled but quickly fell silent. His gaze drifted away, as if peering into a memory.

"I used to have honor," he responded. "I have loved and been loved. And I chose power over it all."

Zara watched him, her lips parted in shock. In all the years she had known the male, this was the most she had heard about his past. "Was it the War?"

Erebus scoffed. "Everything is about the War."

His past must have been difficult to discuss. It was why she never pushed him on it. She understood the difficulties that came with sharing those raw, imperfect parts of oneself.

Zara sighed. "Well, I am glad you are here. You are probably the only archangel I find tolerable in this godsforsaken realm."

His sensual lips curved. "I will always remember when I first saw you. The fire in your eyes."

A memory emerged in her head. The castle looked bigger back then, most likely because she had barely reached eighteen years of age. Still too young. The High King had commanded her to duel his Hand, the guild forced to watch from the shadows. Raziel was looking for a *warrior*, a personal assassin, someone to protect the streets during the hunt. He wanted to see how King Idris had prepared his adopted daughter for the seasons to come. She recalled the deities watching her from the dark corners of the throne room. How their silver ether coasted above them like a veil.

Back then, Zara knew of the tensions between Ikarria and Elios. She was also aware of where she stood in the eyes of the High Throne and the Council. How she was a living embodiment of Idris's defiance. And she would not risk tainting her pater's nor her home realm's honor.

She wasn't sure how she'd managed it. The Hand had been a flash of snow and light, blade poised for her chest. The previous five years of training, spent under the Ikarrian sun and within the old forests, screamed through every nerve in her body. It had not been an easy battle. There had been a dangerous *snap* at her side, a wheeze escaping her. Erebus was merciless, eating up the space between them with every vicious bite of his sword.

Something had rumbled awake within Zara's core during that duel. She had felt it unravel. A breath of untapped power. So, the adopted daughter of the elven king leashed it for her own purpose. The strength whispered to her veins, sinking deeper with every heartbeat. It was still too weak to be seen but she reveled in it regardless. The floor beneath Zara's boots cracked as she lunged toward the charging archangel. A gust of energy swept out from where they collided. Erebus hadn't expected the surreal strength that followed her movements. How the teeth of her blades had slashed up the archangel's chest. A ribbon of red shimmered under the natural light, an array of gems shattering.

The High King had approved of her skills, and Zara had felt a surge of pride. Of all the Horizons in the Continent, *she* had been selected. It was her opportunity to prove to the High Throne that even though she was of Valenzian blood, she was loyal to their laws.

How quickly that feeling dissipated. She remembered—gods, she remembered standing in a pool of blood. It belonged to her first set of marks as the Rogue. A heaviness had drifted over her shoulders, the weight sinking through her, holding her heart hostage. It was at that moment that the reality of her fate had begun to reveal itself.

Zara did not feel like a warrior. What she did was cruel and abhorrent. Nothing like the honor that Hakim described from the mercenaries of old.

Erebus had been there as well. She remembered the night sky had caused his long hair to gleam silver, his ivory cloak billowing gently, mirroring the shifting waves beside them. He was a beacon of light, one that told her she had done a job well done.

That was the beginning of her life as the Rogue.

It was also that night the fyrebrand's voice first came to her.

Zara's skin chilled as the memory shifted to that godsforsaken moment. She had been walking down the halls of the Elios mercenary temple by herself. A presence had brushed along her senses.

Fool, the voice had said.

She had spun around to the empty hall, shouting to whoever was there to reveal themselves. The presence had returned, closer in a way she couldn't fathom. It was in her *mind*, slithering in the passages of her thought, claws clicking within the caverns of her very being, leathery wings that beat through the quiet of her head.

Her fyrebrand had begun to burn, light beaming through the ink, just as Raziel's voice emerged in her thoughts. *Did you honestly think you were going to be a warrior made of honor?*

Zara had shouted, staggering back until she slammed into stone.

The presence sighed as if impatient. *How impure you are, Zara Santos. To think more of yourself. It's quite embarrassing, truly.*

Zara's lungs had constricted, the air squeezing out of her. The words left her trembling lips as she begged for answers. She had only received a single response—the beginning of her end.

I am yours and you are mine.

Zara had to brush the memory away and focus on the present, lest the ether inside her awakened. She forced herself to smirk at the archangel in front of her. "I remember knocking you on your ass."

The Hand of the High King chuckled. "I might've let that happen."

Zara rolled her eyes and leaned to the side when he attempted to playfully swat her with his wing. "That was when Raziel's interest in me began. He saw me fight, held on to me like a prized possession and hasn't let go since."

Erebus's lips thinned. The shine in his eyes dulled. "I believe he saw the same potential that I saw in you. A spark that could be guided into greatness."

"Or carved into a weapon," she mumbled. Shame burned her throat.

The archangel hesitated. "Do not let that fire go out, Zara."

She had no intention of letting the forces inside her wither. There was a different taste of power within that anger. It satiated a darker hunger.

Perhaps that was why she craved the fight. It was a desperate attempt to regain some sense of control. To make her believe that she had *some* freedom. A wicked smile touched her lips. Luckily, she had the head of the Sombra Quarter to hunt down. It would be a good distraction from her fate.

Her fingers were already itching to spill blood.

PART II

THE PATH OF SILVER AND RED

TEN

Unlike the unruly fire burning within her sister, Daria Calderón had been made by a gentler flame. The palms of her hands had not known the pommels of swords or daggers. The elven princess of Ikarria came with intellect and a sharp mind. A greater weapon than the average blade.

Hands clasped over her abdomen, Daria tilted her head up. Soft columns of daylight poured through the slits in the etched ceiling of the Primordial sanctuary in Ikarria. Leaves from the ancient trees poked through the openings, reaching for the statues of the gods and goddesses that towered above her.

"Your Highness," the priestess murmured. "Could you tell me who the Three Sun Gods are?"

Daria inhaled as the urge to roll her eyes swelled. She had nearly forgotten her instructor was there. There was *always* someone there. Such was the life of a princess.

"Must we? You and I have gone over this many times," she replied, keeping her voice small and soft.

The priestess raised a finger. "It is important to remember our culture as well as our histories."

Daria returned her gaze to the statues of the Primordials. They had been carved from ivory marble into a range of body types and styles, from armor to gowns, mere strips of clothing to complete nudity. Torches flickered along the limestone walls as burning incense curled its pale smoke toward the high ceiling.

Pools of water lined the stone pathway Daria walked on, petals floating on its clear surface. The gown she wore trailed behind her like an emerald waterfall. It clung to her tall body and complemented the dark complexion of her skin. Strands of her black hair were braided while the rest swayed against her back.

She looked from one pedestal to the next, to every otherworldly being bestowed with the immense power of unfiltered ether. The Primordial of Wisdom, the Primordial of the Hunt and Harvest, the Primordial of Trickery, the Primordial of Divinity and Prophecy . . . There was still so much they did not know about them and perhaps never would.

To think mere *deities* had bested the Primordials. Celestrea resided on the other side of the Jade Sea. Its Gates led to the ethereal realm, where every god and goddess owned their own kingdom and territory pertaining to their calling. The celestial city of Asheras had thrived along the beaches that led to the Gates, but it had been demolished when the opposing deities won. It shouldn't have been so simple for the deities to seal the Primordials on the other side. But they had. An unsolved mystery that would have scholars racking their brains for centuries.

"Princess." Her instructor's voice interrupted her train of thought.

Right. She had been asked a question.

Daria stopped before the Three Sun Gods. Power seemed to emanate from the marbled trio. Her gaze went to the statue on the left, surveying its headdress of blades, skulls, and feathers. She wasn't sure why, but her fingers always seemed to curl at the sight of the god of Death. He was patron to the Horizons, though honoring the Primordial didn't seem to have brought much fortune to the mercenaries. Especially to her sister . . .

It had been one week since the braver half of her was forced to depart for the hunting season. Even though, as of late, Daria had felt a rift between them. Her sister had become more distant with every passing year. There was something that loomed over Zara's shoulders—Daria could see it. A burden her sister wouldn't share with anyone.

"Mikatán." Daria gritted her teeth, pointing at the skeletal warrior. "He who is Death and oversees the Otherworld."

The priestess nodded, flipping through the tome she had been carrying. Her eyes went from the page to the statue on the far right. "And who is this?"

It was of a large, feathered serpent. His scales seemed to glimmer under the amber light, giving the appearance he was floating above his pedestal. Fangs poised to the sky, the tip of his tail full of feathers.

The princess smiled. "The Primordial of Nature, Aspidis. God of the soil, the skies, and the animals."

Daria pointed to the final statue at the center before the priestess could. "And my favorite. Genesis, the Primordial of Life."

The goddess's curvaceous figure wore a gown that sprawled past the pedestal. The neckline plunged deeply, almost reaching the Primordial's navel. She wore armlets and hand rings, and atop her head was a crown that resembled the sun. The architect behind the statues of the temple had certainly outdone themselves.

The priestess looked appalled. "You're not supposed to have favorites, princess."

Daria's smile widened. "Do you know why she's my favorite? Not only does Genesis represent the source of all life, but she was also a *dragon rider*. She broke the chains of what was expected of her as a Primordial. Fascinating, isn't it?"

The priestess—bless her heart—sighed, closing the tome in her hands. "Yes, our goddess made a pact with the scaled beasts, creating a bond that would be passed on to those who are Ikarrian born."

Daria felt a ripple of disappointment as her expression fell slightly. "It is too bad the dragons disappeared."

"And long before the War of the Skies, too."

"What impeccable timing," Daria muttered, feeling a knot of bitterness in her chest.

How the Ikarrian royal bloodline had been blessed with the gift to forge bonds with dragons was never confirmed. According to scholars, there had been strife in the mortal world, which had caused the elves to seek the strength of the winged beasts. And since the dragons had their own history with Genesis, they had been willing to stand alongside the Ikarrians.

It had been one hundred years since the sacred beasts had disappeared. Another mystery.

Daria jerked her chin to the two empty pedestals that rested behind the Three Sun Gods. "I've always wanted to ask, who is supposed to stand there?"

The priestess made a sound in her throat. "No one knows. Those pedestals were created but never answered for."

Odd.

"Though there are those who believe they belong to Khaos, the Primordial of Fate and Time, and Deimos, the Primordial of Dread and Terror."

That piqued Daria's interest. "I remember learning of them, the ill-fated lovers. Their story is tragic. Khaos had fabricated the cosmos and was a cherished goddess among the Three Sun Gods, almost considered a daughter. Her beloved, Deimos, betrayed the Primordials, so the two were torn apart by the Three Sun Gods."

The priestess sighed. "Yes. As I said, princess, it is just a theory. Who knows who truly belongs on the two empty pedestals."

A soldier scurried into the memorial, her gray scaled armor clinking with her movements. The sight of it tightened Daria's chest.

The soldier bowed. "Pardon me, princess, but the king wishes to see you."

Daria cocked her head. "Isn't the advisor meeting about to begin?"

"Yes, he wants you to attend."

Her heart pounded against her ribs. It was unlike her pater to wish for her presence in these gatherings. "Something's happened."

Daria was greeted by the fresh morning air as soon as she stepped out of the Primordial sanctuary. It was still on royal grounds, the castle within walking distance. The princess picked up her pace through the ash trees, the ancient Ikarrian forest looming at the edges of the property. The occasional soldier or staff could be seen moving amongst the woodland.

The advisor meeting would begin shortly. Daria's stomach flipped with worry over why her pater had asked for her to join. She had always wanted to be more involved in such matters but had always been denied. This invitation now was unnerving, and sweat began to dampen her palms.

Daria entered the castle, passing the throne room. There was no court today, so the area was empty save for the tall torches that illuminated the wide space. A crimson runway bled from where she stood, across the dark marble floor and up the dais.

Her eyes landed on the obsidian throne.

Its black spires struck the air like the rays of a rising sun. Ornate designs of dragon scales gave the seat a light sheen under the soft candlelight. Wide windows stood behind it, revealing a clear sky.

Thanks to her academics, Daria had learned that the enormous throne room had once held dragons. She wondered how it must have looked during their time. The reigning Ikarrian ruler sitting on the black-spired seat with their bonded dragon curled behind them. Reptilian eyes that would watch the courtiers fall to their knees in front of them.

Daria braced herself for the sensation to hit. It always happened whenever she laid eyes on the throne. The world trembled beneath her feet. Her heart pounded through her ears. She stared at the seat, unable to look anywhere else.

In the distance, she heard something . . . like voices whispering. They spoke a language she did not recognize. A deep growl resonated through the throne's dark glass, growing louder and louder—

Daria gasped as she was slammed back into reality. The sounds of the castle staff returned to her, the scent of burning wood and tea wafting in the air. Breathing through her nostrils, Daria clenched the fabric of her dress.

Suns, she would never become accustomed to it.

The sensation had first occurred many years ago, when she had

just reached adulthood, while her pater hosted court. Daria could recall how terrified she had been, how the fear had struck every nerve
in her body. No one had seemed to experience what she had, so she
had always kept it to herself. As of late, the mysterious sensation was
occurring more and more often.

The princess was going mad, she was sure of it. Daria brushed
the thought away, unwilling to unravel what had just happened, and
turned her back to the throne.

Daria rested her hands on her lap, fingers interlaced. Her chin was
poised at an angle as she watched the advisors of the realm settle
around the meeting table. It was made of black glass, reflecting the
dragon etched above them. The head and tail of the scaled beast protruded from the ceiling as if it was stepping out toward them.

Her pater sat in the head seat to her left. An obsidian crown was
tucked within the pure white braids of his hair. He wore a dark gray
coat that draped over his shoulders and pooled on the floor. His tunic
was clean of any embroidery, matching the tone of the coat.

The king's face was cold and unmoving as he addressed the room.
"We have much to discuss, but something quite intriguing presented
itself this morning." A guard stepped to the table and placed an opened
letter before him. Idris gestured to it. "Ikarria has been invited to the
Summit."

The room buzzed with the advisors' mumblings and whispers.
She eyed the letter, feeling the room spin.

An advisor, whom Daria recalled worked on the political affairs
of the realm, rested her elbow on the table. "Your Highness, this has
never happened before. Why is Elios inviting us now?"

Idris ran a hand over his short-cropped beard. "In the invitation,
the High King states he would like to put our differences aside and
have Ikarria see the efforts the Aligned Realms have been making.
I assume it is yet another attempt to have Ikarria join the Alliance,
though it is hard to say for sure."

"Do you plan to attend?"

The king's gaze did not betray his emotions. "I do. I am leaving in two weeks."

Daria shot a look to the king—to her pater.

No. This was why he wanted her here. It was worse than she could have imagined. He was about to leave her, to walk into the snakes' den. The only thought that provided a mild sense of comfort was that Zara and the guild would be there, too.

The advisor didn't seem pleased by that, neither did the others. "May I inquire if it is a wise decision to attend?"

"It isn't." Idris's voice rumbled so deeply even the goblets on the table seemed to shudder. "However, if I do not attend, it would be seen as a grave insult to the Aligned Realms. They may feel less inclined to continue business with us."

A valid concern. Ikarria still had citizens to look after. If the kingdom were to lose those connections with the other realms, then resources would become limited. Daria was tempted to nibble on her bottom lip but forced herself not to. Underneath the table, she twisted the rings on her fingers.

Another advisor spoke. "You must not go alone, Your Highness. In addition to the guards who will escort you, who else will stand by your side?"

More voices interjected, growing more urgent and tense.

"Ikarria does not participate in the political relations of the Continent."

"What if it is a trap?"

"Who will mind the realm?"

Fists banged on the table. Questions and theories spewed back and forth.

Flames from the candles and torches suddenly hissed, rising higher and brighter. The sudden show of ether rendered the room silent. The flickering light illuminated Idris's unmoved expression, the tattoos on his face seemed to darken.

Daria lifted her gaze, meeting the king's, as the fires surrounding them slowly lowered. She saw the message in the lingering embers in his eyes, and understood what her pater was asking.

The words flew from her mouth. "I'll go, too."

Every head in the room turned to her.

After a moment of silence, an advisor spoke from the far end of the table. "We cannot have Ikarria's sole heir leave the safety of our kingdom."

The daughter of the draconic throne. Heir to the dragon-less kingdom.

"Name me as the ambassador of Ikarria," she said.

The king leaned back his seat, turning his gaze to the table. "We've been waiting for an opportunity like this. Since the treaty was drafted, Elios has been hard at work in bringing the other realms to serve its needs. Adrastea's soldiers now roam the streets of their capital. In order for us to maintain our neutrality and independence, we must know what Elios has been up to. My daughter has been preparing for such a moment, I trust no other."

The words caused Daria's heart to swell. Her sister had the obligation to appease the treaty, her pater had his responsibility toward a kingdom—all had a duty to their family.

This would now be hers.

She straightened and addressed the advisors. "There must be a reason why the High King invited Ikarria. The Summit is essentially a large festival, is it not? All the kings and queens of the Continent, as well as the nobles and other powerful patrons, will be in attendance. It is a chance to learn more about the politics of the realms. Not to mention the actual meetings of the Summit are between the royals and the political delegates. Ikarria does not have any representation there."

Her pater watched her. No, not pater. Her *king*. "I know that look. It is the same expression your mater would get when she'd set her mind to something. What do you hope to learn, Daria Calderón?"

She felt a surge of pride at the mention of her mater.

The queen of Ikarria had been a warrior of silver and blood, charging the battlefield, her king at her side. She had been killed in the War. The night Idris lost his wife, he had gained a daughter. Daria could still remember her confusion. How her eyes had blurred with tears when she saw her pater enter the castle not with her mater but with a young girl holding his hand.

The night Zara had come into their lives.

She lifted her chin, an act she'd seen her sister do countless times, hoping it would lend her courage. "I wish to learn more about the Council. They are an enigma. A group of deities who now sit in the highest seat of power behind the High Throne, who defeated the Primordials so easily. While the entire Continent is satisfied with its present state, our realm does not have privileged knowledge regarding the Council's future intentions. Our realm's independence serves us well, but even fourteen years since the War we know little to nothing about these rulers. We have become complacent, and it is our duty to see what their vision of the *new world* entails."

She could've sworn a dragon's shadow lurked in the king's fierce eyes.

"A sort of spy," he said with an amused smile, looking at the advisors. "What do you all say?"

Silence. Flames flickered, papers crinkled. Daria dared to let her gaze coast over the table. And one by one, the advisors agreed. A heavy breath escaped her—she hadn't realized until then how tightly she had been squeezing her hands under the table.

Daria nodded. "Thank you. I have been learning what it means to be a ruler for years, but how can I rule a kingdom if I don't even know what lies beyond its borders? How can I preserve a realm if I am not familiar with the other territories surrounding it?"

Slowly, like the shifting of a fire, something like pride gleamed in the king's eyes. A gentle brightness that she would gladly take into herself. "It seems we are all in agreement. Daria Calderón, I formally name you as ambassador of Ikarria."

The evening light kissed Daria's cheeks. It crowned her dark hair, lighting the gown she still wore in a blazing ripple of green. The effects of the meeting hadn't left her all day. She should've felt elation. A sense of accomplishment that she'd managed to make purchase on something worthwhile. Instead, she was in a pensive mood. And maybe a little nervous.

Her feet moved on their own accord, the marble beneath her slippers turning into dirt and grass. Daria looked up, embracing the glow of the setting sun and welcoming the brush of the leaves against her face.

In the center of the castle's front courtyard stood the Watcher, the largest of the ancient Ikarrian trees. The width of its trunk was so grand that it had been made into a watchtower. Its old wood was strong enough to have stairs built along the outside and posts on the inside. Ikarrian guards walked throughout the tree, silver armor winking under the golden sky.

Her hand traced the smooth bark, the soles of her feet beginning to scream with every step. The air grew clearer, sharper, the higher she climbed the Watcher. Soldiers acknowledged her and returned to their business. They had stolen curious glances at her when she first started making these treks up the Watcher, but now paid her no mind.

Daria didn't know how long it took to reach the top. The struggle to scale the massive tree always took its toll on her and she never seemed to be able to properly time herself. No matter how exhausted she was, it never failed to hinder her euphoria when she reached the top.

An arched opening cut through the tree trunk, a platform stretching beyond it. Proper climbing gear would be needed to track its branches to the top. No soldiers patrolled this height now, but the tree had once been a resting place for the dragons.

Daria raised her hand as if she could touch the red sun. Her head and heart were thrumming. She thought of her sister and her pater, the roles they each held and the energy they put into the safety of their family. The thought alone was enough to strike a hunger in her.

Her life had revolved around being the most knowledgeable of cultures, religions, and governments, honing her intellect into a weapon on the political battlefield. Her pater had prepared her for this. It was a test, to see how she could manage the vipers that wore crowns and fancy tunics.

Daria knew this, and yet the prospect of venturing outside her home realm had awakened a primal, selfish need inside her.

More. There was something that called out to her. For what, Daria couldn't tell but she hoped becoming ambassador would appease this need for change.

Perhaps she wanted to feel like she was contributing to her family. Perhaps she wanted to touch the sky. Perhaps she wanted to feel the exciting bite of the world outside of Ikarria. Daria opened her palm and a blossom of flame appeared, hovering above her skin.

Perhaps she wished to burn.

ELEVEN

Zara Santos felt lighter, despite the reason they were visiting the Machai Forum.

She was quickly realizing that the lawless corner of Soleira sang to her jaded heart. Citizens—of all races—filtered throughout the taverns, pleasure houses, and whatever parties were taking place. It was home to the rebellious hearts, where one could drown in their vices.

A cracked archway made of limestone towered over the guild's heads as they entered. They had to meander through a bustling night market, wading through a variety of smells from sage to chili powder, before they reached the heart of the Machai Forum. Lanterns and torches dangled along their path until the shopping stalls morphed into pillared buildings, where unruly gatherings were being held. The ground and air vibrated with boisterous energy.

Red light flashed in the Forum's center. Fire dancers spun their bare feet on the dirt, twisting with ribbons of flame. Their ether mirrored the liquid movement of their arms and legs. Their red dresses blended with their fiery light, becoming one with the flames, as musicians pounded on war drums.

Zara was so mesmerized by the sight that she almost didn't realize that her hips were swinging to the beat.

"Remind me, why have we never come to this place before?" she asked.

Axar had his own gaze transfixed on the night market. "I assume it is because we would never get anything done."

Hakim glanced over his shoulder. He had been in front of them, alongside Eshe. The head of the Ikarrian guild rolled his eyes. "We will meet with the Messenger in the Siren's Song."

They approached what looked like a government building, its triangular roof sitting above columns that lined its entrance. Drunken patrons mingled along the dusted white steps, while more music and cheering blasted from its open doors. Zara's lips parted as they entered the Siren's Song. The property had been refurbished into a tavern.

It had three levels, all filled with raucous citizens, the upper two with balconies that surrounded a four-corner center on the ground floor. Moonlight beamed from the open roof onto the platform, patrons practically clamoring at its border, cheering and clapping. Axar nudged Zara's arm as they drew closer. The sound of breaking skin and tossing coins was all too familiar.

Zara grinned. A fighting ring. Maybe this hunting season would be more tolerable. Maybe later tonight she could—her smile faltered when Hakim shot her a look that growled, *we are working.*

Fucking Suns.

The citizens seemed begrudgingly aware of the Horizons. She supposed the mercenaries being strapped to the teeth with glinting silver didn't help. Though Zara was sure they weren't the only ones who carried weapons here. Gods knew what sort of criminals roamed free within these halls and the streets of the Machai Forum.

Her thoughts went to the Sombra Quarter at that, excitement racing through her blood. If there were to be a place for illegal business, it would be this one.

Eshe jerked her chin. She had drawn her hood, hiding all but her profile. "I think I found our contact."

A human male with a shorn head stood underneath an archway. He leaned against the wrought iron fence that faced the fight, drinking from a mug. His brown eyes slid to them.

Hakim walked over to him, towering above the male. "Are you who they call Hermès?"

Zara realized the male had been staring at her before he forced his gaze to Hakim. "That'll be me."

"Is that an actual name or a title?" Eshe asked. She'd rounded the human so stealthily that he jumped back.

He ran a hand over his chest, most likely trying to stop his racing heart. "I must keep my identity a secret. The spies of Elios all use a codename."

The way the male moved—the human eye wouldn't have been able to catch it, but she could. She could also smell the ether radiating from him. The spy wasn't human. He was a shifter, and from how he slowly cocked his head, she theorized he could transform into some type of bird.

Zara gravitated to the back of the group to stand guard with Axar. They observed the tavern as Hakim and Eshe handled the conversation.

She kept her eyes on the candlelit tables, watching those who seemed unaware or simply did not care for the mercenaries' presence. "Do you think this place is supported by the Sombra Quarter?"

Her question was quiet enough for only Axar to hear. He angled his body toward her, turning his back to a pair of women who had been casting flirtatious glances his way. Zara was unsurprised. Axar always managed to have a flock of admirers wherever he went. As for herself, she'd garner some attention but the permanent scowl on her face always seemed to scare the fools away. Not that she minded.

"Or is it the other way around and the Siren's Song supports the Sombra?" He countered.

She folded her arms. "It's going to be difficult to hunt down the head of the shadow markets. They have a loyal following."

"It may be beneficial for us to learn more of how the Sombra conducts their business and understand why the people favor it so much."

Zara arched her brow. "Critical thinking, young alpha. I'm impressed."

Axar rolled his eyes, a smile playing at his lips. They stood in

silence, hardly paying attention to the conversation the other mercenaries were having when the crowd erupted in applause.

He looked toward the fighting platform. "Shit, that looked brutal."

She followed his gaze. An unconscious archangel was being
dragged from the courtyard, while the winning winged male raised
his bloodied fists and roared in triumph. Her heart danced at the sight.

The victor flapped his powerful wings, the feathers a deep-sea
green. He lifted himself off the ground, the crowd cheering and en-
couraging him. Zara's gaze followed the male's ascent as something
flickered in her peripheral. A shifting of wings.

On the furthest balcony of the second floor was another archangel. He sat on a lounge chair, half-covered by shadow and firelight,
focused on something at his table. She couldn't decipher much of his
features from that distance, except for the strands of black hair that
fell over his brow and a jawline that was taut with tension. Another
male with light gray wings sat beside him, chugging a large mug of
ale. He was more rugged than the first archangel, though they both
looked like they'd seen actual battlefields, unlike the common ring
fighters here. Zara observed the dark fighting leathers that clasped
their powerful bodies. Their attire was so polished and expensive—
they clearly carried some form of authority. *Warriors.*

Her eyes went back to the first male, to what had first grasped her
attention. Black wings, like midnight. So dark the feathers cast a deep
blue shine, a night sky. She could've sworn she could see stars there.

Something tugged within her. A call, a whisper. The ether in her
blood shifted, purring through her veins. Zara pressed a hand to her
chest and forced her power to silence. For her energy to rebel against
her was not uncommon, but it was different this time. *Calmer* than
what she'd experienced before.

Zara's hearing caught a part of Hakim and Eshe's conversation
with Hermès. The Messenger sounded *angry.* "—I will ask you again.
Is that the Rogue within your guild?"

Fucking Suns. Zara slowly looked his way. The male's face burned
with hatred as he met her gaze, his nostrils flaring. "I thought it was
you the moment I saw you."

Her lips slowly dragged into a dry smile. "A pleasure to make your acquaintance."

Axar braced himself beside her. He knew she could handle herself, but the wolf shifter was always ready to come to her defense. Something she would ever be grateful for.

It was Hakim who planted himself between her and the spy. "Enough. You were informing us of your time with our mark. Where does Cadoc reside?"

Hermès's lips twisted into a sneer. "The Hand of the High King failed to mention the Rogue would be part of this ordeal. She *killed* my sister."

Well. The past was sure to rush her at some point. Zara smoothened her expression. "Whatever I have done, it was by the High King's command. Take your grievances to him. You are the one who still serves him."

The male spat. "Do you truly feel no remorse for those you have slain? I am merely a Messenger. What about you? You're a monster . . . a beast."

Monster. Beast.

Hakim snatched the collar of the male's tunic. "That is *enough*. Speak to her like that again and I will grind your teeth against the wall."

The fyrebrand chuckled in her head. *They never care to see what is right in front of them. No matter what, they will always blame you. It is your fault, Zara. You are what he says.*

Zara's body trembled—and not in fear.

Hermès breathed heavily through his nostrils. "I will fulfill my duty to you, only if she accepts my challenge in the ring."

The head of the guild snarled. "You're a fool. Do you wish to still have the ability to walk?" When the male stayed silent, Hakim shoved him toward Zara. "Then challenge her properly."

She watched as the male puffed out his chest, throwing daggers with his eyes. Zara couldn't blame him. Not entirely. The agony was evident beneath the rage. The grief of losing a loved one. At *her* hands.

The blood that stained her palms—her heart—was too thick to be able to decipher who belonged to whom.

Hermès bared his teeth. "I challenge you, Rogue."

Zara lifted her chin. The male was taller but somehow she still managed to stare him down. "Until you yield, Messenger."

It was hardly difficult to arrange the fight. Axar spoke to the officiator, who was more than happy to have a Horizon entertain the crowd.

Zara stood on the central platform. The white ground was stained with hues of red. Her boots glided above the marble as she prowled to her side of the ring. Her fingers went to the clasps of the cloak, letting the dark fabric float to the ground.

Cheers pounded against her ears. There were those who spat on her name. Curious that they directed all their pain onto her when she was not the only mercenary present. She unsheathed her khopesh blades, handing them to Axar as he also grabbed her cloak.

Eshe's voice rose from beyond the platform. "Teach the male how to properly address a woman, little warrior."

Those words reminded her of where she stood. Of what she was about to do. The world fell mute to her ears. There was only the racing of her heart and the sigh that escaped her lips.

Zara grinned and lifted her fists. At the sound of a bell, she charged Hermès. The air hissed at her ears as she slid to the side, bypassing the male. He twisted around and threw a fist. Zara took another swift step back and ducked every swing of his arms.

He growled in frustration. Her lips twitched in amusement. *The fool called you a beast. Show him your claws.*

Zara snarled. She lashed out, hitting his face, chest, and torso. Blood spewed from his mouth. His lacking skill set was as painfully obvious as the trail of red that trickled down the corner of his eye.

The fight didn't last long. Zara entertained the crowd. She baited the Messenger's attacks, dodging every single one. Her knuckles bruised, the sensation thrummed through her senses.

Monster. Monster. Monster. Every split of pain upon her skin helped drown her weak, internal voice down, down, down.

More blood splattered the ground. The male's eye had swelled, but he did not stop charging her. He shouted, the sound twisting with another type of pain. She evaded him and swept out her leg, knocking him onto his back.

Zara pounced, ramming her forearm against his neck. His legs thrashed but he was too weak. The skin of his face began to purple, and his eyes bulged. She waited for the words, for the tap of his fingers, but he did none of that.

The crowd banged their drinks against the railings. "Yield! Yield! Yield!"

Zara clenched her teeth. "Say it."

There was no need to summon her ether. Not with how the male quickly gasped out the words. "I yield."

The crowd roared and amid the chaos Zara continued to hold him down. "I believe you owe us some information."

"Why did you hold back? Why didn't you make it hurt more?" His voice cracked and she felt herself still. The male's grief had driven him to the point where he wanted to feel pain. Something she was all too familiar with.

"I wasn't commanded to kill you," she responded. Gentler, *kinder* than she intended.

He stared at her with his blood-soaked face. If her words meant anything to him, she couldn't tell. Hermès breathed out a sound like needles rattling in his lungs. "From what I gathered, Cadoc lives in the upper side of the outer district . . ."

When he finished providing the details of their mark's residence, the spy rested his head on the ground. "Be warned, mercenary."

Zara narrowed her eyes. "Why?"

"The Sombra Quarter. They are *everywhere*."

She felt the hairs on the back of her neck rise. Her ether stirred, rushing through her blood. It hummed at the feel of another's gaze on her. As if unseen hands had curled under Zara's chin, she lifted her face to the upper floor.

The archangel with wings of midnight had been watching her.

TWELVE

Zara was ready to kill something.

The moment she and the guild started their assignment, a blood thirst had risen inside her. It had lifted its ugly, powerful head—and she liked how it felt. There was a sense of strength when those who had done wrong feared her.

Gods. She may be just as bad as the High King.

The blue tiles of the rooftop nearly cracked beneath her boots. Trees in the dirt paths of Elios's outer district swayed. Citizens ambled about the neighborhoods and children played on the stone steps of crumbling apartments. Stray dogs scurried away into dark corners.

Zara kept her gaze across the street, her hood casting a shard of shadow across her face. String music strummed from the private feast Cadoc was hosting in his residence. Guests entered the limestone building through its main entrance, laughter and singing filling the road. Guards were posted about the property, including the three marks standing on the flat rooftop, keeping watch to another entryway that led into the building.

Through the open windows, Zara could see bodies mingling either against or on top of each other. Cadoc was currently fangs-deep in an elf's neck. There were two other floors below the vampire's party, which Axar would be raiding within moments.

"I only see the three guards. There will be more inside," Zara observed.

Eshe crouched beside her, her hood partially hiding her face as well. "It seems quite lively this evening, doesn't it?"

The elf made a face. "The festivity is practically on the cusp of an orgy."

Eshe chuckled. "Remember to question the mark. Wring out as much information from him before you kill him." She slid her alabaster bow from her back, her slender fingers brushing the feathers of an arrow as she nocked it. The movement was so agile and smooth. Silent with a promise of violence. "Are you ready, little warrior?"

Zara unsheathed her throwing daggers. The silver danced between her knuckles as she twirled the handles. "Cover for me."

She sprinted toward the edge of the rooftop. Power strummed through her muscles, and her thighs strained with every stride of her legs. Ether rose from the depths of her core, barely scraping the surface and remaining unseen. She mentally latched onto its strength before letting it launch her into the open air.

Zara careened over the street, her arms slashing downward, letting every dagger free, as she was suspended in the air. They struck a guard just as one of Eshe's arrows whistled past her, taking another one down. Zara rolled onto the rooftop, the last guard spinning around to face her. She swept past him, dust swirling in her wake, and shoved her hand in his hair, forcing his head up for another arrow to pierce his face. Blood spattered across her cheek.

"Beautiful execution," she murmured, dropping the body.

She unsheathed her twin khopesh blades, welcoming the familiar surge that ran through her blood. The wicked curves of obsidian were an extension of her blackened heart. They were her teeth and claws.

How good it felt to bare steel fangs.

Zara kicked down the rooftop's door to enter the building, excitement humming through her veins. Her heart thundered with the music, growing louder the farther she prowled the hall.

More guards blocked entry to the feast. They reached for their swords but Zara drove her khopesh through them. She speared the last guard through his gut, placed her boot on his chest, and kicked him off her blade. His body fell through the open doorway and into the ongoing festivities.

Screams erupted. The elf Cadoc had been drinking from tore away from him, sprinting across the room. Other bystanders were throwing drinks and toppling tables as they ran for the exits.

Zara's sharp hearing caught more commotion from the level below her. Of glass breaking and skin ripping. Axar must've made his move already. She didn't have much time.

Cadoc hadn't stirred, staring at her with wide eyes. A dark laugh escaped her as she sauntered toward her mark. "Your sins are catching up to you, shadow dealer."

The vampire balked. He snarled, revealing bloodied fangs as he got to his feet. "What is this nonsense? I am no longer a shadow dealer! I have gone legitimate."

Zara sheathed one blade and spun the other in her hand. "High King Raziel doesn't seem to care."

His face blanched. Instead of fighting, her mark bolted. She laughed once more, as the ether inside her began to race, and lunged after the vampire. Faint whispers of light brushed over her legs as her power pushed her forward. She appeared before the mark. The wood of nearby chairs splintered, and the decorative pottery shattered from the sheer force of her presence. Zara caught Cadoc by the nape of his neck and slammed him against a table.

"Listen to me," she crooned. "Your first mistake was falling into an agreement with the High Throne. That is already a mark on your soul—"

Red spit flew from Cadoc's lips. "My only desire is to see the Sombra Quarter *rot*."

She hushed him, pressing the edge of the black blade to his throat. "And the second mistake is believing that you could demand more from Raziel. Once your purpose wears out, he sends someone like me."

Cadoc snarled. "If I am to be killed, then you will get nothing from me."

"I thought you wanted to see them rot."

He snapped his teeth like a rabid animal, trying to pierce her neck with his fangs. She withdrew her blade enough to throw a punch against the vampire's face. *Ah.* The skin of her knuckles would bruise. Zara grinned underneath her hood.

"My patience is wearing thin," she hissed. "How about this? After you tell me what I need to know, I will give you a head start."

Her mark froze. The white of his eyes blackened with the urge to drink. Cadoc's lips thinned—he was considering it. All prey tried to take a chance at survival.

He struggled against her. "The shadow dealers conduct many of their businesses in the Machai Forum. Markets, blood centers, tailor shops—nearly everything there is used as a front. You only need to know the right individual. I had a spy who managed to gain access to their inner circle. He discovered where the Sombra's leaders lived, but was killed before I could meet with him."

Zara made a thoughtful sound. "So, you are truly useless then."

She lifted her khopesh blade once more, trailing to the place above his heart and dug through the skin there. *Yes.* Raziel's voice—the fyrebrand's voice—whispered in her head. *Make him squirm.*

"Fuck you, mercenary." The vampire snarled. "They have a warehouse somewhere along the harbor."

It was something. Another crumb in the hunt for the shadow dealers. She exhaled through her nostrils. "When you were with the Sombra Quarter, who did you trade with and where?"

Cadoc slammed his hands against the table. The vampire strength was enough to crack the wood. He shouted the words. "Everywhere! We did business everywhere, especially within the—"

Something silver flashed between them. Zara's senses screamed at her and she threw her head back in time to avoid the tip of a dagger before it pierced the wall.

Her head whipped around to the arched window, seeing a figure rush by. She couldn't determine who or what it was—but she *felt* them. A purr of power, a strike of lightning. Her ether hummed at the sensation and it set her on edge. Zara had never felt her strength react that way before.

It seemed that she and her guild weren't the only ones seeking Cadoc. Zara's teeth clicked. "It looks like our talk has been cut short." She narrowed her gaze on the vampire, her lips curved as she slowly loosened her grip.

"Run," she whispered.

Cadoc was fast, and rammed his head against hers. A beam of pain burst on her forehead, and she felt the sharp sting of teeth grazing the skin of her neck, his sour breath close. Zara threw a fist against his lower jaw. The vampire stumbled back before darting for the lower level.

Pain pulsated from her head and down her neck, but Zara couldn't fret over her injuries. She flew down the steps to the next floor and saw Axar lunge. The mercenary and vampire rolled across the ground, broken glass and ceramic nipping at their bodies. Lifeless guards were strewn about the destroyed space. Axar certainly had had his way with the place.

The vampire punched Axar before the wolf shifter managed to kick the mark in the stomach, sending him skidding across the floor. Cadoc quickly got to his feet, took one look at Zara and dove out a window.

She paused beside Axar, watching him struggle to his hands and knees. "You let him go."

He only groaned and collapsed onto his back. "Fucking vampires. I forget they are stronger than they look. I'm fine though, thank you for asking."

"Someone else attacked while I was questioning him." She bit out.

Axar cursed aloud. "Fuck. Go after him, Santos, before they do. I will be there shortly."

Zara careened out the window and into the open street, following the fear-drenched scent of her mark. Air hissed at her heels as her lungs began to burn. Red stained her knuckles and blood dripped from the blade she still held.

All while she reined in the ether that craved to taste the night.

THIRTEEN

Shit.

Ronan knew he had tempted the Fates by throwing the dagger. The mercenary's senses were too sharp for their own good. What stung his pride the most was that he had fucking *missed*. He needed to start training again. But his stubborn ass couldn't bring himself to face any sort of battleground.

Not yet.

His shadow dealers had discovered that Cadoc was the traitor's contact. The vampire had been one of the original shadow dealers before Ronan swept in and overthrew the Sombra Quarter. It shouldn't have come as a surprise that the male's thirst for retribution hadn't waned all these years.

Ronan should've killed that bastard when he had the chance.

The archangel had flown to the outer district of Soleira as fast as he could. Only to find terrified crowds spilling onto the street from the vampire's property. It was sheer luck that he had arrived before Cadoc could reveal anything else.

His wings were tucked tightly behind his back as he stalked the alleys, tracking the vampire.

All the sweat-drenched effort to ensure the Sombra Quarter's success. It was for the sake of survival. Ronan thought of those in the Stone Orchard and those he was caring for. He needed to protect and provide.

Breaking rules and hindering royalty.

That was the only way he knew how.

With shallow breaths, he stepped into a clearing among pillared buildings. No torchlights lit this part of the crumbling neighborhood. Another stroke of luck. The less witnesses, the better.

Moonlight splashed on the stone ground, weeds protruding from the cracks. It was silent, save for the occasional breeze. At times, he could smell the brine from the sea.

Ronan fumbled with the straps and buckles of his black fighting leathers. His hand paused above the pommel of a blade he hadn't used since the skies had turned red. Engravings of suns trailed along the thin sheet of silver. The scar on his lips tingled as his fingers brushed the weapon, the faint sounds of battle he had once led echoing in his mind. He left it sheathed at his hip.

Gods, the War had ruined him.

Cadoc burst into view. The vampire stumbled upon seeing a lone archangel standing in a pool of silver. His eyes widened as he recognized the Sombra leader. "*Shit.*"

A dark smile spread over Ronan's lips. "I like how my evening is turning out. How are you, Cadoc?"

The vampire snarled, turning back in the direction he came. The male was never one for a fight. Instinctively, Ronan shot out another short dagger before Cadoc could twist around. The small blade struck him square in the chest. Not enough to kill a vampire, but Ronan didn't mind a little entertainment tonight. His wings slowly unfurled, the black feathers blending with the night.

A flash of silver caught his eye and he turned to see a dark figure hurtling across the rooftops. The stars shined behind it, gentle light touching its dark gray scaled armor. Ronan cursed under his breath. He had run out of time.

He returned to the shadows. And waited. Suns Above, what was he waiting for? The archangel should've left. He should've turned back and met with Orion—who was most likely on the verge of seeking him out. Ronan should have counted his losses and prayed to the Suns that the Sombra Quarter would be safe.

Yet he couldn't move. His silver eyes clung to the mercenary. No, not mercenary. *Horizon.* That was the proper term for someone who took the oaths and joined a guild. The common folk nowadays were simply too lazy and hardly called them by their proper name. Yes, Ronan might have been living in a secret city, but he knew his history.

A morbid fascination took root as he watched the vampire run straight into the obsidian teeth of the Horizon. He could tell by the frame of the mercenary's body that she was a woman. A hood was drawn over her face, her head tilted to the side as she twisted her wicked weapons deeper into the vampire.

Ronan reached for his sword, the movement feeling odd and unpracticed. His fingers wrapped around the handle when the ether inside him slowly shifted. The power chained deeply within the crevices of his soul moved. It curled weakly and *sighed.*

His body tightened, preparing to fight or flee—he wasn't sure. When the lifeless body of the vampire fell to the ground, the mercenary hissed in pain, light shining from her wrist.

Zara tried to bite back another groan and failed. Sparks of silvery ether burned from the fyrebrand, its light suppressed beneath her leather bracer but still too damn bright. Soon, Raziel would know that the Ikarrian guild had killed their mark. Another death. Another completed assignment.

Her jaw clenched as the last of the fyrebrand's pain dissipated. "Fucking Suns."

Silence. The hunger inside her abated, but the fire within hadn't waned. More. She needed more.

"The poor bastard didn't stand a chance."

A voice.

Deep as the night.

Rough as the Kairos dunes.

And entirely unknown.

Zara struck out her arm, raising the khopesh toward the sound. In an alley, draped by the darkness, was a male. She could barely make out the broad outline of his shoulders as he leaned against the wall. Moonlight traced the edges of a massive wing.

An archangel with black wings . . .

She suspected it was the same male from the Siren's Song. For him to be here was not a coincidence, she was sure of it. It was more than enough to keep her guard up.

The liquid dark voice returned. "Easy, Horizon. I was appreciating your handiwork."

A slight accent touched his words, a melodic roll as he spoke. It was familiar but she couldn't recognize it.

Zara couldn't help but scoff. "A fan of the hunt?"

The archangel paused. "Perhaps. I must admit I have never met a mercenary before, especially one so far away from home."

He must've recognized her armor. It wasn't difficult to tell which realm a Horizon represented. Zara wondered why an archangel was here, but the familiar purr of power told her his presence was the same as before, in Cadoc's residence. She also recognized the way the ether in her veins softened, like it had in the Siren's Song. She needed to learn a bit more about this mysterious male.

Her eyes dragged to the body under her boot. A blade poked out from the dead vampire's chest. Her fingers curled around its pommel and she yanked it free. A stream of crimson followed as she lifted the weapon to the silver light.

"Are you missing a dagger?"

The stranger hummed a sound. "Several, actually."

Zara thought of the knife that had been thrown between her and Cadoc, interrupting her interrogation. How convenient that her mark ended up with one embedded in his chest.

Her lips curved up as she tossed the blade toward the archangel's feet. The steel rang against the stone ground. The tip of his boots hit the light and she caught a peek of black fighting leathers.

Zara didn't hesitate. Ether flared throughout her body, quaking every tendon. She careened toward the archangel and slammed him against the wall. His hard body hit the stone but the male didn't try to fight back.

A strip of moonlight now slashed across his face, though the darkness still greedily clung to him. She could only see locks of black hair that fell over both sides of his brow, the sculpted plane of his cheekbone, and a single gray eye. The color was glinting steel, a brewing storm waiting to be unleashed.

The tip of her khopesh pressed against his ribs. "I've seen you before. You were in the Machai Forum."

Brilliant teeth flashed under the sliver of light. "And you were the woman who caused half of the males in the Siren's Song to shit their pants."

Zara began to smile. Cold and unnerving. "Why were you after my mark?"

The blade was knocked from her hand. Air swooshed from her lungs as she was swept off her feet. The world spun before she was pinned to the wall. She froze in shock, her heartbeat racing against her chest.

Shit.

The archangel was too quick—that realization was staggering. His hand slammed the wall above her head, shielding the world from view. Zara squirmed against him but stopped when she felt the cold kiss of steel against her abdomen.

"Oh," he purred. "How the tables have turned."

She gritted her teeth. "You are from the Sombra Quarter."

The archangel was tall, his wings rising high, ready to touch the stars. He lowered his head until she met his storm gray eyes. His gaze was measured, surveying the opponent before him.

"What makes you say that?" He asked.

Zara's knees threatened to buckle under his grasp. "There is no other explanation as to why you would be here, trying to silence someone who was once a shadow dealer."

The male leaned forward and tightened his grip on his weapon.

She lifted her chin, throat bobbing as the tip of his blade grazed her leathers.

"I would tread carefully, Horizon," the archangel said quietly. "If you decide to battle me here, only the shadows will witness your demise."

Zara tensed. Of all the threats she'd heard, it was the first she truly believed. He wasn't her mark, but this was enough to justify bleeding him out. Her hood still managed to stay draped over her head, boots planted on the ground. She silently called to her ether, the power trickling through her legs and torso.

The male braced himself. He crouched down, like a panther preparing to leap. It was as if he had sensed the power thrumming through her.

"What are you doing?" He growled.

A ripple of energy pulsated from her body as she pushed off the wall. It ran through the air, shoving the archangel off her. Zara kicked the sword from his grasp.

The archangel was thrown back into the clearing. His wings flared, preventing him from rolling over the stone ground.

She could see him clearly now. Black hair and deep olive skin. Broad shoulders angling down to thick thighs. Fighting leathers capped at the shoulders revealing muscular, tattooed arms. The dark ink continued up the length of his neck. With what, she couldn't tell.

"Such pretty threats from a pretty archangel," Zara said.

He smirked and she caught the scar down the left corner of his mouth. "The Horizon has bite, like a wolf."

Zara kicked the sword toward him and unsheathed her second khopesh. "Pick it up."

The moment the archangel grabbed it, they lunged. His speed matched hers, long legs eating up the space. Their blades rang out within the clearing. The male's footing at times seemed sloppy, and she could feel his faltering grip on the sword. His teeth gritted in discomfort as he maneuvered around her. He growled in frustration, leaping back to sheathe the weapon and taking out a pair of long daggers instead. They circled one another. Two beasts clad in steel and leather. Every strike she made, he met with equal ferocity.

The sensation was . . . exhilarating. A new challenge that sang to her blood. Although his fighting skills were rough around the edges, there was a different sort of strength behind the archangel's movements. It echoed the power that ran inside her. While elves were given ether in the form of the elements, archangels had a different sort of power, more ethereal in nature. Ether in the form of shadows and light, illusion and mind-speaking. Though only a small number of archangels—like High King Raziel—had the ability to imbue ether into physical matter, such as the tattoo ink that made the fyrebrand.

Zara wondered what sort of power resided within this archangel. "Who are you?"

He was breathing heavily. Perhaps a little too much in her opinion. Sweat rolled down the side of his temples, trickling down his tattooed neck. But there was a spark in his eyes that hadn't been there before.

The archangel bared his teeth. More akin to a smile than a snarl. "This is the first time in years I have felt such excitement to raise a blade."

She knew he wasn't going to answer her, nor did she understand what he meant by that. Not that it mattered. Before she could shoot a retort, a voice shouted from between the buildings. A voice she recognized.

"Zara!" It was Axar.

The archangel paused. His gray eyes glinted. "Zara."

Her name rolled from his tongue as if this new piece of information was the most exquisite treasure. She silently cursed Axar.

The archangel's wings swept up, lifting him from the ground. He jerked a chin to the lifeless body that had been forgotten in the clearing. "I helped you with that kill, you know." A mild touch of arrogance blended with the humor in his voice. "It was a group effort."

This time Zara snorted. The thrill of the evening was overwhelming. It had been too long since she'd been away from the guild.

She sidestepped toward the sound of Axar's voice while still facing the archangel. "Hardly."

"You and I will meet again, little wolf."

Zara responded in the only way she knew how. Her fingers snatched onto a throwing dagger, firing the small weapon. The archangel batted the thin slate of steel to the ground, the sound of deep laughter growing distant as he took to the stars.

FOURTEEN

It had been two weeks since the invitation to the Summit had arrived. Two weeks for Daria Calderón to burn every Elios law and policy into her brain.

Even then, she still had not gleaned much about the Council. There were five deities who made up the ethereal body of authority: Nadira, Hadeon, Arwan, Saija, and Lucian. There was little information about the figureheads, except that when Celestrea still had access to the Continent, they had served the Primordials. They had been the first to acknowledge the ethereal realm's abuse toward the mortals. Now they were revered as saviors.

Her pater's voice dragged her attention from her thoughts. His white braids swayed to the gentle tousle of their iron carriage. "We are in the outer district of Elios."

Daria stretched her arms, her muscles aching from their travels, and peeked out the gray shutters. The air was a mix of seawater and sweat. And there was so much *noise*.

Ikarria was a large kingdom, but it was not cluttered like Elios. The columned buildings here were stacked too closely, the streets too narrow. Thick pillars of smoke curled in the air.

She frowned as she noticed the cracks in the columns, the withering drapes on the market stalls. The only finery that seemed to survive this place were the statues of the Primordials. The marble a pristine beam of white among the gray.

"I see," she whispered. "The High Throne claims it wants to create a new world. I wonder if this is what they had in mind."

Her pater grunted. "Elios is known to be quite protective of its own peace. Some may question the kingdom's methods, while others claim it provides the most effective results."

Idris's mood darkened the closer they got to the capital. Books were scattered about the iron chariot. His nose had been practically stuck in pages since they left Ikarria.

She eyed the titles on the tomes. *Myths and Legends of Genesis. Creatures of the North.* The skin between her brows furrowed. Her pater had hardly ever cared to read for leisure. Something was bothering him.

"Pater, you never said why you've taken up reading—this intensely at least. What's wrong?" Daria said.

Idris closed the book in his hands, setting it aside. "I didn't realize that me picking up a few books would concern my daughters so much." He smiled, but it didn't reach his eyes. Guilt and something like shame shadowed his expression as he looked at Daria. "My storm is out there serving a masochistic archangel while I am sending you out to infiltrate his very court."

He let out a humorless chuckle. "What a parental figure I am."

Daria sensed that her pater was avoiding the topic, and it was enough for her to drop it. But his words reminded her that he was both a king and a single pater. The laws of the Continent bound his hands, no matter how much he tried to fight it. Ikarria had been weakened by the battles, he was in no position to negotiate any more than he did.

Idris was left with two daughters to raise and a kingdom to rebuild.

"You should've known the forces you were raising," she said, giving her pater a warm smile. "We are women who will blaze our own path. You taught us how."

The king of Ikarria looked at her now, as if realizing that she was no longer the little girl who waited for his return from the ashes. No, he had given her the tools to be who she was now. And it was up to her how she wanted to forge her path.

Someone screamed in the streets, shattering the comfort that blossomed in the chariot. Wine red cloaks brushed the afternoon light. The insignia of a rose sitting in the center of two crossed strands of eucalyptus rippled in the dusted air. Vampire soldiers of Adrastea marched through the forum in melted bronze.

Her nose wrinkled at the smell of metal. A bitter taste formed over her tongue. Her blood turned to ice when she realized the scent.

Fear.

It was so prominent, thicker than the smell of urine and waste. A vampire stood at the helm of the soldier unit. His hair was so long that it reached his waist, dark with a faint hue of deep violet. Tall, with high cheekbones and a sharp, elegant curve to his jawline, the vampire looked as if he had been sculpted by the Fates. Though clad in Adrastea's armor, no blades adorned his person. His teeth were weapons enough, Daria supposed.

Gloved hands clenched tightly into fists, the vampire shouted a command and soldiers spilled from either side of him. They tore through random shops, throwing chairs and tables. Other vampires lunged onto the buildings, crawling along the walls and scaring the bystanders. Animals in small corrals and tied to posts screeched in fear. Citizens fled from the unit's path.

Daria froze at the horror. Her pater spoke from behind her. "It's called a rousting, where the vampire soldiers destroy whatever is in their path as an attempt to incite fear and obedience among the lower class."

She looked back to see the king staring out the window from his seat. Fire flickered over his skin, illuminating the tattoos on his face. "The Adrastean king, Matías, created this practice. I am not sure why Raziel allows it, perhaps to appease his partnership with him."

Her stomach twisted. If she had stayed in Ikarria, she would not have known the atrocities committed beyond the safety of her realm.

A part of her was grateful to witness this, it made her purpose burn brighter and harsher.

Daria's gaze gravitated back to the vampire general who was watching his soldiers drag people to the ground and shatter their belongings. His lips curled to a snarl, and she almost shrank back in her seat at the sight.

A second vampire stood beside the general. He spoke to him, too low for Daria to hear, before belting out a cruel laugh and stalking through the street with outstretched hands.

His voice filled the street. "This is a warning from High King Raziel. Reveal the Sombra Quarter, turn in the shadow dealers, and these roads will know peace once again. If not, then expect more than what we are showing you today. The hunting season is upon you, the guilds already stalk your streets, and they will show no mercy to sympathizers of the Sombra Quarter."

Cold shock flooded through her. She could only imagine what her sister was doing at this moment and shame began to burn her bones. Daria had wanted to know more about Zara's involvement with the hunting season, but this mere peek caused her to understand why her sister evaded such topics.

Her pater's voice was low. "My storm."

He was thinking of Zara too.

Meanwhile the vampire general's jaw had tightened with an unwavering look of disgust. He grabbed the base of a statue—one of the few in the outer district—and ripped it from the ground. Citizens shouted as the sculpture of a Primordial shattered like broken pale gems on the ground.

When the king and princess reached the domed castle, they were escorted by a pair of archangel soldiers to their suites. It had been Daria's first encounter with the winged race, as none resided in Ikarria. She tried very hard not to stare at their wings, but their brilliant colors were too astounding to ignore.

Hours later, when the sun was low and the sea winds were calm, Daria entered the castle's main courtyard. It was conjoined with the royal garden, long drapes of deep green and ivory decorating the various pillars.

Throngs of royal advisors, court members, and other important figures were already gathered. Musicians strung their harps and flutes while servers coasted about, silver platters on their open palms. There were some who held wine glasses filled with red liquid. Daria knew they were meant for the vampires in the crowd.

It was the feast to commence the Summit. She studied every face, trying to identify which nobles belonged to Elios and which to the other realms. It seemed her academics were benefitting her.

Her heart stopped at the sight of the deities. There were many among the guests—they were hard to miss. They looked human, except for the wisps of silver ether that resided in the irises of their eyes. Though many resided throughout the Continent, she had never come this close to any before.

Daria was both amazed and intimidated and couldn't help but stare as she walked with the king.

She wore a form-fitting crimson gown that spilled over her tall body like wine. It had a squared collar that nearly suffocated her. Sitting atop her head was a thin crown, obsidian gems entwined like branches with a single diadem of ruby red at its center.

Her pater wore something similar to match with her. His white hair had been washed and braided into multiple strands once more, the top half of his hair pulled back by a simple leather band. He wore a crimson tunic, embellished with small images of the sun along the lapel. A dark cloak hung over an arm, the entire ensemble lined with black thread, the obsidian crown of Ikarria tucked comfortably upon his head.

The draconic king and princess. That is what would be said after this night. *The realm of no dragons*. The mere thought sent a ripple of bitterness through her.

Still, the curious stares caused her cheeks to burn. It was Ikarria's first appearance to the Continent since the War of the Skies. It had been so long, they were practically outcasts.

A woman strode through the crowd. The guards flanking her wore helmets in the shapes of animals, from hawks and cats to jackals and crocodiles. Her shoulder-length black hair was decorated with a thin headdress, a simple plate of gold engraved with feathers. A thick turquoise and bronze necklace rested against her collarbone. She wore an ivory gown, a thin veil flowing behind her that glittered like sunlit sands. Kamari, the queen of Kairos, Daria realized. It was said she had armies of jackal shifters with blades made of red steel. That was something she knew Zara would be fascinated with.

It seemed she wasn't the only one staring at the royal of the dunes and oases. Deities watched her every move, their eyes reflecting like the wild beasts of the night. She wasn't sure if she would ever get used to that silver gaze. The queen of Kairos headed to the opposite end of the garden and as soon as she disappeared, a swarm of the other feast's attendants approached Daria and her pater.

Many of the royal business men and women made their introductions to King Idris. He was polite, though she knew her pater was on the verge of gouging his own eyes out. Daria listened to every name uttered, every word that was spilled. She would learn everything about this place. She would fulfill her true purpose here and prove her worth.

A male archangel appeared beside her. "Princess of Ikarria, welcome."

Her lips parted in surprise. He was a beautiful archangel with wings as white as the snow-capped mountains of the Dragon's Teeth and long silver blonde hair. Elios's emblem embroidered over his expensive tunic.

Daria's face lit up. "Are you Erebus, the Hand of the King?"

His ice-blue eyes gleamed. "I see Zara didn't fail to mention me."

She smiled. "I am so happy to meet you. Any friend of Zara's is a friend of mine."

"I am glad to hear it, Princess Daria. She told me a lot about you as well."

"When do you think I can see my sister?" The princess asked.

Erebus chuckled. "Straight to the point. You and Zara are alike, I can already tell. Soon, I imagine. I can send word to her. I know the High King has been keeping the mercenaries busy."

Daria felt as if she was getting a peek into Zara's second life. To meet someone her sister knew outside the borders of their home made her feel closer to her.

Her pater turned to them then, and Erebus quickly dipped into a bow. "Your Highness, it is an honor to finally meet you. High King Raziel requests to see you at your convenience."

Idris gave a small bow of the head. "Please, lead the way."

The Hand of the King guided them through the crowd, past the dance floor. Daria saw more of the deities and wondered which ones were members of the Council. It was difficult to tell.

They approached a small dais, a tall seat of marble upon it. An archangel with golden brown wings sat on the royal chair. The male was obviously handsome, an alabaster crown on his head, streaked with glowing gold that suited his red hair. He bore a curved smile on his face that oddly reminded her of Zara.

Beside him was another male wearing a crown of silver thorns melded with iron that resembled eucalyptus strands. The insignia of the rose told her all she needed to know. He was Matías, King of Adrastea and Lord of the Vampires. He was an older male who looked to be in the midst of his fourth decade. Gods knew his real age—it had been a few hundred years since Adrastea had held a coronation. His dark hair was swept back, baring a dusted jawline. Matías bowed to her and her pater.

The High King didn't, and looked a little too happy to see the Ikarrian king. "Idris, it brings me great pleasure to see you joining us for this year's Summit."

Her pater offered a close-lipped smile and lowered his head. She quickly followed the gesture. "The honor is mine, High King. I look forward to becoming more accustomed to the workings of the new Continent."

Something shined in Raziel's eyes. "I am happy to hear it." His gaze slid to Daria, causing the hairs on her neck to rise. Her hands went to her abdomen and she interlaced her fingers, trying to keep her nerves at bay. "And you must be the princess of Ikarria, Idris's true daughter. I must say that there has been little mention of you."

True daughter. For the first time in gods knew how long, Daria felt the urge to curl her lips into a snarl. She did not turn to see how her pater reacted, but she knew he would be writhing with fury inside. The High King knew of Zara and for him to disgrace her so casually . . .

Her voice remained steady. "I am Daria Calderón, princess and ambassador of Ikarria, sister to Zara Santos."

The air about her pater seemed to warm as he spoke. "I wanted to raise *both* of my daughters with as much privacy as possible. Allow them that reprieve before they reached adulthood."

Raziel tilted his head, still observing her. "It is fascinating to know that you have a daughter kept in fine dresses and always surrounded by guards, when the other is always in armor, constantly fending for her life."

The words stung her, whipped against her heart. As nasty and blunt as the High King's words were, Raziel wasn't lying. She hadn't had to go through years of rigorous training. She didn't have to serve a hunting season. Shame scorched through her.

Daria could've sworn the air spiked in heat. Her pater's ether was teetering on the edge. The High King seemed to feel it too. Daria thought she saw the king's lips twitch, fighting back a grin.

She subtly brushed against her pater's arm. The flickering heat surrounding him lowered.

His voice was soft, a promise of wrath lacing his words. "My daughters are both strong, despite their different upbringing. And I believe Zara currently fends for her life as an honor to you."

Raziel's expression did not change. "Ah. You are correct. Zara serving the hunting season was my doing."

The way he said it. As if it didn't mean anything to him—while Zara wrangled with whatever darkness that haunted her. Daria had never sworn a day in her life but a slew of colorful words were on the tip of her tongue.

The vampire king cleared his throat. "We are all very appreciative of Ikarria's part in the treaty. It is why we wished to extend the invitation to the Summit. Since your mercenaries are serving the hunting season, it only seemed fair to have you partake in the conversation at the table."

Idris didn't hesitate. "Will the Council be joining the Summit as well?"

"The deities might visit some meetings, but Raziel will handle the proceedings. The Council supports the High King. Any decisions made for the Continent are decided between them."

They needed to tread carefully. It was an opportunity to learn more about their neighboring kingdoms. If Daria wanted to gain access to the mysterious Council, then she needed to act accordingly.

Daria offered a shy smile. "I am looking forward to seeing more of your beautiful capital, High King. As an ambassador, I wish to learn more about Elios, and Soleira as well."

The lines that were slowly emerging on Raziel's chiseled face disappeared. He smiled, wings rustling behind him. "Speaking about my beloved capital, there has been much unrest within our streets caused by the Sombra Quarter. That is who your dear sister and the guilds are searching for, princess."

Daria wasn't sure how to read the High King's tone. He waved a hand and a shadow moved from behind the two kings. Daria didn't look away, Raziel's golden gaze pinning her to the floor. "With the ongoing hunting season, there are many dangers lurking within the capital, including the inner district. Since your father will be attending the official gatherings during the Summit, I want to ensure the safety of my esteemed guest with a personal bodyguard."

What in the Three Suns . . .

Bodyguard? Absolutely not.

A voice practically purred. "It is a pleasure to meet the future heir of Ikarria."

Daria jumped. She twisted around and peered up through her lashes. She could've sworn she heard a sharp inhale.

Sharp cheekbones. Elegant jawline. It was the vampire general she'd seen in the rousting. Her heart raced, and not in excitement. Up close, she could see the vampire's eyes were a rare dark violet. A gaze with the power to pierce hearts. Or eat them.

There was a sophisticated fierceness about him. While she observed him, she didn't realize that he had also been surveying her. His lips parted and the tips of fangs appeared.

The vampire bowed low before her. "I am Ares Valdemar, General of Adrastea."

His voice was beautiful and rugged. The words were gentle off his tongue, resembling a soft growl.

Daria blinked before giving him a tight smile. "Flattering to think I need an army general to guard me." The words flew from her mouth. She bit her tongue, mentally scolding herself.

Ares's lips twitched upward, but it was Raziel who responded. "We wished to have the most skilled guard to take this duty. Ares is more than capable of protecting a princess."

Ares hadn't looked away from Daria, but she was sure a shadow flickered across his gaze. A slight tightening to his mouth.

Her pater raised his chin and eyed the vampire general, who seemed to straighten under the king's burning stare.

"How generous of an offer," Idris responded. Daria could see impatience brimming beneath her pater's stoic face.

Daria certainly did not want a vampire—a vampire general, at that—to be stalking her every movement. Though if she was to learn more about the Council's motives and the goings- on of the High Throne, then she supposed she would need to overcome whatever obstacles were placed before her. She unlaced her fingers and curled them into fists at her sides.

Ares Valdemar was simply another opponent on the political battlefield.

FIFTEEN

The following morning, Daria awoke to a subtle throb at her temples. The silk sheets were cool beneath her fingertips. The shutters from the windows on the opposite side of the room were peeled open, allowing the young ocean breeze to waft in, sunlight pouring over light blue furniture lined with gold that surrounded her bed. Daria rubbed her eyes as the events of last night flooded back to her.

It was no dream, she was in Soleira. Far away from her home for the first time in her life.

The princess slid off the bed and entered the bath chamber. There were no handmaids to tend to her—precisely how she wanted it. Not even in Ikarria did she have such services. In her world, where there was little to no privacy, she appreciated the moments of solitude.

After Daria had bathed in rose scented waters, she dressed in a blush pink day gown. The collar slipped off one shoulder, the fabric billowed gently around her arms and legs. She wrapped her hand around the bronze handle of her bedchamber and paused. Her sharp hearing caught the presence of another on the other side.

Dear Suns, she had almost forgotten Raziel's *gift* to her for her stay in the High Realm. Daria swung the door open, grumbling, her gaze down. The mere notion that she needed—

"Good morning to you, too, princess."

Daria froze at the threshold and slowly looked up to find the vampire general looming in the hallway. Ares Valdemar was taller than she recalled. He was leaning back against the ivory wall, his arms folded. His lips parted enough to reveal the tip of a fang. She couldn't tell if he was amused or upset. The brown and maroon tunic and leathers clung to his lithe frame. That luscious hair with its dark purple sheen seemed smooth to the touch. Too beautiful for his own good.

"You mock me," he said.

Daria clamped her mouth shut. She had been so caught up with her thoughts that she hadn't realized she had scoffed out loud. "I apologize, general Ares. It wasn't towards you."

A sore attempt at a lie—the vampire seemed to know it. His expression sobered as he stepped away from the wall. The general towered over her; even though she was taller than the average female she still had to raise her chin to meet his eyes.

Daria's gaze went to his fangs. How many throats had he torn apart with those teeth? Alone in a hall with a formidable predator, she felt the urge to take a step back but willed herself not to.

Sunlight poured through the openings in the stone ceilings, gilding the edges of his waist-length hair. His violet eyes seemed more luminous as well.

"Right. Come along with me. We are going on a tour this morning."

Ares walked with the prowess of a soldier, and Daria hurried to keep up with him.

"Where is my pater?" The princess asked.

Ares sighed, sounding almost irritated. "The king of Ikarria has left to join the other royals. They will be occupied with their own agendas for most of the day."

Daria's lips thinned. It was clear the vampire did not want to be here just as much as she didn't. But she would not let this stop her. The Summit's official proceedings had already started, and she would handle the task she had set out to do.

Ares cocked his head at her. "Is there something you are concerned with, princess?"

Daria blinked at his question. "I'm sorry?" she stammered.

"Or is it me? Are you afraid of me?"

Her cheeks burned. She was tempted to duck her head. Gods, she had held formal discussions in front of dozens of court members back in Ikarria, it was no time to get flustered.

Daria cringed. "I am not afraid of you. I'm sorry, I suppose so much has been happening ever since I arrived that I'm a bit overwhelmed."

Ares exhaled through his nostrils, as if disappointed. "That's too bad," he said. "You should be."

He did not say it unkindly, his expression remaining unmoved. His voice was smooth and polite, but there was a coldness along the edges that Daria didn't know what to make of.

The vampire quickened his pace. "Keep up, Princess Calderón."

Daria watched the male walk, the muscles of his back shifting beneath his tunic. She remembered that he was not the average vampire. Ares was a general of *war* and for the High King to assign such a personage to her, meant that she couldn't so easily drop her guard. It caused her to wonder if the High Throne had sent Ares to keep an eye on her, a royal of Ikarria, rather than to guard her.

Whatever the reason, Ares's words echoed through Daria's thoughts. He had said she should be afraid of him.

A small shameful part of her admitted that she was.

Daria lost count of how many yawns she'd had to smother. She had been trailing Ares the entire morning as he droned on about every hall, room, and crevice of the Elios castle. He would charge ahead of her as if marching into battle and wouldn't look back to see if she followed. Her feet still ached from last night's constant walking and dancing.

Eventually, they went to the breezeways leading to another wing of the castle, made of arches of pristine stone. The morning light bathed the marble path in liquid gold, the sun making the specks of stone glimmer. Gardens and small pools of water stretched out from where they stood.

"I'm sorry, princess. Am I boring you?"

His voice was flat and emotionless. Daria peeked up to see Ares fold his arms and rest a hip against the stone railing.

She placed a hand at her waist. "Well, it may help if you put more enthusiasm in your tour."

Ares's brows jumped as if he didn't expect her to be so abrupt. "Apologies. I'll be sure to consider your feedback during my actual position as general."

Daria sighed, feeling a sense of defeat. "I understand. You did not wish to play bodyguard."

"I will admit I did not imagine I would spend the glorious Summit celebrations watching over a mysterious princess."

Daria frowned. "Mysterious?"

Ares pushed off the stone. "Yes. Daria Calderón, heir to the draconic realm. No one knows anything about you for years but, suddenly, you appear as an ambassador."

She gestured toward him with her hand. "What about you? I hear no songs about the *bold* Ares Valdemar, war general of Adrastea. I don't recall any ballads of your bravery and heroism."

His lips curled, fangs gleaming. "There is no heroism in bloodshed, princess."

Daria's eyes narrowed. "I am not naive, vampire. My point is that you are as unknown to me as I am to you. As far as my role as ambassador, when we received the invitation to the Summit, my pater thought it was time for me to partake in the Continent's affairs. I want to bridge the gap between the realms, especially with Elios."

"Spoken like a true politician," Ares responded. She didn't miss how his lips twitched with disgust at that.

He strode out of the breezeway and into another hall. Daria had in mind to simply turn the other way but thought better of it. Soldiers meandered about the foyer. The majority were vampires and bowed to the general, who barely acknowledged them other than with a wave of his hand.

Daria made a mental note to learn more about her bodyguard. He seemed a handful of years older than her, perhaps around his early to mid-thirties. She picked up her pace to walk beside him.

"So, how would you normally spend your Summit celebrations?" Daria asked.

Ares looked at her sidelong. "Either blood drinking or fucking . . . or both."

He said it plainly, as if speaking about the godsforsaken weather. Daria wasn't sure how her face looked, but she imagined it was akin to shock because Ares began to chuckle. The sound was velvet and mischief, entwined in one.

"What, was I too crude for you, princess?" He leaned toward her, hands clasped behind his back. "Have you not heard the words: sex, fuck, or cock?"

Daria felt her face burn. "*No.* I'm no prude."

In truth, she hardly ever gave herself the opportunity to explore the more primal, sexual parts of herself. Yes, when she had just reached adulthood she had lost her virginity to a nobleman's son, but that was the end of it. A tender experience but nothing more. She was in no rush to pursue more salacious encounters, even though desire made frequent visits. Especially alone in bed, when her hand would drift between her legs—

Daria cleared her throat, attempting to wipe her damp palms on her dress. "If you've had your fun, vampire, I'd like to visit with the court members."

There was still a hint of amusement on his face. "How come?"

"Well, I should become more acquainted with the other diplomats. I wish to see what efforts they are making for the citizens of Elios."

"I can tell you right now, princess." Ares tilted his head as he observed her. Like one would to a potential opponent on the battlefield. "Shit. They are doing shit for their own kingdom."

Daria was surprised to hear Adrastea's general say such a thing regarding the High Throne's realm. "I'm sure some good has occurred since Raziel and the Council came to power."

The vampire shook his head, a ghost of a cruel smile touched his lips. "Debatable. Regardless, princess, meeting with royal officials sounds positively tedious."

She folded her arms. "You've been acting disinterested all day, what's one more dull occurrence?"

"Suns, have mercy on me," Ares muttered as he turned his back to her and started down the hall.

Ares was right. The first official Summit assembly had been boring, though she would never admit that to him.

As the first meeting started, her eyelids grew heavy with the constant droning of one of Elios's advisors. The poor male was young, probably at the beginning of his career, and kept stumbling on his words, sweat cascading down his neck. As the first gathering amongst the Continent's diplomats for the Summit, this was merely a summary of the political, environmental, and social initiatives each realm had started the year prior. The information was valuable to her, since she had no clue as to what the kingdoms had been doing for their people. If only it were less painful to listen to. Time was slowly peeling away, torturing her and every other attendant.

White marble made the large circular table of the meeting chamber. Every seat was occupied by representatives of the realms. Beams of light pierced through the grand windows, allowing a slight heat into the room. Archangel guards lined the edges of the space, their wings dipped in daylight.

The advisor still droned on.

"They should serve drinks here. Strong drinks," Ares grumbled.

Daria had almost forgotten about the vampire seated beside her. He didn't stand behind her like the other soldiers did with those they were charged with. She didn't look his way as she whispered back to him. "Don't be rude."

"To think you were complaining about *my* tour." He glanced at her, shaking his head. "At least you weren't falling asleep, like you were just now."

She briefly closed her eyes, feeling a twitch in one of her eyebrows. "I was *not.*"

"Liar."

"For someone who is normally so quiet and brooding, you're awfully chatty right now."

"That is how you know I am quite bored, princess."

Daria rolled her eyes, fixating her attention back to the meeting. She clasped her hands together atop the smooth marble surface. The light glittered off the patterns that swirled across the table. Streams of crystalline rock danced under the sun.

"Now I present Maira Iryndel to take the helm of our first assembly."

The advisor slipped out of sight as a woman strode to the center of the table. She wore a soft green gown that flowed like water. The dress had no sleeves except for the fabric that draped over her shoulders as a cape, cutting down between her breasts. Gems were embedded in her long black hair, and it was difficult to miss the silver ether glow among the soft blue of her eyes.

Daria's jaw slackened.

A deity.

There was an aura about the lesser god, as if her olive skin had been kissed by stardust. Power seemed to radiate from her person, a subtle heartbeat of energy that was beautiful as well as terrifying. Daria wasn't sure she would like to witness a deity's ether unleashed.

"You're gawking, princess."

Gods. Daria's lips thinned as she dared a glance at the vampire general. He was leaning back in his seat, his long legs extended underneath the table. A full representation of arrogance and boredom.

She couldn't reveal that she had been tasked to learn more about the deities and its Council. That would cause suspicion around Ikarria. Despite Ares's crass behavior and apparent skepticism regarding those in charge, he was not to be trusted, but she could still use him for his knowledge.

"I didn't realize the deities were involved with the proceedings amongst the mortal diplomats," she said.

He raised an eyebrow. "The deities are citizens of the Continent like the rest of us, and some of them work in politics. Most either live here in the castle or in the capital—primarily in the inner district—while the rest live throughout the expanse of Ribera. They tend to stick to their inner circles, but I would say they are quite involved with the kingdoms."

"I see." Daria nodded, turning back to the deity.

Maira's gaze was sharp as a blade, piercing through every pair of eyes set on her. She settled on Daria for a moment, which caused the princess to sit straighter. "Ikarria has joined us. Welcome."

Daria wasn't sure if it was said as an insult, but the deity sounded . . . genuine. She bowed her head. "I am honored to be here."

Maira's lips turned up and she addressed the other members. "I am sure by now your kingdoms have received word of an abnormal amount of crops perishing before harvest. It has been brought to our attention that the ether in our soil is not as strong as it was when the Primordials had access to our world."

She paused, tension lining her delicate mouth. "I mention this only so you're aware of why there'll be less food at the marketplaces over the next months. Now I am primarily speaking to the representatives of Elios, as this is affecting our realm the most—"

A wave of energy rolled through the air as a group of individuals entered the chamber. There were five of them, three males and two females. The men wore golden wreath crowns upon their heads, while the women wore circlet crowns of white gold that gleamed across their foreheads. Silver burned in their irises.

The power that emanated from them felt almost tangible. The hairs on Daria's arm rose. Her own ether, the same fires that writhed in her pater and passed down by birth, festered within her. She rarely tapped into her own energy, its presence surprising her at times.

Ares stilled, as if turned unto stone, violet eyes set on the approaching deities. "The Council."

Daria's eyes widened as she watched the powerful figures stroll past. They were the rebelling deities who had rallied enough support to overthrow the Primordials. Who had done the unimaginable and removed the gods from the mortal world.

One broad-shouldered male deity glanced at the assembly as they passed, silver rippling and brightening in his dark eyes. "Ether is *not* dying."

Ares sighed under his breath. "And that is Hadeon."

The Council stopped halfway through the meeting chamber as the one called Hadeon stepped closer to the marble table. He smiled, his eyes warm. It startled Daria, she wasn't expecting the deity to have such a welcoming demeanor. "In case the message gets lost in this meeting, know that the natural ether of this world is not at risk. Despite what acolytes and common believers may say, it is solely a temporary change in the workings of our Continent. Since we took the world for ourselves, there is bound to be some adaptation and evolution. There is nothing to fear, we assure you."

Hadeon glanced at Maira and bowed his head. "I apologize for the intrusion. I only meant to reassure our fellow leaders of the Continent."

Maira's manner was refined, a soft lilt to her lips as her eyes bore down on the male deity. "Of course," she responded before addressing the delegates. "I only endeavor to address the people's needs."

Maira shot a look to Hadeon, but he didn't seem fazed. The male deity bowed again and joined the rest of the Council.

He gestured to his companions. "We, the Council, made the vow to preserve this mortal world. We upheld that promise during the War of the Skies, and this matter will be no different."

As Hadeon spoke, Daria observed the other members of the Council. She knew their names, but couldn't tell who was who. One female deity caught her eye; she was a mirror-image of Maira. She had the same oval-shaped face, with long black hair pulled high up with a dark leather band. Light scars could also be seen across her cheekbones and neck. Unlike Maira, there was a razor sharpness to her blue eyes.

It must have been the famous Nadira Iryndel. She didn't realize that the Council member had a twin. Nadira didn't look her sister's way, not even when Hadeon excused himself, the rest of them following suit.

Once the deities left the meeting chamber, the remnants of their powerful presence still crackling in the air, Daria sagged in her seat. Maira gazed at the closed door they disappeared through, as if deciphering a puzzle. And maybe with what looked like a flicker of longing.

SIXTEEN

After the meeting, Daria felt drained. She had been thrown into an entirely different world in Soleira compared to Dae Asari. A part of her thrummed with excitement for this new venture, while another piece of her mourned her home. The quiet mountains and gentle forests.

Ares had been silent beside her, especially since the Council had left. For the remainder of the assembly, Maira had discussed potential initiatives for flourishing regions of Elios to provide humanitarian aid to more unfortunate areas. Daria was astounded with how the deity had formulated such ideas to assist those in need, but the meeting concluded with advisors wanting to mull over the next best course of action without doing anything.

The princess and general continued to walk till they reached the gardens. They faced the sea, the salty air running fingers through her hair. She could smell the blossoms and lemons from the trees.

"What did you think of your first official meeting as ambassador?"

Ares's voice sounded bitter. Daria's brows furrowed, eyes shooting daggers at him. "I thought it was productive. Maira seems very intuitive and plans to do much for the people of Soleira, and all of Elios."

He scoffed. "You cannot rely on words alone, action must reflect the truth of what they say."

She arched her brow. "On that, I agree. What are your thoughts on the Council? You didn't seem enthused with their promise for support."

If there was an opportunity to pry into the dynamic of the rebelling deities, she might as well ask her bodyguard. Daria turned her gaze to the castle staff tending to the olive trees in the open courtyards, feeling his stare on her skin.

Ares's voice was cold. "The Council's doings are not my priority. As I said to you before, princess, the diplomats of the realms are doing little to nothing. All they do within their lavish meetings is give pretty words and empty promises."

Daria wasn't sure what to say to that. Her fingers clenched into fists. It was beginning to dawn on her that her experience in politics was more inept than she thought. She turned to see his expression shift into that same look of disgust.

"Let me guess," he said. "You spent all your years studying how to be a ruler but have never visited those you were meant to rule."

"That's not true," she started to say, "I am acquainted with the citizens of Dae Asari. I often visit the public establishments and—"

Daria shut her mouth, stopping herself from saying more, suddenly feeling embarrassed.

The princess may have had acquainted herself with the citizens of Ikarria's capital, but she certainly had not visited the far corners of the realm she would one day rule. Unlike her sister.

Ares, however, didn't look smug. The lines around his mouth tensed. "Let me show you something, princess."

The vampire turned on his heels and her eyes flicked to his waist, noticing the lack of weaponry on his leathers. A broken statue flashed in her mind as well as the vampire who had torn it from the ground.

"I noticed you in the district forum," Daria blurted out.

The general froze, his shoulders stiffening. His hands were still clasped behind his back, his knuckles now a bone-white.

"I saw you wreak havoc on the streets, terrorizing those innocent people," she whispered.

He was too silent, too still. Ares slowly turned to face her with a look that was enough to skewer a soldier into the ground. She was no soldier, though.

Daria crossed her arms, her voice sharpening. "I am not as oblivious as you thought. I hope you understand who you are up against."

Those violet eyes pierced through her, slowly looking her up and down. The vampire general's voice rumbled through her bones. "You may be right, princess. I do not know who I am up against . . . yet."

Much to her surprise, Ares took her to the inner district. Shifters, vampires, archangels, elves, humans, and even deities filled the white streets. They meandered about the outdoor markets, strolling in and out of shops.

Daria squinted against the beaming sunlight, sweat already dotting the nape of her neck. She kept close to her silent bodyguard as they walked through the crowd. Even in the inner district, where the wealthy and upper middle class primarily lived, Ares was revered.

Citizens nodded their heads, keeping a respectful distance. Suddenly Daria had an inkling as to why the vampire king had assigned Ares as her guard. But those violet eyes—they were not as guarded as he thought; she saw flickers of irritation and distaste. There was more behind that controlled gaze.

Ares still said nothing as they reached the inner district's forum. No statues resided in the center except among the slew of market stalls, draped with cloth the color of copper. Large hyenas, patched with rough hide and fur, pulled carts. Ares swept a hand to the side, guiding her back as one trudged past them. The hyena's hot breath pressed against her skin, snickering as it did so.

"Incredible," Daria breathed.

Ares glanced at her, with more curiosity than anything, and she felt comfortable to ask, "Why are we here?"

"While you royals drone on and on about a brighter future, every day of inaction is a day of consequence for those who are waiting for your help." He searched her face. "You saw me *wreak havoc,* as you so eloquently put it, but you only witnessed a *fraction* of what really occurs outside the castle's pretty walls."

Ares continued forward, leaving Daria with a sinking feeling in her stomach. She reached after him, wanting to tell him that she wished to learn and be better than the average ruler, when an enormous plume of dust exploded from within one of the shops.

Vampire soldiers beckoned the passersby to make way, clearing a section of the forum. Chips of wood and stone fell from the clouds. There was a scream, followed by something that sounded wet.

Red wings emerged from the pale smoke. Daria's lips parted as she watched an archangel pin a man to the ground, a sword deep in his chest. The winged female, who had a scar down one side of her face, was beautiful—if not utterly terrifying. The Horizon bore white and bronze armor with a drifting pale cloak behind her, indicating her loyalty to the Elios guild.

More screams erupted from within the shop. A handful of citizens scurried out into the forum, while other Elios mercenaries charged after them. Random onlookers watched with horror as the Horizons speared, stabbed, and sliced. Blood splattered on that immaculate ground. The red would seep in between the cracks, forever staining the city.

One male broke from the fray with a cry, steering toward her. He didn't seem to be paying any mind to where he was going, so long as it was away from the mercenaries. Daria's heart raced when she noticed the meat cleaver he was swinging in his hand. The male's only thought was survival and it seemed he was willing to bash his way through the crowd.

A hand pushed her back and Ares lunged forward, sunlight shining across his violet-hued hair. He grabbed the man's back—no, not grabbed—*punctured*. Daria saw the spray of blood in the air as Ares's nails pierced through the male. The runaway was still alive, gasping out red saliva.

Ares swung him back to the forum, straight into the arms of the red-winged archangel. The Horizon snatched the male by the shoulder and drove her blade through him. Her expression was like stone, similar to how Daria had seen the vampire general hold himself. It caused her to wonder if it was common for those who had seen so much pain and violence to shield how they truly felt inside. If they still felt anything at all. The archangel didn't give the general a second glance before tossing the body into the pile that had grown behind her.

As quickly as the rampage had erupted, life in the capital moved forward. The bystanders resumed their businesses, even with a bleakness overtaking their expressions.

A shadow fell over her. At her peripheral she could see red trickling down long, pale fingers.

"It was their kill to make," Ares said. He gestured with his bloodied hand to the wreckage. "Tell me, princess. Do your textbooks and spreadsheets tell you about *this?*"

Daria's eyes hadn't left the scene in front of her. The mercenaries grunted as their fyrebrands burned a bright light. Nor could she stop when the capital's soldiers began to clean the mess the guild had left behind.

Such bloodshed. She had never seen so much blood and . . . was that a liver? Daria's face blanched. Her insides contorted, the contents of her stomach rising up her throat.

Daria felt that shame return to her with a vengeance. This was a test. She knew the world was imperfect, but it was massively different to witness it firsthand.

Ares ushered her away. It wasn't long before she was back in her bedchamber retching everything she had eaten since breakfast. There was another truth that sickened her even more. She had the power of ether, in the form of fire, and in the face of danger she hadn't even tried to summon it.

Another dinner feast was being hosted in the castle gardens. One of many celebrations in honor of the Summit.

The Ikarrian princess had managed to freshen up for the occasion, and dressed in an evening gown. It was form-fitting to her long torso and hips, the buttery soft fabric the color of the blue sky. Daria pinned her hair up, allowing several stray strands to fall along her cheeks and neck. The princess's crown sat proudly atop her head.

After being surrounded by new faces for hours she was more than relieved to reunite with her pater. They were both seated at a small table in the garden, tucked in the corner and away from prying ears.

The setting sun nearly blinded her as it cast shards of gold on the ocean's surface. A breeze tousled her hair, sending her gown fluttering around her legs. Torches burned brightly and blossom petals were scattered along the limestone pathways. In the center of the garden was a small group of musicians playing string instruments. One played the harp, singing odes of love and new beginnings while a pair of dancers took to the floor. Daria grinned when she noticed the tendrils of water that followed the elves' movements. The elemental dancers were popular among feasts, especially in Ikarria. It felt like a piece of home.

Ares was off-duty for the evening, but he was still attending the feast. Gods knew what he was doing at this moment. He had assigned his Second, Silas, to assume the night shift.

Silas didn't hover like Ares. He lingered along the edges of the garden, speaking to fellow guards, but she knew that he kept an eye on her. His face was more boyish, with curly brown hair and dark eyes. Daria could see the black slowly fade from the white of his eyes—a sign of bloodlust—as he licked something red from his finger.

Daria returned her attention to her pater, who had been going over all the meetings he'd had with the other royals. More wrinkles seemed to have appeared around his eyes and mouth since they'd arrived in Elios.

Idris took a sip out of his goblet. "It has been beneficial to see how Ikarria can strengthen trade and partnerships while remaining out of the Aligned Realms. I was almost concerned that King Matías would try to push for Ikarria to swear fealty, too."

The mention of the vampire king made her think of Ares again. "Pater, do you know the history between Matías and his general of war?"

Fire sparked in her pater's eyes. He cast his gaze about the feast, most likely looking for the vampire general. "I only know that he was born and raised in Adrastea. Recruited to the vampire army when he was just a boy."

"Interesting," she mused. "He is respected by the public, but he doesn't seem to bask in that sort of attention."

It almost seemed like he hated it. Not to mention the politics of Ribera. Daria didn't dare voice that out loud.

Her pater gave her a warning look. "Careful with that one, firelight. He is still a soldier, and a loyal one to Adrastea and Elios. They call him King Matías's favorite."

Daria nearly choked on her water. "Now that is intriguing. How are you discovering all the gossip?"

"It's quite shocking how much political representatives are willing to talk behind closed doors." He picked at his food, looking around the garden and people gathered once more. "There will be games hosted in the coliseum throughout the Summit's season. Many of the deities will be in attendance."

Daria leaned back, hands resting on her lap. "A perfect opportunity, then, to become acquainted with them. The Council made an appearance during my meeting with the diplomats."

She quickly went over the details of what the assembly entailed. When she finished, Daria stabbed a cooked vegetable with her fork and plopped it in her mouth. "The Council seems to be dedicated to their people, even if they seem a bit self-absorbed. Perhaps I can use my acquaintance with Ares to get a closer audience with the deities."

Her pater stared at her. "Be cautious as you proceed. What we need to understand is what they hope to gain with the High Throne at their side."

She wondered if that was something they could even discover. Finding out surface facts about the Council members was simple, as it was public information, except for their histories. Daria had written everything she learned and kept the notes hidden in her room.

Idris's gaze went back to his plate, a shadow flickering across his expression. "Have you heard from Zara?"

Daria slowly placed her fork down. After they had settled in

Soleira, she'd had Erebus send a request to her sister to meet, but Zara hadn't responded.

"No," she mumbled. "Not yet."

Her pater hesitated, eyes darting away. "I see."

Daria felt the guilt return. "I can't imagine what she is going through, but I still hoped she would be willing to see us."

The king sighed. "I feel that Zara has become more withdrawn."

Daria looked at her pater sharply. "If an opportunity arises to remove her from the hunting season—or at least away from the High Throne's spotlight—you must take it."

Idris nodded, lifting his chin. "I will, firelight."

The way his amber-brown eyes sparked with determination, his jaw clenching, ready to drive a blade through someone's chest, was the same blaze the king of Ikarria had bestowed within his daughters.

Daria felt that burning resolve now. She may have come to Soleira in search of knowledge regarding the mysterious Council, but she would abandon any obligation if it meant helping Zara.

As the night grew late and the drinks flowed, Daria caught her first glimpse of Ares leaving the feast alone. Storm clouds seemed to loom over his shoulders, a weight that he shouldered.

Her pater's previous words whispered through her head.

King Matías's favorite.

She was curious to know what the general had done—what he was capable of—that had made him so valuable to the Lord of Vampires.

Ares Valdemar paused to mutter something to Silas. She knew he was speaking about her as his Second looked her way, but the general did not meet her gaze.

Daria could only watch as her guard melted into the darkness.

SEVENTEEN

Ronan stood along the edges of Soleira's outer district. The sweet smell of wild blossoms clung to the empty villas. No one had lived in these parts since the end of the War, which made such meetings like tonight possible.

His wings rustled, shaking off a soft cloud of dirt. The Stone Orchard rested within the hills that bordered the Estrella Territories, and it had nearly taken him the entire day to fly here. Ronan didn't mind the journey, it was a blissful escape to lose himself within the sky.

He stepped into the familiar abandoned temple. A Primordial statue of Aspidis stood at the center of the courtyard, the feathered serpent clawing at the dark sky. Ronan could only imagine how magnificent this place had been during its prime. Worshipers would have visited day and night, burned their offerings and paid homage to the Primordial of Nature.

Out of all the gods, Ronan reserved the most respect to the one who stood for the life of not just animals but the trees, the oceans, and the grasslands. The purest forms of being.

He saw a tendril of red smoke and caught the scent of root with a faint twist of copper. A figure sat at the foot of the statue. Ronan smirked.

Ares Valdemar rested his head against the statue, his eyes closed.

A small roll of parchment was tucked between his teeth as he took another drag of the bloodroot.

"It's interesting that you can fly everywhere and yet I *still* arrive before you," the vampire rumbled.

Ronan swaggered into the courtyard. "Convenient you left out the fact that I had to travel a lot farther than you. Admit it, you were just eager to see me."

"You might be right." Ares scoffed and opened his eyes. "And that is saying something, if I am voluntarily meeting with a criminal such as yourself."

Ronan went to sit beside him, mindful of the wildflowers that grew between the brown tiles. "You may have not wanted to start these meetings at first, but you quickly realized that this *criminal* is a lot more entertaining than those stuck-up soldiers of yours."

The vampire blew out another plume of blood-red smoke and gave Ronan a sidelong glance. His violet eyes seemed to deepen under the starlight. "Our little secret here has proven to be useful for the both of us."

Ronan tugged a leather bag loose from his belt and tossed it to Ares. "The dosage should last another month."

Ares pulled out a vial of purple liquid. His long fingers turned the clear tube around, watching the medicine whirl. The expression on his face was shadowed, his emotions hiding behind that steel wall.

"Thank you," he said roughly before tucking it back into the pouch.

Ronan nodded, knowing full well who that vial was intended for. He didn't bother asking Ares on the matter since the vampire never wanted to speak about it.

Instead, the archangel jerked his chin. "I brought a little something for you as well."

Ares's lips curled into a sly smile as he lifted a small canister from the bag. He clicked it open to reveal deep red powder. "You wicked bastard. Just when I was about to run out."

"Only the purest bloodroot for you." Ronan sagged against the stone. Yes, Ares was very aware of Ronan's illegal livelihood. It was the reason why they were meeting in an abandoned temple. He tipped his chin up, watching the stars shine. "Do you have anything for me?"

The tip of Ares's roll burned bright. "The High King is sending all mercenary guilds after the Sombra Quarter."

Ronan was silent for a breath. He was aware of the yearly hunting season, a time when his shadow dealers would keep the lowest profiles. "That explains it," he muttered.

Ares looked at him, raising a brow. "Care to elaborate?"

"You're aware the High King has been at our throats for some time, sending traitors to gather information on our whereabouts. Earlier this week, I encountered one of the Horizons. She and her guild had been tasked to hunt down a target of mine who used to be a shadow dealer. I suspect it was to find clues about the Sombra Quarter."

The vampire shook his head. "Gods, the mercenaries work fast. Who did you come across? From what guild?"

"An elven woman from Ikarria."

Ares shot upright, his fingers almost crushing the bloodroot. "Ronan, how long have you been in that hidden city of yours? That was no mere mercenary. They call her the *Rogue*—personal assassin to the High King, do you not remember her?"

Ronan had heard word of the hunter who owned the shadows, how just the mention of the Rogue struck fear in the cold streets. He thought of the Horizon who had raised a blade against him, the tip of her foreign obsidian sword threatening to pin him to the wall at his back. Though it may have been some time since he'd practiced with the blade, she was clever and cutthroat in a way that he hadn't experienced before.

"Fitting that the vicious elf is the infamous *Rogue*," he said, his lips pulling at the side. "No wonder the High King chose her for that role."

Ares snorted before taking another drag of his bloodroot. "Only the gods know the answer to that. That is another thing I wanted to tell you: he personally assigned her to hunt the leader of the Sombra Quarter down. She is after you, Menodora."

Ronan's gray eyes darkened. "Is that so?"

Zara. The name drifted across his thoughts like a ripple of water. Ronan remembered how her voice had sounded, throaty and deep, her Ikarrian accent strong, and with a sultriness that was all her. She had seen his face but had not known who he was. Ronan had mulled over their encounter just as much as his experience with the possessed mortal from the destroyed city of Huerta. Two obstacles had now been set before him. It seemed the Fates had lured him into a false sense of security. Shit.

Ares rested his head back against the stone. "Just be careful."

"It almost sounds like you care about my safety, vampire."

The general made a disgusted noise. "I am merely giving you information in exchange for your shadow market goods. Consider it a heed of warning, as danger never seems to leave you alone."

Ronan's voice sounded distant. "I suppose that is true."

"Something has happened, hasn't it?"

He chuckled mirthlessly. "Are you sure you are not part wolf? You always know when something is wrong."

Ares waved a hand. A tendril of red spun into the air around his fingers. "Fucking Suns, do not compare my skills to a *shifter*. I think you and I have spent enough time together that I can tell when you are worried."

Ronan sighed, running a hand through his hair. "The Estrella Territories are being attacked."

He and Orion had discovered more abandoned establishments throughout the Territories. Though they hadn't seen any other mortals with cerulean eyes—thank the gods.

Ares frowned when Ronan had finished recounting. "What kind of ether was it? It couldn't have been that of a demon, could it?"

He shook his head. "It was no demon. At least, I do not think so. There was something about its presence. The power that emanated from it. I recognized it."

Ares seemed to consider his words. "There have been no reports of this at the castle."

"News is bound to reach the High Throne soon. I rather you not say anything about it if you can. These incidents are interrupting business and trade with the Sombra Quarter. I would like to sort them out before the High King's forces intervene."

Ares smirked. "So be it. It is not like you don't have much to deal with already. With the guilds hunting for your shadow dealers and the Rogue after your neck, you are very popular."

"Extremely," Ronan said dully. "Be careful, vampire. You can't bring it to the castle's attention—they will question how you came to that information."

"Archangel, are you worried for *my* safety?"

"Bastard," Ronan mumbled. "Maybe."

A smile twitched at Ares's lips. He raised the bloodroot to the sky and watched the embers dim. "I have more news."

"I'm brimming with excitement. I hope it includes some of your wild adventures at those parties."

Ares gave him a dry look. "I haven't been able to lose myself in pleasure houses and feasts like I normally would. Ikarria was invited to the Summit." When Ronan's mouth parted in surprise, the vampire rolled his eyes. "Would you care to hear more about it, or are you going to blabber more nonsense?"

Ronan raised a hand in surrender. "Please do."

Ares relayed the details regarding the draconic realm's attendance to the Summit. "I have been so accustomed to doing what I pleased until Matías commanded me to act as a bodyguard to the spoiled Ikarrian princess. The woman is already a thorn in my side."

Ronan fought back a laugh. "Good. I hope she is. You need someone to keep you on your toes—gods know those soldiers are no match for you."

He rolled his eyes before his expression darkened. "I think my king has some sort of plan, but I cannot see it. It makes no sense for him to assign me this duty."

Ronan growled. "Matías is hardly *your* king. He, Raziel, and all the fucking deities that sit within those royal walls are *not* your rulers."

Ares sighed and glanced down at the soft brown fighting leathers fastened over his dark tunic. He pressed a finger to the insignia of a rose sitting over crossed eucalyptus strands etched over his heart. "As long as I wear this, they *are* my kings."

Something twisted inside Ronan's chest at that. His voice fell into a whisper. "You don't have to keep doing this. You can turn your back, leave all this behind."

The vampire shook his head. It wasn't the first time they had this conversation. "You know I can't."

"You can bring *her*. I can help, give her access to proper medical treatment."

Ares's darkened expression shuttered. A crack in the walls that looked something akin to devastation.

"The danger is too great," he responded softly. "Matías is a proud male and would send every soldier after me. We would be on the run, and everything we worked for would fall apart. To flee would be irrational and too risky. He would never let me go."

Ronan cursed under his breath. "I hate this."

"Let's keep these meetings as they always have been, archangel. A temporary escape."

They both looked to the sky. The Fates seemed to stare down at them in silent judgment.

Ares turned to look at him. "You are plotting something, aren't you?"

There was a subtle clench to Ronan's jaw before his scarred mouth slipped into a smirk. "I think I may have something in mind."

"And I am assuming you're going to need my help."

Ronan raised his brow, flashing Ares a smile. The vampire sighed. "If I knew what a pain in the ass you were going to be, I never would've helped you escape."

Ronan knew very well what he was referring to. It was, after all, how their budding relationship began. In the wake of the War, Ronan had been taken prisoner by Elios's soldiers. He was broken and defeated. Had lost everything and everyone.

His fingers drifted to his neck, still able to feel the phantom chains that bound him. How his wings were strapped to his back for gods knew how long. He remembered sitting in his cell, his head hung low as he lay in a pool of his own waste, when a pair of boots appeared before him.

Young Ares had been assigned to clean his wounds, to feed and watch over him. Ronan wasn't sure what the vampire ever saw in him to even decide to speak to him. It might have started out of pity, but eventually he discovered that Ares had his own darkness. His own duties that tied him to corrupted crowns.

Years after Ares helped him escape—which had encompassed careful plotting that led the High Throne to believe he was dead or missing—Ronan had found the soldier again. By then, Ares was the general of war while Ronan was preparing to overthrow the original leaders of the Sombra Quarter. Being in command of the vampire armies, Ares had access to trivial information about the criminals slinking around Elios's corners and was able to help Ronan claim power within the shadow markets.

Somehow, the Fates wove the strands of the suns and stars, causing the two young males to grow close enough to put their allegiances aside. Their odd companionship was a way for them to seek peace in the heap of shit that was their lives.

Ronan's lips twitched into a grim smile.

"Liar," he replied.

Ares chuckled deeply. No, the vampire would've helped him escape again and again.

"So," the general of war drawled. "Tell me this plan of yours."

"You're not going to like it."

EIGHTEEN

The guilds of Elios and Adrastea were gathered in the temple's training ground. They watched as an Adrastean shifter dug her ebony nails against the colored tiles, puncturing the painted suns. Axar's gray wolf was crouched at the opposite side. His hairs bristled and saliva dripped from his fangs. In the blink of an eye, the sound of snapping maws began to echo in the circular room.

Hakim leaned toward Zara. "I bet Verena will knock Axar on his ass."

The wolf named Verena was much older than Axar. Her brutal strength practically sent him flying across the room every time. What he lacked in experience, he made up with his agility. He lunged for the wolf and flipped her to the ground. Mercenaries had to leap out of harm's way, barely dodging the giant beasts.

Zara smirked. "Have a little faith."

Axar's voice echoed in the temple. "*Both of you, shut up.*"

Verena snatched him by the neck and threw him as if he were a rag doll. Hakim gave Zara a sidelong glance and she shrugged. "I said have a *little* faith."

He chuckled and brought up the map he had been holding. It was wrinkled and well-used. The Continent of Ribera was shared amongst the six mortal kingdoms, save for the single ethereal realm that resided on its own slice of land to the North, divided from the rest of the territories by the Jade Sea. Zara's chest tightened as she saw Damalis and Valenzia resting in the northern borders of the Continent, the guardian realms on the coast opposite Celestrea. Palm trees dotted the water's edge, stretching into the unknown mountain ranges. Many of the landmarks were unnamed due to the sister kingdoms' demise. They had truly been forgotten by the rest of the world.

To her knowledge the northern regions of the Continent were uninhabitable, due to the aftermath of the War of the Skies. When Zara first arrived in Ikarria all those years ago, she didn't dare even look back at her home. But seeing the map now, a small part of her desired to see what remained of her homeland.

Hakim pointed at the smeared ink that outlined Soleira's harbor. "Back to more important matters, it has been nearly a week and we have found nothing. Maybe Cadoc lied."

The Ikarrian guild had been tracking nearly every warehouse along the sea border. With the additional marks the High King had been assigning them, they were making little progress in finding the shadow dealers.

Zara sighed, brushing her hair over her shoulders. "The bastard wasn't lying. He told the truth because he believed it would help his chances in surviving the night."

Eshe leaned on one hip, her eyes on the tousling wolves in front of them. "Maybe our little warrior's winged friend could offer more insight on the matter."

Zara rolled her eyes before she could catch herself. "He tried to kill me. I highly doubt he would make an appearance again after that. Besides, we haven't searched all the warehouses yet."

Hakim nodded, still staring at the map. "You are right. It is a wonder you managed to run into someone from the Sombra Quarter. By now, we can assume they know the guilds are after them, thanks to Zara's new friend."

Zara frowned. "I'm beginning to wonder if you both misheard how my encounter with the archangel went. My *friend* tried to kill me."

The mercenaries shared an amused look which only caused Zara to sigh and rub at her temple.

Within the first month of the hunting season, there had been reports of the Horizons tearing down shops and businesses that were suspected to be in alliance with the Sombra Quarter. Chaos had erupted in the streets. Some citizens had tried to protest, but were quickly silenced by the official Elios guards. A bleak reminder to stay out of the mercenaries' way.

"Speaking of the guilds, where is Kairos?" She asked.

"Kairos hasn't been seen since our first night here." Eshe responded. She had forgone the head wrap today, her hair tied into a knot, and only wore silver hoops earrings. "I can only assume they have been tending to their own hunt."

Zara was sure the Kairos mercenaries were adamant on receiving Raziel's gift. The other guilds had been hungry to draw blood as well. Not that she could blame any of them. The mere possibility of changing their futures drove them. It was all they had.

Eshe bent to catch her attention. "Will you be meeting with Daria? She's sent requests."

Her stomach dropped. Erebus had informed her that Ikarria had been invited to the Summit. The fact alone had been enough to send Zara reeling with worry. She knew she needed to see her family, but there was a stubborn—no, a *shameful* part of her that stopped her. She couldn't face them. They had never seen her . . . like this.

Zara's voice fell low. "I don't know if I am ready."

The guild understood her apprehension and had never judged her for it. Eshe rested a hand on her shoulder and squeezed. "As you wish, little warrior."

Clouds of dirt plumed from the ground, obscuring the wolves. Axar emerged, his big form atop Verena, paws pinned to her chest, fangs within inches of her neck. By the Suns, he had won.

The wolves shifted in a burst of light and Axar helped Verena to her feet. She smiled as he bowed his head to her before jogging back to the guild, while other mercenaries started more sparring matches in the training ground.

"Doubt me again," Axar said, flicking a finger against Zara's arm, "and we will see who's laughing when we return to the hunting field."

She lightly shoved him back. "A bet, then. Next time we are on the kill, we'll see who takes the most marks down."

A wolfish grin. "So be it."

Hakim groaned. "Fates Above."

Zara's lips lifted into a smile. The motion of it was stiff and foreign. It was the beginning of genuine joy. Whatever seed of light she felt quickly flickered out in one swoop when she caught sight of white wings. Erebus lingered at the training ground's entrance, his blue eyes pinned on her.

She had to skirt around Hakim, who always tended to gravitate to her—one arm outstretched as if to push her behind him. To hide her from the High Throne. There was a roaring in her ears as she approached the Hand of the King. A bitterness coiled over her tongue.

The look in Erebus's eyes told her all she needed to know. He wasn't seeking Zara Santos today. He was seeking the Rogue.

And that understanding sent a flare of frustration through her. It spiraled down her veins, setting aflame a desire to distract the pain that haunted her. She eyed the archangel and noticed the tunic he wore, the patch of carved skin underneath. *Easier to rip off.*

Zara walked past Erebus before he could speak. The look she gave him was enough of a message for the Hand of the High King. He followed her into the mercenary temple's strategy room.

Erebus closed the door just as she twirled to face him. "I came with another assign—"

Zara crashed her mouth against his, flinging her arms around his neck. The archangel groaned, his hands at her back. It seemed he was also on edge. His hands dove for her waistband, and he began to unlace her fighting leathers.

"Tell me after," she breathed.

Erebus answered in a growl, pushing her farther into the strategy room. The archangel swept off the trinkets and instruments from a table before he hauled her onto the wooden surface.

They were gasping for air, quivering with need. His strong hands ripped her fighting leathers open, allowing Zara's body to be bathed by the pouring sunlight through the glass ceiling.

Erebus slid a hand down her abdomen as he pressed his mouth against her aching core. His long silver-white hair brushed along her skin, white wings extending. The sound of his leather trousers being undone had Zara shaking with anticipation.

This was what she needed, her mind no longer agonizing over her impending tasks as the Rogue.

And as the Hand of the High King sheathed himself in her, Zara knew that for the time being, she was free.

Rain had begun to fall. Dim torchlight managed to survive underneath tarps and against doorways. Citizens filtered through the muddied roads, disappearing between the alleys and inside various buildings. The crowd was thin. There were no night markets tonight. A blessing, Zara thought. Especially for this evening's hunt.

Her blood pulsed with the song of unsheathed blades. As if she were crafted for bloodshed. Beads of water trickled down the sleek obsidian of her weapons.

She stood at the edge of a rooftop. Her assignment had taken her so deep in the outskirts, the border of Soleira was within eyesight. The hills and stretches of forest leading to the Estrella Territories were mounds of ash from this distance.

The Rogue's marks were runaways, an elven male and a human female. From what her missive advised, they were traitors to the High Throne. They had stolen something. What that something was, it was never explained, but Zara didn't have the luxury to question it.

They were last seen escaping the inner district, and she suspected whatever they stole had come from a wealthy contributor of the throne. She had been scouring every run-down street, monitoring every tavern and pleasure house possible. From her own tracking, she discovered they had hidden in various shops and homes. Their routes of escape timed well in terms of the city guard rotations. They were receiving help, that much was clear. Her marks were clever.

Zara anticipated their path would lead to the Estrella Territories. She knew this because she would do the same. Run to the farthest place from the High King's grasp.

As if summoned by the trail of her own thoughts, two cloaked figures emerged on the sodden road.

Fear with a tang of determination trickled through the rain, and the subtle glint of weapons peeked below their garb. Zara leaned forward into a crouch.

"There you are," she crooned.

Zara scaled the buildings, sending thin ropes of rain to whip the air. She leapt from rooftop to rooftop, skidding along the slick ledges. Her unseen ether sent her speeding past the marks below her.

A female voice hissed from below. "We are being followed."

"Keep moving. Do not stop."

Her lips twitched at that. They could sense her. Zara willed her power, tendrils of dawn whispering over her body. She was alone, no one to witness her ether here. Cracks of energy sparked around her and Zara became a flare of red light, moving so quickly it was as if she had teleported. Her marks were too busy scanning the buildings to notice she had materialized before them, blocking them from their path to freedom.

From beneath her hood, she surveyed them. Faces beaten and clothes that used to be fine were stained and dirty. Who were they?

Something felt wrong but she shoved the sensation away. The fyrebrand tingled her skin, telling her to *kill, kill, kill.*

The elven male stepped around the woman. He ran his fingers through the air and ether in the form of ice danced between his fingers until he created a makeshift sword. He swept his legs into a fighting stance.

"Mercenary, I beg you." His voice was like gravel. As if his throat had been torn. Like he had been screaming. "Let us go."

His brown skin was weathered with age, but it was difficult to ignore the old scars that covered his body. Zara's heart tried to speak to her, but the fyrebrand gnawed on her soul. It dug its talons deeper into her essence. Painfully.

Close that heart of yours, the voice hissed. *You have your own to protect.*

Zara's face remained cold. She—the Rogue stepped through the curtain of rain, mists of night flanking her. Her gaze was fixated on the male. A wolf who had found its prey.

Something indecipherable flashed in the male's eyes before he struck. Pain ricocheted through her arm as the tip of his ice sword nicked her arm. *Fucking Suns,* it stung. Zara parried his attacks and circled him.

The elf raised a hand as he kept his blade up. "Please. We are not traitors to the Continent, we are trying to save it."

Zara remained silent, her twin swords angled toward him. She had little interest in what her marks needed to say.

The human girl hissed from where she stood. A meager knife in her trembling hand. "Why are you trying to talk to her? She is the High King's pet, she won't listen to you."

Fury burned through Zara's blood. She glared daggers at the young woman, whose face paled.

The elf tried again. "I do not know what you were informed of, mercenary, but we did not steal anything. We discovered a dark truth and were imprisoned for it. Nothing is as it seems—the War of the Skies was only the beginning."

Zara's curiosity perked up but her fyrebrand's presence pushed against her conscience.

Hunt.

She lunged at her mark, their clashing weapons sparking with ice and ember. Zara was closer now and could see the gashes that riddled the elf's body. Hardly healed, she noted. Not to mention that he knew his way around the blade. In a past life, this male had been a fighter. Whoever stood before her now was a ghost of that.

A voice that was *not* the fyrebrand curdled her thoughts. A voice that dared to question whether this male truly deserved to be killed.

No. The fyrebrand returned with a vengeance. *You are not to fail.*

Her grip tightened on her blades' handles. She saw the faces of her guild—Hakim, Eshe, and Axar. Her sister and pater appeared. The Ikarrian realm rising from the depths of her mind, too. Everything that was at stake if she didn't succeed. This was why she hunted. She repeated that truth, no matter how much it tainted the air she breathed.

Zara steeled herself, exhaling a steady breath. Whatever power had managed to restrain her broke, and she unleashed herself upon the elf. Her khopesh eventually snapped the ice off his blades. She bashed a pommel into his face and he crumpled to the ground, groaning.

The woman cried out. She was younger than Zara, but not too far from her age. Her nostrils flared as she held out the knife. The grip was weak, the angle off.

Zara stalked toward her, sheathing her twin blades. Something tried to tap the back of her mind, but the fyrebrand's grip—the *High King's* grip—on her was ironclad.

You are not free to decide for yourself. You are solely an executioner.

The human tried to swipe the knife at her. Zara sidestepped, the tip of the steel hissing at her ear. She batted the back of her hand against the human's wrist and the weapon fell into a pool of mud with a splash.

Zara swerved around the human so that they both faced the elf and placed her hands around that delicate head and neck.

The elf was still on his stomach struggling to get himself to his feet. But he stopped moving when he saw how Zara held his companion. His eyes turned wide. "*Don't.*"

"Help me." The woman was breathing heavily. "I don't want to die."

He stumbled forward, clawing his way toward them. "Please!"

His cries reached for her, threatening to pierce through those thorns that guarded the most vulnerable parts of her being. Zara's heart screamed along with him as she snapped the human's neck. The body slipped from her hands, landing in that same pool of mud. The elf let out a sob and bowed his head to the ground. His hand slowly reached for a weapon tucked underneath his tunic.

Zara unhitched a longer dagger from her thigh strap as he charged for her again. The movement was sluggish. There was no passion or desperation for vengeance. It was utter defeat.

She grabbed hold of the male, her dagger thrust deep in his gut. The elf lifted his head and met her eyes for the first time. And his own tortured expression slowly fell.

"You," he said. The skin between her brows pinched at the disbelief in his voice. His voice became more ragged as his blood spilled onto her hand. "I know you. Somehow, in some way. Do you not feel the call of the ether within the winds, the sky, and the soil you walk upon—the urge to protect the Gates?"

The beating of her heart must've stopped. She felt suspended in time. The water cascading from the sky seemed to pause as moonlight lit the features on the male's face.

His green eyes shined. "We recognize our own."

Valenzia. He was Valenzian. She had never met anyone from her home realm. It had been so long that she almost believed there were none left. Zara couldn't breathe, she couldn't—

She tore her gaze away. Like a fucking coward, she looked away. Zara stared at the darkness ahead of her, holding the dying male, and listened as his broken breaths slowed. Until the beating of his heart stopped.

It was seconds, minutes, or even hours before she gently placed him on the ground. The sound of squelching flesh wrenched her ears as she pulled her dagger out. Zara cleaned her weapon and pressed its tip against the male's chin.

Lifeless green eyes met her. She quickly pulled away and went to her feet.

Well done, the fyrebrand sighed.

Rain pounded her head and plastered strands of hair to her face. The roaring of her heart grew loud as her tattoo stung her skin, burning another kill off her ledger.

She should've felt her stomach twist with disgust or the color leach from her face. But the heartache she had experienced while her marks were alive suddenly vanished, leaving a void inside her. A nothingness that almost terrified her.

The familiar sense of being watched prompted her to look up. Something stood behind the sheets of rain.

Gleaming fangs and piercing eyes.

It was a wolf, black as the shadows and night. It was larger than the common animal but nowhere near as big as a shifter. Zara didn't move. Couldn't so much as raise her voice. Her ether began to rush through her bloodstream. Energy seeped into her, beyond her. Caressing and beckoning.

The black wolf took one step toward her. Puffs of air billowed from its nostrils. Zara found herself leaning forward, ready to walk to the large creature.

She blinked and the animal disappeared. For whatever the reason she could not understand, her heart sank.

Alone. She was alone once more.

Her cloak drifted behind her, the veil of a mourner. Emptiness expanded inside her once more, and every step felt heavy. Something wet fell along her cheeks, but Zara was sure it was only the rain.

NINETEEN

Silver flames flickered along the pillars in the throne room. Ethereal light stretched out from the tips of Raziel's crown. The golden veins on the High Throne seemed to glow, as well. Zara hated the sight. She lifted her chin, keeping the hardened mask of indifference. Her boots echoed on the dark marble, a trail of red following her, her grip bone white around the burlap sack, a dark red splotch at its base. Dripping and dripping and dripping . . .

The Council was gathered in the throne room, their faces partly obscured by the dim light and the ether mist that coated the air. Velvet cloaks were draped over their shoulders. Expensive gowns and tunics upon their person. Their eyes rippled with glowing silver, tracking her every move.

Zara smothered her confused look before they could notice. She had rarely crossed paths with the members in the past, only in passing. The hunting season caused her to be away from the castle a lot and the deities hardly ever ventured outside the walls. Did the deities not sleep? It was still late into the night. The rain had been relentless, nearly flooding several of the poorly maintained streets of the city.

High King Raziel was reclined in his seat of power. Red hair spilled over one shoulder. The way he glanced at the Council and then her made her believe he wanted a spectacle. To show off his influence and power. So fucking be it.

"Rogue," Raziel greeted her.

Give your master what he wants, the fyrebrand whispered.

A savage grin stretched over her lips. Zara pulled her hood back and tossed the bloodied sack to the base of the dais. "My king."

The deities didn't look at the bag that contained the marks' heads. They didn't stare at the red that stained her hands. Their eyes were only on her. Zara couldn't bring herself to meet their gazes, something about them unnerved her.

Raziel's gaze sharpened. She could've sworn he grinned at seeing her this uncomfortable. The king stood and moved closer, his glorious golden brown wings arched behind him as he stepped down from the throne.

"Look at her," he purred. "My Rogue. You fulfilled your latest assignment within one night. Our realm is safe once again, thanks to your efforts."

Anger rose its fiery head inside her. She wasn't sure what true danger the human girl and elven male would have wrought on this godsforsaken kingdom, if any.

Raziel curled his fingers around her shoulder. She fought every urge to pull back. "How goes the hunt for the leader of the Sombra Quarter?"

Zara raised her chin. "The shadow market hides well, but I believe we are making progress."

His eyes seemed to shine at that. "Erebus will provide you and your guild with more marks to eliminate. It may bring some assistance in identifying the Sombra. While the guild of Ikarria is commanded to slay as many shadow dealers as possible, I expect the Rogue to conduct the final blow against their leader."

She felt the finality of his words—the command—within the fyrebrand. The lick of fire that singed the skin of her wrist. Zara focused on her breathing to distract herself from the burn.

She bowed her head. "As you will, High King."

"Who do you serve?"

The question was sudden. The silence that invaded the throne room was suffocating. She felt the curious gazes of the deities.

"You, High King," she whispered. "I serve you."

Raziel rumbled in approval. "Remember your place and how much I value you, my warrior."

Yes.

Raziel gestured to the Council. "Well, you wanted to see her. This is Zara Santos."

Wisps of pale smoke curled from the ground. Zara only blinked before a deity appeared where the ribbons of white gathered. Her dark hair was smoothed back, magnifying the sharpness of her cheekbones. The deity looked human, near her age, with deep blue eyes. The difference being that the anomaly before Zara would have the power to rip the sky apart.

The deity eyed her, nostrils flaring. Was she . . . sniffing her?

"Word of the Rogue has grown much over the years, we thought it was time to take a closer look at the mysterious woman you have called to be your *personal* assassin, Raziel. Though we continue to overlook the fact that she is the daughter of the Ikarrian king."

Zara stiffened. She fought to keep her expression neutral, having been accused of excessive eye rolling and looks of disgust by her guild.

Raziel replied, "I am sure you can see that I have a keen eye for strength."

Despite the flicker of anger, the nerves in Zara's bones rattled as the deity prowled closer till the mercenary could make out the clouds of silver light in her irises.

The deity cocked her head. Sniffed again. Her lips began to curl. "Indeed."

Raziel cleared his throat. "If you are satisfied, Nadira, I ask that you step back from my mercenary."

The deity named Nadira retreated, still facing Zara. A twisted smile appeared on the female's delicate mouth as she addressed her. "I look forward to seeing how your strength prevails this hunting season. We will be watching."

Zara gave her a bemused look. Nadira only chuckled, the sound that of darkness.

When Zara left the throne room, Erebus waited at the doors, searching her as if looking for wounds.

"Are you well?" He asked.

The archangel tried to reach for her, but she evaded his touch. She couldn't formulate words. There was a fire brimming inside her. Her hands tightened into fists. The skin on her knuckles pinched with pain from the bruises and cuts of her recent kills. It wasn't enough.

Zara swallowed. "Yes. I will see you soon."

Erebus called out for her, but she couldn't look back. Zara walked until the rain found her. Red misted the corners of her vision. A pain inside her howled.

She needed . . . she needed . . .

A wicked smile graced Zara's lips as she threw herself into the throes of sweat and blood. Welcomed every lash of pain. The crowd thundered, waking each sense of her being. Her lips were cut, the corners bruised. Her body ached in the way she craved.

Zara limped out of the fighting ring. An involuntary groan escaped her when she reached the bar. A human tended to the drinks and brought her a short glass of clear alcohol. Her battered fingers curled around it, hardly pausing before she tossed the drink to the back of her throat, hissing at the burn.

She couldn't bring herself to return to the mercenary temple quite yet. When she had left the castle, she had found herself entering the Siren's Song. The pain that ricocheted through her now was enough to distract the torment within. What a way to celebrate the cheap winnings of tonight's fight.

The atmosphere seemed to crackle as a presence sat next to her. Her ether purred—she recognized the other's power. Her hand flew to the dagger at her thigh when a dark, velvet voice stopped her.

"Is that you, little wolf?"

Zara slowly turned her head to the male with black wings and stormy gray eyes. The same one from the night she killed Cadoc. A smirk danced on his lips. Her gaze snagged on the pale scar that ran over the left corner of his mouth. Her grip tightened around the dagger's handle.

The archangel barely moved. "Careful. The Elios soldiers aren't the only ones you should be worried about here."

Zara scanned the tavern. Most of the patrons looked rugged and stood out from those who looked too clean and refined, most likely naive to the bloody realities of the world they lived in. She caught the male's insinuation but couldn't discern who was part of the Sombra Quarter. There were no insignias or matching armored uniforms.

If the archangel was here to kill her, then she would be outmatched. Anticipation tingled through her sore muscles. The adrenaline from the fighting ring still lingered, just as the alcohol that still quietly burned within her center. She would have to bide her time before she could finish the brawl they had started.

Her voice remained steady. "I do not worry about guards nor soldiers of any kind."

That smirk curled higher, a hint of white teeth peeking through. "No, I suppose you do not."

Zara left the dagger at her thigh. "Tell me what you want, archangel. I have a busy night ahead of me."

Those gray eyes flicked to her bruised mouth. The smirk faded. "I've been looking for you, actually."

She braced herself. "I am sure it is not to sit there and gawk at me."

"We must speak in private," he said.

The shift in conversation was so sudden Zara almost laughed. "I'd rather not."

There was no amusement in the archangel's gaze now.

"I wouldn't do this unless I felt it was absolutely necessary." He leaned forward, large shoulders bunching. "I can assure you that it will benefit the both of us."

Her eyes dragged over him. "I can think of several alternative ways in how you can prove useful to me, archangel."

That silver gaze searched hers. A question lingered in his eyes.

Zara arched a brow, gesturing to the empty glass she twirled with the tip of her finger. The archangel finally caught on what she was insinuating, his smirk returning. He signaled to the barmaid to refill her alcohol and slid a silver mark across the bar.

The mercenary did not remove her gaze from the male as she took another swig of her drink, emptying it. The archangel rested an arm along the wooden surface. "Now, did I pay my dues for your audience?"

She was faintly amused by that. Her gaze flicked to the pommel of her dagger for a breath. "For now."

His expression turned serious. "Horizon, you will want to hear what I have to say but, I cannot speak about it here. We will have our privacy, and you will still have your weapons. Not like that would matter. I am more than confident you can skewer me with a fucking fork."

Zara found herself actually considering this. He seemed genuine, and she would be damned if she wasn't curious about what he had to say. It was reckless of him to present himself to her like this, and that only spurred her interest even more.

Unless it was a trap. Still, if this was an opportunity for her to discover who the head of the Sombra Quarter was, then she would take it. And as he said, if the situation called for it, she would find creative ways to end the archangel.

His voice dropped low. "I will not harm you. Regardless of what you may think, I am a male of my word."

Zara folded her arms across the bar. The male was her greatest lead into the Sombra Quarter. Several scenarios played in her mind, as she contemplated the best path to pursue.

The mercenary couldn't help but notice the inked designs of jasmine flowers on his neck were entwined with leaves and stars.

Her eyes narrowed. "If I sense any trickery, I will—"

"Stab me? Gouge my eyes out?" Light shined in his eyes. "I understand, *Zara*."

The sound of her name surprised her. She had nearly forgotten that he caught it the first time their paths crossed. No thanks to Axar.

With that, the archangel pushed himself from his seat and

gestured to her with a tattooed hand. "The night is hardly young. If your plans were to continue sulking here for hours, a breath of fresh air may help."

Zara rolled her eyes. The male was relentless. She slammed her palms on the bar, the wood cracking underneath the pad of her fingers. She brushed her long hair over her shoulders and waited for him to lead on. There was not a chance under the Three blazing Suns that she would let him walk behind her.

His lips twitched into a half-smile. "Ronan."

Zara blinked in surprise. "Excuse me?"

The archangel placed a hand over his chest. The tattoos flexed over the veins on his large fingers. "Since I know your first name, I thought it was only fair. My name is Ronan Menodora."

There was no second thought as she responded. She pressed a finger to her own chest, covered in sweaty leathers. "Zara Santos."

TWENTY

Gods, what was she doing?

Zara was walking—by her own freewill—alongside someone from the Sombra Quarter. She should've stayed behind and kept drinking.

Ronan Menodora led her to the upper floor of the Siren's Song. Patrons of the tavern gave a subtle dip of their heads when they saw him. She thought it odd that they would acknowledge a random archangel, unless he was a frequent visitor. But when they noticed her, blood seemed to drain from their faces, and they rushed to get out of her way. It only amused her.

She studied the winged male before her. The dark fighting leathers strapped to his broad body made him blend in with the darkness. Light from the torches lined his frame in molten red. They approached arched double entry doors, greeted by images of horned sea monsters. A pair of males idled near the entrance. One of them was another archangel with deep gray wings. Zara immediately recognized him as the male who had sat beside Ronan during her first visit to the Siren's Song.

The archangel's attention dragged to hers. He was stunning, with golden brown skin and dark eyes. His gaze was assessing, roving over her face and the weaponry on her body. Then he went back to his conversation with the other individual. Zara couldn't help but feel wary.

Ronan didn't acknowledge the males and pushed the double doors open, stepping aside to allow her in. To her surprise, a small set of stairs led up to a secluded floor of the tavern.

Arched windows had been carved out along the red stone walls. Round tables and chairs were set about the room, as well as a lounge area with bookshelves. A desk stood to the right, positioned in the center of the long wall. The entire space was an office, she realized. An expensive looking one at that.

"Who are you, really?" Zara asked.

Ronan brushed past her. She was careful to dodge his wings when they almost touched her arm. He gave her a sidelong glance, a dark lock curling over his brow. "Someone with loved ones to protect."

Zara didn't take her eyes off every nook and cranny of this place. Where any routes of escape were located. What she could use as a weapon if her own were apprehended. The need to survive, to always stand on the blazing edge of defense, was second nature to her.

The archangel turned to face her, leaning against the desk while tucking his hands into his pockets. He seemed quite at ease. Those steel gray eyes settled on her and she arched her brow.

"What do you know about the Sombra Quarter?"

Zara glanced outside to the sea of twinkling lights below them. Felt the distant hum of music in her bones. "It is an illegal network of trade," she said simply.

"Horizon," Ronan chided with a dry chuckle, "I would've thought you had done more research on your marks. We are so much more than that. Why do you think the High King is so gods-bent on getting rid of us?"

She cocked her head. "There is not much I need to know. I am given a mark, and I hunt."

His stare intensified. "Yes, you do hunt. That is exactly why I must speak with you. Something is happening to the Estrella Territories. People are going missing, entire towns abandoned."

"It is not unheard of for people to migrate to other lands."

Ronan shook his head. "What I say to you does not leave this room. I understand you will need to bring it to your guild's attention, but no one else outside of your ranks must hear of it."

Zara barked a laugh. "Trust that I would never repeat *any* of this to the other guilds. They would go rabid if they knew where I was. For one, I am standing here with you, a member of the Sombra Quarter, and haven't killed you yet."

The archangel rolled—*rolled*—his eyes at her. "I have seen a type of . . . *creature* in the Estrella Territories. It was a human woman. She was dead but . . . alive. Her eyes glowed with a strong form of ether. I suspect the human woman was possessed by a type of power that I don't fully understand. But I *felt* it. It was ancient and powerful."

Zara's expression slowly sobered as she listened. She would have to give credit to the archangel if it was something he'd made up. She had to admit that it kindled a small flame of interest in her. Though the male could still be tricking her.

Fucking Suns, she needed a drink.

"You realize that I cannot simply believe you. I would have to see the woman for myself," she deadpanned.

Shadows seemed to flicker around him. "I had to kill her. Trust me when I say death was a mercy." He folded his arms, a cord of muscle along his neck flexing. "I understand that you will need proof, but that is something I cannot provide yet."

Zara huffed in disbelief. She should've wrung information out of the male like with her previous mark, but a larger part of her knew that would not have been possible. The archangel was not her average opponent. "You do not bring evidence but expect me to take you at your word."

He raised a hand as if in surrender. "I have not come across any other affected mortals like the woman before."

"Perhaps whatever form of ether you saw was a one-time occurrence."

A dark edge took his voice. "Unlikely. I found other abandoned towns with footprints leaving their borders and no sign of any citizens."

Understanding dawned on her. "You worry that other creatures like her are roaming the Territories."

The lines around his scarred mouth deepened. "Exactly."

The mercenary was silent for a moment. "How does that involve me?"

Ronan met her gaze, held it. His voice was firm. "I want to hire you and the Ikarrian guild to help me track these missing people, help me find out what is happening in the Territories."

Zara blinked before she tipped her head back and laughed. That same cold, bloodless sound. "You are in no position to hire me, much less an entire guild. We are in the midst of the hunting season. Not to mention," she added, unsheathing a single blade, "we are supposed to be hunting the Sombra Quarter. The very entity *you* are part of."

The archangel didn't move. Didn't even flinch. It mattered not to her though. Her suspicions had grown. She could sense the two males still lingering outside the doors to the office. Guards, perhaps. Ordered to protect the mysterious, *important* male before her.

Zara slowly raised her blade. "What can you offer me? What is worth betraying the High Throne?"

The archangel's expression hardened. There was a rumble in the air. "Your freedom."

The torchlights outside seemed to dim. The thrumming music quieted. The world beyond her seemed to fade into darkness as everything in her stilled.

Ronan jabbed a finger toward her left wrist. "I can help have that fyrebrand removed."

"Impossible," she breathed.

"Nothing is impossible."

She couldn't entertain the thought, nor would she acknowledge the small light of hope. The High King had made his intentions with her clear since the day she was promised to the guild. Since she became his killer within the shadows. A reaper of the realm. Raziel's current award still stood. If she completed her task, she and her guild would be able to *reduce* their servitude. And she would not risk losing their chance at freedom.

Zara didn't realize she had voiced it out loud as Ronan began to laugh. His black wings flared slightly as he tipped his head back.

"Little wolf, I can assure you the High King is not that *generous*. Everything he does has a purpose." His expression softened a fraction. "Be honest with yourself. Do you think he would allow you or any other powerful mercenary one step closer to walking away from him?"

Zara's lips parted, ready to shout her affirmation. Yet, she hesitated. Deep within the bloodstained walls of her soul, tucked within the thorns that guarded her heart, a flicker of doubt held her tongue.

Raziel had made her into the Rogue. Would he truly release her from this life?

Ronan's jaw clenched. "Raziel has the ability to work ether into objects and liquids. He put *that* brand on your wrist, and you really believe he would let such a rare power go to waste?"

The grief and panic fused into anger. The curved sword in her hand shook. "What you are asking of me—of the guild—is too dangerous."

"It is a risk for me as well. I wouldn't be asking if I wasn't desperate. These disappearances risk my business, and my business is how I save those I care about."

"Why me? Why the guild of Ikarria?"

A breeze wafted in from the windows behind the archangel. It brushed through his dark hair, the dark locks at the sides of his face rippling. Ronan's gaze remained steadfast on hers, as if he was seeing into her—into the depths of her thorny heart.

His voice was deep and strong. Midnight and steel. "I saw you after you killed Cadoc. The fyrebrand glowed, causing you pain. It reminded me of just how deep the chains run through this realm. Ikarria is still independent from the Aligned Realms, though it is becoming more involved with the Continent. Compared to the other guilds, yours would have more opportunity in doing work outside of the hunting season without garnering too much attention."

Ronan's words rushed back to her. *These disappearances risk my business, and my business is how I save those I care about.*

Her grip tightened, voice laced with steel. "You said *your* business."

He was an unmoving shadow, the lights outside casting a line of deep yellow around his wings. "I did."

The beating of her heart quickened as the skin on her neck dampened. "I can assume you were still speaking about the Sombra Quarter."

A pause. "Yes."

"Who are you really, Ronan Menodora?"

He stared, his arms still folded across his solid chest. "Is that a no to my offer? Do you wish to continue being a puppet to a king who only seeks to control you, for a slim possibility of freedom?"

Zara felt every muscle begin to tighten with fury until she was quaking with it. There had been war in her heart, for as long as she could remember.

Her voice went lethally quiet. "What do you know of the Horizons, archangel? Little to nothing? Then let me educate you. The mercenaries had purpose once, before the War, during the Age of the Primordials. But times have changed. Needs have changed. You do not get to judge the means for survival we have had to take."

Ronan slowly lowered his arms. His fingers flexed and she understood the movement. He was readying himself. As was she.

His voice did not hold any form of hostility. It was low and melodic, unlike any she had heard so far. "Ask me again who I am."

Zara released a hitched breath as the air between them thinned. A silence that seemed on the verge of exploding. It was the break of lightning. The howl of raging winds. Ronan's black wings widened the longer they stared at each other.

The conclusions she had been drawing since she had agreed to speak with him crashed down on her. She'd seen it in the awe-stricken gazes of the people in the Siren's Song. The lingering sense of respect that followed the archangel. The way Ronan walked with power and purpose. The concerned look from the archangel outside the office. And the office itself.

These disappearances risk my business, and my business is how I save those I care about.

All the pieces clicked together and Zara smiled, a cruel edge to her lips. "Ronan Menodora, *leader* of the Sombra Quarter."

Flickers of power seemed to flash across his gaze. His own smile widened. "I heard you've been sent to kill me. Is that true, Horizon?"

Zara snapped forward in the blink of an eye. Blade raised, ether heightened. And Ronan met her with equal force. He lashed out with his sword; the sound of their colliding steel could've cracked the very walls. Shouts exploded outside the office before the brawny archangel with gray wings smashed the doors open.

Ronan shouted. "Stand back!"

Zara grasped the opportunity and kicked him square in the chest. He stumbled back a few steps. Hunger for blood sparked life inside her. This was her moment. Her only chance. She was not going to lose it.

She sheathed her khopesh and lunged for him, tackling him and sending them both through an open window. The space was narrow. His wings scraped the sides of the arches, batting against the stone. Dust exploded in the air, clogging her nostrils.

The mercenary struggled to hold onto the archangel as they plummeted toward the ground. His wings snapped out in an attempt to hold them midair before they crashed through the tarps of a closed stall. Pottery smashed beneath them, chipped pieces of glass and clay nipping at her hands and cheeks.

Zara rolled to her feet, maniacally looking around for anything to slow the archangel from charging her. She ignored the painful pull of her muscles as she grabbed at the array of ceramics and began throwing them toward him.

Ronan struggled to stand, dirt and blood smearing the side of his face. His eyes widened as he tried to avoid the projectiles aiming for his head. "For the love of—"

He ducked before a clay vase could smash his face. "I didn't realize a Horizon would resort to such antics!"

"Can you not keep up, archangel?" Zara hissed as she threw another pot.

The sound of pottery breaking filled the air, Ronan managing to dodge it. He grunted and reached for a pair of silver platters and threw them her way. Zara stumbled to the side, her hip smashing against the stall's main table. She cursed out loud.

"Is the Horizon losing her edge?" Ronan taunted.

Adrenaline soared through Zara's body. It was addicting. She threw another vase, only for the archangel to snatch it midair and swing it right back at her. The mercenary cursed as she slid across the broken wooden table and headed out of the stall.

In the rush of the moment, Zara dropped her fight's winnings within the rubble. The poor seller of this stall would need to replace what had been damaged.

She stumbled onto the dusty, empty road and unsheathed her khopesh blades once more. Ronan emerged from the ripped tarp, breathing heavily. He spat on the ground and lifted his sword.

They crossed their weapons once more. Pushing and pushing. Zara's boots slid against the ground before she managed to force Ronan a step back. His footing was awkward, it was as if he was trying to remember a proper fighting stance. It was easy for her to gain the upper hand. Odd that a leader of an illegal organization was rusty in a battle.

Their eyes met above the steel.

"It's a shame, really." She bared her teeth. "I was hoping the head of the Sombra Quarter would be a woman."

Ronan laughed darkly. "I'm also disappointed. A lot more would've been done otherwise."

Small rivers of strength powered through her bones from the tips of her toes to the pads of her fingers as Zara felt the ether rise, melding against her being. A mirror of her own self, rippled in dawn light. Something only she could see in her mind's eye.

And the mercenary began to push once more against the archangel. Ronan's eyes slowly widened at the feel of her strength.

His brows pulled forward. "What are you doing?"

The fyrebrand crooned. Claws wrapped over her shoulders.

Death is near. Yes, yes, yes. End him. Kill your mark and be done with it.

Zara gritted her teeth, twisting around to pin Ronan Menodora against a wall. He grunted at the impact, wings splayed out on either side of him. He lifted his chin as their crossed blades neared his neck.

"The offer still stands," he said through clenched teeth. "Even now. I need your help and you need mine."

Zara snarled. "I work with my own. We do not need to risk the king's wrath."

Ronan pressed forward. His footing gained ground and she felt herself stumble back.

The voice echoed. *Weak.*

The archangel managed to slide his sword down the face of her khopesh and twisted the blades free from her grip. All their weapons clattered to the dirt.

Ronan took two long strides toward her. Before she could back away, his hand wrapped around her wrist and lifted it between them. The fyrebrand hidden underneath her bracer.

"Ether has natural laws that it must abide by. If there is a way to bind it, there is a way to break it," he said. "That I know to be true. I can help you free yourself. Consider my proposition."

Don't listen, the fyrebrand slithered behind her. Like a viper, it coiled around her. Round and round. *Lies. They always lie.*

She faltered a step, her chest heaving. A trickle of sweat ran down her spine. She was amid an internal battle. Always in a fight with her head and heart. A part of her—albeit a small one—lifted its child-like innocence at the prospect of being liberated from the fyrebrand. To be able to wield the sword by her own choosing.

You will never be rid of me.

Zara was silent. Too quiet. Ronan must've assumed she was considering his offer as his grip on her slightly loosened. A dagger from her thigh strap found its way into her palm and she punctured Ronan's side.

Her power caused the steel's edge to tear through his leathers and skin.

The archangel jerked back and hissed. "*Fuck.*"

Zara fought to catch her breath. The strength in her limbs was waning. It was the most she had used her power in a given evening, and she wasn't going to be able to hold on to it for long.

"Why?" she asked again.

There was a twinge to her voice. Almost like a plea. Much to her distaste, Ronan caught it. Even then, with his hand covering the bleeding wound, there was a flicker of softness in those gray eyes. "Like I said before. I have those I need to protect. I assume our situations are similar."

Her lips thinned. "The Rogue isn't for sale."

Ronan's scarred mouth twisted into a sneer. "I am not seeking the Rogue—I am seeking *you*. I've heard the rumors of how the Rogue came to be, yet I saw you in the fighting ring. I know a formidable will to survive when I see it."

Zara's eyes snapped to his. The night clung to him as he stood in the empty road, the darkened buildings looming at either side as the stars gleamed above.

"Do not forget what we've discussed. The offer still stands," he said.

It was ridiculous. She couldn't believe what she was hearing. "No, Ronan. I already have my mark."

Something icy bled over her senses, dissipating whatever bravado she had felt before. *Fear.* The punishment of going against the sole purpose of the hunting season was worthy of death. To decline his offer was the only answer she could spew in that moment.

"Go," Ronan said gently. "Leave this place."

Her body quaked. She had summoned too much ether at once. Having to bottle her power every day and keep it underneath her skin was taxing. It took as much from the mind as it did from the body. "You know I am assigned to hunt you down. Why let me go when I am at my most vulnerable?"

She wasn't sure why she was giving him ideas, but that didn't seem to matter. Ire flashed in his steel gaze. "I told you I wouldn't harm you. I *am* a male of my word."

Zara retreated a step, refusing to turn her back on him. She slowly bent to pick up her blades. Every movement caused her muscles to scream. When she reached an intersecting path, she finally turned to flee.

"Zara," Ronan called out.

She twisted around to see the archangel standing in a strip of dust and night. A cloak of stars ready to drape over his shoulders.

"I wish you luck on your hunt." His voice was low, *sinful*. "I do like the chase."

It was then that a truth settled over her—it nicked at her pride. She gritted her teeth. The only reason she had even set eyes on him was because he had searched for her.

The leader of the Sombra Quarter had *wanted* to be found. Only by her.

The temple was silent. The red and purple sky guided Zara to her guild's suite. Her mud-caked boots left prints on the floorboards, but she didn't notice. Zara's mind was flooded with the events that had transpired that evening.

Ronan. The High King and the Council. The two marks she had killed . . .

What lingered the most was Ronan's proposition. While the offer was tempting, the realities of her situation were difficult to ignore. By accepting his proposition, she would be risking the safety of her guild, pater and sister. Even the safety of Ikarria.

Not to mention the fyrebrand's Reckoning. If she didn't kill the archangel, the tattoo would poison her mind, body and soul. It had been slowly killing her spirit all these years, but it would give the final blow.

Still. Shards of her soul had always dared to dream of a life where she wouldn't have to follow the High King's demands. A life without the hunting season, where she could live with her guild in peace. Glimmers of the fantasy she had created had come in the form of an archangel she was supposed to kill. Ronan Menodora was her only other option, beside trying to reduce her sentence in the hunt. But would Raziel truly allow her to go?

Fucking Suns. She had met the head of the Sombra Quarter. Her mark. The one destined to meet her blades. Zara would have to let the guild know—but not tonight. Her body was on the brink of oblivion.

The fyrebrand tarnished her thoughts. *What makes you think you deserve to free yourself from this pain? How many lives have you ended?*

Leave me alone, she seethed.

I think not.

Her eyes lifted to find the guild in the foyer. Her mercenary family had waited for her. Eshe held heaps of blankets in her arms; Axar leaned against the wall beside the fireplace, his face stern and shadowed.

And Hakim—

His massive arms looped around her. Zara couldn't move, her eyes blinking blankly at the floor. He pulled back and bent to meet her gaze. "Remember who you are, Santos."

She only stared at him.

Hakim's brows pinched together. His hands grasped her face. Tenderly. Affectionately. As a pater would to a daughter.

"You are a Horizon. You are the roar of the thunder and the power of the wind. You are *more*."

Those words wrapped around her: they were warmth and love, the comfort she didn't know she had been seeking. No words found her lips. For the first time, she wanted to throw her arms around Hakim and the others and let them share the weight she carried. She had shown affection before, but never like that.

Zara's lips trembled. "I'm so tired."

"I know." She thought she saw Hakim's eyes glisten. "I know you are."

He stepped away so Eshe could unhitch the blades from Zara's body and replace them with a blanket around her shoulders. The archer gently nudged her toward her private room. Zara cast another glance toward Axar, catching a glimpse of his back disappearing from the guild's suite. He might've gone to meet the other mercenaries within the temple. Anywhere was better than here, in this dreary atmosphere, she supposed.

"The bath has already been drawn," Eshe said.

Zara managed to speak. "Thank you."

The vampire rubbed her back, a delicate smile curling her lips. "It is hard, little warrior, but you have been so strong."

For whatever reason, those words twisted her heart. "When will it be over? When will we be free from this?"

She lifted her wrist, the fyrebrand tucked beneath her leathers, and Eshe's expression softened. "From all the years I have known you, you have never quit, nor have you faltered. Don't you start now, Zara. We will find a way. We always do."

She left Zara to her bath and those words to mull over. Zara sighed as she felt the sting of the hot water.

Afterwards, when she had donned her nightgown, a knock sounded at her door. Axar was there, holding a wooden platter of cooked slivers of meat and a small pile of rounded flatbread. In his other hand was a tall flask of water.

"You look like shit," he said. "I thought you'd like some company. And food."

Zara spat out a chuckle and pulled the door wider. Axar gave her that wolfish grin. By then, that hum in her heart had returned once again. That soft song that seemed to find her when she felt a moment of peace.

Her guild. Her family. They had given her that peace.

TWENTY-ONE

I t had been a week since Daria arrived in Soleira. She spent the days in meetings or social gatherings, learning more of the High Throne's policies and plans for its capital and kingdom. Much of its agenda revolved around an effort to rebuild from the long-lasting effects of the War and remove anything to do with the Primordials. A pang echoed in her chest when she heard of such endeavors.

The thought of Genesis, one of the Three Sun Gods, being torn down from the temples unsettled her. Thankfully, the High Throne's plans did not extend to independent Ikarria.

Sunlight blinded her, yanking her attention back to the paved road in front of her. Daria squinted as she crossed the copper gates from the inner district to the outer district. The streets were still busy with citizens, bustling in and out of shops and businesses. Livestock meandered about the alleys as their owners herded them through the old buildings. Few groups of soldiers patrolled the roads, their white armor glaring underneath the blue sky.

Ares was a shadow at Daria's side, silent and ever-watching. His eyes tracked anyone who walked and breathed within her radius. While he remained true to his duty, the vampire seemed sullener than when she'd first met him. Since their mild debate regarding the worth of a ruler's words he had kept to himself, obliging her request to attend any and every formal meeting within the castle.

The princess hadn't inquired where he had disappeared to the night of the garden feast. Not that he was obligated to tell her his whereabouts, but curiosity still prodded at her.

"Can you tell me why you wished to visit the outer district?" Ares asked.

The near-silent rumble of his voice almost caught her off-guard. Daria glanced at him to see his violet eyes piercing through her.

Daria held his gaze. "You sound surprised that I asked such a thing."

"Considering that the past week all we've done is listen to lectures and write notes, yes. I didn't think I would see a princess walking about the lesser parts of the capital."

There was no judgment in his tone, but genuine interest. Ares truly didn't think someone of royalty would be willing to visit those outside of their social circles. Unless it was to punish them, no doubt.

She hoped she would be better than that. Daria faced the busy streets, inhaling the smells of cooked meat and garlic. "Our last visit to the capital's streets stuck with me. I witnessed some gruesome realities when you took me to the inner district. Your words stayed with me every day, because you are right, all my ledgers and spreadsheets do not tell me the truth of what happens in the streets of our realms."

It was true, she hadn't forgotten the sight of the Horizons tearing through the inner district's forum. How the smell of blood still clogged her nostrils when she thought of it.

"So that is why I am here. To learn from observing. I want to see how the citizens of Soleira live, see how their lives can be improved, in both districts."

Daria didn't turn to see his expression, whether he believed her or not. Her priority was her duty to her kingdom.

To find her place in the world and, one day, to be a worthy ruler.

Ares was silent, as if mulling over what she had said. He stepped closer to her side as they pressed farther into the forum. "As much as I appreciate you taking my words to heart, you might find that your experience here will be less pleasant than our last outing."

Interesting that he described their visit to the inner district as *pleasant*, when it had involved murder. "What makes you say that?"

"Look around us."

Daria scanned the crowd. Citizens averted their gazes and quickened their pace. She realized that no one had come up to shower Ares with their praise, to thank him for his service to the realm. Instead, they tried to avoid them entirely.

While the people of the inner district respected the vampire, it seemed those within the outer district *feared* him.

She wanted to slap a palm to her face. Daria should've known they would not be so keen to see the general. It was here, after all, that she had seen Ares lead the vampire roust. Though she couldn't see any residue of that wreckage, she was sure the people hadn't forgotten.

"The realization on your face is almost comical," Ares said. "It is fine, princess. They may not like me within these parts, but I can't control what I am ordered to do."

Her brows bunched together. "Why does King Matías command such things? And why does the High King allow it?"

Ares guided her to cross to the other side of the road. The heat beat down on her face, but she relished in its warmth.

"For control, mostly," her guard responded. "Like with any ruling authority, there are factions who do not agree with their leadership. The vampire rousts are to quiet those voices and ensure obedience."

Daria did not agree with such an act, but there was little she could do to sway the High Throne.

They wandered down another street of shops away from the main forum. Daria caught the smell of sweets and baking bread. It was enough to make her mouth water.

When they'd almost reached the last building on the corner, she noticed a string of citizens—humans—lined up outside its front doors. There were many young people among the crowd; they looked moderately healthy, but it was difficult to ignore the faint sense of unease among them. A chipped green door at the other side of the building swung open as a vampire exited. Then another and another. While humans entered the structure on one side, vampires emerged from the other.

Daria cocked her head. "What is this place?"

Ares didn't answer at first, and the princess thought he hadn't heard her. She whirled toward him but halted mid-step upon seeing his face. He was still as stone, those violet eyes heavy on the green door. She could've sworn a light sheen had spread across his brow.

She grew concerned. "Ares?"

The general swallowed, throat bobbing. "It's a blood bank, princess."

Daria was aware of such establishments, as there were some in Ikarria. Nonconsensual skin-on-skin blood drinking was illegal throughout the Continent. These businesses had started to still provide vampires with their life source while giving donors another method of receiving wages.

But the general looked as if he had seen the spirits of the dead. His face grew pale as a flash of anger passed over his eyes.

She frowned at him. "Are you well, Ares?" He blinked before clearing his throat as his gaze settled on her. Daria took a step toward the vampire. "Have you come to this place before?"

Ares's lips curled into a sneer. "Not this one in particular, but these blood banks in the poorer areas are not cared for in the way they should."

"How so?"

"A lack of funds results in overworked staff. Blood can become contaminated if the donors lack proper treatment. Sometimes the contributions are mishandled, combined, and of low quality. That doesn't stop these businesses from selling to a vampire in need."

Daria observed the green door from where vampires exited the old building. If they lived within the outer district it must have meant they were in a lower social class, just like the humans who were donating. Both struggled in life, and it was only through the blood bank they could find support.

"This makes you angry," she said as she met his gaze again.

He didn't look away from her. Those small flares of fury now burning a bit brighter. "It does."

Daria nodded. "There's more to it, isn't there? The color has leached from your face. Not only do the blood banks frustrate you, but they also make you worried."

Ares ran a hand down his chest, his Adrastean emblem basking in the sunlight. Whatever distress he had shown disappeared, replaced by that familiar coldness. His mouth thinned as he turned away from the building.

The vampire's expression was shadowed, and there was a faint rumble to his voice. "No. These people mean nothing to me."

Lies.

Daria was beginning to see another part of her bodyguard, and it piqued her curiosity. She dropped the subject, not wanting to aggravate him. She wouldn't force him to talk on things he wasn't ready to.

Hours passed, Ares's mood soured as she finished observing other parts of the outer district. The princess of Ikarria mulled over what she had seen as they returned to the castle. A part of her had to admit that she had been hoping to catch the mercenaries at work again, more so to see Zara. But what she had discovered was useful as well.

Daria thought it was time she started practicing her duty as ambassador.

Soleira's coliseum was a beast of glimmering bronze and ivory. Firebirds screeched as they perched on the massive statues of archangels and the pillars surrounding the structure. In honor of the Summit, the official games had started: entertainment for the highly wealthy and influential.

It was late in the afternoon, the sun making its way over the large amphitheater. Daria and Ares had returned from the outer district to attend the games. A spectacle that hosted battles of the sword and ether, as well as athletic, musical, and equestrian competitions.

Ares had escorted her to a wide, covered section of the coliseum stands dedicated to royals and esteemed guests, closest to the grounds. Lounge areas stuffed with pillows and throws were filled with nobles and other court members. Servers paraded down the halls with silver platters of food and drink. The rest of the citizens cheered and roared from the higher tiers of the amphitheater.

They sat within their private viewing area. The arena was so close, along with the smells of saddles and sweat, Daria couldn't move her eyes away from it. It was filled with soldiers on pegasi who either took to the sky or cantered along the makeshift racetrack. The officiator's voice shouted over the cheers, announcing the first event.

"The pegasus riders are new to Elios," Ares said, following Daria's gaze. "They are part of the kingdom's armies."

Her eyes stayed on the winged horses, their sleek coats blinding under the sunlight. "Are the riders vampires?"

Ares barked a deep laugh. The rich sound snatched Daria's attention away from the creatures. Seeing the general smile, the flash of fangs in his grin, especially after how he'd been since the venture with the blood banks, baffled her. "Gods, no. Vampires are too prideful to take on a mount. No, humans tend to bond with the pegasi. Some elves, too, but they are few."

There was the sound of glass breaking and silver clattering to the ground. Spilled food and drink surrounded a group of deities who seemed to be in the heat of an argument. Daria had noticed the ethereal race the moment they had entered the veranda. She had been watching them from a distance, curious to see what they were like in a casual setting. A male with ether-flared eyes was speaking to a female deity. They weren't too far from where Daria and Ares sat, so it was easy to hear their debacle.

"You bring shame on our kind," the male deity hissed. Daria

couldn't see the female's face, but she recognized the long black hair as well as the deity's sharp tone. "Your ideals will hinder our success. Continue down this path, Maira, and you will see the consequences it will bring."

"Lower your voice, Hector. With all the ruckus you've caused, it is you who embarrasses us, not I. What you fail to understand is the path we are currently on will not provide the *success* you are all so keen on obtaining."

Maira Iryndel.

Daria felt herself rise from her seat, but Ares grabbed her arm. "Stay away from them, princess. I know you've been interacting with the deities in a professional setting, but the ancient race is not so accepting of others. They do not care who you are or where you come from."

She wrestled out of his grasp. "So what, we do nothing? He's harassing her."

Her mouth snapped shut when she saw the fury in Ares's eyes as he stared down the male. The tension bracketing his tall body was like a drawn bowstring, ready to launch.

"Stay right here." His voice was near-quiet yet thunderous.

The vampire stormed after them. Daria knew she should've heeded his warning, but when she saw the deity grab Maira's arm she didn't think twice.

Daria hurried forward and reached her just as Ares stepped in between the two deities. The male roared in outrage, spewing a variety of insults at her bodyguard. She couldn't care to hear what they were saying as her attention focused on Maira.

She inspected her, keeping her hands to herself. "Are you well?"

A magenta gown flowed over the deity's soft body, complementing her olive skin tone. Up close, Daria noticed she had long lashes and sun-made freckles scattered across her nose.

Maira blinked in surprise. "Daria Calderón of Ikarria, you helped me."

Daria's brows pinched together, amusement touching her lips. "Well, my bodyguard is currently doing most of the confrontation."

Servers drifted by, seeming oblivious to the ruckus within the hall, while other court members stared. The crowds in the stands erupted in cheers, followed by the sound of a blaring horn.

Daria felt eyes on them and pointed to the private seating area she and Ares had sat in. "Would you care to sit with me?"

Surprisingly, the deity obliged and seemed to glide across the ground before taking a seat. Daria settled next to her. Maira crossed her arms, looking out to the arena.

The deity's jaw clenched. "I apologize that you had to witness that. Unfortunately one of my colleagues suffers from a feeble mind and I must remind him of his place."

Daria cocked her head. Deities were notorious for being seen as united beings. To hear one of them insult one of their own was not what she expected.

"You have nothing to apologize for," Daria said.

The deity returned her gaze, causing Daria to freeze at the sight of her silver-imbued irises this close. "You've been making yourself quite known among the court, princess."

Suddenly, Daria wasn't sure if she should've felt bashful or worried. Flustered for being under the heavy attention of a deity, or more concerned with how those with influence viewed her.

"Ikarria has never had an ambassador before, and I hope I'll make a good impression of my home realm."

Maira reached to pluck a piece of bread from the small, round table in front of them. "Such is the way of politics. I can say with confidence that the halls whisper the Calderón name. You are a wonder and curiosity to the diplomats."

Before Daria could ask more on the topic, a cold voice made of ice interjected. "What is this?"

Daria's jaw slackened as Nadira Iryndel stalked toward them. The deity was just as wickedly stunning as her twin sister. Her hair was glossed back, tied with a leather band. She wore a tight black gown that dipped low between her breasts. A thick necklace of gold wrapped around the deity's throat.

Daria also didn't miss how Maira winced at her sister's tone.

Nadira narrowed her steely gaze on her twin. "You already bring dishonor to us by being one of the weakest, and now you need *elves* fighting your battles."

Maira snapped her gaze to the deity. "Leave me be, Nadira."

Nadira scoffed, fixating those cold eyes on Daria. She observed her for so long that Daria had to fight the urge to shrink back into her seat. Suddenly, Nadira's lips spread into a smile; the sight sent chills up Daria's arm.

"You are a Calderón, aren't you?"

She drew her arms across her abdomen. "Yes."

The deity leaned forward and *sniffed* her. Daria's feet were frozen to the ground, and she briefly wondered where in the gods' names Ares was.

Nadira straightened and inclined her head, her hair slashing through the air with the movement. "There's something about you. Something foreign to me."

Daria's brows jumped. "Is that a good thing?"

Dear Suns, what was she saying?

Nadira smiled once more. "I haven't decided yet, but you're certainly more tolerable than your sister."

The way she mentioned Zara sent Daria's fingers curling into fists. "What is that supposed to mean?"

Maira was watching her sister with a look of disdain. "Nadira, leave."

The deity gave her a cold, lingering stare before strutting off into the crowd. After several moments, Daria slowly exhaled. "Your sister is . . ."

"A bitch."

A chuckle escaped the princess before she could stop it. "I was going to say intense."

Maira smirked. There was a softness to her demeanor, unlike her brawny twin. Remembering Ares's warnings about dealing with deities, Daria still kept her guard up.

Her brows pinched together. "Speaking of sisters, she knew of mine. How?"

The silver hue in Maira's eyes seemed to deepen. "As you're aware, Nadira is on the Council. My sister is a bit more cutthroat and deals with battle-related matters of the realm. She most likely dealt with the Rogue in that capacity. Since you're from Ikarria, I am assuming that is who we are talking about."

Suns Above. Daria perked up in her seat. "I wasn't aware the Council was involved with the guilds."

"They normally don't concern themselves with trivial mortal matters," Maira responded. Her brows pinched together in thought. "This year is different. They've been taking more interest in the mercenaries, though I am not sure why."

Something must have happened for the deities to have gained interest in the Horizons, and from Nadira's reaction it seemed Zara had made quite an impression. "Maira, I can see why your services are needed for the High Throne. Your expertise regarding the Council and Continent is unmatched. It is not fair that other deities treat you so disrespectfully."

Maira looked amused. "I've been helping oversee the policy-making for the realm since the War of the Skies. I've come to have some influence within the court. Though at times they seem to forget that."

Daria surveyed the deity. "That was fourteen years ago. Forgive my ignorance, but you seem to be quite young."

The deity chuckled. "I've been alive quite longer than you. I am still young in terms of a deity's lifespan, mind you, but I'm nearly double your age." When Daria's jaw dropped, she smiled. "I've been groomed for this position all my life back in Celestrea."

The news was shocking enough. If that were true and the deity had been alive for fifty-two years, then the rebelling deities may have been planning to overthrow the mortal realm for some time. The deity currently owned a position that had not existed before the War of the Skies. Daria tucked that information away for later.

Another horn rang from the arena. Ribbons twirled in the air as the spectators stood from their seats. The crowd had thinned within the halls, but she didn't look to see where Ares had gone.

Her eyes caught movement beyond their seating area. Ares's long hair seemed to shine under the natural light as he was stopped by a handful of his soldiers. His eyes lifted to hers. He searched her face, most likely looking for any injury of any kind. The general noticed Maira sitting beside her, a wary look overtaking his stern expression.

Daria quickly leaned forward toward the deity. "Maira, in our first assembly meeting you had mentioned initiatives to help the citizens of Soleira, yes?"

Interest gleamed within the deity's eyes as she leaned in as well. "I did."

Daria glanced at the general and back to Maira. "Before my broody guard arrives, there is something I'd like to ask you."

TWENTY-TWO

Two shadow dealers—human males—were strapped to their chairs, struggling against their restraints. Chains bit into their wrists, red welling underneath. Zara paced in front of them, a dagger steady in her hand.

Eshe lingered in a dark corner behind her, perched upon a barrel. The vampire nomad swung one leg over the other as she propped her arm on one knee.

"How much longer?" Eshe sighed.

The first mark spat on the floor by Zara's boots. Bruises and gashes botched his face, a sneer slicing through his teeth. He had been the subject of her torture for some time, but the male hadn't broken *yet*. She paid him no mind as she drove her knife through the second shadow dealer's thigh. His screams were muffled through the rag shoved between his teeth.

The harbor could be seen beyond the wooden doors. Fishermen tended to their ships, oblivious to the torture that was occurring within their neighborhood. Maybe they could hear the cries but turned a deaf ear.

Fishing nets, hooks and spears hung about the pale blue walls. The Ikarrian guild had finally found one of the warehouses of the Sombra

Quarter. On paper, the establishment worked in standard sea trade. Only that it also transported shadow market goods.

Zara looked at the first mark and smiled. "I still can't believe we managed to find not one but *two* shadow dealers. Now, will you speak or must we continue this dance? I have nowhere else to be."

The human peeled his lips back into a snarl. "The Sombra Quarter does not tolerate the corruption of the High Throne. You are evil as you serve evil."

She made a face as if contemplating his words. Slowly, she pulled the dagger from the second male's thigh. His eyes bulged, the veins on his neck were on the verge of bursting.

"What about you?" Zara cooed. "What do you have to say?"

With the bloodied silver tip, she tugged the rag from his mouth. He heaved for breath, lips trembling. Sweat rolled down his face with his tears.

"You fucking bitch!" He cried out.

Zara tilted her head and tapped the flat surface of the dagger against his cheek. Blood smeared on his sweaty skin. "Careful. If you hurt my feelings, I may get more creative."

Tears and snot mixed with his muffled voice. Zara let the edge of the dagger skim down the skin of his neck.

"What was that?" She whispered.

The shadow dealer shuddered. "We have a trade route, under the guise of Soleira's official path, from the capital to the Estrella Territories."

"Shut up!" The other snapped.

Zara held the mark's gaze. He was in the palm of her hand, ready for her to mutilate. "What cities do you have business with?"

The first human thrashed in his seat. "Stop! Don't you fucking say another word!"

"You will tell me. As well as whether the head of the Sombra Quarter ever visits those locations."

As the mark's eyes widened, he jerked his head back from her reach. He couldn't get far. The chair groaned underneath him. The binds rubbed against each other, searing deeper into his skin.

He breathed heavily, managing to steady his voice. "Return to your *master*, Rogue, you do not have power over me."

Zara closed her eyes as she tried to brush the sting of his comment away. The mark was not wrong but having to hear it constantly was chipping away at her restraint.

The fyrebrand snickered. *Oh, that anger. It has been residing within you for so long, but it never fails to please me when you lean into it. Let it free, Rogue. Hide your agony underneath the gritted teeth of your fury. Swallow the remains of your heart and become a living blade.*

Since the night of Ronan's offer, she'd felt as if she was being pushed farther toward the edges of her fear and anger. It was exhausting having to show control when all she wanted was to lash out at the world.

So Zara obeyed the voice in her head and opened her eyes.

Good.

The familiar emptiness embraced her, snuffing out the light from her eyes. She prowled toward the mark, and he shrank back into his seat.

"Wait," he blubbered.

Zara slashed her knife across his leg once more. His cries fell on deaf ears as she continued to slice into his body. Blood ran down the legs of the chair. Her anger was silent, echoing behind every swing of her hand.

A hand latched onto her wrist. "Santos."

Zara froze at Eshe's voice, the edge of her dagger hovering above the mark's face. The world around her and the male's sobs slowly returned to her ears. She glanced at the vampire. Eshe's eyes bore into her own as if she was reaching into Zara's soul and plucking her heart from deep within the void.

"Let me have a try," the vampire said.

Zara cleared her throat and lowered her dagger. She stepped back as Eshe took her place. Both marks went still. Something dark had pooled in between the legs of the male Zara had been terrorizing.

She pursed her lips, feeling her bravado return. "Eshe, you made him piss himself."

"I'm quite sure that was your doing, little warrior." The vampire reached for Zara's mark, brushed a finger against the wound on his thigh, and ran it over her tongue. "It has been some time since I've fed, and you taste so sweet."

"Now you've done it," Zara mumbled, meeting the shadow dealer's frantic look. "Since you haven't been helping me, you're going to have to deal with the vampire."

Eshe prowled to the first male, temporarily ignoring the other. She crouched in front of him, revealing her fangs.

"You have been so loud today. Fighting for the secrecy of your shadow business. Do you think you are part of some grand rebellion?" She asked.

The male whimpered. "We are. We fight against the High King's injustice toward the lower classes by providing them with what he will not."

Zara grinned from behind the vampire. "Did you know that your beloved Sombra leader tried to recruit our guild's services?"

He shouted another curse. "Lies!"

She shrugged. "The truth can be bitter."

Eshe took out an arrow from her quiver. Her slender fingers brushed the jade green feathers, and she brought the stone tip between them.

"Something I like to do is decorate my arrows," she said, her voice like velvet. It soothed and lured. A viper and a siren. Over the years, Zara had built much of her own swagger simply by observing the archer.

The tip of Eshe's arrow drifted to the base of the male's collarbone. He leaned back as far as the chains would let him. "For instance, this one here is doused in the Tears of Datura, sometimes known as the Fates's Trumpet. A very poisonous plant from my travels. Maybe that is something you have smuggled as well? It is truly rare. And expensive."

The second shadow dealer cursed. "The city of Adira! That is the trade route's rendezvous point. We make transfers there."

Zara smiled. "See, this one may be sitting in his own piss, but he is smart."

Tears relentlessly streamed down his face. "And I do not know if the head of the Sombra goes there. He rarely makes appearances. Most of the other shadow dealers do business at the meeting points, though. They will be there, if not him."

"Shut your mouth, you idiot," the first mark yelled.

Him. Ronan Menodora. It was a start. They could track him from there. Zara had informed the guild of the archangel's proposition, but they had decided they would discuss it after tending to their current assignment.

Eshe dragged the arrow across her mark's chest. Steam rose from the cut, and his skin sizzled. The male bucked. He nearly tipped the chair over so that she had to hold him down. Screams tore from his throat as he gagged on his own saliva.

"Disappointing," she muttered as the shadow dealer died in his seat.

Zara took a step back, knowing all too well what would happen next. Eshe lunged at the other human. Her fangs ripped into his throat as she drank and drank. His cries were cut short with a *snap* and his body slowly slumped, head hanging low.

Eshe straightened and cleaned her mouth with a cloth that she pulled from her belt. "Sometimes, you frighten me with how merciless you become when hunting."

Zara blinked in disbelief. "I didn't tear a man's neck apart."

The archer arched her brow. "I mean you no offense. I only worry. Sometimes, you have this . . . emptiness in your eyes. It's not you."

Zara was silent as she cleaned her dagger. "It makes it easier," she said simply.

Eshe sighed. "Tread carefully on that path, little warrior. We cannot force you to stop drowning your sorrows in your drinks or in your fighting rings. I understand the need to cope, but you are stronger than that."

Zara's eyes strayed back to the mutilated bodies. She had been so transfixed on her assignment. So drunk on bloodlust. So far under that darkness had prevented her from seeing what she was truly doing. It was a form of protection, so she didn't have to be reminded of what she had become.

No, she wasn't strong at all.

Gods. The truth *was* bitter.

The armor and sword would always be an extension of her. Battle would always be her air. Without these things she was . . . no, she didn't know the answer to that.

Zara shut her eyes and tried to focus on the sailors shouting outside, the waters sloshing against the stone walls of the harbor, and the spike-tailed seabirds cawing in the distance.

The back door opened, and a blood-drenched Hakim entered, the gloves on his hands sodden with gore. Behind him, Axar's wolf poked his head in, the fur surrounding his muzzle stained with red.

Hakim looked at the mess she and Eshe had made. "Your marks screamed louder. I couldn't hear mine over yours."

"Most of the credit goes to your accomplice there." Eshe jabbed a thumb at Zara. "You taught her a little too well."

The head of the guild smirked. "A compliment, in my eyes."

In unison, ether glowed from each of their wrists. Axar jerked his head, shifting back into his human body. He clapped a hand around the bracer that covered the fyrebrand. The muscles in his bare arms clenched.

"Fuck the Suns," he growled. "The Sombra Quarter's followers may not be so wrong in rebelling against the High King."

The mercenaries stared at him and he scoffed. "Really, are we not going to discuss what Zara had revealed earlier this week? We finished our task, I think it is time we address the more intriguing news to date. She met the *actual* head of the shadow markets."

"The only reason I was able to meet him is because he was seeking me," Zara pointed out.

"To hire us," Hakim added. He wiped his dirty gloves with a cloth Eshe handed him. "It could very well be a trap, a way to sell us out to the High King if we accepted his proposal. Did he offer anything in return?"

Zara sighed. She had been unable to share all the details with the guild before they were sent on another hunt. "Our freedom. He believes he can find a way to break the fyrebrands."

Axar cursed. "Is that possible?"

Hakim ran a hand over his dreads. His earrings jingled with the movement. "How would he know? There is nothing recorded on how to break such binds."

Eshe picked at her fingernails. "There might not be anything in our current texts. Didn't the High King banish all books to do with ether from the kingdoms?"

Hakim made a sound. "He had many tomes destroyed and kept the rest in his castle. Isn't that interesting?"

Zara's heart skipped a beat. Could it be possible to remove the fyrebrand?

No, it whispered. *It is almost endearing how much you wish otherwise.*

She looked up, eyes darting to the mercenaries. They remained unmoved, as if they did not have their own fyrebrands haunting their waking thoughts.

How special you are.

She took out a dagger and a thin slate of flint, slashing steel against rock. Zara thought of the archangel and his promise to free her. Another deal dipped in red. Not the first male who'd desired to seal her into an arrangement.

Her life was already bound. The High King had already succeeded in that.

Sparks flew. Smoke began to curl.

No. She would not be lured by sweet falsehoods. Ronan Menodora was her target, and she always completed an assignment.

Zara smiled as fire hissed to life. She turned her back from the Sombra Quarter's warehouse as the flames devoured everything in their path.

TWENTY-THREE

Days after she had destroyed a part of Ronan's business, Zara found herself tucked in a corner booth in one of the inner district's taverns. Hakim had wanted the guild to prepare before launching a hunt on the town of Adira. If Ronan or any other shadow dealer were to be present, they needed more information.

Erebus hadn't visited them with another assignment, so Axar and Zara took it upon themselves to meet with several of Elios's Messengers. The spies of the capital were resourceful, but they all seemed at a loss at finding more concrete information regarding the shadow markets. Their skill set turned out to be limited.

Axar hunched over his plate, piercing the slices of meat with his fork. He shoved the food into his mouth and chewed for mere seconds before adding another bite. Zara watched, her nose wrinkling, her hands wrapped around a cup of water.

"We are supposed to be *working*," she hissed.

Axar grunted. "How am I supposed to do that on an empty stomach?"

Zara blew out a breath and returned to the Messenger sitting across from them. The meek-looking young man blushed when her eyes landed on him. He was their last meeting of the day and had been much more useful than the others. He had identified the trading route schedules, learned when the smugglers would leave Elios and join the merchants.

She gestured to the young man. "If there is nothing else, I think we have all we need."

He nodded furiously, skidding the chair across the floorboards. He stacked the parchment he had brought with him and shoved it in his leather bag.

He stopped, hesitating. "One other thing, if I may. Have you heard of the Three Sun Gods?"

Zara stared blankly at him. "What sort of question is that? Of course we have."

The Messenger shook his head. "No, I mean have you *heard* of the Three Sun Gods? In my line of work, I hear many things that are happening in the world, and apparently there have been sightings. Ethereal beings wearing crowns of silver fire have been seen stalking the wild lands."

The description made her pause. It didn't surprise her that the Messenger had caught word of such mysteries before the public. Zara recalled her last night in Ikarria when the acolytes had preached about the return of the primary Primordials. How no one believed them. Messengers were more likely to keep in mind all rumors they heard, no matter how outrageous.

"Wondrous theories," she drawled, leaning against her seat. "Why mention this to us?"

He clasped his hands together. Something she had seen her sister do too many times when she was nervous. "There are such things as demons and wraiths on our Continent, but they are nothing compared to these foreign beings. These occurrences have been so rare and far between that it hasn't spurred much interest from the High Throne. But I thought if anyone else should be made aware, it would be the Horizons."

Zara was tempted to wave off the young man, but seeing the awe-struck gleam in his eyes, she couldn't bring herself to do it. He seemed to be an admirer of the Horizons. Instead, she nodded. "We will keep it in mind. Thank you for your time."

The Messenger bowed to the mercenaries and left. The smell of cooked meat and sage touched her nose. At this point, she was on the verge of taking Axar's plate for herself.

The wolf shifter cleared his throat, thumping a fist against his chest. Zara slid a glass of water to him. "I didn't see you take one breath during that entire meal."

Axar rolled his eyes and drank. "With that boy ogling you, I couldn't intrude."

Zara snorted and began to pick at his leftovers. When she didn't respond, Axar leaned forward. "What do you think of the supposed return of the Three Sun Gods? Do you think it's true?"

"I'm hesitant to believe it. If the three main gods most of the Continent worshiped had returned from the *broken* Gates, then wouldn't there have been a sign of some sort? Wouldn't more people know about it?"

Her mercenary brother seemed to ponder that as she ate. "We will never know if it's true unless the Three Sun Gods reveal themselves. And if they have returned, then it may mean war once more. The Primordials would want to take back the mortal world, restore their order of power and remove the Council."

Zara chewed on her food as she mulled over his words. She was too young to remember the last War. Only flickers of a red sky remained in her memory. But the idea of witnessing a repeat of the War of the Skies, this one brewed from revenge between the rebelling deities and the gods sent shivers down her spine.

The sound of a fork clattering on a plate ringed in her ear. Axar had dropped it, discarding his plate before glancing her way. "I've been meaning to ask you. How long are you going to continue ignoring Daria?"

She . . . wasn't expecting that. It had been nearly two weeks since her sister had arrived in Elios. Zara sighed and leaned back in her seat. "You and Eshe need to stop gossiping."

"Answer the question."

"We need to meet with the others."

He shook his head. "Don't run away from me, Santos. Daria has sent multiple requests to meet with you. Why haven't you visited her?"

Zara clenched her jaw. "I am not—fucking Suns, you are not going to let this go, are you?"

He gave her a dazzling smile. "Why would I let you off the hook? You and I are stuck together, stars made by the Suns."

Her lips twitched into a smile, remembering when Axar had first said those words. They had been in the Ikarrian temple, gazing up at the pink sky with their legs dangling over the terrace's edge, scores of trees resting below them. The stars were faint that evening, growing brighter every inch the sun lowered. She and Axar had just made their oaths, bound their hearts to the ways of the Horizons.

Axar had pointed up. *That is us*, he had said. *We made oaths not only to our guild but to each other, you and I. We are family and we will always share the same sky. We are the stars made by the Suns.*

Her heart clenched at the memory. She tapped on her glass with her finger. "Daria knows I am a mercenary, but it is not like she has witnessed it. The bloodshed I have committed."

The concern etched in Axar's brow slowly disappeared as understanding flooded his expression. "The bloodshed *we* have committed. You are not alone in this."

His large hand enveloped hers, but she shook her head. "My sister is too innocent for all this. She would see me for what I truly am."

Axar paused. "And what are you?"

Like a match lighting a candle, the fyrebrand flickered to life. The essence breathed out from the corner of her thoughts. Unseen claws tapped at her consciousness.

Mercenary. Rogue. Monster.

Zara's gaze turned vacant. The words were whispers in the wind. The dying embers of burning wood. "Nothing."

Axar's hand squeezed hers. His hazel eyes burned with intent, forcing her to look at him. "You are more, Zara. You are *more*."

She had heard those words before. Hakim had said them, Eshe had tried to echo them. But she didn't understand what they meant.

What is it that you seek? Redemption? Don't be so naive, Rogue.

I hate you.

No, I am your truth.

Zara pulled away from Axar's grasp. She tried to latch onto the words, no matter how weak the tether was.

How she yearned for more.

It was evening when Axar and Zara decided to return to the mercenary temple. His arm was slung over her shoulder as they strolled up the steps of the steep slope. Zara closed her eyes, listening to the thunderous waterfall that roared beneath her feet. The smell of the blossoms below surged upward, filling the air.

She felt a presence ahead of them and opened her eyes to see Erebus waiting for them. With his white wings extended, the archangel looked like a guardian of the temple.

Axar's hold on her tightened as he waved to the Hand of the King.

"Not tonight, my beautiful friend," he drawled. "My sister here will not be taking any marks tonight."

Zara was tempted to laugh and embrace Axar for coming to her defense, even in a small way such as that. Erebus, however, did not seem amused.

A shadow darkened his gaze. Those water-blue eyes honed in on her, a sort of manic look pooled in there. His jaw was so tight that Zara thought she heard the crack of teeth.

Erebus opened his mouth as if trying to formulate the words. Zara's stomach sickened. The Hand of the High King hadn't spoken yet, and she already feared what he would say.

TWENTY-FOUR

Daria's lurching heart jolted her awake. Her hands bunched the silk sheets. She felt the cool salted kiss from the sea on her face as well as the knots in her stomach.

Something wasn't right.

The floor was cool beneath her bare feet as she padded to the windows and pushed the wooden shutters open. A soft mist lingered above the water's surface. Hues of orange and purple brightened the sky.

Unable to keep still, Daria quickly dressed herself. The ivory dress was long-sleeved, snug around her ribcage. It would keep her warm from the crisp bite of the morning. She slipped into her flats and opened the door out of her room.

"Ares, I couldn't sleep—"

Another voice responded, a softer one. "Not Ares, thank the gods."

She took a step back, hand sliding against the door. The war general's Second, Silas, stood where the broody vampire normally would. Daria hadn't interacted much with him during the night of the garden feast and still wasn't sure what to make of him.

He seemed a few years younger than Ares but, with the beam of sunlight that pierced through the ivory hall, she could see a faint stubble across his jaw. His curly brown hair was brushed back in an elegant style, and he had thick brows and brown skin.

Silas grinned, and Daria realized she was taking too long to respond. Gods, the vampires were so attractive it was almost unfair.

But still, seeing the Second of the Adrastean army here caused her to worry for her broody bodyguard. "Where is Ares?"

He squinted his dark eyes as he hummed in thought. "Probably balls deep in a pleasure house somewhere."

Daria's expression twisted in disgust. "Never mind, I'd rather not know."

The words were a half-truth. It may have been due to her lack of experience, but she couldn't help her curiosity. She wondered how Ares, the callous and insensitive soldier, acted in a more *intimate* setting. Was he gentle? What was it Zara had said before? Oh. There were males who enjoyed it rough, where they bend their partner over and—Gods, Daria didn't know what she was thinking. She tried to shake off the image. But it didn't stop her mind from conjuring full lips trailing over her collarbone, the tip of a tongue running up her neck—how her fingers would dig into a bare chest. She felt long, silky hair caress her cheeks. A mouth that pressed a kiss at the base of her throat with a slight *prick*.

And violet eyes meeting hers.

Heat rushed to her cheeks. She shouldn't be entertaining such thoughts. It was easy to see why she would think of Ares in such a matter. He was—objectively speaking—an *attractive* individual.

Daria cleared her throat, hands resting across her abdomen. Silas observed her expression, a smirk on his lips, like he knew exactly what she had been thinking. She didn't know the male, but so far, he seemed a bit more talkative and friendly compared to Ares and she might as well make the most of it.

"I'd like to take a walk," she said.

He cocked his head, dark curls falling over his brow. "Isn't it a bit early, princess?"

Remembering how unsettled she had felt when she awoke, Daria knew she couldn't go back to her room anytime soon. She shook her head before following Silas toward the gardens.

Mist still streaked its gray fingers across the sky. Though it was early, castle staff swept the pathways that trailed through the grove of trees and hedges around the domed castle. The air smelled of soap from the laundry that was being done.

Silas walked beside her, his hands clasped behind his back. An awkward silence fell between them. She had become so used to Ares that it unsettled her to have someone else as her shadow.

Daria surveyed the emblem etched onto Silas's cloak. "How long have you been a member of Adrastea's forces?"

The wind brushed through the brown curls of his hair. "Eighteen years, princess. I was in the ranks before Ares was even drafted into the Academy."

And Ares was promoted as general instead, over many other soldiers who had been there longer. She didn't say the words aloud, but she wondered if this was something that bothered Silas. They veered toward the stone edges of the gardens, where the remainder of the capital stretched toward the harbor.

"Did you know him well during that time?" Daria asked.

Something predatory gleamed in Silas's eyes. "Of course, all the soldiers knew who Ares Valdemar was. There is little compassion within the Academy. It is the place where your will to survive is truly tested. Recruits will kill each other to secure their place in the Adrastean army. You could be on the training ground, sleeping, or taking a shit, and your life still isn't guaranteed. Ares made sure his name was known; it was easy to see why he became the general of the vampire army so quickly and so young. He was fearsome back then—he still is."

King Matías's favorite. Daria wondered if this was how Ares had received the title. To hear from his Second how merciless he could be dumbfounded her. She supposed he would have to resort to such lethality to conduct things as a war general, but the impression she had seen from him was not quite the same.

Silas slipped his hands into the pockets of his trousers. He gave her a kind smile. "That being said, I hope my general is behaving well as your personal guard. How are you enjoying Soleira?"

The princess fidgeted in place; the unease that had startled her awake hadn't left her. She kept walking, Silas falling into step beside her as they strolled along the garden edge.

"Soleira has a lot to offer," Daria said. "I believe the capital will continue to teach me lessons I didn't know I needed."

Statues of archangels appeared as they rounded a corner. Their wings and carved armor towered over her but provided her some comfort. They reminded her of the Primordial sanctuary in Ikarria.

A part of her wondered why she felt a seed of relief when Ares emerged. His long hair swept to the side with the breeze. Lean muscles shifted with every stride of his legs.

When he drew closer, she noticed the lines that bracketed his sensuous mouth. It certainly wasn't the look of someone who had been to a pleasure house. Or maybe it was, and she was too inexperienced to see it.

"I was looking all over for you." His voice was strained.

Ares gave Silas a firm nod who in turn bowed before leaving them alone. The vampire general was still. Too still. His gaze drifted to the ocean, fixed on the waters. The skin around the corner of his colored eyes tensed.

"I can take you out into the capital," he said. "There are many shops you have yet to see—I have a few places in mind that you may like."

"What's wrong?" Daria took a step toward him.

He didn't move. "I can take you to the outer districts again. There is a lot of work to be done worthy of an ambassador—"

"Ares," she snapped. "Tell me what is going on."

He closed his mouth, slowly turning to face her. Wind swept between them, and she caught that rose and ocean scent that was becoming familiar.

Ares stared at her with an unreadable expression. "There will be an execution today."

Daria's breath hitched. In Ikarria, executions were rare. The last one that was held had been so long ago that she barely remembered the splatter of red on the ground or the head that had rolled from the stone. Now that she thought of it, her pater might've protected her a little too well from the realities of her world.

Ares searched her gaze. "The High King has ordered all in the castle to attend. It will be held in the coliseum, but I can still take you out of here. You will not have to see—"

Daria raised her hand. "There is a reason why Raziel wants us present. I will not shy away."

"Princess—"

She cut him off. "No. Tell me when it will be."

The general of the vampire army hesitated. "Now."

The stands of the coliseum weren't full, but that didn't prevent the heaviness in the air. An executioner platform had been erected in the center of the arena. Erebus and a small squadron of soldiers were positioned around it, facing the crowd.

From where Daria and her pater sat, she had a direct view of the High King. Raziel sat in the royal suite in the center of the coliseum stands, while the Council watched from the formal balconies at the ground level. Their eyes glowed so bright they looked like spirits.

Daria clasped her hands across her stomach, acutely aware of her vampire bodyguard sitting at her side. He had made another attempt to get her to avoid the execution, but she wouldn't hear it. If her pater was to be here, then so would she. She wouldn't shrink from the duties of her royal blood.

Her pater wore his obsidian crown, his white hair unbound over his shoulders. Embers burned in his amber-brown eyes, like the Ikarrian forges.

"They didn't tell me about this," he rumbled.

Erebus raised a hand and the coliseum silenced. His face was like stone, voice cold. "Bring forth the prisoner."

There was the sound of wailing chains as two vampire guards

hauled forward a male whose hands were shackled behind his back. The tunic he wore was tattered and soiled, his face obscured by an alabaster mask etched into the shape of an owl.

Her blood iced at the sight. The owl was an omen of death. What a cruel, godsforsaken joke.

The prisoner limped up to the platform, landing on his knees with a pained groan. Erebus's gaze was downturned, a flicker of something Daria couldn't discern passing over his face.

"The accused standing before you has been found guilty of high treason, on the grounds of rebelling against the High Throne and the Council's new world. It was discovered that the traitor was preparing a violent riot against the inner district's shops and businesses. Let this be a warning and an example to those who wish to dismantle the peace our High King, Council, and fellow soldiers have fought to maintain."

Daria shared a worried look with her pater. Erebus's eyes landed on her as he spoke, his words piercing through the fabrics of her soul. "The High King calls for his personal assassin: the Rogue."

The color drained from her face. Whispers rippled throughout the crowd. Fascination and horror, entwined as one.

No, it couldn't be, Daria begged the Suns.

Her sister stepped into the arena. She did not wear her Ikarrian armor. Gleaming plates of white covered her body, bronze stretching across her breastplate like the roots of a tree. A thin veil flowed behind her.

Zara's face was also hidden by an ornate headdress, blades that resembled feathers lining its crown. The mask rippled with gold and white and was shaped into a humanoid skull.

It was symbolic to Mikatán, the Primordial of Death.

A mockery. It was all a mockery of the Primordials, the treaty with Ikarria—and *Zara*.

Fire brimmed underneath the surface of Daria's skin. Steam rolled from her fingertips. Ether hissed from within her, a dragon uncoiling from its sleep.

She had never felt such a surge of her abilities before, the bounds of her fire still unknown to her. Out of all the academia, it was the ether residing inside her that was the most troubling. There were hardly any books that advised ether-wielders on how to bend and manipulate the elements.

Idris kept his power at bay, but she could tell he was livid. The air heating around them was evidence enough. Raziel was spiting them, the realm of Ikarria. He was showing them his true hand by parading a member of their family as his own prized possession.

In Zara's hand was a bone-colored blade. She prowled forward, like an ethereal beast of Celestrea. Sunlight shattered on her body, making her a beacon of white light. The male prisoner moved his head as she neared. The owl gazing upon the Primordial of Death.

They stared at one another. Slowly, Zara lifted his owl mask with one hand. It clattered to the ground, revealing an elven male. His brown skin was slightly wrinkled with age, jawline dusted with facial hair.

He never peeled his eyes away from his executioner. Not as she raised her hand to her own mask.

Daria's breath hitched. It was Zara—but she was not the sister she knew. A cruel light seared through those green eyes, swallowing any hint of the girl—the woman—she had grown up with and come to love. It was as if she could see the Primordial of Death standing behind Zara, with his skeletal face and headdress of feathers.

Fire cracked between Daria's fingers. She couldn't sit here and allow her sister to be degraded like this. Flames hissed around her hands. Never had she lost control or tried to use her power properly, but she knew she could wield it. She was the heir to the Ikarrian throne, blessed with the ether of the dragons. She could unleash it all right here—

A hand wrapped around her wrist. The scent of rose and ocean wrapped around her. The coolness of Ares's skin soothed the burn of her own. Comfort. A mild one, but a comfort, nonetheless.

Daria's fire banked.

She hadn't noticed him leaning toward her. The touch was a message. That he was there with her.

Ares's voice brushed against her ear. "You are from Ikarria, the kingdom of dragons. You are just as powerful as one, and you will not break."

Daria sucked in a shuddering breath, his words seeping into her. If it were any other day, they would've been a balm to her breaking heart. But not then—not as she fought the scream that climbed up her throat. Anger and horror *for* Zara. This was the atrocity that her sister had been subjected to all these years. Daria knew—by the Suns, she knew—that it must have been awful for her sister. But she hadn't known how much. This was an abuse of the treaty, of what had been agreed upon on behalf of their guild.

Zara stepped behind the male. He lifted his chin, baring his throat to the cruel world. The Rogue stared at the crowd as she slit the prisoner's neck. Daria gasped, the sound echoed by her pater at her side.

Ripped flesh, spilled blood. Daria hadn't remembered how vicious a throat being cut open sounded.

The princess wasn't sure how composed her face looked as she tried to contain the overwhelming emotions. But it was too late—her sister found her gaze. Zara's expression shuttered. The bone dagger slipped from her fingers, the clatter echoing throughout the coliseum, penetrating the thick silence of the crowd. Daria clutched onto her seat, ready to tear through the stands to Zara. But her sister turned her back to her and left the arena.

All while the High King grinned.

TWENTY-FIVE

After what felt like hours of scrubbing blood from her scarred hands, Zara ended up in the stables of the Elios temple. Her fingers slipped against the latch into Río's stall, stumbling toward the warhorse. She wrapped her arms around his thick neck and inhaled the earthy smell of hay and damp wood.

Her heart hadn't stopped thundering. Not since she had left the castle. It was beating so fast that her chest began to ache. She braced her forehead against her horse's fur.

Too much. It was too much.

Sucking in a sharp breath, Zara reached for the reins.

Río lunged over the tall blades of grass. His hooves pounded the earth, sending them straight into the moonlight's embrace.

Zara had no direction. Aimless as her heart. She loosened her grip on the reins, allowing Río to conquer the silver-streaked glen as he saw fit.

Her voice echoed within the webs of her mind, reliving the hours before she had stepped onto that execution platform.

"You can't ask this of me."

She had stood before the High King. His private courtyard was encompassed with hedges and small groves of trees. He watched her with an unreadable expression. The gold in the alabaster crown on his head gleamed as if mocking her.

"You can't ask this of me," she repeated.

Raziel's face remained unmoved. "I do not believe it was a request, Rogue."

Her gloved hands clenched into fists. If her nails could've pierced through the leather, she would've drawn blood from her own skin. She had done many gruesome things, so dark and twisted the average soldier could not even fathom. All of that had been bringing her to the edge of an abyss.

What the High King had requested—commanded her . . . It would be the beginning of her end.

The fyrebrand heated on her skin. It warmed to the point that it scalded her flesh. Sweat began to bead across the nape of her neck. The High King may be causing the fyrebrand to harm her. Gods, he may have made it into a sentient being and have his own voice haunt her. She couldn't tell what was true. Reality was slowly breaking into fragments.

She had already been losing parts of herself all these years.

Zara's lips trembled. "I cannot do a public execution."

The High King's bronze wings snapped in the air. His golden eyes pierced her to the ground. "You can and you will. This is simply another mark I have assigned you. One that I am delivering to your feet. You will execute the criminal in front of the entire court and that of the Summit."

Bile curled in her throat. "Please."

The thing she most feared. She would have to strip whatever dignity she had left and leave it at the king's feet. She would bare the scars that riddled her essence to her family.

Raziel's lips twitched. "I'm disappointed, Rogue. I thought you were better than this. Do I need to remind you that you have no choice in the matter? Your soul was given to me, daughter of Idris."

Zara breathed heavily through her nostrils. Her gaze turned into a glare. "Why me? I am *no one*. You only wanted my servitude because I am a daughter to a king who refused to bow to you."

He grabbed her arm. A soft smile touched his lips. "Him adopting you all those years ago meant little to nothing. I could've rained the bowels of war upon him and what remained of that kingdom." His fingers dug deeper into her arm to the point that she flinched. "Idris refusing to honor the High Throne means nothing to me. I wanted you the moment I felt your presence."

Zara tried to jerk away from him, but the High King forced her still. "Do you not remember? I was there on that ruined battlefield when Idris found you."

She remembered. Gods, how could she forget?

Those golden brown wings that had unfurled from the clouds of ash. The tattooed elven male who had stepped in front of her.

Her lips curled into a sneer. A tremor seared through her bones. Whatever boldness she didn't know she had found its way to her again. "I will destroy you."

The High King did not balk, nor did he shrink away. That gentle smile never left his face. "I think it is a little too late for that. We are both already ruined."

The memory shifted, Zara's grip on Río faltering through her slick hands.

Elven ears. A bone-colored blade in Zara's hand. A skeletal mask discarded on the floor.

The prisoner's lips moved. *Do it.*

Suns, help me.

When the blood had begun to pour over her boots, she had lifted her head. Zara hadn't meant to look into the crowd. Gods, she hadn't wanted to. But it was too late. The world had stilled when she met the gazes of her sister and her pater. As they watched her in horror and absolute fury.

Río galloped through the tree line. The rush of mint and sweet honey snapping her back to the present. Her hand went to her chest. Too much. It was too much.

Zara pulled on Río's reins, the horse skidding to a stop. Her breathing had become ragged and heavy. She slipped from the saddle, her fingers curling into her leathers.

"Fuck!"

Ether exploded from her skin. It was a shield of red and deep purple. Energy waved through the seams of her power. The ferocity of it shocked her; it pulled and pulled from her essence. Zara closed her eyes against the force of it as it lifted the weight from her shoulders, chipping at the heaviness in her chest.

There was a sound of twigs breaking, and her eyes snapped open.

A black wolf lingered across a creek. The same wolf from before. The warhorse's ears perked up at the sight of the beast, his nostrils billowing as he took one powerful step closer to her.

"You can see it too," she whispered. Gods, she wasn't going completely insane.

The wolf stood within the bushes and trees near the gurgling stream. Its large tail swept the forest ground, tossing leaves into the air. Starlight dappled its fur, casting a blue sheen over its dark coat.

"What do you want?"

Zara didn't know why she called out to it. For whatever reason, it had been following her. She couldn't recall feeling any sort of presence after that first night she had encountered the wolf. Zara dared not to look away for fear of losing sight of the animal.

Once she blinked, though, it was gone.

Zara staggered back until she landed against a tree. Ether pulsated from her, soothing the ache from within. She rubbed small circles over her chest.

The fyrebrand's presence seemed to land over her shoulders. *Stop pouting. You've done what you were ordered to do—*

Enough. For the first time, in gods knew how long, it was her own voice that rendered the fyrebrand silent. *I've had enough of this.*

When her hands found Río's reins once more, Zara had already made her decision.

TWENTY-SIX

Zara stared at the star-shaped flowers around her. Their centers glowed a soft yellow, filling her lungs with a sweet scent. Only at night would the glades within the Estrella Territories shine bright. From where she sat, it was a sea of twinkling lights that rolled in waves.

She pushed herself to her feet. In the distance, the city of Adira was a splash of vibrancy in the stretch of darkness, the blue painted buildings impossible to miss. Even from where she was, Zara could see the flowerbeds that filled porches and lined walkways, the cobblestone roads that ran up and down the city's slopes. It was one of the largest settlements in the Territories, a popular visit where its roads split toward the various realms.

The guild stood at her sides, their presence warm and powerful. Her brows were pinched together and had stayed that way since they'd left the capital. After the execution, the mercenaries had thrown themselves back into the hunting season . . . in a way.

Zara exhaled a ragged breath. They had gone over this many times. She had shared her desires and fears, presented them in her callused hands. Unsurprisingly, the guild made quick work to prepare for the journey.

As if sensing her trepidation, Axar moved closer. "Give it a rest, Santos. This was our choice as much as yours."

The gentle glow of the wild blossoms illuminated half of his face. Its light touched the dark patterns of his tattoos. His smile was warmth, the press of his hand against her shoulder reassurance.

Zara's voice turned hoarse. "I can't lose any of you."

Axar's eyes warmed. "Have you not been listening all this time? You are not alone. We are in this together."

The fear for the guild's lives was palpable. It was tempting—so fucking tempting—to succumb to it. To continue her years serving the hunting season, to live her days as the Rogue until her sentence met its natural end.

But she had had enough.

Had they not done their part in satisfying the treaty? Hadn't she fulfilled the terms that Raziel had laid out in order for her to live as an Ikarrian? Zara knew the High King didn't respect her. He'd pushed her onto this death-filled path. And for years, she had been willing to let herself be used, hated, insulted if it meant keeping the agreement between their kingdoms, thus ensuring the safety of her family.

No more. They would risk their lives and get their freedom on their own terms.

Hakim and Eshe watched her now. Hoods drawn over their heads, faces etched with determination. No, she wasn't alone.

How that thought chipped at the thorns surrounding her heart.

Hakim gestured to her fyrebrand. "The High King commanded that *you* deliver the final kill. It won't be long before the ether in the tattoo sickens you if you don't obey. It will drive you mad, Zara. I will not risk your safety. If it comes down to it, you must strike the archangel down. Damn the consequences."

To her, the Reckoning was just another obstacle to overcome. One that she would inevitably face. Whether she would fight or embrace that fate she hadn't decided. That was for later.

Zara lifted her chin. "We work with the Sombra Quarter. If Ronan Menodora is unable to uphold his end of the deal, I will kill him."

Zara kept to the shadows. Río and the other horses waited outside the border of the city. She was unsure how aligned Adira was with the Sombra Quarter, but they didn't want to take any chances.

Hakim and Eshe kept a vantage point on top of the buildings. Their bird calls communicated to Zara: when to cross the roads and hide from night patrols. Axar's eyes shifted between human and wolf as he navigated through the streets, flanking her.

Thanks to the continuous meetings with the Messengers, the mercenaries knew where the Sombra's business was normally conducted. They reached a pillared warehouse with a roof made of glass near the town center. Zara found purchase along the stone ledges of the building and started to climb. Chipped pieces of rock and brick plummeted to the ground. Axar waited below, keeping watch from the streets.

Her grip tightened around a blue ledge and hauled herself over it. The flat surface scraped at her tough skin, and specks of blood had already gathered in her palms. Zara heard another fluttering sound of a bird, a message that warmed her chest as she stepped through the open window of the balcony into the warehouse.

Inside was a massive, open space. Starlight shined through the high glass ceiling, revealing towers of boxes that covered the floor. Papers were sprawled on desks. Curiosity overwhelmed her, to the point that she went to the crates first. With her superior strength, she snapped a lid open. The force of it was a little too much as the box snapped in half.

"Oh well," she whispered, picking broken pieces of wood and putting them aside.

She found a variety of items, from weapons to jewelry, artwork to grain, seeds, and roots. Her fingertips skimmed over the crates, delving deeper and deeper into the supply room.

Voices murmured on the other side of the wall, and she crouched in the darkness, tugging the hood farther over her head.

"We must act more quickly. Have the funds made the trip?"

That voice.

Ronan Menodora.

"Yes. The shipment has made route to—"

Whoever was speaking to him was cut off. Silence. A rustling of wings.

Zara's body stiffened. A curse left her lips as the thin wall exploded. Black wings unfurled from dust. It was all she saw before she was lifted from the ground.

Ronan held her with an arm clamped around her back. Her stomach flipped as she watched the floor grow farther and farther away as they almost reached the glass ceiling.

Her legs dangled in the air, chest pressed against his hard body. Her breathing quickened, hands tightening around the fighting leathers on his torso. She felt the tip of a short dagger graze her chin as she was forced to meet silver eyes, glinting like the honed steel now at her throat.

Those scarred lips curled. "Zara Santos, how unpleasant it is to see you."

She forced a dry smile on her lips. "Shame. I thought you would be delighted to see me."

His smirk grew even wider. "After you killed my men and destroyed one of my businesses, I've grown some reservations."

Ah. Zara supposed she couldn't blame him there. "I've had some recent epiphanies," she managed to say, fighting the urge to look down. Gods, she was not meant for negotiation, especially from this height. "I've come here as a truce between the Ikarrian guild and the Sombra Quarter."

Ronan's arm tightened around her as his beating wings continued to hold them midair. "A lie." His voice rolled down her skin. "Have you come to kill me, Horizon?"

Zara gritted her teeth. "No, much to my disappointment. We want to take your offer."

He angled his head. Shadows cascaded over his face, his steel gaze turning a shade darker. "Why the change of heart?"

"I would love to explain myself in a more civilized manner."

Ronan chuckled deeply. "There's hardly anything civilized about you."

She reached for his wrist that held the dagger. "I gave you a good chase though, didn't I?"

Ronan's eyes brightened. "This could be a trick."

"If it was, the guild would have gutted you already."

Their gazes were caught in a silent battle, save for their ragged breathing and the flapping of his wings. Then, Ronan slowly helped her to the ground and released her.

Zara was about to speak when an icy wind swept through the room. It was so cold that she could see her breath. Rain started falling from the sky; it pounded the roof in vicious sheets. The realization stunned her. It had been a clear night sky, no indication of a storm.

Ronan bristled. "Is this you?"

Her eyes widening, she pointed at her chest. "Do you think I am controlling the weather? What sort of creature do you think I am?"

He gave her a disbelieving look. "You are an elf, are you not? Doesn't your kind manipulate the elements?"

"Elves can control a *single* element. We cannot command the matters of the world, we are not fucking gods."

Blood curdling screams rose in waves from outside. The distant sounds rolled closer and louder. Zara met Ronan's gaze before they unsheathed their weapons in unison.

A door on the other side of the warehouse slammed open and an elf stumbled in from outside. They were hunched over, arms wrapped around themselves. Zara took one step before Ronan struck out an arm to stop her.

He slowly shook his head, gaze heavy on the elf. "Are you well over there?"

Zara heeded the warning in his tone as she raised her blades. The elf twitched and rocked side to side, a snarl curling from their lips. Their head jerked up and her heart nearly stopped.

It was a woman, and her veins were lined with a bright blue hue. Eyes glowing like sapphires with unnaturally pointed teeth. She roared and lunged toward them.

Ronan skirted ahead of Zara, raising his blade to block the assailant. The elf clung to his arm, her sharpened teeth pinned around his sword. Zara yanked the elf by the hair and pierced her khopesh through the woman's back.

The cerulean glow in her eyes dimmed. The colored veins remained but, from what Zara could tell, there were no other abnormalities about the elf.

Ronan was at her side. "Are you alright?"

She gave him a confused look. "What in the fucking Suns was that?"

The creases over his brow deepened. "I suppose it is good timing that you are here, Horizon. What you saw is the very reason I need your help."

Zara blinked, struggling to formulate a response. She and the guild had stumbled upon something graver than they thought.

Collapsing stone, entwined with shrieks and roars, echoed from outside.

The guild. Zara spun the blades in her hands and strode for the door. "Be sure to keep up, archangel."

They stepped outside to find the city of Adira flooded with citizens screaming in terror, running for their lives. They toppled over one another, pushing through the streets. Within the chaos, scores of blue eyes shined, wisps of ethereal light following the mortals who were no longer themselves as they chased the other citizens.

A male paused in the streets and turned to face her. Human. His lips curled back to reveal sharpened teeth that were made of metal. Odd, the woman from the warehouse hadn't had these. He charged her but, before he could reach her, Zara ducked low, driving her blade forward.

Blood splattered the ground. More of the seemingly possessed creatures launched themselves upon them. Ronan moved in a wicked dance of black and silver. Agile despite his large body. It was a wonder how he managed to maneuver himself so easily with those wings.

Her fighting leathers were drenched with blood now. More possessed humans, elves, and some vampires met her blades. They began to overwhelm her, forcing her back toward the town center, Ronan behind her.

He didn't turn her way as he shouted. "Brace yourself, Horizon. We will need to take to the skies."

"Wait—"

"—We don't have time."

Arrows whistled through the air and the first row of the possessed mortals fell. Zara and Ronan took the opportunity to push through, gutting and slicing. Another array of arrows pierced the surrounding attackers. Zara thought it was her guild when she noticed the golden and ivory feathers on the arrows.

Not Ikarrian. Zara managed to steal a glance at the rooftops to the hooded figures there. They were too far—shielded by the darkness—for her to see who they were. Their archers raised their bows once more, the arrows like black birds against the dark clouds. More of the possessed surrounding her fell.

The archangel latched onto her arm, not bothering to think twice on the help they had received. "I am going to pick you up. We need to get out of there."

She wrestled against him. "I *need* to find my guild."

Ronan growled. "We will search in the air, but we have to *move*."

The rain pounded harder on the cobblestoned streets. Clusters of ice managed to flutter through the moisture. And a voice. It was soft yet pained; gentle with a touch of sorrow; a mother's hum twisted with a mother's anguish.

"Children. Where are my children?"

The swarm of creatures dispersed as if afraid and fell back to the corners of the city. Ronan's hand landed on her shoulder, his eyes on something above her head. She followed his gaze to the rooftops and her heart flipped.

Three figures stood within the sheets of rain. In the center was a woman draped in veils of white and cerulean armor. Her skin was milky white with a touch of blue, as if Death had drained the blood from her. She looked human, though her face was mummified. She had no nose and pale eyes. The veils she wore melded to her body, fluttering behind her bare feet.

The two standing on either side of her were clad in cloaks and black armor. The one to the left had a skull for a face, two horns curling over its head, and a spear strapped to its back.

To the right stood a warrior. It resembled the statues and carvings of the gods that served Mikatán. Its skeleton face shined with a bronze hue. A hood was drawn over its head, its cloak draping over a bulky frame strapped to the teeth with blades. A large scythe peeked from where it hung across its back.

Each of them wore a crown of silver that gleamed like fiery stars.

The acolyte's words rang in Zara's head. *Prepare for the new world, the Three Sun Gods have returned!*

Even the Messenger had shared something peculiar. *Ethereal beings wearing crowns of silver fire have been seen stalking the wild lands.*

She fought the quiver in her knees, swallowed back the bile that rose in her throat.

It couldn't be . . . could it? The Primordials' connection to the world no longer existed. It was not possible for the Three Sun Gods to be here.

The woman raised her armored arms. Her voice was loud despite its wraithlike, whispery sound.

"*Come, my children.*"

The possessed citizens who had been enraptured by whatever ether was at work began to move. They gathered, snapping at each other but otherwise keeping in line. And they marched through the city.

Zara stumbled back, meeting Ronan's chest. His hand wrapped around her arm, voice low in her ear. "Brace yourself."

He launched them into the air. Rain pelted Zara's face, icy wind howling in her ears. Ronan's wings flapped once, twice, before he swerved to the side.

"Look out!"

A spear hissed past them. The three ethereal creatures watched them now, the one who had thrown the weapon lowering its hand.

The skeletal warrior with the scythe stepped forward. It braced, the air rumbling about it.

Zara clutched onto Ronan tighter. "Shit. Fly faster!"

He shouted back at her. "What do you think I am doing?"

The archangel's wings sliced through the rain as he climbed higher and higher. It was too late—the creature careened through the air and smashed into them, Ronan losing his grip on her. The warrior's gloved hands grabbed Zara by the throat, empty eye sockets staring at her as they tumbled toward the ground.

A deep, male voice reverberated around her. "*Child of the Ether. Maker in the making. You have been lost but no longer.*"

Zara's eyes widened, his words sending ice through her veins. She threw a punch at the ethereal warrior, and its head snapped to the side. The ground was rushing toward them, wind whipping her face, and she closed her eyes for the impact.

A howl in the distance. She recognized the sound. Axar. In that space of time, where she was falling and the world was rushing to meet her, relief swelled in her chest. If the guild was safe, nothing else mattered.

She closed her eyes, prepared to meet her godly patron. Suddenly, the skeletal warrior was knocked away from her, the impact causing his grip to tear at her fighting leathers. Zara screamed and worked at her ether. The power inside her seemed to crouch, ready for release but she found herself cradled against a chest, arms fastened around her.

Ronan was breathing heavily. "I don't understand what we just witnessed, but we must go. I will take you to my stronghold. It will be the safest place from the High Throne, as well as whatever those things are."

Zara glanced behind the archangel. "Do we leave them?"

He knew she was referring to the surviving townspeople. Something like guilt flashed across his face. "Adira is lost."

Ronan soared past the city's borders, lowering closer to the ground. Zara heard a familiar thunder of hooves and paws and looked down to see the guild racing toward her. Río galloped past the others, his head tossing with the wind. Ronan glided even lower, letting Zara slip from his grasp and onto her horse's saddle.

The guild of Ikarria and a criminal archangel tore through the hills, their hearts pounding with the tremor of the Continent. The farther they were from the ethereal creatures, the quicker the rain drew to a stop.

TWENTY-SEVEN

If anyone had told Ronan Menodora that he would be escorting a guild of mercenaries—a guild of *Horizons*—to the place he now called home, he would've called them a fool.

Perhaps he was an idiot for trusting the Horizons. They might have been planning to drive a knife into his back. Ares had nearly keeled over at this absurd idea of his to ally with them. But what he had witnessed so far had only confirmed that he needed the mercenaries.

The Sombra Quarter did not have the forces or the skill set to track the ethereal creatures. Ronan also couldn't bring himself to entrust his average soldier with a matter such as this. Many would be willing to blindly follow him, but he couldn't afford to wonder which of his own men and women had been bought by the High Throne. At least with the guild, he knew exactly what he was up against.

Ronan led the mercenaries toward the hillsides, the capital's borders emerging in the distance ahead of them. The familiar scent of smoke invaded his nostrils. He could see the Stone Orchard's night watch, could remember every crevice and spot throughout the canyons and hills they were posted in.

Much to his surprise, the Horizons had also spotted the guards. Their hands flew to their weapons but, at Ronan's direction, they relaxed. He had to remember that they were not average mercenaries. Their senses and intuition had been sharpened a thousand times over.

The mercenaries gravitated toward each other to guard their blind spots, the movement so natural Ronan was unsure if they noticed it themselves. The large wolf kept to the back of the group, the shifter's gaze steady on his back.

At the entrance to the cavern, Ronan landed. The limbs and muscles within his feathers ached as he rustled his wings and gestured to the guild.

"Welcome to the Stone Orchard."

Guards watched as the mercenaries entered the tunnel with such bewildered expressions it was almost comical. Ronan led them to the smoothened path that sloped down the length of the cavern walls.

When the passage opened up to reveal the city below, Ronan heard the mercenaries gasp. Amused, he watched as they stared open-mouthed at the adobe buildings splayed about the flat landscape and carved along the canyon's walls. At the gentle river glittering in the moonlight. At the stone bridges and lights, at the people walking about, children laughing. Music filled the air. Smoke curled toward the high rocky arches through which the night sky could be seen.

The sound of clopping hooves drew closer to where Ronan walked at the front of the group. The presence cracked the air: it was the brewing of a storm, the tremble of the earth; it hummed against his blood, touched the lonely ether in his soul.

"Did you create this place?"

Her voice. Rough like steel and battle. Ronan glanced back and found Zara watching the nightlife, those green eyes wide with wonder.

He nodded. "I did. Many years ago."

She gave him a wary look. "Why would you trust us with the location of your stronghold?"

"I requested your aid and offered mine in return. As long as we are in alliance, I will give you the roof over my head and the food on my table."

Her lips twisted, the skin around her nose pinching slightly. "That sounds utterly ridiculous."

Ronan shrugged. "It was the way I was raised."

"Didn't you create the shadow markets as well?"

Ronan ran a hand through his damp hair as it fell over his brow again. A bemused expression touched his mouth. "A grave misconception. The shadow markets have been here long before I was. I simply took it and made it my own."

"And these people." Zara gestured to the shops and homes around them as they walked on. "They are your allies."

He grunted. "In a way. They are more indebted to me. These people you see are a combination of families and loved ones of other shadow dealers, as well as those seeking refuge from their corrupted realms."

She whirled to him, the green of her eyes igniting. "Refuge? Are there people from Elios?"

"There are many from Elios and from Adrastea as well. And from the far corners of the Continent. Victims of the War, either enslaved or wrongly imprisoned. This place is their new beginning. They work either here or in the outside world, but they have a place they can call home."

Something fell over her face. A touch of shadows—something tortured. "I have killed many . . . I wonder if any of them intended to come here."

Ronan didn't respond. He felt something nudge his arm and he moved his wing to see Zara's horse let out a snort. He was a beautiful stallion with a dark yellow pelt and black mane. The animal touched him again, its nostrils billowing a gush of warm air.

Zara leaned forward. "It seems Río approves of you."

Ronan lifted a hand and gently rested it above the horse's snout. "A pleasure to meet you." He looked up to see Zara's confused look and smiled. "Río. I like his name."

They exited the main city and approached the river. A small ferry waited at its bank. Ronan looked at the large wolf. "You may want to shift for this part."

The shifter seemed to snort as light exploded from beneath its fur. A lithe male stood in its place, muscular and tattooed. The male's gaze on Ronan was stone cold as he approached Zara to help with Río.

The ferryman, a water-wielding elf, outstretched her hands and the waters obeyed, pushing the small boat farther across the river. The horses neighed as the ferry rocked gently.

Ronan noticed the tall, bulky mercenary looking over the boat's edge, watching the water bend at the elf's command. Flickers of ether light weaved within the waves. During their trek to the Stone Orchard, Ronan had learned the names of the other Horizons.

Hakim had been silent for most of the journey, as well as the archer called Eshe. Ronan didn't miss how she eyed him. He was not so much of a fool to think that the mercenaries wouldn't attack. If it came down to it, he would fight them. He may bleed out and lose his wings, but he would win against the guild. The mercenaries were not the only ones with historically exquisite training.

Hakim folded his arms, admiring the scattered lights. "It is amazing what you have done here." The mercenary slid his gaze to him. "Who are you really?"

There it was. Ronan had formally introduced himself earlier, though he suspected they were asking more than just his name now. He only shrugged. "A nobody. A survivor. Take your pick."

The mercenary narrowed his eyes. Ronan held still under the scrutiny. Maybe the male could sniff out the lie. Well, half-lie.

"You have an unusual surname," he said. "Where are you from?"

Ronan refrained from letting his jaw clench. "Nowhere now. The War obliterated what I knew as home."

Hakim went silent. His dark eyes flipped to Zara—who watched them from the opposite side of the boat—and back to him. Ronan thought to distract the Ikarrian from where the conversation was heading.

"I've heard of you, Hakim. The Dragonheart of Ikarria," he said.

The Horizon grimaced. "I suppose I shouldn't be surprised that my reputation from my battling years has reached these parts of the Continent."

Ronan leaned against the railing, his expression morphing into slight admiration. "You are a legend among soldiers. Even amongst the archangels. For a human to have bested many skilled warriors who could summon ether and such, it is beyond impressive."

Eshe smirked as she nudged Hakim. "He is more modest than he seems." Hakim grunted.

Ronan's expression sobered. "So, from what we all experienced in the Estrella Territories, do you understand why I sought your help?"

The shifter—what was his name? Oh, Axar—snorted. His eyes reflected under the night, revealing the wolf within his skin. "This is no mere hunt, leader of the Sombra," he pointed a finger toward the Stone Orchard's entrance in the distance, "What happened out there was an *annihilation*. It begs the question, what exactly are you bringing us into?"

He lingered at Zara's side as if he was her shield. Perhaps he was. The elf said nothing, but her brows drew forward as she waited for his answer.

Ronan couldn't blame the shifter for his caution. He sighed, strands of his hair drifting over his eyes. "I do not know what is happening, but I cannot rely on my forces alone for this. I've seen one of those . . . *possessed* people before, but those creatures with the crowns? That was my first time. I can't guarantee your safety."

Axar's jaw clenched, unsatisfied with what the archangel had said. "This situation is bigger than us. It's otherworldly. I hope you are not bringing us to our deaths, archangel."

Ronan felt his stomach twist. Gods, he hoped not as well. He refused to believe it.

The ferry docked on the other side of the river where more adobe homes sprawled ahead, shielded by the canyon rocks. Lanterns swayed in front of their entryways, pastures and gardens attached to the properties. Ronan took a narrow path up a slope, the mercenaries following.

They approached a villa that had a corral and stable for the horses. He opened its wooden door and stepped inside. Pottery and woven baskets were neatly arranged along the red-brown plastered walls.

"There are three rooms. There's some water in the jugs, but you can get more at the river. There is always a night watch if you need assistance to cross the ferry, and food and clean clothes will be brought to you. We will reconvene first thing tomorrow."

Ronan left the guild to settle in, the night air pressing cool palms along his cheeks as he stepped outside. Perhaps his mind was playing tricks on him, but he could've sworn he could smell the sand and palm trees.

He made his way down the slope from the villa's property when he felt Zara's energy ripple through the seams of the realm. Unseen tendrils of chaos and unfiltered strength. It was a foreign sensation to him, unlike anything he'd felt before.

Zara stood under the pale moonlight, a blade of darkness in a pool of white. He could see the tattoos that decorated the top of her hands disappear underneath her leathers. It was too dark to tell what the designs were, but it was enough to pique his attention.

"Thank you," she whispered. "For saving me."

Ronan thought of the ethereal creature in Adira, how it had slammed into him from the sky. In that moment, he had been thrown back to that constant feeling of helplessness. A reminder of his failures. It had threatened to overwhelm him, but when he saw her in the creature's clutches, something inside him snapped.

It awoke a feral hunger to prove that he still had a *sliver* of worth. That he could save someone. He wouldn't tell her that, of course.

Ronan kept his voice light. "I can't have you dying on me yet, Horizon. I need you."

Was that a smirk? He couldn't be so sure. His wings unfurled and he rose from the ground. "I wish to show you this place and its residents while you are here. I think you will find that we are not as different as you may think, Zara Santos."

PART III

BLEEDING LIGHT ON THE HORIZON

TWENTY-EIGHT

Zara stood in a field where the sky was a clash of dusk and dawn. Trees and hills and mountains, as far as her eyes could see. There was no end and no beginning. And the wolf appeared before her. It padded a few steps through the gentle grass, pausing to look over its shoulder. Zara wanted to move toward it, to reach a hand and ask what it wanted.

But the black wolf only watched her with its orange-red eyes as she slipped from the ground, the sky rushing to meet her—

Zara lurched upright in her bed. Her hand flew underneath her pillow, grabbing the dagger she had tucked there the night before. Her eyes scanned the room as she fought for breath. There were only the reddish-brown plastered walls, the woven baskets that hung on the walls as well as the painted water jugs on the floor.

After several moments, she lowered the weapon and ran a hand over her face. The wolf she had seen on the outskirts of Soleira had returned to her.

Her hand rubbed circles over her chest. The ache inside felt like she had experienced loss, like she yearned to be reunited with the creature.

The next day, all that happened the night before came hurtling back: the ethereal creatures wearing crowns and armor; the one who had taken her from the sky, his scythe flashing like lightning under the rain—and the cold fear that flooded through her veins. She couldn't remember the last time she had felt something like that.

Zara brushed the thought away as she observed the city. She wasn't sure why this place was called the Stone Orchard, but the mere fact that an entire civilization thrived under the High King's nose without his knowledge was too good to be true. Ronan had arrived at the villa in the morning and was currently escorting the mercenaries somewhere they could speak in private.

Many of the elves in the Orchard—just like back home in Ikarria—used their ether to sustain the territory. The earth wielders moved stone and rock, creating new pathways for the river to water the crops. Fire wielders worked the forges, alongside a few archangels. It was a wonder to see any of the winged race working against the High Throne.

Ronan led them up a slope away from the city to an entrance built into a cavern. Darkness dwelled inside, save for the flickering torches on the walls. There was no door, solely stone steps and two statues on either side crafted from the rock. Much to Zara's surprise, the statues were skeletal warriors, massive creations that stood from the ground to the ceiling.

"These look like the guards of Mikatán," she observed.

Ronan stopped in front of them. "It is because they are. I am not sure what this place used to be, but it must have belonged to one of the civilizations from the Age of the Primordials."

She turned her head to look at him. "The time when the races first entered Ribera. How do you know so much of the Continent's history?"

Daylight made the steel in his eyes seem more like shimmering water. "I like to read, little wolf. Is that so shocking?"

"Quite frankly, yes."

The air whispered to them as they entered the cavern into a grand hall. The floor changed from loose dirt to what felt like tiles; it was paved with pale-colored brick, creating a design that Zara could not decipher.

There were more broken statues carved along the walls, the space oddly resembling a temple. Ronan led them into another corridor and pushed a pair of stone doors open, letting the guild inside. Zara's breath hitched at the sight of the mural covering the entire wall. It was whittled into the pale stone, etchings of more skeletal warriors and feathered creatures stretching toward the cave's ceiling.

"It's like the one from Dae Asari's temple," she whispered.

Hakim patted her shoulder and headed to the stone table at the center of the chamber. She didn't realize there were two other males waiting in the room. One was the same archangel with light gray wings from outside of Ronan's office. Zara's suspicion must've been correct, he was someone of importance here.

As for the other male . . . he looked too otherworldly to be human. His cheekbones were high, delicate yet strong features crafted on his face. He had long dark hair that held a dark purple tint and reached his waist. His eyes were also a deep violet, and he watched her with a sharpness she found herself staring back at, her chin raised. He must be a shifter or a vampire. Zara even thought she recognized him, but couldn't recall from where.

Ronan sat at the head of the table, motioning for the guild to follow. He gestured to the archangel and then to the mysterious male. "Orion Solterra and Ares Valdemar. I trust both with my very life, and they will be the only ones privy to what we will speak about. I have already provided them with the details of what we witnessed."

The archangel called Orion made to sit next to Ronan, but he held a hand up. He pointed a tattooed finger to the empty seat. "For Zara."

Orion blinked at him but didn't seem to object as he moved to the seat that would be on her other side. Zara wasn't sure why Ronan would do such a thing.

She sat down and he answered her unasked question. "You are my guest, Horizon. I was the one who asked you to work with me."

Zara glanced at Orion. His black hair was not in a braid today but tied up in a knot at the top of his head. He was a very rugged, handsome creature with scars that riddled his muscular brown skin. He gave her a sidelong glance.

She couldn't help but raise a brow and lean against her seat. "I feel like you and I were overdue on introductions."

Orion surveyed her and let out a short snort. "I know all about you, Rogue."

Zara tried to not bristle at the title. Her gaze slid to Ronan, who had been watching their encounter, and tossed him a look of boredom. "What now, head of the Sombra?"

Ronan's lips curved upward before he addressed everyone at the table. "About a month ago, Orion and I found several abandoned towns. There were signs of struggle but no evidence of death, except for the one possessed mortal we came across. The same as the mortals from yesterday."

"So we agree that what we saw last night was an act of *possession?*" Hakim asked. "The glow in their eyes, the coloring of their veins . . . That's no mere sickness, nor your usual form of ether."

Ronan ran a hand over his jaw. "I suspect the same. As I said yesterday, it was my first time seeing those other ethereal creatures, though. I do not know who or what they are."

"Is there a way we can find out?"

Ronan gestured to the violet-eyed male. "Ares holds significant power in Soleira, and he can obtain information that is not accessible to us. He has offered to be a resource should we need it, and could provide us a way to learn more about these creatures, as well as how to eradicate the fyrebrands."

Significant power in Soleira. An intriguing frame of words. Zara had been eyeing the mysterious male during the conversation. "Where do I know you from, Ares Valdemar?"

Those colored eyes flicked to hers. His voice fell like a purr, deep and alluring. "I hear suspicion in your tone, Horizon. I am your ally."

As he spoke, she caught sight of vampire fangs peeking from between his lips.

"No," Zara drawled. "You are clearly someone in a position of influence. Someone who could betray us easily. If you do not wish to share, then I see no point in maintaining this partnership."

"Ares," Ronan rumbled.

The vampire sighed. "I am the general of the Adrastean army."

Ah. That was probably why he looked familiar, Zara had most likely walked past this male several times over the years when she visited Soleira. She met Ronan's gaze, eyes wide. "You have friends in very high places. I'm impressed."

"I am no friend," Ares growled. "I am merely an ally. As I mentioned."

Zara looked between the archangel and vampire. "Could you also *mention* why you, Adrastea's general of *war*, are here with the Sombra Quarter?"

Ares curled his lips and revealed his fangs. "I do not need to explain myself to you, mercenary."

Ronan shot the vampire a look, but the male only glared at her. She caught something like a flash of sympathy on the archangel's face. There was history between the males, that much she could see. She didn't have to know their life story to satisfy the needs of their arrangement.

That didn't stop her from baring her teeth. "So be it. But if you dare utter a word about my guild and I being here to the High Throne or anyone who breathes in that castle, I will not hesitate to throw your name in too, so that your vampire king may rip out your innards."

Ares met her threat with a composed demeanor, though it felt like he was holding back. His nostrils flared and he squared his shoulders. "We both have something deadly over each other's heads. It looks like we are in agreement."

Ronan ran a hand over his face. "Look at us being friendly. Can we move on now?"

Zara relented. "Speaking of those ethereal creatures, I had heard word of the Three Sun Gods returning to the mortal lands. I feel as though those *things* wearing crowns are what started the rumors."

Ronan's gaze darkened. "If that's the case, then all the more reason for Ares to research exactly what these beings are."

Orion interjected. "In the meantime, how can we find out what those townspeople are actually possessed with?"

"We catch one." Axar's voice echoed in the chamber hall. He rolled his eyes when everyone looked to him. "Gods, isn't that why you wanted us mercenaries here? We track the missing people as far as we can and hunt one of them down."

Hakim began to nod. "Agreed, but let's avoid those three beings until we learn more about them. They are not your average monster."

Ronan drummed his hand on the table. With his dark sleeves rolled to his elbows, he looked like a member of Celestrea's legendary winged legion.

"I can show you the abandoned towns," he said. "The footprints may not be there anymore but anything you can glean may help. Orion and I have tried to track them, but it is as if the people are constantly migrating."

Zara began to mull over what they would have to do. She thought of the High King and the hunting season, the fears and anxieties that polluted her mind. "I know that your end of this arrangement is to help us get rid of the fyrebrand, but this is a great risk for us."

Ronan watched her. His gray eyes gleamed with interest. "I feel as if you're on the verge of making demands. What else would you like?"

She shrugged. "Pay us. The rules of the hunting season prevent us from taking assignments outside those of the king. Since we are well beyond betraying the High Throne, not to mention the heightened risk of danger with those unknown creatures, I think we should be compensated at least."

Orion tensed. "We can't possibly—"

"Done."

Ronan held her gaze in a silent challenge that thrummed through her blood. "Only if you agree to withhold hunting shadow dealers for as long as you can."

Her jaw clenched. "Not possible. If we are provided with an assignment, we must follow. Otherwise the fyrebrand will punish us. It is another reason why we need it removed."

His eyes fell to her wrist. The tattoo was hidden beneath her leathers, but she still had the urge to clasp a hand over it.

"I didn't know that," he said, his voice low. "In that case, would your guild be willing to stay in the Stone Orchard during the time of our allegiance?"

"Why in the gods' names would you want us here?"

"Well, if you plan on skewering me in my sleep, I'd like to be prepared. Keeping your enemies close, that sort of thing."

Her lips began to curl. "You can try to gain the upper hand, archangel. But if I were to kill you, it wouldn't be something so dull."

Zara felt the curious stares from the others at the table. None of her mercenaries intervened, and she had a sense they were entertained by her altercation with the head of the Sombra Quarter.

She cleared her throat and sighed. "Fine. We shall stay in the Stone Orchard, but we will need to make appearances in the Elios temple to avoid suspicion."

Ronan's face gleamed with victory as he winked. She gritted her teeth. "Thank you, Horizon," he said.

She rolled her eyes as the others went on to discuss the logistics of the plan at his lead. The guild would stay to help track and capture a possessed mortal, all while they continued to serve the hunting season. They needed to tread carefully—Zara would still be expected to report as the Rogue.

A part of her, however small, did wonder if this temporary alliance with the Sombra Quarter may lead the way to a life where she and the guild would no longer have to bow to the High King.

Lies.

The fyrebrand rose from the depths, its claws sinking into the jagged parts of her mind. *Be brutally honest. Deep down, you do not believe there is any hope of being rid of me. You are only here to kill.*

Zara Santos's gaze slid to Ronan. Whether this partnership succeeded or failed, it mattered not to her. She would either be free of the fyrebrand, or her blade would find its way into the archangel. Consequences be damned.

TWENTY-NINE

The secret city of the Stone Orchard was like no other. A string of buildings with flat roofs stacked either along the dirt paths or against the canyon walls. Colorful tarps—blue, green, and red—were erected over stalls and open-air shops. There were even banners made of parchment flapping above the streets, the sight reminding Zara of home.

Flocks of birds could be seen soaring above the arches of rock that created shadows over the city, a waterfall cascading down from the rocks, the sounds bringing her a sense of peace. The river that sliced through the Stone Orchard shimmered underneath the rays of sunlight and was almost blinding to the eye, hiding the stretch of adobe homes on the other side.

Zara had seen some of the city when she arrived last night, but the beauty of it in broad daylight left her in a trance. After the meeting with Ronan and his inner circle, the guild was left to explore. The archangel Orion was with them as a guide, but she had a sense he was here to keep an eye on the mercenaries.

She couldn't blame Ronan for taking precautions. He had stayed behind to escort Ares out of the hidden city. Zara was curious about the vampire general. There was more to understand about his role and connection within the Sombra Quarter, but by her deduction, one fact remained clear: Ares Valdemar was not loyal to Adrastea and Elios. Perhaps he was a mole for the shadow markets. Zara tucked that information for later, it was a weapon she could use against Ronan if the situation called for it.

Someone lightly shoved her, and she looked up at Hakim. He had left his dreads free from the leather band and kept his usual arrangement of jewelry. His fighting leathers were tight on his large frame—a common issue for a male his size.

The head of the Ikarrian guild's eyes gleamed. "I have to say, I am impressed with what Ronan has accomplished here."

He gestured with a gloved hand to the city that surrounded them. They were in the center of the markets and dining places. The citizens here merely glanced at the mercenaries, and they went on their way. Knowing that most residents here had escaped hardships, they seemed at ease even with a guild of Horizons walking amongst them.

Orion gazed out at the city. The pride in his face was subtle, a twinkling light in his expression that told this place was precious to him.

"Yes, my brother has done well," he said.

Zara thought to ask the archangel about his relationship with Ronan when Axar darted past her. He was dragging Eshe along with him by the arm, the archer feigning annoyance but Zara could see the amusement in her eyes.

Axar pointed at a stall with jewelry, woven blankets, and baskets. "Eshe, don't these seem like something made from the nomad clans?"

The archer leaned over the seller's table as she observed the array of goods. "Gods, this is nostalgic. The nomads must have sold these to the shop. Look, little pup, this talisman is made of copper."

Hakim chuckled as he watched the mercenaries fawn over their discovery. Orion followed his gaze and cocked his head.

"A pair of Horizons giddy over *trinkets*," he said. "I never thought I'd see the day."

Hakim crossed his arms. "There are many things that are more than what meets the eye."

The archangel nodded, a knowing shine in his eyes. A human male approached Orion, saluting him. He was dressed in simple fighting garb and Zara suspected he was one of the soldiers charged to protect the Stone Orchard.

The human muttered something to the archangel, and Orion addressed the mercenaries. "Excuse me, it seems I am needed. Feel free to explore the shops, and I will find you shortly."

His wings tucked tighter over his muscled back as he followed the soldier through the lively street. Hakim nudged Zara along again, steering her toward the stalls. She eyed the variety of rare art pieces from all parts of the Continent. The shadow markets must have been selling similar items, since the Stone Orchard was supported by those businesses.

Hakim tensed beside her. "Incoming, little warrior."

Zara reached for her dagger, gripping its handle. She noticed a group of men and women storming toward where Axar and Eshe were. A male led the entourage, his forehead drawn into a scowl.

He stopped in front of Eshe, his hands on his waist. "We heard there was a fucking *guild* among the safe streets of the Stone Orchard. How did you find this place? Your type should not be here."

The passersby around them gave them a wide berth, tossing them nervous glances. Eshe seemed unfazed as she finished placing gold marks in the seller's hand. The mercenary straightened, the sound of leather stretching. She had left her bow at their temporary villa, but the vampire nomad was more than capable of ripping bones from flesh.

Eshe gave the male an exasperated look. "We were given passage here by your leader, Ronan Menodora."

The male snorted. "He would've informed his shadow dealers if that were the case, and I personally have not received word of this. You mercenaries have been killing my associates all hunting season. How can you expect me to just let you go?"

The shadow dealer reached for Eshe, but Axar swept in. He snatched the male's arm and twisted it behind his back. The man squirmed as the shifter held him in place. Bystanders gasped as the other shadow dealers unsheathed their weapons, their blades aimed at Axar.

Zara raised her dagger, ready to throw it in between someone's eyes.

"*Stop.*"

Ronan stepped out from the throng of people, his black wings flaring, battle seeming to echo behind his every step. The other shadow dealers balked at the sight of the archangel. They lowered their weapons, blades trembling.

Zara's eyes widened as she witnessed the fear on their faces. Ronan glowered at the shadow dealer Axar held. "I see that word spreads quickly. Is there not enough to do outside these walls that you must resort to gossip for entertainment, Erasmus?"

The male called Erasmus tried to wrench away from Axar's grasp but failed. "You will have to explain yourself, Menodora."

Ronan's expression turned cold. "Are you trying to command me?"

The shadow dealer began to stammer out nonsense, but Ronan ignored him. Zara stilled when his eyes went to hers, as if he had known where she had been standing the entire time.

He stood there, a symbol of rebellion, about to show her what he was truly capable of.

Orion emerged in time to yank Erasmus from Axar. He shoved him to his knees before Ronan, who hadn't looked away from her. Slowly, he lowered his gaze to the shadow dealer.

"You bring this feud to *my* streets? In front of *them?*" The promise of wrath was laced through his low voice.

He waved a hand toward the crowd and Zara understood the true reason for his fury. Ronan was angry that the citizens were having to witness this. Citizens who had already gone through so much.

His teeth clenched as he brought out a dagger and pressed the edge of the blade to Erasmus's ear, digging into the skin. The shadow dealer hissed and clamped his mouth shut.

Ronan held the blade there and eyed the other shadow dealers. "Let it be known that the guild of Ikarria has been granted entry to the Stone Orchard. No one is to threaten or attack them. If I hear word of it, you will be banned from the shadow markets and the Stone Orchard."

He returned his attention to Erasmus and cocked his head, pressing the dagger deeper against the male's ear. Bystanders cowered as the shadow dealer screamed. Ronan snapped his head up as if just remembering there was a crowd surrounding them. He released the crying shadow dealer, who pressed a hand to the bleeding wound. Ronan blinked and shook his head before leaning down to where the male covered his half-hanging ear. "I will remove the rest in the meeting hall. Be grateful that I did not cut off your tongue."

He stepped back, cleaning the blade against the leathers on his chest. "Gather the leading shadow dealers; it looks like I will need to discuss some rules."

Zara's heart pounded. She almost didn't recognize the archangel before her. Cunning and merciless. Ronan met her gaze once more, as if he could feel the curiosity buzzing inside her head.

The steel in his eyes sharpened. "We leave tomorrow, Horizons."

The archangel turned away. Orion nodded at the mercenaries before following Ronan, hauling the shadow dealer with him. Zara watched as Ronan disappeared, her mouth agape.

She had witnessed the true leader of the Sombra Quarter.

THIRTY

The outer district of Soleira was teeming with its usual business, except for the flow of archangel soldiers marching behind the Ikarrian princess. Their boots thudded against the dirt, vibrating through the nerves in her limbs. Daria didn't know this but, through the eyes of the citizens and of the children staring up at her, she almost radiated gentle sunlight. The blush pink of her gown flowed with the autumn wind as the wings of the Elios soldiers unfurled behind her. She was a fairytale made real.

Daria's eyelashes fluttered as she pressed a finger against the ache in her temple. Today was not a day to wallow in pity, though the sleepless nights of the past few days did not help. The execution still lingered behind every blink of her eyes. She couldn't stop seeing those masks, gleaming with gems of red. Nor could she stop thinking of Zara, when her sister had gazed out at the realm, bloodstained and immoveable. A queen of death and ruin. The blank stare in Zara's eyes was not something Daria had ever witnessed. It was as if her sister had been a shell of herself; all that existed within her was Raziel's obsession with power.

Ares Valdemar was taut with tension beside her. His hardened gaze scanned every corner and pathway of the city. The poor citizens cowered back whenever those violet eyes crossed theirs.

He angled his head toward her, never removing his gaze from the road ahead of them. "I was informed that the princess of Ikarria had created a campaign to help the outer district, but I was not told what exactly. Care to explain, or do you still intend to keep me in the dark?"

Daria gave her bodyguard a sidelong glance. His arm brushed against hers as they walked, and she was reminded of how he had leaned closer during the execution. He had noticed her discomfort and offered himself as support. Even before then, he had tried to deter her from attending. Duty aside, the vampire probably didn't know how much those simple acts had helped her. She felt her heart squeeze at that.

For the past two weeks, they had fallen into a comfortable normalcy. They ate every meal together and explored the inner district. While she tended to her official duties, he would wait for her, sometimes in the same room of her meetings, or even sit right next to her. It was only at night where Ares would disappear. Though he never shared where he went, Daria always knew when he was gone.

His presence was different from the others. A coldness that didn't bite but soothed.

Daria gave her bodyguard a knowing smile. "Do you not like surprises, general?"

Ares finally met her gaze. He searched her expression as if trying to read behind her smirk. "I am not particularly fond of them. Are you trying to surprise me, princess?"

She faced the street ahead, leading him and the squadron of archangel soldiers deeper into the outer district. "I specifically requested that no one breathe a word of today's initiative to you."

He faltered a step. It was almost comical to see the general of war taken aback. Daria stifled a giggle and gestured to the soldiers behind them. "Take a look, Ares. You must have noticed what Raziel's archangels are carrying."

Daria knew what Ares would see. Every soldier held either baskets or crates, filled with blankets, food, and jugs of water. What he may not have been able to see were the supply of blood bags packed within.

"I suspected it was to be some sort of philanthropic venture," Ares muttered.

They turned to a familiar road, but Ares was too distracted to notice where they were heading. She smacked her bodyguard's arm. "Pay attention, general. Have you caught on to what we are doing today?"

Ares shut his mouth when he saw the blood bank, the same facility they had seen during Daria's first visit to the outer district. Waiting out front was Maira with a few other patrons dressed in white and a massive crowd of humans behind them.

Daria chuckled at the general of war's confused look. "The deity is here," he said.

She bumped her shoulder against his. "Do you see those individuals dressed in white? They are healers from the castle."

The skin between his brows pinched and realization slowly dawned over his expression. His eyes softened as he looked down at her. "The blood bank is being helped."

The vulnerability in the vampire's gaze took her by surprise. She knew that the blood banks were in dire need of additional support and that Ares had been angry at the neglect. But by the way his soul seemed to crack, allowing her to peer into a quiet ache inside him, she saw just how much this affected him.

She couldn't look away from him. "Not just this one. All the blood donating houses within the outer district will receive support from the castle, courtesy of the Council. They helped make this all happen."

Ares shook his head slowly, his lips parting. He was about to speak when Maira strutted toward them.

"Princess Calderón, it is time to see your efforts come to fruition."

The deity wore a dark gray skirt that fell to her ankles and a white-sleeved blouse. Her black hair was plaited, dirt dotting her freckled cheekbones. Maira was almost unrecognizable outside the castle, among the streets and citizens.

Daria had spent many evenings with the deity preparing for this initiative. Ever since she had proposed the idea to Maira during the coliseum games, they had thrown themselves into arranging the logistics. They presented their plan to the Council in order to receive access to the supplies.

The princess had been on edge with nerves when she approached the powerful group of deities. Their glowing eyes pinned on her had her palms coated with sweat. Daria mustered all her courage and pushed her fear down, down, down. She was an ambassador of Ikarria, but that didn't mean she wouldn't advocate for those within another city.

And what a relief it was to see how impressed the Council was with her agenda. So much so, they even offered their personal healers to assist.

Daria shook her head. "*Our* efforts, Maira. It was by your guidance that we were able to coordinate this endeavor."

The deity smiled and jerked her chin toward the waiting crowd. "Shall we?"

Daria glanced back at Ares before following. He bowed his head, eyes on her. There was a gentle lift to his lips, and his expression was softer than she'd ever noticed before. She couldn't help but feel a warmth spread through her chest. It distracted her from the previous ache that had been present since the day of the execution.

No, she couldn't think about that pain now.

The princess faced the multitude of citizens. Their faces were a mix of wonder and apprehension, and she couldn't blame them. With the ongoing hunting season, their streets were coated in violence every day.

Maira raised a hand and silence followed, allowing the deity's soft voice to be heard across the dirt-paved road. "Thank you all for coming. I am glad to see that word has spread in the short time we have prepared to visit your neighborhood. For those of you who may not be aware of what we are doing this day, I will explain. Your local blood banks have been working all hours of the day and night in ensuring your donations are treated healthily and compensated well. However, the lack of funds and support have shown a deterioration in the blood banks' success."

Daria could feel Ares's suspicious gaze on her. Yes, her bodyguard had seen her working all this time, but he had been either too oblivious or had not been bothered enough to ask what she had been preparing for. She suspected it was the latter. Ares had made it clear that he did not care for the ways of politics.

The deity gestured with an open hand toward Daria. "Princess Daria, ambassador of Ikarria, saw this travesty and reported it to the Council. They have ordered for additional staff and healers to help with your blood banks, including with the delivery of food, water, and supplies. The Council has extended their deepest apologies in not seeing this issue sooner. They are grateful for the partnership that Ikarria's ambassador has offered and intend to monitor the blood banks from here on."

Applause rose in a wave. The soldiers began to meander about the humans, who lined up to wait their turn to donate, and offered the supplies they held. The castle's healers went to aid the blood bank's staff, and the building quickly grew packed with business. Daria and Maira managed the entire operation, diving in to help whenever needed. The princess also noticed Ares joining the soldiers in handing out the blood bags, specifically to the poorer vampires waiting for their meal.

Come late afternoon, Daria's back ached from being hunched at the front desk for hours. She had volunteered to take position there alongside the other staff to address the humans who entered the building.

She felt a presence loom over her, the scent of roses surrounding her. "Princess."

Daria wiped her brow, turning to see Ares with a mug of water in hand. His long hair had been pulled back with a band, revealing more of his sharp features. She found herself staring longer than intended, only to realize she wasn't the only one. The humans—both men and women—gaped at the tall vampire.

Ares must've been aware of the eyes on him but didn't acknowledge them as he offered the drink to her. "Come with me. You need to rest."

She nodded, chugging the water. They stepped outside, through the green chipped door, and went to linger in the shade between the buildings. Archangel soldiers still wandered the streets with crates and baskets, offering aid to anyone who passed.

Daria felt her knees shake from standing so long. She pressed her back against the wall and slid down. A sigh left her dried lips. "Thank you, I didn't realize how much time had passed."

Ares went to sit beside her, stretching out his long legs. She noticed his empty hands. "Do you not need to feed as well? Come to think of it, I've never seen you eat anything."

The vampire snorted. "Don't fret, princess. I am well fed."

Daria sipped on her water. It was common for vampires, especially the wealthier ones, to have blood sources for skin-on-skin feeding, so long as it was consensual. She imagined it wasn't difficult for someone like Ares to have a willing blood source. He must have had flocks of offerings.

A comfortable silence slipped between them as they rested. Children shouted and laughed in the streets, darting between the winged soldiers.

Ares watched as some of the archangels played along with them. "I see what you did by bringing them here instead of the vampire soldiers."

Daria's eyes softened seeing the interaction on the street. "I thought it would be better received to have the archangels here. They don't conduct the rousts that the vampires do." She faced him, offering a sad smile. "Though, from what I understand, those acts are not of your command."

The vampire flinched at that. "No, they are not, but I am indebted to King Matías. Whatever he asks of me, I will do."

Daria shifted her body toward him. "How did you become his general of war?"

Ares snapped his mouth shut, his gaze downcast. She was tempted to take back what she had asked, thinking he wouldn't answer, until his eyes slid up to hers. His lips parted and closed, as if he couldn't find the words.

"I used to live in the slums of Adrastea," he eventually said. "For most of my life, I stole to make ends meet. Blood bags, blankets—anything I needed to survive, I took. One day, I was caught trying to steal from the local soldiers and they took me to the vampire king."

Daria gaped. "You attacked soldiers with *fangs*. Explain your logic there."

"I have fangs too, princess." He scoffed and showed a flash of the culprits. "But yes, it was stupid of me to do that. Apparently, King Matías liked that I had the gall to steal from his forces, and I was recruited."

"So, he took you away from the slums and now you live a life where you never have to worry whether you will go hungry."

Ares rested his head against the wall. His throat bobbed. "Yes."

She placed the cup on the ground and pulled her knees up to her chest. "That is incredible, what you have managed to accomplish."

His eyes darkened, but Daria caught the flash of pain there. "No," Ares growled. "What's incredible is the work *you've* done here."

She brushed him off. "It was the Council's doing. They were the ones with the resources, I am simply the courier."

Ares searched her face as he had before, that softness returning. "No. This is all because of you, Daria Calderón. I was . . . wrong about you. I thought you were like every other unfeeling politician and royal. But in the short time you've been here, you have accomplished more than the other diplomats."

Daria felt her cheeks heat. Her chest swelled with pride and a gratitude that she had been able to do something worthwhile.

She couldn't find the words, not as Ares continued to gaze at her. "Your eyes burn red gold . . . they're beautiful."

Daria looked down, letting her hair fall over her shoulder. "You're being nice, general. It's unsettling."

Ares chuckled, deep and gentle. She thought the sound suited him.

Gasps from the street yanked on Daria's attention. Flashes of bronze hurtled over the rooftops, wine-red cloaks banners of bloodshed under the blazing sun. It was a guild, roaming the outer districts, most likely in search of their marks. By the emblem of a rose sitting in the center of crossed eucalyptus strands, Daria knew it was Adrastea's mercenaries.

The color drained from her face. The memory of flesh being ripped apart, of blood spilling onto the execution platform, of her sister, whose light had been snuffed out, warred in her mind. The smell of death and fear returned to her with a vengeance. Her hands curled into fists, and she exhaled a shaky breath.

Her bodyguard missed nothing. Ares was crouched before her, his large body shielding her from the memory.

"Breathe in through your nostrils, princess," he coaxed. "Hold and release slowly."

Daria did as he commanded. Eventually the tightness in her chest eased, and she relaxed her hands.

Ares observed her, his brows slashing down into a frown. "It's the execution, isn't it? I suspected that you were struggling with what happened, but you have been so busy these past weeks, I thought you were managing." He swore under his breath. "I'm sorry, I should've heeded my suspicions."

Daria shook her head, waving a trembling hand. "I needed to toughen myself regardless. I have been sheltered for so long, I did not know the horrific realities of life. You were right."

The general of Adrastea looked pained. He tilted his head down, forcing her to meet his gaze. "I was stupid for saying that, princess. While it is true that reality may be difficult to face, and it may be good to understand it better, the world needs more light. And you, Daria Calderón, are that light. One that brings warmth and healing. Your heart is pure, princess."

Ares gave her a soft smile. The sight was enrapturing, as when the sun gilded the ocean, the trees, and the mountains. "Do not let anyone or anything take that away from you. Not even me."

THIRTY-ONE

A s soon as their satchels and waterskins were filled, the Ikarrian guild saddled their stallions and galloped into the burning sun. Ronan flew overhead, a dart of shadow beneath the clouds.

He had been silent since the debacle with the shadow dealers. Zara wasn't sure what the Sombra leader had said to his followers, but the guild had left the Stone Orchard without trouble. It took nearly a week to reach Huerta, the first abandoned town. They spent the nights within the wilderness, passing through rivers and groves to reach the Estrella Territories. While the guild chatted over the fire in the evening, Ronan kept to himself most nights.

Zara knew something was wrong the moment they reached Huerta. The fine hairs on her arms rose at the subtle brush to her senses that had her fighting back a shiver. There was little to nothing within the homes and shops; the painted buildings were either broken or plowed through and dried blood mingled with the debris. Raiders had passed through the place as well, it seemed.

The guild split ways, each taking a different path into town. They would investigate the remains of Huerta and find any information on the ethereal beings. Pieces of pottery and glass crunched underneath Zara's boots. There was a whisper of energy, and it wasn't of darkness. No, the walls shuddered with agony, the shattered stone and wood echoing the cries of those who had lived here. This place had been violated, and the ether of the Continent mourned.

Her power trembled inside her, as if shying away from the desolation. Her hands swept over a dusted wall, the tendrils of energy following her touch. She saw cracks within the stone and a clean slash across the surface.

Ronan drew up behind her. She could always tell it was him with how the air seemed to hum in his presence. The taste of lightning on her tongue. And the scent of jasmine—she could catch it whenever he drifted close.

Zara pointed at the cut in the wall. "That was made by the same spear the ethereal being with the horns was holding. I recognize the pattern, it's clean and thorough. You can see how deep it goes, and then there is a splatter of blood towards the end here. Whoever it was after, it managed to catch them."

Ronan's eyes widened slightly. "Shit. I didn't notice this before."

She cupped her chin, frowning. "Let's continue and see if we can find anything useful."

His brow furrowed as he stared at the gashes on the wall. "Why? What is the purpose of all this?"

Zara waded through the debris, the sun beaming upon her and the collar of her fighting leathers beginning to dampen. "What did you do with the woman's body? The first possessed mortal you encountered?"

Ronan flanked her and started lifting slabs of stone. Dust coated his tanned cheekbones, the black strands of his hair sticking to his sweat-beaded skin.

The wrinkle between his brows hadn't left. "I buried her. She rests within the grounds of the building I found her in."

His voice had turned solemn. As if he hated what had happened to the human, and that he had been forced to kill her.

Zara feared something might be wrong with her. She saw this turmoil, this destruction, and her heart didn't ache. A deadly quiet settled within her, her fingers slowly curling into fists. The most prominent feeling that claimed every tendril of her being was *anger*.

Anger for the innocents who needlessly suffered, anger for the mere fact that her mercenaries were brought into this, anger that they even had to consider this deal for a meager chance at freedom, anger at the great possibility that their efforts would be in vain . . .

Just anger.

For everything.

It festered and gnawed at her soul.

Ronan, however, seemed . . . softer, despite what the scars and black leathers tried to say. Unlike her. Zara almost envied it.

She stopped in her tracks. She didn't trust it.

The mercenary tugged on the heartless being that made the Rogue for the words to come out of her gritted teeth. "Dig out the body."

Ronan's steps halted. She expected to hear poison lace his words, absolute disgust for what she had said.

"Why?" he asked. Instead, he sounded empty, and she wasn't sure if that was any better.

Zara faced him. They stood in the midst of a ruined town, on opposing sides of a silent battlefield.

"We may be able to gather some information from the remains." She gave him a look as if he'd asked a ridiculous question. Because he had. Then she scowled. "Though I do have a question for you."

Ronan watched her carefully. There was no fear or even curiosity in his storm-gray stare.

"Oh good," he drawled, his usual arrogance slipping in, and she could've sworn she felt a vein at her temple twitch. "Feel free to share."

"Why would an archangel, a traitor to the High Throne and the godsforsaken Continent, spend his time *helping* others?" Zara let out a low, bitter laugh. "I've seen the way you handled that shadow dealer in your precious city. You may have fooled your citizens into believing you care about them, but they are a means to an end for you. Their support results in thriving shadow markets which in turn make you more powerful."

Ronan's jaw ticced and she knew she had hit her mark. His black wings snapped open, cracking the air with a force that whipped at her eyes. And suddenly the archangel was inches away from her. The energy around his presence pushed against hers. Nipping and nudging.

Sweat began to form against her skin. What she felt was his power, she could tell that much. But it was a distant roar that reached for her but would never touch her. Zara wondered what that was about.

Flashes of silver flickered in his eyes. "You are free to challenge my standing, I do not blame you. But do not take me as some soulless bastard using the lives of others to gain power. I am not like your High King."

His expression was too raw—a clash of rage, annoyance, and pity. And something else that was so—so broken. Zara couldn't make much of it, and she flinched at the weight of his stare.

"That *soulless bastard* is who I serve," she bit out, looking away. "And I represent him. Though, most of the Continent would argue against your view of Raziel."

Ronan blinked, the emotions in his face edging away. "Everyone has different opinions on their rulers, and I have mine. But," he leaned toward her. "You are not as devoted to the High King as you want to appear. I came to you with that proposition prepared to kill you if it turned out you had undying loyalty to him." He smirked. "I'm glad I didn't have to resort to that. Truth be told, I'd say you fear the High King more than you hate him."

This time it was Zara's turn to clench her jaw. "I do not *fear* him."

He searched her eyes. "Little wolf, I see the reason for your anger. You were reminded of everything that's at stake in siding with me. Spar with me, if you must, but know that I will not hold back either."

Ronan brushed past her, wings whispering at her ear. Zara

stared at the empty space he had been standing in. He truly did see right through her. "I am putting my guild's life in jeopardy." Her lips trembled, but her voice remained steady and sharp as a blade. "You better meet your end of the bargain."

She looked around to see Ronan had half turned to face her, a snarl on the verge of his teeth. "I said I would, didn't I?" The archangel stared at her a moment longer before storming away, his voice a rumble against the ground and sky. "Are you coming or not? You're going to help me dig."

Zara's gloves were caked with dirt, her fingers underneath tender to the touch. She swept back the strands of her long hair, silently cursing herself for not tying it back earlier. Ronan sat on a fallen beam of wood. The archangel leaned forward with his elbows on his knees and bowed his head as he caught his breath.

The corpse had nearly been chewed to the bone. Nature had had its way with the body, leaving behind decayed tissue. Zara had to fight the guilt for ripping this woman from her rest.

She and the archangel had ignored each other for the most part as they dug, allowing their frustration and irritation to die off with every claw of dirt.

Ronan drank from his waterskin, droplets trickling down his inked throat. He suddenly popped the top off and dunked a splash of water over his head. The archangel whipped his hair back up before extending his drink to her.

Zara wrinkled her nose and his lips twitched in amusement. "It's not poison, little wolf."

Her eyes narrowed. "Stop calling me that."

Before Ronan could respond, Axar emerged from another building, whistling. His braids were pulled back, tied into a knot on the back of his head. He rolled his shoulders, muscles flexing over his tattooed body.

The shifter's nostrils flared. "Gods, it reeks."

Zara gave him a dry look and pointed at the body. "I am glad you are here. This is the first possessed mortal Ronan saw. Can you sense anything . . . unnatural from her?"

Axar sank to his haunches, his brow furrowed as he inspected the body. He was careful when peeling some of the torn clothing from the corpse. Zara crouched on his other side, observing the remains as well.

"There is an odd smell beneath the decay and rot," Axar said. "Your senses may not catch it, but a shifter can. It wasn't obvious at first, though now that I've caught the scent I can't focus on anything else. It is stronger than death. Like burning metal, steaming forges and falling ash."

Ronan gazed at the corpse, shadows hiding his emotions. "What you're describing sounds an awful lot like war."

Zara continued to inspect the body. It was difficult to identify anything at this point. She whispered an apology to the woman's body as she lifted another flap of chewed fabric.

She sucked in a breath, her stomach knotting in disgust. "Look, she was also bitten."

On the body's torso were teeth marks—non-human. Like tiny, sharp daggers. Zara felt nothing but confusion.

Axar hummed a sound. "Do you think this bite caused whatever mania that befell her?"

Ronan grunted, shaking his damp hair. "I don't think so. Her eyes glowed blue, the same as you witnessed in the others. It must be ether. You saw how the mortals acted in Adira—they were feral— the bite could've happened after the woman was possessed."

Zara recalled how the mortals had tried to bite her as well. Their teeth had sharpened, and some looked to be made of metal. Her skin chilled at the thought.

"This all tells me it *was* the work of a powerful ether and not something of this world," Ronan continued, a dreary look falling over his face. "Remnants of ether always stay with the body, even if the soul has long left it. This must be an ancient and angry form of power, and wherever this ether came from is certainly not our friend."

"I'd imagine so, seeing as we encountered those three murderous beings," Zara muttered.

Axar added, "With deadly weapons and crowns of silver."

Her stomach sank. "The return of the Three Sun Gods," she murmured.

The shifter snorted. "Stop with that nonsense, Zara. You sound like those acolytes."

She rolled her eyes, noticing Ronan's jaw tighten.

"There's something that has been bothering me," he said. "It is about the weapons the creatures were holding. I didn't get a good look at the steel, but their make did not look like something any of our realms could create."

"What does that mean?" Axar rumbled.

The archangel's eyes flashed, but he looked away. "Nothing. Never mind, I'm just spewing thoughts."

Zara frowned but said nothing.

Whispers of energy swept around her, sinking into her bones with a coldness that was almost paralyzing. She couldn't shake off the sense of unease. Ronan seemed well-versed in the ways of ether, and she was tempted to ask how he had come to know so much.

The sun was lowering over the west, bruising the sky in shades of dark orange and blue. They would have to leave soon and make camp somewhere in the blasted Territories. Zara would rather not stay in Huerta any longer than they needed to.

Hakim and Eshe appeared from the dying light, cloaks waving in the sunset. Their weapons were banners of their presence. Their gloves and faces were smeared with dirt and dust. They must have been searching through many of the abandoned homes.

The head of the guild caught sight of the corpse and, when Zara informed them of their findings, his eyes widened.

"She is the only one in this town, then," Hakim said. "We found nothing else here, except more evidence of the attack. Eshe and I tried to follow the tracks out of town."

Eshe wiped her hands on her leathers, puffs of dirt exploding into the air. "According to the map, there is another city north of here. The tracks seem to lead to it."

Zara looked back down at the woman's decaying body. "Then I suppose that is where we go next."

She was not one to pray to the gods and goddesses, but she whispered another apology and a hope that the woman had found peace. Zara pushed herself upright, feeling the wind brush through her tangled hair.

Ronan watched her. He gave her a look that said, *I see you. You care.*

Zara cleared her throat and addressed the others. "Can we *please* leave this place?"

THIRTY-TWO

Ronan Menodora braced his hands against the edge of the basin in his rented room. The lodge he and the others had found was tucked within a small town north of Huerta. It was night by the time they arrived. Thank the fucking Suns and Stars that he wouldn't have to sleep with the weeds again.

The city was untouched. If the residents had heard of Huerta's demise, he and the mercenaries intended to find out after they had freshened up.

Nothing held any significance to him in that moment as the memories came rushing back to him. It always happened when he was alone. Those familiar screams echoed from the abyss, wrenching out a hand and plunging him into darkness. The cries of his dying family grew louder, piercing through him.

He remembered the rush of power running in torrents through his body as it ripped free, violating him of his autonomy. The bright ether that had disobeyed him, devouring and destroying everything and everyone—

Ronan bit his lip, holding back his own cry of anguish until he tasted copper on his tongue. He was growing tired of this constant torture, but the pain never left him alone.

The granite was cool underneath the pads of his fingers. Calluses scraped the surface. His head was bowed as he poured water over himself. Thin streams of ice ran through his hair, sending chills down his spine. He aimlessly placed the brown ceramic jug down, but it fell over the counter's edge, shattering beside his feet. Ronan gritted his teeth, breathing heavily as he overcame another wave of memories.

Fuck. Had the War truly destroyed him? Would he ever be the same archangel that he once was? The one who never tasted fear. Who would recklessly dive into danger in the hopes of becoming stronger.

He lifted his gaze to the plated mirror: silver eyes that were void of light; skin that had sunken slightly around his cheeks, making them sharper than usual.

Ronan couldn't recognize himself anymore.

Tattoos adorned his bare chest. Etchings of vines weaved with jasmine flowers stretched down his arms to his fingers. Scars rested underneath the ink. He was glad the power of ether could not remove such wounds.

His gray eyes flicked to his lips, to the jagged line across the left corner of his mouth. Yes, scars were whispers of stories.

Power purred beneath his skin; he felt it ripple like a pebble falling into a pool of water. Unfortunate that it would never see the light of day. His fingers brushed the band of ink that wrapped around his left bicep.

The ether that he had been born with, constrained within the tattoo. A chain that he placed on himself. Ronan didn't regret the decision.

He pushed off the basin, walking into the empty room. If he had been back home, his private quarters would have had heaps of armor, fighting leathers, and weapons shoved in a corner or strewn about his desk. Ronan did not have much use for such things nowadays. The warrior within him had died all those years ago. He was a criminal, leading illegal trade. That was his legacy now.

Except when he had raised a blade against the Horizon had he felt that old flame, that long lost love for battle stir to life. His lips twitched, almost into a smile. There had been a flicker of excitement then.

Ronan pushed open the door of his room, sauntering along the dimly lit hall and down the stairs, where warm air and chatter awaited below.

The bowl of potatoes and beef stew had warmed Ronan's belly. He wiped his mouth clean, eyes darting across the busy lodge. There were many travelers passing through, but it seemed the residents of this city dined here as well. It was simple, with a myriad of round and long tables, garlands hanging across the wooden beams overhead and bushels of onions and mistletoe strung across the brown walls behind the lodge's bar. The host was serving drinks to cheery men and women.

He caught sight of the mercenaries within the dining place. Eshe and Axar had paired together while Hakim mingled on his own. They didn't have their Ikarrian armor on, wearing instead simple and less noticeable fighting leathers. It was an opportunity to see if anyone had heard about the otherworldly creatures.

Someone pulled out the empty chair at his table and his gaze landed on piercing green eyes.

Ronan swirled the spoon in his empty bowl. "I think you are lost. The bar is behind you."

"I'm afraid the joke is on you." Zara lifted two mugs of ale into view. He hadn't noticed her carrying them. Smug victory danced across her face. "I've brought the bar here. As a truce."

He eyed the mug and cursed under his breath as he took it. The drink was enjoyable enough, but he guzzled it down. Zara seemed amused and Ronan rolled his eyes.

"Thank you," he grumbled. "I needed it."

She chuckled, draping an arm across the back of her chair. "I figured as much. You should thank Hakim. It was his idea that I come to you and *try to get along.*"

She mimicked the head of the guild's deep voice and Ronan smirked. They had been bickering all the way to this city. Pure entertainment for the other mercenaries, at his and Zara's expense.

The Horizon before him had cleaned herself of the muck and grime. Her dark brown hair curled, smelling of soap and sweet orange—he didn't recall having this fragrance as an option in his room. The tunic and trousers beneath her plain leather garb were form-fitting but she wore her cloak, hiding most of her outfit from view.

Zara took a sip of the ale and her lips twisted in disgust. "Gods, save me. They didn't have wine. Can you believe that?"

"The horror," Ronan said dryly. He jerked his chin to where the other mercenaries were scattered. "Have you gathered any information on the possessed creatures?"

She cocked her head, gaze going distant. "Not yet."

Ronan was puzzled. "What are you doing?"

"Were you so busy stuffing your face with food that you didn't notice the merchants at the table beside you?" She muttered.

He glanced around to see a pair of males, two elves, amid a lively conversation.

"—Not that these new trade routes are doing us any good. The problem with the barren soil hasn't gotten better and there is a lot less activity in the marketplace—"

Zara straightened and waved at them.

"Excuse me, I'm sorry to intrude." Her voice was much softer than Ronan had ever heard it. He blinked to hide his shock.

The elves turned, their lips peeling into a growl at the interruption. When they saw Zara—was she batting her eyelashes?—their faces softened. Typical male behavior. The mercenary knew what she was doing; Ronan was impressed.

Her mouth parted and, under the candlelight, he noticed a light gloss over her lips. "Both of you seem the types to have ventured to many parts of the Continent, have you not?"

One elven male nodded, practically puffing out his chest. "We have traveled from Ikarria, all over the Estrella Territories, and to Elios."

She beamed and reached over to rest her hand over Ronan's. He stilled at the touch, fighting the urge to look at her.

"How wonderful," she said. "My betrothed and I are heading to

Elios. I wish to visit several parts of the Territories before we reach Soleira. Have you been to Huerta? I've heard it is such a lively place for first-time travelers."

Clever, little wolf. Ronan stifled a smirk.

The elves shared a look with each other. The second male answered, "It may not be good for you to head there, miss. Huerta is no longer there."

She made a worried face. "How come?"

"The entire town was ransacked by beasts. We haven't been to see it, but our associates have. Apparently, others in our trade have spotted groups of people marching through the plains."

Ronan shifted in his seat. "Was it the people of Huerta moving to another city?"

The elves looked at him as if just realizing he had been sitting there all along. The first male responded, his face ashen. "We aren't sure. Our friends saw them from a distance but . . . there were three *figures* with them. Sadly, my associates couldn't tell who they were, but they wore crowns of fire. Odd, isn't it? Maybe they are part of some cult."

The second male shook his head. "I wouldn't be surprised. The most concerning part is that they had people bound, hauling them in carts.

Ronan couldn't help his scowl. "And this wasn't reported."

The elf snorted. "No offense, archangel. You may be able to handle yourself in the wild, but we are lowly merchants. We will avoid any sort of trouble at all costs, our associates included."

Ronan supposed he couldn't blame them. They wouldn't have been able to do much. A part of himself was relieved that it hadn't been shared with officials yet. Word may be spreading, but any delays were worth it.

Zara sighed. "A mystery, indeed. Thank you for your time, gentlemen."

They nodded, preparing to leave their table. The first elf glanced at her again. Zara stiffened the longer the male stared, and Ronan felt his body tense, ready if the elf decided to try anything against her.

Though he had a feeling she would be more than happy to skin any potential attacker herself.

When the elf finally looked away, her shoulders loosened. "I thought he recognized me."

Her voice had fallen so quiet he knew it was intended only for his ears. The skin between Ronan's brows pinched as she gestured to her apparel. "By me, I mean the Rogue."

Ronan nodded. He felt like he should've known that. The Rogue had killed many from Soleira over the years, as well as throughout the Estrella Territories, as those lands were provinces of Elios. There was always the risk she would be recognized by many who feared the infamous Rogue. He was losing his sharp edge. Perhaps it was because of the latest assault of his memories, leaving him more weak than usual. At least that was what he told himself.

He mulled over what the merchants had said. "It sounds like the creatures have also captured people."

The statement sounded more like a question. Zara tapped a nail against the table's surface. "Bound people in carts and what not, yes. But why? The possessed people we encountered didn't have any *normal* mortals among them."

Ronan felt his body tighten with stress. "There are probably more of these monsters than we suspect."

"That's a terrifying thought."

Ronan looked at his hand where Zara had touched him earlier. His mouth quirked to the side. "So . . . Betrothed?"

She gave him a dry look. "It was the best I could come up with."

The archangel dug out a gold mark and slid it across the table to her. He smiled even wider. "To treat yourself, my darling. I must be able to spoil my future wife."

Zara's jaw dropped in shock before she placed a hand over her mouth to smother her chuckle. Ronan had hoped for a full laugh, but it seemed he would have to wait a bit longer.

They stayed in silence, the sounds of the busy lodge taking over as people conversed and servers paced about.

Ronan looked at the mercenary again and decided to take his

chances. "May I ask how you came to be the Rogue? I've heard of you over the years, but I never knew who it was underneath the hood."

Zara took another gulp of her ale, her expression twisting. She wiped her mouth before scooting her chair back.

"I think we've done enough work tonight. I'm going to get some rest," she said, swiping the gold mark he had offered her. Zara lifted the coin as she turned her back to him. "And I will definitely be *treating* myself."

The Horizon walked away, and the archangel gazed at the two empty mugs. It had been a failed attempt to get to know the mercenary, but he didn't mind that.

He only wondered if he would be able to sleep tonight, or if the memories were waiting to haunt him.

THIRTY-THREE

Daria wished she could say that she had mastered the horror of the execution. It wasn't so much the stench of spilled blood that preyed upon her now, but the despair that had reverberated within Zara's eyes.

She was managing it, pushing through the bitter twist in her abdomen. It came in intervals that grew greater with every passing day.

Today, however, bitterness mixed with her defeat. Her gaze lingered on the latest letter she had drafted, Zara's name glaring at her. Daria had lost count of how many times she had sent requests to see her sister since arriving in Soleira.

How many had Zara answered? None.

Daria decided she would send one last letter. The sound of crinkling parchment rang in her ears as she scribbled on it.

It's not like Zara would answer, but she had to try.

A rumble sounded within her heart. A faint vibration, a tremor that spoke of flames and skies. In the center of Daria's mind she saw mountains, sharp as teeth, surrounding her. It was a brief image, one that she couldn't grasp before she was plunged into darkness. There, she saw the glow of an ember—it pulsed and flickered. Claws curled over the fire, a reptilian eye opening just beyond it.

Daria shook her head, bringing herself to the present. The ocean rolled gently in the distance, the skies painted gray with clouds. Soleira was loud today, the sound of its citizens buzzing in the air.

She placed a hand over her chest, feeling the steady beat of her heart. Yes, it was her ether reminding her of its presence. It wasn't something she could ever forget. Except that she had. For so long Daria had disregarded her fire-born power, never thinking to hone it. Had the audacity to believe she didn't need to.

That all changed when she saw Zara on that execution platform.

"May I ask you a question, princess?"

Daria glanced at Silas. He rested an arm across the stone ledge of the garden and was giving her a measured look. Ares had left her under his watch while he ventured to do gods knew what. Ever since the initiative with the blood banks, the court had been in a flurry of excitement. Daria had been pulled back and forth, meeting more and more royal staff members and other diplomats from across the Continent. The days had become so tiresome she barely found a moment to escape. Thankfully, she had received a respite today. Daria nodded at the vampire.

"You hail from the kingdom of dragons, do you not?"

She felt a pit in her stomach and the words came out strained. "I do."

Silas didn't seem to notice her discomfort. "What happened to Ikarria's dragons?"

Daria had heard the whispers that floated past her since her arrival in Soleira. She knew that her pater had felt them as well. He was the king of the *dragon-less* kingdom.

"Scholars have their theories," she responded, fiddling with the jewelry on her fingers. Her eyes landed on the obsidian ring around her thumb, a black glass that was very popular in her homeland. "Some believe that when the dragons made the pact with the Primordial Genesis a time limit was set for how long the beasts would walk amongst the mortals. Others say that the elves of long ago betrayed the trust of the dragons, severing the bonds they had forged for so many years."

Silas gazed at the capital. "Intriguing. I don't suppose your kingdom has ever thought of bringing them back?"

Daria kept her gaze down. Shame held her tongue. Oh gods, she hadn't even considered the possibility. Could the dragons return?

"We haven't tried," she said softly. "It's not possible."

The vampire sighed, keeping his gaze on the world before them. "That's too bad."

Nothing but sea winds and distant bird caws answered. Daria was grateful for it. Ikarria's history was something she knew well, but the dragons had always remained a mystery. There was evidence of the scaled beasts having been among her kingdom. Ridges in canyons, jagged spaces big enough for their talons to dig into. Even the castle walls had dragon marks if one knew where to look.

A sad part of her kingdom's heritage that would remain lost.

Several painful moments passed when that silky voice drifted to her. "Am I interrupting?"

Daria turned as Ares stepped through the soft ocean mist. The strands of his hair were damp, small droplets trickling down his cheekbones.

Those violet eyes landed on her. "Silas, you may take your leave."

The soldier cast a look at his general before he strutted back to the castle. Ares still watched Daria, scanning her face.

He must've seen something because he asked, "Was he bothering you?"

She waved him off. "No, he did nothing wrong. I am fine."

Ares took the place that Silas had stood in. The deep purple in his eyes deepened. "You will tell me if he does."

Daria found herself nodding her head. "Do you not trust your own soldiers?"

"I hardly ever give my trust to others, princess."

She noticed he was holding something behind his back. Ares didn't miss her gaze and cleared his throat. "I'm sorry for disappearing," he said. "I actually . . . have something for you."

Ares placed a box on the stone ledge. It was thin and long, made from dark wood with a string wrapped around it.

As she began to untie it, he cleared his throat again. The vampire general of war sounded *nervous*. "I know the past few weeks hurt you, as well as your family. I've seen how low you've been, persevering while you managed the work for the blood banks and other duties, and I thought this would lift your spirits."

The wooden top slipped off with ease and Daria gasped. Lying in soft white cloth was a dagger. The blade looked to be made of dark steel, its edges jagged and the handle crafted with obsidian. A ruby sat at the hilt's center.

Words couldn't describe how she felt. This was a weapon—*her* weapon. She had never thought that someone like her could ever own something like this. Daria was an academic at heart, always safely tucked among bookshelves and in study rooms. But this spoke to another side of her. A part where even a dragon could reside.

Ares was still rambling. "I know this gift will not rid you of the pain from the day of the execution. I just—"

"I love it," Daria said.

He closed his mouth and ran a broad hand over his cleanly shaven jaw. Behind his fingers, she thought she saw the hint of a smile.

She grasped the handle of the dagger and raised it to the sky. "I love it," she repeated. "This is the most thoughtful gift. Thank you."

Ares's eyes shined. "It is long overdue that you learn how to handle a weapon."

Daria gave him a dry look. "I know the basics."

"Sure," he drawled. That shine hadn't left him. His lips curled to reveal the tip of a fang. "Perhaps I could help you with some training. And maybe you can show me that ether of yours."

She had forgotten that he must have felt her power during the execution. How her emotions had nearly snapped her fire free. "You do not wield ether, how would you help?"

Ares arched a brow. "Blade combat and ether-wielding all contain the same foundation training. It begins with the balance of the mind and body. Ever since the execution, I figured it would be good for you to know some techniques in case I am not there."

Daria admired the weapon in the palm of her hands. Growing

up she hadn't followed the rigorous regimen her sister had. She had learned how to defend and apprehend an attacker, but it had been so long.

"Fine." She would use this opportunity to help carve the new path she was undertaking. Mark a place for herself to the world.

And it seemed the vampire general of Adrastea was not so heartless as others made him out to be.

The Summit was filled with formal proceedings every day. The kings and queens of the realms had made several appearances at court, but their time had been consumed by the High King and Council, so Daria had barely seen her pater.

Another feast was being held within the gardens and courtyards of the castle that night, and Daria was able to reunite with her pater for dinner. Idris had managed to establish more trade and partnerships for their realm, promising the other rulers that the ambassador of Ikarria would visit the other kingdoms of the Continent in his stead.

"Apparently, the deity Maira has spoken well of you at court," her pater said, lifting his goblet. Pride glistened in his amber-brown eyes. "The Council seems to be intrigued by Ikarria's heir now. It may be a good opportunity for you to delve even deeper on who they are."

Her heart beat with excitement, enough to bruise her ribs. The prospect was invigorating, and Daria felt she was at last contributing to her family and realm.

She tilted her head, drawing up her arm to rest her chin on her palm. "Wouldn't you be able to get closer to the deities than me?"

"The Council refrains from attending royal meetings. Though, they seemed quite interested in the effort you made in Soleira's outer district. They might be more amenable to having a conversation, at least."

She pursed her lips in thought, nodding. "The Council hasn't shared their long-term plans for the High Throne, but perhaps now I can find out more. Their support with the blood banks was enough to give me a sense of ease that they are prepared to make the necessary improvements for the people."

Her pater nodded as he refilled their goblets with white wine. "One victory at a time, firelight."

The moon rose and the drinks kept flowing. Idris had gone to converse with some fellow politicians and Daria was ready to retire for the night. Ares was off-duty, as he usually was in the evenings, but Silas was nowhere to be found. She could've escorted herself to her rooms but didn't want to risk upsetting any one of her vampire guards.

The soldiers were gathered toward the edges of the castle's cliff-side, half-hidden behind the hedges and statues surrounding it, so the princess started heading there.

Vampires, male and female, were splayed across stone and wooden benches, donned in either armor or simple tunics. Glasses were passed about, filled to the rim with red liquid. Daria didn't miss several humans strolling about the group.

There was a man sitting on a vampire's lap while he drank from his neck. A woman was sprawled on a table extending her arms to two others. Daria also didn't miss the sound of moaning and panting. Vampires and humans alike mingled in the corners, pressing their bodies against each other. One couple was writhing against a statue for all to see, sticking their tongues down each other's throats.

Daria felt a blush rush up her face. *Suns*, she needed to get a hold of herself.

She peeked round a hedge and found Ares leaning against the cliff's stone ledge. His back was to the moon-streaked sea as he faced the soldiers. A thin roll of parchment was tucked between his lips, its burning end a cherry red. The scent was so strong, a mix of copper and some sort of root, that Daria scrunched her nose.

A human woman swayed toward Ares and went to stand between his legs. She turned to press her back against his chest, his hand going to the slender column of her throat. The woman closed her eyes as if that touch was intoxicating enough.

Daria couldn't peel her eyes away. She wasn't sure why she kept watching, it was curiosity and a heady thrill wrapped together. She recalled what he had said, how he would normally spend his Summit celebrations.

Blood drinking. Fucking. Both.

Gods, he was allowed to enjoy himself when not shadowing her every move and she should give him his privacy—but she couldn't tear her gaze away.

Ares exhaled a puff of powdery red, holding the roll in his fingers and dragged his lips down the woman's neck, her lips parting as he grazed her with his teeth. When his fangs pierced through her skin, she arched her back with a moan.

Daria swallowed. The act seemed so intimate that it made her lower abdomen tighten. She didn't realize words had left her lips until it was too late. "Oh gods."

Ares's violet eyes snapped up to her and the world froze for a breath. All Daria saw was a gaze full of *hunger*, and it pinned her to the ground.

Daria bolted.

She barely made it to a breezeway when the general appeared in front of her. He had moved so quickly that a short gust of air blew through her hair, together with the scent of roses and the sea.

Ares wiped blood from the corner of his mouth with his thumb. "Were you enjoying the view, princess?"

Daria stumbled back and tucked her chin low. "Apologies. I solely wanted to return to my room."

He cocked his head, moonlight rippling over his dark hair. "I think you *were* enjoying yourself, perhaps it even made you want to give it a try."

She scowled. "Do not flatter yourself, vampire."

His eyes seemed to glimmer as he took a step forward. "Wouldn't dream of it."

Daria couldn't move. Her legs felt numb as she watched the vampire prowl toward her. He stopped just close enough that she could smell the ash and copper from his clothes.

Her eyes snagged on his parted lips—on his fangs. The image

of Ares and that woman flashed in her mind. How the human had arched against him, a look of ecstasy on her face as he bit her.

Daria's skin tingled and her throat bobbed. "I didn't mean to intrude, I only wanted to give you the courtesy of letting you know that I was leaving."

Ares loomed over her, his gaze assessing. "Where's Silas?"

"I am not sure. I did not see him."

Her guard's eyes dragged over her, from her form-fitting gown to her face. "That idiot can be reckless sometimes," he muttered.

Daria was unable to look away from his mouth. That heat returned to her lower abdomen. "I'm sure he can be."

Ares didn't step back, nor did he move any closer. But his presence was all-consuming. Dominance and danger all wrapped in one.

"Did you enjoy the feast?"

Daria dared to look up at his eyes. Only to find that he had also been staring at her lips. His gaze slid to hers.

She opened her mouth, struggling to find the words. "I did."

There were no words except their breaths, each one more shallow than the previous. It was getting harder for her to formulate a thought. "You can go back. I am sure she is waiting for you."

He didn't respond at first; the silence was agonizing.

His voice went lower. "I prefer where I am."

Daria wasn't sure what came over her. Whether it was the boldness of taking on the world outside of her home or if it was pure, outright stupidity.

She took another step toward him, and maybe she had imagined it, but it sounded like Ares sucked in a breath.

The general of Adrastea held her gaze and she was swept away. Galaxies of constellations and power roared behind those eyes, a cosmos of pain and savagery as well.

There was so much more to him than she'd first thought. She knew this in the core of her being, but she wouldn't voice it. Not now, at least.

For a moment, as quick as a comet splitting the night sky, she wondered what it would be like to *taste* him.

Ares seemed to drift closer. His lips mere inches from her own. So close that she could smell the rose and ocean from him. And the faint scent of the root he smoked. She liked it.

Daria's breathing grew uneven, wondering if she should close the space between them. Ares lifted a hand, and she wondered what he was going to do, if he would brush the hair from her face or trace a slender finger along her jaw.

The vampire general lowered his hand to her waist, pinched the fabric of her dress with two fingers and rubbed it. "Where is your dagger?" he asked roughly.

Daria blinked through the haze of . . . of whatever she was feeling. "In my—in my room."

A deep growl tumbled through his chest. "You must carry it with you at all times, especially in places like this, where vampires are feeding."

That was enough to clear her head. She hadn't thought about the possibility of vampire soldiers losing control. It was rare but did happen.

"Yes," she whispered.

Ares dropped his hand and turned around. "I will escort you to your room, princess."

Daria followed the general of Adrastea, fighting to regain her breath. Though none of it helped because she could've sworn that the last look Ares gave her before facing away was one of genuine affection.

And hunger.

THIRTY-FOUR

Ronan was impressed with the Ikarrian guild. He and the mercenaries had spent the following three days tracking the creatures. The mortals' prints were hardly visible, but the Horizons were able to read the land well enough to see that the possessed mortals were heading to the East.

On the third night, under a starry sky, Eshe began recounting a story of her travels with the vampire nomads—the fact that she had been of them was unsurprising to Ronan. The hooped jewelry that pierced the archer's ears held markings of the dune people. Not to mention the amulet—a single coin of copper tied to a string—that hung around Axar's neck. It was enough to tell him that the objects both originated from or held some connection to the East.

"The desert wraiths are pricks," Eshe said, flicking a speck of lint from her cloak. "Sometimes they would block our clan's path and the only way to pass them was to solve their riddles. Other times they served as a distraction so certain groups of the Kairos people could ambush you. The latter was the most popular option. And *that one* was a pup at the time, completely useless," she jabbed a finger to where Axar lay beside Zara. "But he would find ways to follow me and other fighting partners and cause chaos as we eradicated our attackers."

The shifter tsked. "I was only trying to help." His smile turned bright. "Though, you did have to save me a few times while fending off those bastards."

The buttons of his fighting leathers were unhooked and peeled back to reveal a sliver of his tattooed chest. He rested on his back with his arms crossed behind his head. There were times throughout the evening when he would glance up at the unsuspecting Zara Santos and whack her arm. She would hiss and thump him on the chest with a fist. Axar's teasing brought a light to her face, a shine that Ronan hadn't seen before.

"Careful," Hakim warned. He had been sitting on a stump, eyeing the two mercenaries with amusement.

Eshe merely shook her head, her lips on the verge of a smile.

Sibling behavior, Ronan realized. Seeing it made his heart deflate, as he mourned a fading memory. Suns Above, he was almost starting to forget how his younger brother looked.

Hael had been fourteen at the time of his death. Didn't he have gray eyes like him—like their father? No, he'd had darker eyes, almost black, the same as their mother's. But he had the same midnight hair as him, with deep blue wings . . .

Ronan held onto the weak image as tightly as he could.

The campfire flickered, sending sprays of embers toward the sky. The sight of the flames unnerved him. Had since he had started on this journey with the guild. But he held back the urge to cower at the sight of the fire. He wouldn't give into that deeply embedded pain. Not in front of the Horizons.

Zara suddenly stood up from her side.

"We are being called to the capital," she grumbled. Darkness shadowed her features, devouring the brightness she held moments before.

Ronan saw the soft glow emanating from her wrist. It didn't take long for the others to receive the same signal from their fyrebrands.

"Do you have to go back?" he asked.

Zara mindlessly fumbled with the bracer that covered the etherlaced ink. She flinched as if she had been scolded. The movement was quick, too fast for the other mercenaries to notice.

"We must," she muttered. "We have no choice."

His wings rustled as he shifted his seating position. "Do you truly not have a choice?"

She huffed, jaw tightening. "This was part of our agreement. You knew we had obligations to the High Throne while playing rebel with you."

"This entire journey is no game, Santos, we are not *playing*," Ronan gritted out. "It's just . . . when the fyrebrand called you back to the capital just now, you seemed sad."

The other guild members shared glances with one another while Zara's gaze sharpened.

"Would you be able to ignore this assignment, or even delay it?" He pressed.

Her hardened expression fractured, and he saw the sadness once more. The quiet plea for mercy and escape. Ronan's chest tightened.

Gods, he knew that look. Understood it.

"We have to obey, Ronan," she whispered, and he found himself leaning forward. "Otherwise our fyrebrands will punish us."

His eyes narrowed slightly. "I remember you mentioning something about this. How will it punish you?"

Zara sighed. "During the hunting season, if a Horizon were to ignore or delay an assignment set by the High King, then the bearer of the tattoo would eventually become sick. Sick to the point where they go mad, either killing themselves or having to be put down by their guild for their and others' safety. It is called the Reckoning."

Ronan cursed under his breath. "Does anyone else know? Has that ever happened before?"

"No, I imagine something as gruesome as this is not openly shared with the public. Raziel had to put some rules in place to ensure the hunting seasons were honored." Her gaze went distant. "The Reckoning hasn't happened in some years."

Zara glanced at Hakim. He folded his arms. "I remember when it first happened. A mercenary from the Adrastean guild started having frequent headaches that turned agonizing. He kept seeing figures, shadows walking about, ones that only he could see. The pain was so overwhelming he eventually drove himself off the edge of a balcony of the Elios temple."

Ronan grimaced. "How soon after an assignment is given would the Reckoning begin?"

Zara interjected, her long hair swaying. "There is no designated timeframe for when this would occur."

He mulled over this new discovery, wondering how long it would be before Zara Santos decided to forget their truce and drive her foreign blades through his chest.

The hunting season summoning the mercenaries would temporarily halt their tracking efforts, so Ronan decided he would return to the Stone Orchard.

His eyes went back to Zara, to the unseen shadows that enveloped her. That much they had in common.

Ronan heard the near-silent cries of his ether in the distance, lost to the veil of this mortal plane.

"So be it," he said, looking at every mercenary before him. "You have kept and will continue to keep your end of the deal. You serve your High King as I find a way to free you."

He was a male of his word. The truth of his promise seared through his veins. While the other Horizons murmured their thanks, Zara Santos simply looked away.

Ronan headed to his private quarters after yet another tiresome gathering with the shadow dealers.

Before Ronan had left for the Estrella Territories with the Ikarrian guild, he had threatened to skewer every shadow dealer who decided to go against him. They complied, though they began bombarding him with questions. Apparently, the other guilds of the Continent had been hunting down their shadow dealer subordinates, slaying them in the streets.

There was little Ronan could do about that. The hunting season was still in effect and, though he had made a pact with the Ikarrians, there was no guarantee for his followers' safety. If the guild were assigned one of his own shadow dealers, he would have to let nature run its course.

By some grace of the gods, Ronan had managed to appease them. Spewed weak promises of future stability and wealth while carefully avoiding the fact that the Ikarrian guild had already killed some of their own. Every leading shadow dealer at the table left the meeting chamber with the understanding that they oversaw their own trade's survival during the hunting season.

Ronan stepped out of the Stone Orchard's grand hall. The shards of the sky above bled into an orange red. The smell of cooked meat and burning wood began to thicken, indicating the rise of nightlife. He sighed, a heavy weight slowly sliding off his chest.

He made his way to the secret city but found himself looking to the Stone Orchard's entrance. A week had passed since the Ikarrian mercenaries left for the Elios temple. He was sure they were busy killing off many marks that were somehow connected to the Sombra Quarter.

Such was the agreement and sacrifice he made. He would have to lose some of his followers to save his people. All for his home.

Ronan wondered when the Horizons would come back. They never said. Something pulled within his chest.

The archangel let out a bitter chuckle, brushing back his hair with a tattooed hand. "Gods, my loneliness must be making me mad. I can't be *missing* the Horizons."

He continued forward, silently making plans to meet with Orion. There was a good chance his brother would be out drinking with his soldiers, ready to indulge in his vices. Maybe that was what Ronan needed to soothe whatever fucking ache had blossomed in his chest.

But he still looked to the Stone Orchard's entrance, as if the silhouettes of cloaks and blades would appear.

That night, nightmares eventually found him again, keeping him awake.

More screams. More fire. More chains.

The cool night air ran gentle fingers through the loose long-sleeved shirt he wore. He had barely had the strength to tie the waistline of his dark trousers before he made his way to the stone grove. Ronan inhaled and exhaled as he walked, every breath willing the images away from his mind. He saw his mother's eyes, heard his brother's screams, and his father's wings . . .

Relentless. Whenever he believed he had gained some control, the memories always managed to return to spite him. And he would carry this burden for the rest of his long, miserable life.

The trees bowed over him, shielding and comforting him. He walked and walked until he saw a lithe figure along the edges of the grove. He stopped.

Zara Santos stood underneath a thin strip of stone trees. The rest of the Ikarrian guild must have returned as well. Though right now, it was just her.

Her head was bowed, the hood of her cloak nearly covering her face. Dark gray scales clasped the curves of her hips and breasts.

And she was drenched in blood.

It wasn't hers. He could smell a mixture of different scents over her armor. Zara swayed slightly as she moved. And when she lifted her head—

He inhaled sharply, the sound almost silent. Bruises mottled her face, dried bits of blood coated the corner of her lips, and cuts ran over her brow. The usual spark of annoyance could not be found in those green eyes.

No sign of the witty woman he had been getting to know.

No, there was an emptiness there that was so viscerally familiar.

Zara didn't seem to notice that she was within the carved trees. Suns Above, she didn't seem to have noticed him either.

But he couldn't stop looking at the wounds on her face. At the hollowness of her expression.

Eventually, Zara resumed walking. Ronan could only watch as she disappeared down the slope into the city. She may have believed that everyone outside of her guild despised her, and he couldn't speak on behalf of those she had been assigned to kill.

He only knew that he didn't.

THIRTY-FIVE

Zara's ether had been aggravating her lately. She felt the threads of light uncoil from the abyss of her mind, as they pressed red hands against the surface, yearning for release. It was why it was so difficult for her to unscrew the ointment canister. The muscles in her fingers spasmed with every flicker of her power.

None of the mercenaries were in the villa when she woke—she suspected they were exploring the Stone Orchard. Not that she minded the silence. The morning light streamed through the wooden shutters, reflecting off the blue tiles that decorated the brown water mugs. The plate of breakfast Axar had left for her was now empty and discarded on the table. In the distance, she could hear the horses neighing in the corral as well as the rush of the river.

Zara hunched over the counter, her temple throbbing from last night's alcohol. And perhaps from the fight. The distractions helped to block out the marks she had killed. They had been smuggling supplies into the ships before she unleashed herself upon them. So much blood had pooled in the seawater.

There was a knock on the villa's door and the sound ricocheted in her head. Maybe if she ignored it, they would leave. Power crackled within her bones, causing her to drop the canister. She pressed her hands on the counter and bowed her head, groaning.

Another knock.

"What?" she snapped.

The door clicked open—gods, why hadn't the mercenaries locked it? Axar's doing, she suspected. A soft wave of jasmine reached her nose and that was enough to tighten the muscles on her back. Her fingers dug into the counter, the restless ether causing cracks to crawl out from where she touched the tiles.

Ronan had seen her last night. She had barely noticed him through the haze of her drunkenness and lingering bloodlust, but somehow the look of sadness, the etch of concern that knitted his brow—it had stayed with her longer than she liked.

She twisted around to face the archangel, a scowl already on her face. "Can a mercenary not be bothered on their day off?"

There was that smirk. "You're so cheerful in the morning."

Ronan stopped before the kitchen's entrance. He blinked as if seeing her for the first time since he'd entered.

He cleared his throat and gestured to the door. "We have some things we need to discuss."

The way he stared at her caused Zara to glance down at herself. Gone were the fighting leathers and armor from the day before, replaced by black form-fitting trousers with a white sleeveless top, a black leather corset strapped above it. Truth be told she felt naked when not wearing the guild's usual attire. Though that hadn't stopped her from hiding an array of daggers and throwing knives within the folds of her outfit.

She picked the canister back up. Her fingernails dug underneath the lid. "Why in the blazing Suns would I go out there? Also, where are the others?"

"I have introduced them to the Sombra Quarter's soldiers, at Hakim's request." He stepped into the kitchen area, eyes scanning her face. "Are you well?"

Her teeth clenched as another ripple of power shuddered through her fingertips, preventing her still from getting to the *damn* ointment.

"I'm perfectly fine," she gritted out.

Ronan sounded closer. "The bruises on your face say otherwise."

Zara cursed under her breath as the canister slipped from her fingers once more. A large hand swept underneath, catching it before it could clatter on the floor. Ronan popped the lid off, and the smell of mint and lemon curled into the air.

"Do you need help?" He asked.

That softness. She wanted to snatch the ointment from him and tend to herself. But her ether quaked, and she didn't trust herself as she tried to tamp her power down. She stayed silent.

Ronan took another step. "May I help you?"

She clenched her jaw and forced a stiff nod. The archangel said nothing as he scooped some of the ivory cream. Zara hissed as he began to dab it along her cheekbones.

"Sorry," he mumbled.

Ronan was surprisingly gentle. His thumb swept at the corner of her eyes, brows furrowed as he concentrated. She took the moment to observe the archangel. Her gaze gravitated to the tattoos on his neck, designs of vines and jasmine flowers that decorated his sun-kissed olive skin. He wore a dark sleeved shirt, its buttons open to reveal a muscular chest also covered in ink. She couldn't help but stare at that pale, jagged line over the left side of his lips. It gave him a harsh edge, betraying the true gentleness that rested beneath the surface, the care he had for his people. At least that was what she had experienced so far.

How very unlike what the leader of the Sombra Quarter was expected to be.

"Your elvish genes are healing you nicely." His deep voice pulled her from her thoughts. "I assume your ether helps in that regard as well."

Zara folded her arms while he continued to smear the cuts on her face with ointment. "Yes."

His lips twitched, fighting a playful smile. "Are you going to show me your power?"

"You have ether as well. Are *you* going to show *me*?"

He chuckled. "You have me there, little wolf. I can't show you all my cards now, can I?"

The pad of his finger drifted to the corner of her lips. She flinched at the sensitive wound there. At least, that was what she told herself. The touch was . . . foreign to her. The members of her guild had always cared for her, but this was an intimate gesture from someone who was not one of her own.

Ronan's breaths became shallow as if he realized how *affectionate* the act had become. Zara was prepared to rear back when she felt a shimmer of energy where the cream covered her skin.

She gasped. "What is that?"

He searched her eyes and his lips tilted up. The expression on his face was as if he discovered a tantalizing secret. "Did you buy this from the shadow market, Horizon?"

Zara scoffed but then groaned at the slight pull of pain. "Yes—purely out of convenience."

The archangel gave her a full-out grin. "The ointment is infused with ether. Don't ask me how that was done. The healers of the Continent are quite skilled in manipulating the otherworldly properties into available medicine."

She flinched at another vibrating touch from the cream. The sensation was uncomfortable at first but quickly dissolved into an iciness. One that soothed the dull pain behind every bruise and cut.

"This isn't available in the average market, is it?"

Ronan shook his head, putting the canister away. "No, it's a luxury if bought in the official business places. But through the Sombra Quarter, the average citizen could afford it."

"I thought shadow markets were supposed to overprice their resources," she said.

"Not us, Horizon." Ronan took a step back, a shadow flickering over his gaze. "Now tell me, how do the fighting rings help you?"

No one had ever asked her that question. Every year, her fellow mercenaries encouraged her to change her habits, but they hadn't delved deeper on it with her. They couldn't nor would they force her to stop. It had to be up to her. She knew she always had their love and their support to lean on.

But that step, that godforsaken leap, it had to be her own decision.

"They fill what I cannot," she replied. There were many meanings behind those words. "And I can't bring myself to stop."

Yet. It was the unsaid word that they both heard. Time. She needed time.

There was no judgment in Ronan's face, and he mercifully dropped the topic. "Is there anything else I can help you with, little wolf? Maybe you need help polishing your boots?"

Her eyes narrowed. "Why do you call me that?"

For a split second, his expression shifted. Gone was that teasing light replaced by an openness she wasn't sure she liked. "When I saw you in the fighting ring for the second time, you could've easily beaten down your opponent. He was hardly a fighter, but you *let* him land a hit. Why did you?"

Zara took a step back but hit a countertop. The fact that he had noticed such a trivial detail only told her that he had been watching her for some time.

Her jaw tightened. "I don't need to confide in you."

The steel in Ronan's eyes sharpened. "You may be part of a guild, but I suspect you fight many of your own battles." He pointed at his chest, the place over his heart, as he said, "You are resilient and cunning. Like a wolf."

It sounded awfully like a compliment. Zara shifted in place. Other than with her guild, for someone to say something like that about her—it had never happened before.

She kept her voice even. "Most people hate or fear me because of what I do."

"I am not most people." There was a bite to his words. Zara held his gaze. After a pause, he cocked his head. "So, are you going to tell me how long you've been a Horizon?"

It was far too easy to slam those walls back up. She felt herself withdraw and folded her arms. "We do not need to do this."

Ronan leaned back on his heels. "Do what exactly?"

Zara gestured between them. "This idle chatter. Our working relationship will function better without having to get to know one another."

"I disagree."

"Wonderful."

He chuckled, the sound like warm winds between the sands. "I believe our work will be more efficient if we are able to trust each other. Do not worry, Horizon. I am not trying to uncover your deepest, darkest secrets."

She arched her brow just as the ointment nuzzled into her skin, healing the remaining wounds. "Is that what you tell the shadow dealers who work for you? Trust is the basis of a good work relationship?"

Ronan began to pace about the kitchen, edging toward the main living space. "I do not trust the shadow dealers," he said. "It is why I made the risk to appeal to you and your guild."

"You would rather take your chances on the Horizons?"

The archangel stopped. His short hair fell on either side of his brows. "My shadow dealers are not true warriors—unlike you. So, yes. I'll take my chances with a Horizon."

Zara wasn't sure if she would call herself a warrior. That term belonged to those who served with honor. The others were more deserving of that.

She looked away, the word a mumble from her lips. "Rogue."

Ronan stilled. "What?"

A frustrated sigh escaped her. "I am not a warrior, I hardly qualify as a Horizon as it is. I am the Rogue."

He didn't respond immediately. The silence was almost torturous, but she refused to look his way, her gaze lowered to her feet. She thought she would hear a flurry of pretty words that wouldn't truly reassure her or change the position she was in.

Instead he said, "Is that why people fear and hate you?"

That was a stupid question. One that she didn't need to answer, though she found herself saying the words aloud. "They see me as their villain because it's easy to. They do not care to see the true creators of the monster before them."

The silence made her look at Ronan. He slowly shook his head. "You are surviving in chaos. You could've let it destroy you, but here you are, being made from the ashes."

Her heart clenched at the words, and she found herself giving a half-hearted smirk. "Poetic."

The archangel smiled and beckoned with his head. "Now that I *saved* you this morning, will you join me?"

Zara frowned, ready to fire some witty retort, but thought better of it. "Thank you," she said with a grimace.

Ronan gave a close-lipped grin. He looked a little too pleased by her words. "A criminal archangel helping a mercenary? How archaic."

THIRTY-SIX

"Can you remind me again why Ronan enlisted the mercenaries' help?"

Orion leaned against the stone wall of the meeting chamber. The etchings of the feathered beasts stretched out from where he stood making him look like one of the warriors in the mural. He was speaking to Ares, who propped the tip of a boot on the table's edge, fumbling with a match. Zara recognized the copper and earthy scent as bloodroot.

She folded her arms, arching her brow. "Please speak as if one of those mercenaries is not standing in front of you."

Ronan had dragged her into a gathering he had arranged with Orion and Ares. She wasn't sure what the purpose was for yet, but she was bound to find out. Her encounter with the leader of the Sombra Quarter earlier that morning had left her on edge. Someone outside the bounds of her guild and family was concerned *for* her, they were trying to see past the blades and blood on her soul.

It was unsettling.

That same archangel had disappeared, temporarily leaving her alone with two males. One of which was being quite protective as Orion continued to stare her down.

Ares, however, seemed bored. "From what I hear, they've been quite useful."

Orion's eyes narrowed. "Until they decide that he's better off dead."

Ah. She couldn't blame him for his wariness. To kill the leader of the Sombra Quarter was still an option. Zara was biding her time with this hunt for the mysterious creatures, for that sliver of hope that she may be able to be rid of the fyrebrand without having to still serve the High King.

If all else failed, then she would resort to bringing the archangel's head to Raziel.

A part of her shifted uncomfortably at the thought. It was the same voice that challenged her when she was hunting the human girl and the elven male with the green eyes. Zara grounded that thought with the heel of her boot.

She gave a wicked smile, instead. "It's yet to be decided, Orion Solterra."

The archangel growled but said nothing. Ares lit his roll of bloodroot, shielding it with his hand. "If the Rogue manages to slit Ronan's throat then maybe he deserves to die."

"I heard that." The head of the Sombra Quarter entered the meeting chamber, holding a worn leather tool bag. Ronan pierced the vampire with his gaze. "And do not call her by that title, Ares."

Orion pushed off the mural sauntering toward the stone table. A wild grin spread across his mouth, his eyes on the bag Ronan held. "Finally."

He reached for the hem of his tan shirt and slipped off the top to reveal his burly chest. Zara's jaw slackened at the sight of muscled brown skin. Battle scars claimed his body, at least she assumed they came from fights that involved blades and ether. She wondered what the archangel had seen in his lifetime, what misery he had beheld.

There was more to him as well as the other powerful males surrounding her.

Orion laid himself flat on the table's stone surface. His magnificent gray wings draped over the sides, the feathers nearly touching the ground. Ronan was rummaging through his bag and took out a glass canister of dark liquid as well as a folded leather piece that stored needles.

Zara's heart skipped a beat. She recognized the type of tools. "Those are for tattoos," she said, cocking her head at Ronan. "You are an ink artist?"

Under the dim light of the torches that lined the walls, shadows caressed his face. The archangel's black hair fell over the sides of his brow, nearly touching his eyes. He wore a form-fitting shirt that capped at his shoulders. She couldn't help but notice a thick band of ink wrapped around his left bicep. It was a stark contrast compared to the design of vines and jasmine flowers that filled his arms and neck.

His dark wings folded as he approached Orion. "I'm hardly an expert, but ever since I took the Sombra Quarter ink art was something I began to dabble in."

An array of tattoos already sat on the brawny archangel's back. It was an incomplete design of whorls and sharp edges mingled with a language that Zara couldn't decipher. Her legs moved of their own accord and she took the seat across the vampire, the two archangels taking up the other half of the table.

Ronan prepared his needle, the material was dyed black but seemed to be made of bone. It was different compared to Eshe's set of tools which were made of jade stone. The archangel hunched over Orion's back and began to dip the ink onto his skin. His brows pinched as he focused while Orion closed his eyes and sighed. Zara was sure the large male could fall asleep if he wanted to.

Ares exhaled red smoke, the scent of the root filling the air. "You forced me to come this way, Menodora. What do you need from me?"

Several beats passed as Ronan worked. The only sound was the clink of the needle dipping into the canister and the subtle shifting of wings. His voice went low and rough. "I have scoured the shadow markets' archives for information on how to remove the fyrebrands. I hoped to find something about the ether-laced tattoos, but there wasn't anything worth mentioning. I know we had talked about this in the past, but I'm going to need you to look at the royal library in the Soleira castle."

Zara's stomach twisted at the topic. Her fyrebrand tingled against her skin as if it knew what was being discussed. She braced for the voice to berate her, but it never came.

"Did you even think it was possible to remove the binds when you promised the mercenaries?" Ares asked.

Ronan's teeth clicked, still working on the tattoo. "I *know* there is a way. Histories have said that if ether-laced tattoos can be created, they can also be destroyed. It is only the matter of its manufacturing that determines how to break it."

The vampire shared a look with Orion who looked up from his daze. "Ronan has had a more extensive education than you and I."

Ares plucked the bloodroot from his lips and exhaled red clouds. His eyes went to Ronan's left bicep where the thick tattoo rested.

"I supposed he does," he murmured.

Ronan seemed to have finished his work. He reared back, admiring the whorls he designed before signaling for Orion to get up. The large archangel moved slowly, his skin still tender.

Ronan cleaned the needle. "We will also need you to investigate those mysterious creatures we've come across. I've described them to you so maybe you can see if any text mentions their kind. Is this something you can do?"

"I can and I will," Ares said, tapping the ends of his roll with his pinky.

Zara watched the discussion from her seat, observing the males' mannerisms. The vampire was straight-edged and stoic, a war general. But someone who seemed efficient in his doings. Whatever history existed between him and Ronan, it was obvious the leader of the Sombra Quarter trusted him.

Ronan offered the vampire a grim smile. "Thank you."

Ares shot Zara a wary look which only intrigued her. "In regard to the royal library, I will search for answers about the fyrebrands.

Though it'll be difficult considering my daily duty to guard the . . . princess."

She felt ice bleed through her veins. A dangerous quiet silenced the beat of her heart and the thrum of her thoughts. The mercenary growled the words. "What princess?"

A voice of battle and storm. She could see Ronan placing his tools aside. His stare burned her skin, but she refused to look his way.

"This is why I brought you here," the archangel said.

Her gaze was heavy on the vampire. A predator catching sight of its prey. "Does this happen to be the draconic princess?"

Ares's eyes slightly widened and that was enough of a confirmation for the mercenary. She flipped out a dagger and pointed it at him. "Harm her or fail to do your job and you will find my blades down your fucking throat."

"Violent little wolf," Ronan said. He almost sounded amused.

Ares looked to Ronan with a plea in his eyes, as if he, the *vampire general*, was asking for assistance.

Ronan simply folded his arms and jerked his chin. "It's none of my business. You have the honors."

Ares glared at him before responding to Zara. "I was assigned to be Daria's bodyguard. I have been with her since she arrived in Soleira."

Fucking Suns. Just when she thought that her sister was far away from the harms of the hunting season and whatever violence that has been occurring outside the capital's borders. Danger was threatening to creep closer to her family and she couldn't bear the thought.

Her voice went lethally quiet. "And you haven't told her of your affiliation with the Sombra Quarter?"

The mercenary and vampire general stared at each other like prowling beasts. Orion snickered, his voice echoing within the meeting chamber. "I wouldn't mind seeing the mercenary put Ares in his place."

Ronan chuckled, the sound deep. "I agree."

"No," Ares bit out, ignoring the archangels' jabs. "At the time I didn't see a reason to. Daria has been quite busy trying to familiarize herself with the castle's politicians."

Zara caught the soft lilt he gave as he said her sister's name. Her gaze turned thoughtful. "I do not want my sister getting involved in any of this."

Ares took another inhale of the bloodroot. "It will be difficult to avoid it. Daria is persistent. I will have to do my part for Ronan immediately. She will find out soon enough, and will want to help." His eyes flashed with something Zara couldn't decipher. "And you must speak to her regardless, mercenary. She's been disappointed by not hearing from you."

His last words stung, harsher coming from a male she hardly knew. It was true, Zara had still avoided responding to Daria's requests. After the execution, she was sure her sister was terrified of her. Zara couldn't bring herself to face anyone from her family.

Now Daria would be dragged into this mess. All because she wanted to spite the High King.

Tension bracketed Zara's mouth. She felt Ronan draw closer to her side of the table. His large presence was impossible to miss. "I promise she will not be in any danger whether she knows the truth of everything here. It is your decision."

The torches hanging about the meeting chamber flickered. Zara tapped the table with a nail, considering any possible outcomes in involving her sister. The vampire guard had kept his relationship with the Sombra Quarter a secret from Daria and—if she suspected correctly—it seemed that Ares held a shred of fondness for her sister.

Eventually, her lips curled upward and pushed herself out of her seat. Her gaze slid to Ares, but she spoke to Ronan. "I understand that we can't avoid Daria finding out about all this, but we will go about it my way."

Zara chuckled that empty sound she used when hunting her marks, looping her arm around Ronan's. She gave the archangel a sidelong glance. "Though I have a feeling your vampire friend will not like it."

Ronan grinned, his curiosity peaked.

Ares's eyes jumped between them and shook his head. "Trouble. You are both trouble."

All the while Orion stared at Ronan as if he couldn't recognize the male in front of him.

Fishers were taking to the waters. Citizens tended to their small gardens outside of their adobe homes while children scurried between the narrow paths. Red and black tapestries drifted over the market stalls.

Zara couldn't help but think that Ronan had taken this route on purpose. To show her the Sombra Quarter in its full extent, that the underworld was not as dark and terrible as one might think.

The meeting with Ares and Orion had long ended, the former returning to the capital while the latter went to meet with the rest of the guild who were still with his soldiers. Ronan, on the other hand, had asked her to follow him to gods knew where. She was too exhausted to argue with the archangel and trailed along.

They had formulated a plan for Ares to begin his research about breaking fyrebrands and ether-laced tattoos as well as the ethereal beings, which meant they had to inform Daria of Zara's involvement with the Sombra Quarter. It also meant she would have to know what had been occurring within the Estrella Territories.

The thought of having her sister be involved in this aspect of her life, no matter how small it seemed, terrified her. Zara wanted to fight against it, to keep her sister at arm's length, but the vampire's words struck her harder than she wanted to admit. Daria had always wanted to know who she was as a mercenary, especially within the hunting season. It was long overdue, something Zara should've discussed with her sister a long time ago.

Still, she was adamant to the males that Daria would not be any more involved than researching the fyrebrands and the creatures.

Zara and Ronan passed the forges, the ash and smoke so strong that her eyes began to water. Sparks of ember flashed, bright and fiery. It was so quick that she almost missed it—how Ronan flinched at the sudden burst of flames.

He cleared his throat. "We are almost there."

"Where, exactly?"

"It's a surprise."

She arched her brow. "Are you taking me somewhere to kill me, archangel?"

His stormy gaze slid to hers. "No, that's supposed to be your job," he said dryly.

Charming.

Soon they were on the main path toward the cavernous grand hall, and Zara could see the statues from their distance. Ronan, however, steered her down a slope onto another path. She hesitated. Ronan must've sensed her wariness as he turned around and continued to walk backward.

His expression held a touch of mischief. "Would you like to know why this place is called the Stone Orchard?"

Zara's eyes widened when she noticed the trees, an entire grove made of stone. She had passed this area last night, how could she have missed this? The branches were bare, made of smooth gray rock. They were clustered together, casting shade from the columns of sunlight. She jumped ahead of Ronan, spinning on her heels as she observed every trunk and root.

"Amazing," Zara breathed. "Was this always here?"

Ronan nodded as he gazed at the carved canopies. "Yes, all thanks to whoever lived here before. We suspect the grove here represents the floating orchards in Mikatán's realm."

The land of the dead, otherwise mostly known as the Otherworld. Souls had to overcome trials to determine their worthiness to join the land of the eternal skies. It was believed that a soul would know they had successfully crossed the threshold when orchards filled with white-gold fruit were seen floating through the twilight. Zara was confident there was more to Mikatán's domain.

Beyond the gates of Celestrea, the Primordials each had their own kingdom; whether it was in the form of cities, castles, or even open lands filled with mountains and oceans depended on the god or goddess.

No mortal had seen these realms, except for the archangels and deities. Only they were able to travel between the ethereal and mortal realm. She briefly wondered if Ronan had ever visited Celestrea.

He stepped into a small clearing, his wings spread out wide against the beams of daylight. "No one ever comes here. If you wish to fight and train, this space is yours."

Zara's head went silent. She stared at the leader of the Sombra Quarter. "What sort of games are you up to, archangel?"

Ronan's expression turned stern. "Instead of going to the fighting ring, you can fight me here. Should you need it."

Something cracked in her chest. "Are you sure?" She asked softly. Too soft for her comfort.

His face fell. It resembled the pained look she had witnessed when they passed the forges. "It wouldn't hurt for me to pick up a sword again."

Zara walked deeper into the clearing. The air was lighter somehow, the outside world far from view.

In that moment, she had found her resolve. She didn't think about her assignment. The mark who stood before her. None of it. There was that voice again, so unlike the fyrebrand, and it seemed to sigh.

Yes.

THIRTY-SEVEN

Daria grunted. "It's too hard."

"Your hand needs to grip it tighter, princess." Ares's voice was guttural.

"I am!"

"I thought you'd had practice."

Daria groaned and brought up her dagger once more. Sweat dotted her brow, though the ocean breeze cooled the damp strands that stuck to her skin. Her hair was braided into multiple tresses and bound at the nape of her neck.

The trees in the castle garden surrounded them, tucking them against the stone wall that faced the shore. Ares had been instructing her all morning, showing her basic maneuvers in wielding a dagger, as well as the footwork. He made her train in her gown, much to her dismay. According to her personal guard, it would be best to know how to fight while under more constricting clothing and things she would wear every day.

Her goal was to disarm Ares. He slashed his own knife low toward her stomach and Daria managed to step back, bringing down her clenched hand over his wrist. On impact the dagger slipped from her grasp. She groaned and bent to pick it up, before sheathing the weapon between the folds of her dress, hitched against her rib.

Dammit. She was too weak. It had been some time since she had practiced with Zara. Ares watched her, the trees rustling behind him cast him in an orange glow. The corners of his lips twitched. By the gods, he was *laughing* at her.

She glared. "Shut up."

Ares chuckled deeply and slipped his own weapon into his belt. "We will practice more, princess."

Daria wandered over to the wall. A light spray of water tickled her face as she stared at the city and sea below. "Good to know that I have King Matías's favorite to train me."

He snarled. "Don't call me that."

She startled. His reaction surprised her. "I'm sorry. Your reputation precedes you. Why do they call you that?"

Ares surveyed her. "Is the princess curious about me?"

She sighed. "Is it so wrong? You are the only person I've spent time with since coming here."

His expression was unreadable as he watched her before he turned to look back at the water. "I became a general by being the most ruthless vampire in Adrastea's academy. I killed lesser soldiers who were nothing more than liabilities. I made enemies within my own ranks and killed them too. Matías saw this and *loved* it. He personally oversaw my training. Is that what you wanted to hear?"

Silas had mentioned as much. Her blood rushed at the image of a young Ares surrounded by others determined to see his downfall. His elegant face painted with malice as he licked the blood of his opposers from his fingers. Those violet eyes would have burned with a promise for violence, to claim power as his own.

It was no secret that Adrastea was a violent kingdom, she just had not realized how much.

Daria should've been repulsed by it. She should've feared him—and maybe she did. A small part of her knew this male could rip her throat open in a blink of an eye. That knowledge was like standing on the edge of a cliff, knowing the abyss awaited below.

But she was not as helpless as people thought—as her pater and sister most likely believed. She understood the need for survival that had made Ares act the way he did.

Daria opened her palm and a blossom of flame appeared, its tongues of red and yellow licked the salty air. Ares stared at her power with wide eyes . . . and something like awe.

"Beautiful," he murmured.

She felt her cheeks warm and wasn't sure if it was due to the heat of the flames. "I haven't practiced my ether as much as I should've. I have been so consumed with my academics and royal training that I forgot to become familiar with this part of myself."

He observed the ball of fire floating above her hand. "I heard that ether-wielders are able to command their power by manifesting it with their minds."

Daria felt the pulse of her ether. It stemmed from her palm down to her veins. A second heartbeat to her own. She closed her hand and the ribbons of fire slipped between her fingers.

A vampire soldier appeared from within the trees, a rolled parchment in her hand. She placed a fist over her chest and bowed to Ares. To Daria's pleasant surprise, he bowed his head in return.

The soldier did the same to Daria, handing her the piece of parchment. "A letter has arrived, intended for the princess."

Daria read the words over and over again. Her chest swelled with a mix of relief and happiness. "Zara would like to meet with me today."

Since the execution, she suspected that her sister was not in the mental space to reunite. Daria had been willing to wait, having sent one final letter to let her sister know she would be ready whenever she was.

Ares's voice sounded clipped. "Let's be off then, princess." He grumbled under his breath what sounded like, *"Might as well get this over with."*

When she glanced his way, she was sure his face had gotten a little pale too.

Daria felt the color drain from her face as she stared at the doors to the pleasure house. It was in the outer district, at a walking distance from the center of Soleira. The sun was high and beat down on the cobblestones. No matter the early hour, it seemed people still gave the brothel plenty of business. Patrons entered and exited its brick entrance, a bronze plate lining the panel above its doors with the name *House of Roses*.

She kept her head low, hoping the hood would keep her identity hidden. Its velvet fabric was soft against her skin, dabbing at the light perspiration gathered there. Ares hadn't seemed to care to cover himself, and she quickly discovered why.

"Ares!" A voice sang out from an arched window on the upper level of the building. Daria peeked from underneath the hem of her hood. She saw a beautiful human with dark hair and hazel eyes. Her soft flesh was a deep brown, barely covered by thin strips of shiny material.

Her guard lifted a hand in greeting. Daria didn't want to see how his face looked. Of course he was known as a visitor here. And why did that bother her?

"Did your sister mention why we were to meet her in the House of Roses?" he asked.

Daria growled in exasperation and placed the heels of her palms to her eyes. "Who knows what goes through that head of hers. I'm sure once you meet her you will understand."

Ares didn't respond. He leaned down to peer under Daria's hood, eyes glinting with a hint of mischief. "There's no need to be nervous, princess."

Daria's face burned. She tucked in her chin, shoving past Ares to enter the pleasure house. The vampire chuckled, shadowing her every move.

The inside was not what Daria had imagined. To be honest, she wasn't quite sure what she was expecting. Garlands of olive leaves hung from the wooden beams above and along wooden tables. Decorative bird cages dangled from various parts of the walls and ceiling. Bouquets of white roses had been placed beside plates filled with grapes. The lighting within the building was dim. Only some of the arched windows had been left open, while a few lit candles gave the place a dark, sensual ambiance.

In the center of the main floor was a small, circular platform. Some of the staff—both men and women—danced on it, while a musician played the harp in the corner. They were all very close to one another, their hands and mouths exploring each other's bodies as their hips swayed to the music. Daria's face warmed. Patrons sat at the tables, either drinking and chatting or watching the show with heated looks.

The dancers were mesmerizing. She realized she had been swaying to the sound of the harp when Ares nudged her to keep moving, his voice at her ear, slightly muffled by her hood. "About time the princess loosened up."

Daria scowled and stepped away from him. He gently grabbed her by the elbow, guiding her through the main floor. She noticed lavish seating areas and alcoves lining the walls, filled with beaded cushions and silk sheets. They were raised up a step, providing a slightly elevated view of the stage.

Thin dark veils separated each lounging space. Shadows moved on the other side, and Daria caught the sound of moaning.

As well as the sound of skin slapping on skin.

Her face was scalding hot by now. A numbness trickled down her legs, threatening to freeze her in place. Though that would be impossible, as the vampire was tugging her to one of those seating areas.

The thought of being stuck in a small space with him, surrounded by lewd noises . . .

Ares pulled the thin drapes for her to enter. "We will wait here to avoid any attention. I am sure your sister will find us."

Daria released a short, ragged laugh. "Right, because the patrons will surely be interested in us at the moment."

She settled on the cushions, feeling the silk against her damp palms. The vampire closed the veil, though she could still see the stage, the dancers now a blurred view in the candlelight.

Ares settled across from her, picking at the fresh platter of grapes in front of them. The vampire seemed at ease.

He had been here before. How many times? And with *whom?* Daria's mind burned with curiosity, and she hated that it did. It did not—*should* not matter to her. But she couldn't help it.

There were couples on either side of them, barely hidden behind their curtains. To her right, Daria could see the figures of a man and woman. The man was in a sitting position, the woman cradled in his lap. Her legs were spread out on either side of him, arms hugging his neck as she rode him. The man ran his hands along her back, his mouth on her breast. Her head was tipped back, moaning loudly.

While in the lounge area to her left, a man shoved another man's head down into the cushion as he thrust into him. The male cried out, pleading for *more, more, more.*

Daria was glad she couldn't see any of their faces, but that didn't stop her from feeling that heat curdle low, between her legs. A need rose within her, one that craved to be touched and claimed the way the man and woman on either side of her were. Gods, she'd barely had any experience with sex, she didn't even know what she would like.

But Daria would like to find out for herself.

The previous ease Ares had displayed had long withered away. His jaw was tight, eyes pinned to the stage beyond their space. They burned with something she was too scared to identify.

By the Suns, a strong sensation tightened in her core. It longed for—for release. Daria fought the urge to rub her thighs together.

Ares growled. "You have to stay still, princess."

His voice was strained, words laced with frustration. She was sure their little room was growing smaller and smaller. It was becoming harder to breathe.

Daria licked her lips, and she noticed the vampire gaze honing in on the movement. "Is it normal to feel . . . affected by all this?"

Ares hissed out a breath, as if her question had burned his lungs. He closed his eyes, seeming to gather his thoughts. Her guard looked at her again, the fire in his gaze abating as he said the words, "Of course it is. Everything you feel right now is natural."

Time seemed to drag. Daria squirmed in place and Ares ran a hand over his face. "You haven't mentioned your sister much before today. Is there a reason?"

The sudden subject change was a poor and obvious attempt to distract them from the tense atmosphere. Daria had to admit she was grateful for it. She wasn't sure what she would do if it continued like this. "Do I need to spill my life's stories when you hardly speak of yours?"

"I simply find it interesting, as I am sure many others do, that the Ikarrian king has two daughters who live vastly different lives." He did not speak unkindly, but out of what seemed like genuine curiosity. "People fear the mercenary, even the soldiers. I've heard them say that there's a certain . . . energy around her. Like a beast ready to unleash its claws."

Another voice interjected. One that made Ares go deathly still. "That's boring. Do they at least mention the Rogue's unearthly beauty?"

A smile grew wide across Daria's face, the confusing horde of emotions washing away.

Zara appeared at their lounge's entrance, swaggering through the thin drapes. She released a sigh of relief. "I was partly afraid of coming in here and having to cut off the vampire's balls."

Her sister looked . . . good. Better than good. There was color in her cheeks. That light Daria was so familiar with had returned, brighter than she'd ever seen it.

She jumped to her feet, ready to throw her arms around her sister, but stopped herself. The last time they had seen each other had been across the blood-stained arena. She wasn't sure where Zara was emotionally, whether she was ready to be embraced.

Zara seemed to sense her apprehension and extended her arms. A raw expression peeled through the previous cocky persona. "Hello, sister of mine."

Daria crashed into her. Tears pricked the corners of her eyes. It felt as if a knot had finally loosened from within her chest, and she silently tried to tell Zara through her embrace that she did not judge her for what she had witnessed at the execution. That she still loved her. The tremble along her sister's back told her that Zara heard her message.

Zara squeezed her a moment longer before they broke apart, but kept her arm wrapped around Daria's shoulders, the warmth in her eyes bleeding into a bitter coldness when they landed on the quiet vampire.

"Ares, darling," she drawled. "How wonderful it is to see you."

Her sister stared at the general with a wicked grin, as if happily preparing to wage war, while Ares looked back at her with a stony expression.

Daria's brows bunched together. "You two know each other?"

Her sister's grip around her tightened as she nodded. "That's actually one of the reasons I wanted to meet with you."

It shouldn't have surprised the princess. Zara had been to Soleira every year for the hunting season; she was bound to have crossed paths with the general.

Daria braced herself as Zara added, "There's a lot I need to tell you. But we must not speak here. Follow me."

Her sister pulled away, tugging her own hood over her head as she peeled the drapes open. Daria couldn't move at first. She watched as Zara's figure moved through the main floor, heading toward a set of stairs Daria had missed when she first entered the House of Roses.

Ares lingered close, his gaze heavy on her.

He had already met Zara. How long had they known each other? How come he hadn't shared any news or information regarding her sister when Daria had been sick with unease this whole time?

Daria swallowed the flurry of questions that rose up her throat. She would wait a bit, hear what her sister had to say.

Ares took a step toward her. His voice edged with concern. "Princess?"

She found herself unable to look his way. "Not right now, if that's okay. I need . . . I need to process all this."

The vampire fell silent. "As you wish," he said, eventually.

They followed Zara to the second floor where they passed more occupied veiled rooms. The air was thick with the smell of sex and lust. One space was filled with a group of people. Daria caught sight of multiple races within, men and women lost in their pleasure.

She picked up the pace and reached her sister's side farther down the hall. "Can you explain why you had us come here? Not that I mind, it's just this is all so very new to me."

Zara snorted. "I'm sorry, sister. I wondered how flustered you'd be coming here." She led them to a set of double doors, her hands curling around wrought iron handles. Zara hesitated and glanced back at Daria.

Something shadowed her expression and it knotted Daria's stomach.

"So much has happened since I last saw you; there is a reason why I brought you here," Zara whispered.

She pushed through the doors to reveal a wide bedroom chamber. Daria couldn't take in her surroundings. Her eyes were pinned on the fluttering white curtains—on the male with black wings facing the open windows.

Zara gestured a hand toward the archangel. "*He* is the reason."

Daria had no words as the beautiful male turned to face them, as she was greeted by steel gray eyes.

THIRTY-EIGHT

Zara Santos watched as her sister gaped at the archangel beside her. Her nails dug crescents into her palms as she waited for Daria's reaction. This was another step in welcoming her sister into her second life, where danger and hurt lurked around every corner.

Ronan gave Daria a gentle smile, a far cry from his previous irritating mood. A few hours earlier he had rolled his eyes at Zara as she paced the massive bedroom chamber in the hopes of driving her anxiety to the ground.

"We are in a brothel, Santos," he had said, lounging atop the made bedsheets. "Feel free to ease your tension with the staff." The waggling of his eyebrows and his splayed position on the bed shouldn't have been so attractive.

Zara had snapped back. "I should've known you had more businesses in the outer district loyal to you."

Ronan smirked. "Imagine all the times you wreaked chaos in these streets, unknowingly passing by fellow Sombra Quarter sympathizers. The House of Roses allows for my shadow dealers to use their business as a front and in return I ensure the owners and their staff are supported and safe."

He was distracting her from the upcoming encounter with her

sister. While Zara was grateful for his effort, she still allowed herself to lean into the frustration stirred by his words.

"You think that is funny?" She could've sworn her eye twitched.

Ronan merely shrugged. Feeling a surge of rebellion, she placed her hands on her waist. "You know, you are right, Menodora. We are in a pleasure house, and I *should* go relieve my stress."

She marched out the door, heading to where the veiled rooms were. A hand latched onto her wrist and yanked her back. Zara's reflexes acted on their own accord as her leg swept toward her assailant.

Ronan was too quick, twisting his body to the side to avoid her attack. His own reactions had sharpened since they'd first started sparring. In that moment, Zara regretted helping the male. He still held onto her, his fingers nearly trembling around her skin.

Her eyebrows slanted downward. "What? You were the one who gave the suggestion."

Ronan's jaw tensed, an unreadable expression shadowing the planes of his face. "You can if it's what you truly want. I just . . . stay with me instead."

His gray eyes seemed to glow under the dim light. They still stood in the hallway and Zara had nothing to brace against the rush his words sent her way. Ronan didn't seem to insinuate anything by his words.

She wasn't used to that.

If it had been Erebus, he would've followed her into one of those rooms, and let her drown her worries with mindless sex.

With Ronan, however, it was . . . different. In a way she didn't quite understand and was hesitant to try.

"Why?" she asked. "Don't you want to enjoy yourself? This place is practically your business, I imagine the leader of the Sombra Quarter would have flocks of lovers waiting for him."

He gave her a stern look, the candlelight embracing his wings and one side of his face. His mouth was lined with tension as he gently tugged her closer.

"No. I haven't had a lover—even a casual one—in some time," he said. His grip on her tightened. "Stay by my side, instead. Let me hear you pace the room. I want to hear you grumbling about how you can't stand this and how you want to stab that. I'll listen to whatever you need to say."

Zara searched his gaze, her own cowardice winning over. She forced a dry smile. "You would've been lonely without me, is that it? I understand, I am quite a joy to be around."

The humor was a weak attempt to mask the waver in her voice, but Ronan still caught it. He paused, her words sinking between them, creating the rift she so foolishly desired. The haze that had fallen over his face whisked away.

His lips spread into a smirk, and he let her go. "That's what it is."

And Ronan had done exactly what he said he would. He had listened to Zara ramble on about her worries on involving her sister, and she had even shared stories of their childhood. And now, the archangel was looking at Daria with a tenderness that said he knew how important this woman was to her, to Zara. It punctured something in her chest.

But before anyone could speak, it was Ares who stomped past her sister. His violet eyes aflame on Zara. "What is *he* doing here? You did not tell me you were bringing him too, mercenary."

She stretched her arms. "You agreed to work on my terms, I just happened to change them halfway."

Ares growled in response. Ronan crossed his arms and cocked his head at the vampire. "What gives? I thought you'd be happy to see me."

Daria's gaze flicked between the two males, her jaw still wide open. Zara called out to her sister and jabbed an elbow against Ronan's ribs. "This is Ronan Menodora. He is the leader of the Sombra Quarter."

"The . . . The Sombra Quarter?" Her sister hissed. Daria shook her head and put up her hand. "Wait, let me see if I understand this correctly. You're involved with the shadow markets, and you *all* know each other?"

She looked between all of them, though her gaze lingered on Ares a moment longer. Something strained and shattered in those amber-brown eyes.

Zara swallowed back the thick emotion gathering in her throat and gestured Daria farther into the room. The bedchamber was wide enough to include a small parlor. They went to sit at the table, the two males lingering close. Ares wandered to the shelves behind Daria while Ronan drifted toward Zara.

Her stomach sickened as she started. "You have asked me many times what my life is like during the hunting season, and I could never answer you. Truth be told, I didn't want to. This part of myself is so disgusting and twisted. I would've continued withholding this side of me for as long as I lived, but Raziel changed it all that day in the arena." Zara could see her sister's eyes glisten. She continued. "Not only that but there is a darkness growing within the Estrella Territories. I didn't want to have to involve you, though seeing as your pretty vampire guard over there is deeply connected with the Sombra Quarter, we thought it best to inform you. And *I* wanted to be the one to explain it to you."

So, Zara told her everything. From her being assigned to hunt down the leader of the shadow markets to Ronan proposing an alliance. From the day of the execution that sparked her decision to quietly revolt against the High Throne to the guild staying at the Stone Orchard—something that Ronan had agreed to share. And finally, from the abandoned settlements in the Estrella Territories to the possessed creatures and ethereal beings.

When she finished, Daria slumped back in her seat. She ran a hand over her face. "Gods—I—I don't know what to think or say. Are you sure these creatures are not some forms of demon?"

Zara shook her head. "I've experienced my fair share of demons, and these things are unlike anything I've encountered before. The energy about them screams . . . *unnatural.*"

Daria interlaced her hands across her abdomen, most likely trying to wrap her mind around the idea of mortals turning feral. Eventually, she reached for Zara's hand. Her sister felt soft and warm, skin that did not know the pommel of blades and knives. Palms that did not know bloodshed. The reminder almost made Zara flinch back. Unlike Daria's, her hands were likely rough and cold. Stained and bruised.

Her sister's expression softened, oblivious to the war in Zara's heart. "And this Ronan, can you trust him?"

Zara saw Ronan raise a hand in her peripheral. He spoke to Ares. "We are invisible at this point."

The vampire still loomed beside the shelves, his eyes on Daria. "So it seems."

Zara's lips thinned. "I can never fully trust someone, sister. At this moment, however, I believe he will do anything to protect his business and people. And us by association."

She could feel Ronan's gaze on the back of her head, but she ignored it.

Daria nodded, the amber in her eyes seemed to brighten. "I appreciate you telling me all this. So, what is it that you need Ares to do that involves informing me?"

Zara winced, feeling a rush of guilt. "We need to learn more about the ethereal creatures, as well as find a way to break the fyrebrands. While Raziel burned many of the old books in the Continent when he won the War, there may be some he missed. Ronan believes that the answer lies in the royal library. A place only Ares can gain access to."

Ronan took a step forward, addressing Daria. "You will not be anywhere near the dangers lurking in the Estrella Territories, princess. We intend to continue hunting for these creatures in one week. Enough time to see if there is some insight already available in those texts. Time is not on our side."

Daria nodded. "Then that means I will join the effort and help Ares look. If there is anything I can do to help my sister leave the High King, I will do it."

Zara could only stare at Daria. The princess before her was not the same woman she had left in Ikarria. There was something more ...elevated about her. Mature. Daria's commitment to help her softened her heart.

Her sister glanced at Ronan. "If I may, could Zara and I have a moment to ourselves?"

The archangel bowed his head and went to yank the stoic vampire by the shoulder. Ares looked like he wanted to protest but said nothing. When the door closed and their footsteps drifted away, Daria sighed.

"I thought I would also take this time to tell you what brought me and pater into Soleira," she said.

Zara leaned in. "I was meaning to ask. I only heard that the High Throne invited Ikarria to the Summit."

Daria quickly told her about the invitation to the Summit and how she planned on learning more about the Council. She mentioned the little progress she had made, including meeting Maira and her twin sister, Nadira.

At the mention of the Council member's name, Zara's lips curled into a sneer. "She is dangerous, Daria. All the Council are. They may be helping their people and the realms, but they are still very powerful and power-hungry beings."

Daria gave her a weary look. "I've gathered that much, though I am starting to doubt if there is anything we can truly learn about them."

A sly smile appeared on Zara's lips. "You must be craftier, sister. You are used to following rules and doing what is expected of you, but you are sneaky when you want to be. Tap into that skill and use it to your advantage."

Her sister nodded, but Zara caught the flash of hurt across her eyes. "Are you alright? I'm sorry I've dragged you into this—"

"Stop apologizing, it's odd coming from you." Daria's lips tilted up in a small smile. She was still holding her hand and gave it a soft squeeze. "I hate to admit this but a part of me is hurt that you didn't share this from the beginning, that you haven't spoken to me since I arrived in Soleira. And that Ares never mentioned he already knew you or about any of the things that are happening. I feel as though I've been left in the dark, which is silly because I can understand why you didn't tell me and that you kept me at a distance because you were worried for my safety. I know your life is not an easy one, sister."

Zara tried to pull back, the guilt stronger than before, but Daria held on.

"I tried to find out more about your mercenary life without considering how it would make you feel," Daria said softly. "For that I am sorry. I wanted to support you, be there for you, but I should've known that I could've done that without having to know every detail of your life."

Zara's throat bobbed. Though there were times when she felt envious of her sister's upbringing, Zara was thankful that Daria would never have to experience the hardships she had. A part of her, however, still longed for the safety and comfort her sister had.

Zara had also wanted to ask how their pater was and knew he would have been asking for her presence as well, but she was reminded of the twinge of resentment she felt toward him every time she prepared to leave for the hunting season.

That was for later.

Gods, she was weak. She was a mercenary, she had fought and killed—she could not afford to be like this.

But right now, in this moment they had stolen from their obligations, they were just two women finding a way to maneuver through their complicated reality. And gods, Zara was grateful to have a sister like Daria.

A soft smile touched Zara's lips. "Thank you. It means more to me than you know."

They conversed a bit more until Ronan and Ares returned. It wasn't long before the vampire urged the princess to return to the castle in case someone searched for them.

Zara held onto Daria a moment longer than usual. Her sister's eyes held a sheen to them as she turned to leave the room. The vampire held the door open for her, and Daria brushed past him without a second glance. Ares's lips were a thin line as he gave a stiff nod to Ronan and Zara before heading after the princess.

It seemed the general of Adrastea had his work cut out for him.

THIRTY-NINE

There were so many questions. Too many for Daria to comprehend.

The truth had been laid before her and it racked through her bones. The abandoned towns, possessed creatures, Zara working with an illegal organization . . .

What baffled her the most though, was that Ares Valdemar, general of Adrastea, *King Matías's favorite*, was also an ally of the Sombra Quarter. Not only that, but he was a friend to the leader of the shadow markets.

The general had led a roust in the inner district. His vampire soldiers had unleashed destruction and fear within the streets of Soleira. Surely, a male such as that would not betray his kingdom.

That same vampire had supported her during the execution in the coliseum to the point of gifting her a weapon, advocating for her self-defense skills. Had been there for her.

But he hadn't thought to tell her of Zara's state when Daria was beside herself with worry. Had kept so many things from her. Because she was just a spoilt princess.

"Daria."

She hadn't given him an opportunity to explain after they had left the House of Roses. Daria had marched all the way through the capital. When they reached the castle, she charged into its front court-yard as if going to battle. Ares had flanked her the entire time, keeping a respectful distance from her.

He tried calling out to her again. "Princess."

She raised a hand, not bothering to look back. "Not now."

Leaves skittered across the path and suddenly the vampire stood before her. His expression remained neutral, which infuriated her even more.

He angled his head, eyes searching hers. "You can't keep running away from me. We will have to talk about what happened."

Daria's voice could cut glass. "By all means, general, explain why you kept secrets from me regarding *my* sister."

Ares didn't falter. He checked their surroundings; they were alone, save for the imposing hedges and statues.

The vampire released a heavy breath. "This is a topic we cannot discuss here. There are many eyes and ears in this place."

Daria couldn't argue with his logic. She folded her arms, frowning. "Where do you propose we go?"

A wicked glint rose in his eyes. "I just thought of the perfect place, princess, though it will require you to change your attire."

"Pardon?"

His lips curled. "Be sure to bring your dagger.""

Daria stood in a training courtyard. Located in a lower level of the castle, the grounds faced a part of the capital and the open sea, rocks along the cliffside acting as their fence. It was such a secluded space she would never have known it was here.

The princess wore brown, skin-tight trousers and an olive-green shirt. It was rare for her to wear something like this—aside from the night she followed Ares to the outer district. For her, dresses had always been her armor. She felt bare, unsure, in this attire.

Daria huffed with impatience. She knew Ares wasn't obligated to share every detail of who he was, but now, with what Zara had revealed, circumstances had changed. The vampire before her stood in a different light. She couldn't decide whether it was good or bad—or a blend of both.

"Why did you bring me here?"

Ares paced the courtyard. His boots brushed over the damp rock that made the ground. The ocean wind lifted his violet-hued hair. "Your sister had suggested—well, more like *commanded* me—to reveal my secret partnership with Ronan. I have wanted to tell you for a while but never found the right moment. When Zara decided to tell you herself, I thought she had thrown me to the wolves."

He stopped, the purple in his eyes deepening. "But it seems she threw me into the maw of a dragon."

Daria scoffed. "I thought we could trust each other. I thought you could trust *me*. But Ares Valdemar will always remain a mystery to me." His jaw locked.

"I will tell you everything, princess. How my alliance with the Sombra Quarter started, why I always pretend to be loyal to the Lord of Vampires." He swept his legs and arms out into a fighting stance, his movements like silk and air. The flash of a grin stumped her. "So long as you throw your ether at me."

Her brows furrowed. "My ether? Why?"

"You are angry with me. So show me."

Ares sighed when Daria didn't move. "Princess, I see you. You withhold your true emotions, always maintaining your composure when handling the world. Except when it comes to verbally sparring with me." His eyes shined at that. "I see how you clasp your hands in front of you when you are nervous. I have sensed the ether in you rise when you are angry or distressed. And from what you told me earlier, it seems you do not often allow yourself to *feel* fully. You hold yourself back."

Daria took a step back, shaking her head. "No, you're wrong. I am always aware of my emotions."

The words sounded bland. Empty. Ares didn't look convinced either. "Princess, all that emotional labor must be exhausting. It is okay to unleash the dragon that rests inside you every now and then."

She felt his words fall over her heart.

His eyes softened. "I see your strength, you've been tirelessly educating yourself on how to be a better politician, ambassador—gods, even *ruler*. You care about your people. It is more than what anyone here has done."

Daria had been molded and honed by the knowledge of the Continent. Yet there had always been a side of her she hadn't discovered, the part where her powers resided, the flames that made her soul, and it was only by stepping away from the confines of her home that she had begun to reconnect with that side of herself. Perhaps that was the true reason why she had wanted to come to Elios, to discover what she was missing.

Daria felt the presence of her ether inside her—so alive and *strong*—and she was tempted to have a taste.

Ares seemed to notice her resolve. He grinned with those twin fangs. "Unleash that fire. Let me feel the bite of a dragon."

Flames bloomed over the skin of her hands. Every pulse, every heartbeat—Daria felt it pound through her blood. She closed her eyes for a breath to relish the sensation. The fire was gentle against her, soft and delicate, masking its fierceness.

The power of the world at her fingertips. And another wave of euphoria when she finally released it.

Ares was quick. He dodged the attack with lethal grace and skidded closer to her. He stopped a mere few inches away, his nose nearly brushing the skin off her brow. She could almost taste the scent of roses.

"I never planned on double-crossing my kingdom," he began. Daria jumped back and raised her fire-touched hands, but Ares held her wrists, ignoring the heat of flames that could burn him. "I was still a meager soldier at the time the War ended. I fought in the regiments that protected Elios from the deities who stood against the Council. Then I made my way toward the guardian realms."

Her eyes widened. "Did you fight the Primordials?"

"Gods, no. The ethereal battles were happening near the Jade Sea, but I saw the wreckage on those lands. Nothing could've survived, and when the War ended, any opponents who still breathed were taken as war prisoners. Ronan was one of them."

Daria stumbled back when he loosened his grip. She called to her ether and the flames rose from her palms in two thin pillars. The tendrils of fire began to circle the air—albeit a bit awkwardly—and crashed toward Ares. It was messy and slow, more than enough time for the vampire to roll lazily to the side.

"I never planned to betray my home realm. I was indebted to King Matías. Then I heard stories of this archangel they had brought in. They said that in the battlefields he was more monster than man. A living storm with the power to rend the skies in half."

His gaze darkened. "If such power was possible, I did not see it. What I saw in that cell was a broken young man. He didn't eat. He didn't sleep. Nor did he try to fight the soldiers who beat him. It seemed as if he had given up."

Fire illuminated Daria's face, brightening the light in her eyes. "You found compassion for him."

Ares's nose wrinkled, like the idea of that was abhorrent to him. The warmth that flickered in his gaze betrayed him. "I helped him escape. It took years in planning, but I managed to make it seem like he died. They never found the body, but the High Throne wasn't bothered about a nameless survivor disappearing. By then, the Continent had begun to move on from the War."

He suddenly lunged toward her. Daria had almost forgotten they were experimenting with her ether. Fire lashed out from her hands. It was like an animal that tugged on the binds, pulling and twisting from her grip. Sweat poured down her temples as she focused the flame's direction. It swept around the vampire, enclosing him.

Ares evaded the fire's touch and stood in the center of her burning chaos. He looked at her then, as if she was all he saw within the fire, the world.

There was still a question that failed to ebb from her mind. "So why work with the archangel to this day? After you helped him, you could've forgotten about him."

Ares was a blur of smoke as he pierced through her wall of fire.

She cried out, her power faltering and falling in fiery waves. Her footing slipped against the damp ground, and she lost her balance. A hand caught the back of her head before it could make impact.

All she could see were those violet eyes as Ares searched her for injuries.

"I might've helped Ronan escape," he said softly, once satisfied she was unharmed. "But he saved me in more ways than one. Since starting my life as a soldier, he was the only one who saw me as someone . . . with meaning. Not just some mindless soldier who takes orders, but someone with worth, who could *do* something of worth. After many years, when I thought I would never see him again, we reconnected. That is when we fell into an agreement. I'd help him gain and *stay* in power in the Sombra Quarter, while he provided me with—"

Ares's face shuttered as he broke off and looked away. Daria sat upright and they stayed on the ground for a while, the sound of the crashing sea in the distance. She noticed the fine lines that tensed his jaw.

Her own frustration and hurt waned. Ares and the others had good reason to keep such dangerous truths hidden. Their lives were constantly at risk, and that was not something she could relate to.

She knew the truth now and while it seemed that Ares had more shadows looming over his shoulders, more secrets that had yet to be revealed, she could accept this. Daria had finally been confided in, even by her sister, and she was honored to be trusted with all of this.

Daria inhaled a deep breath, feeling the salted air fill her lungs. "You don't have to say more if you do not want to. Thank you for telling me. I know I can trust you to help my sister."

Ares froze, and it was then that she realized her hand now rested against his cheek. It had happened so naturally: she had seen his flash of pain and hadn't thought twice.

His throat bobbed and yet he didn't pull away. Daria hesitated before she slowly brought her hand down.

"Why do you continue to serve Adrastea and Elios?" She asked.

Ares angled his head, staring into the space her hand had been. "I will show you. Soon. Will that be alright?"

It was more than enough. They were entering dangerous waters by helping those they cared for, but she wouldn't have it any other way.

The corner of his lips curled up. "I know I said I was thrown into the maw of a dragon," he said, brushing a strand of her hair over her ear, "but I like where I ended up."

Daria had to admit, so did she.

FORTY

Ronan winced as he felt the pull of muscle in his arm. "Gods, I swear you fractured some of my bones."

Zara was slouched in her seat, boots on the table. She grinned. "You need more practice."

Yes, the bruises on his body were proof of that. They had begun to make a habit of meeting in the grove, unleashing themselves on each other with their blades until their limbs gave out. He had to admit that it had felt *good* to properly hold a sword again. It was like reuniting with an old part of himself, all while being reborn.

Two elven fighters had taken to the Siren Song's fighting ring, smearing the white platform with their blood and sweat. From the upper level where he and the mercenary sat, they had a perfect view of the chaos below.

It was only Zara at his side tonight. Orion was tending to the soldiers back at the Stone Orchard while the Ikarrian guild had returned to the Elios mercenary temple to avoid suspicion of their constant absence. From what he understood, the other guilds were too busy maiming whatever poor bastards the High King deemed unworthy to live to notice, but the Ikarrians preferred to take extra precaution.

The Horizon slammed her cup on the table. "Another."

The long curls of her hair fell over one shoulder, her sun-kissed skin gleaming under the firelight. Ronan took one look at that smile, the mischief and defiance behind it, and found himself pouring her another drink. It was the most emotion the mercenary had shown within the past two weeks.

"You have a higher tolerance than I do," he murmured.

Zara flipped him a finger as she drained the cup to the damn dregs. A server swept by, and Ronan was sure to hand them the empty wine bottle. The little wolf was relentless, he would give her that.

"Admit that you enjoy my company," Zara drawled.

Ronan hummed, shifting his long legs underneath the table. "I suppose you'll do. Unlike you, I have options."

She frowned. "What is that supposed to mean?"

"Other than the guild, I am practically your only friend."

Zara shook a finger. "Not *friend*, archangel. We are in a business agreement, with temporarily aligned goals."

Ah. *Temporarily.* That was the word that hung between them. They were on amicable terms—so long as they served each other's needs. She hadn't tried to kill him—*yet.*

She dropped her feet to the floor and leaned forward with her elbows on the table, her hands under her chin. "Speaking of your dire need for more training, why is it that a leader of the shadow markets is not as sharp with the blade?"

He grimaced. "It was irresponsible of me. Even after I gained control of the Sombra Quarter, I shouldn't have stopped training. I think a part of me wanted to forget how to fight."

Zara cocked her head at that but she said, "It's obvious that you are familiar with using a sword, though. I noticed your skills when our paths first crossed. Where did you learn?"

Ronan briefly saw the image of his father handing him a sword. The blade had burned bright like a star and sang to his blood. He remembered the vines that crawled along the edges of the training ground, how his father's wings eclipsed the sun after beating him in mock combat.

He blinked back to his current reality, where the air was stale, smelled of sweat and alcohol. "My father was a skilled swordsman," he responded. "He wanted me to know how to defend myself."

Her curious expression quickly shifted into understanding. "My pater did the same. When Raziel enlisted me to live the life of a mercenary, pater rallied Hakim to rebuild the guild."

The name of the High King sent his blood boiling. He saw the chains flash in his mind, felt the phantom weight of them around his wrists and neck. The cold memories of metal slicing into his skin, along with Soleira's soldiers jeering at him, were only some of the many ghosts of his past.

The way Zara had said Raziel's name as well, with such familiarity—he clenched his jaw. Ronan sympathized with her—and anyone who had to tolerate the bastard on the High Throne. The makings of the hunting season were not unknown to him, however the creation of the Rogue had always remained a mystery.

"It sounds like your pater rebuilt the guild as a way to help you. To prepare his own mercenaries," he said. "So, the creation of the Rogue was not your doing?" Ronan asked tentatively, remembering the last time he had tried finding out more about her history as a mercenary.

Her gaze went a shade darker. "Raziel created the persona. My family and I suspect it is because I am the adopted daughter of the Ikarrian king, the one ruler who refrained from swearing fealty to him." She paused and took another sip of her drink. "My history involving the High King is a bit complicated. I was born in Valenzia and, when the War ended, I was bound to face the consequences of my realm's alliance with the Primordials. However, Idris adopted me, saving me from such a fate. This was seen as an offense by those in power, which prompted Raziel to create the hunting season . . . as a compromise . . ."

Ronan pondered on that. The High King was a spiteful male, not one to do things without intention. The news about her being a bloodborne Valenzian was surprising. "How long have you been a mercenary?"

"Nine years. I was adopted by King Idris when I was thirteen and I began my training not long after. At eighteen, I took my oaths as a Horizon."

Suns. She had been thrown into this violent life at such a young age. "And your sister," he asked. "She does not have the same burdens as you do."

Zara shook her head. "As you probably noticed when you met her, her duties consist more of becoming the future ruler of an independent kingdom. I never wanted her to see this blood-ridden part of my life, but I suppose it was bound to happen."

The previous shine in her face seemed to wither away. Ronan shifted in his seat to lean toward her, a playful smile growing on his lips. "According to Ares, she has been testing his patience, which is quite amusing. The vampire bastard deserves it."

Zara looked at him then. Truly looked at him, as if she knew that he was attempting to bring back the momentary bliss from before. He thought he saw the whisper of a grateful smile on her lips.

"It's almost been one week since Daria and Ares started their research on our mysterious enemies. I wonder if they'll be able to find anything useful before we resume our tracking," she said.

Ronan's gaze fell to the map at their shared table. A few drops of wine stained the corners, courtesy of the Horizon next to him who had only snickered and kept drinking after the crime. The towns that had been destroyed were already marked.

Four, he counted. Four settlements had been turned into abandoned cities and possessed creatures.

Zara flicked out a dagger, the thin steel blinding between her fingers. She pointed the tip of the blade at a section on the map.

"This was the last town we inspected, but there are no other settlements for miles. However, the eastern border to the Kairos realm is nearby," she added.

Ronan placed his hands on his knees as he observed the area she had indicated. His large body swallowed the space beside her, the small chair underneath him on the verge of falling apart, he was sure of it.

"Are you saying they might be heading to Kairos?"

Something twisted in his stomach at the thought of the possessed people unleashing themselves on the sand cities. No, he didn't like that at all.

Her lips thinned. "We must find their motives to be able to anticipate where they're going."

"We will."

His eyes caught the tightened skin over her knuckles. Scars nicked her body and the tattoos adorned both of her wrists. They disappeared underneath her clothing, and he wondered just how far they went.

Zara's cheeks had suddenly gone pale, and he waved for the server. It wasn't long before platters of cooked chicken, beans and flatbread were delivered to the table. Tall glass decanters of water set before them.

Ronan poured her cup and pushed the food her way. "You seem restless. Do you have a mark tonight?"

She gave him an odd look—which he chose to interpret as gratitude—and ripped off a piece of the flatbread, using it to scoop up slices of chicken. After a few bites, some color returned to her face.

"Yes," she said stiffly.

"As the Rogue." It wasn't a question.

Zara slid her eyes to him: the brewing of a storm echoing with a tortured plea. Something in his chest twisted at the sight.

"Would you like me to wait for you?"

Her eyes widened slightly. "You don't have to."

"I don't mind." He refilled her water. "Who is it tonight? Someone I might know?"

He said it in a light tone, but she grimaced. "Possibly. Though the marks the High King orders the Rogue to hunt are separate from the hunting season."

Ronan shook his head and lifted his cup to his lips. "After all this is done and over, when you are free—what will you do? What would Zara Santos, *not* the Rogue, like to do?"

A thoughtful look spread over her face. Firelight glowed against her cheeks, and he could see gold flecks within the green of her eyes. Orange burned like fire around her pupils.

"I don't know," she said. Zara lifted her dagger to the light. "This is all I know."

He smiled softly. "Violent little wolf."

She rolled her eyes. "I suppose I'd like to find out."

Ronan was genuinely intrigued. Speaking to her was better than any conversation he'd had with any of the shadow dealers in the Stone Orchard. "Is there anything you enjoy doing? Besides beating me to a pulp while training."

The corner of Zara's lips lifted. "Growing up, I remember that I liked books. I visited the castle library often and read in my pater's office with Daria while he worked." Her expression softened, a quiet radiance to her face at the memory. "And I think I like . . . dancing. When I first came to the Machai Forum, I saw the fire dancers in the street and was mesmerized by their movements—and the music."

Ronan smiled. "Then maybe we should try dancing."

She arched her brow. "We?"

"Don't think so highly of yourself, Zara. I can go without you. I've been leading criminals for over ten years, I would like a change of pace."

The Horizon shook her head, fighting back a grin.

She then let out a ragged sigh, as if the weight of her burdens were too much. They probably were. "My soul feels . . . weary. I'd like to find myself once more. Heal and rebuild."

Zara had been fighting a silent war. Though Ronan was familiar with that, he could never truly understand her position.

He found himself nodding in understanding. His eyes warmed. "I think that's admirable. It shows your perseverance."

Like a wolf.

She almost looked abashed. "And what would you do, Ronan Menodora? If you did not have any obligation to the Sombra Quarter, where would your wings take you?"

He tried not to consider how hearing her say his name, with that rough and smokey voice, had him perking up in his seat.

Ronan's gaze drifted to the fighting ring. Fists were flying, blood spewing. All the sounds rushed around him, and they fell into a dangerous hum. "Fuck. I don't know either. It seems I also haven't been able to consider other paths."

Zara chuckled and he glanced back to find her giving him a curious look. He grasped onto her gaze, held it, hardly breathing, until she cleared her throat and returned to the map. "We should explore the border territory to Kairos. If the groups of possessed people keep moving, we may be able to catch them before they reach the dunes."

"We will need to make sure we bring enough weaponry. I suspect those creatures won't be as forgiving as last time."

Zara sheathed her dagger and slid her chair out. "Perfect. Well, it looks like we accomplished what we needed to for this evening."

Ronan reached for the edge of her seat and dragged her back to the table. "No, little wolf. We are not leaving until you finish your food." He refilled her cup and slid it to her. "As well as your water."

Zara narrowed her eyes but obeyed. The Horizon listened without threatening to skewer him. He would call that progress.

After she had taken several bites, a male voice called out. "Rogue!"

"You, Rogue bitch!" Another voice. Female.

Ronan felt his body still. So still, as unto death. Fury simmered in his veins as he gave a sidelong stare at the couple glaring at Zara. She remained unfazed and continued to sip on her water.

His eyes narrowed on them. "Keep walking."

The male—an elf—ignored him, anger flushing his face a pure red. "You've killed people I cared about. Cut them down in the street like they were *nothing*. I do not care if you are the High King's personal assassin, you don't deserve to live among us. We should do to you what you do to your victims."

Ronan felt a rumble in his chest. An unseen hiss of energy coasted across his skin, testing the limits of his binding tattoo. The blunt nails of his fingers dug into the wood of the table. The couple snapped their heads to him. He prepared to move but had barely lifted from his seat when they finally heeded his warning and rushed away.

A snarl ripped through his clenched teeth, but he felt a hand rest over his own. Zara had that same empty gaze he'd seen before.

"It's fine," she whispered. "They are mourning. Let them grieve."

Ronan gave her a measured look, steadying his breath. "What they said was *not* fine, Zara. It is not as if you had a choice in the matter of your profession."

Zara offered him a small, tired smile. "I appreciate it. Truly, I do.

Someone with higher power may have ordered those deaths, but *I* swung the blades. I am not completely blameless."

"And you still have to suffer the consequences," he gritted out. Ronan ran a hand over his face. "Let's go, I've suddenly had enough of this place."

They left the Siren's Song and wandered toward the street shows. Zara seemed fine, her expression smooth and calm as she admired the parties. But Ronan knew better. He had been a ghost of himself for so long that he recognized when one retreated to a dark place. He was still finding his way out of it.

Ronan cursed under his breath when he noticed the fire dancers. He had been too distracted by Zara that he didn't notice how close they had gotten to the flames. Maybe nothing would happen this time, and he would be able to pass in peace.

A fire dancer pranced across the square, their hands bent and twisted toward the night sky. Flames sparked to life at their fingertips, a fiery ribbon of red flashed and whipped the air.

The brightness of it—the burns—the heat—*the screams*. His family was shouting—

Ronan flinched and looked away from the performance. His wings flared slightly as he fought back a shudder.

"Ronan, are you well?" Zara's voice was soft. Softer than he had ever heard it. Her hand on his shoulder awakened a desperate attempt to fill a need as he leaned into her touch. He couldn't remember the last time someone had touched him like this.

"I'm fine," he rasped out.

Zara tensed. "Shit."

He followed her gaze to a guild of mercenaries entering the Machai Forum, their armor stained with blood and gore. He recognized their garb as belonging to Elios. At their head was an archangel with red wings who was dragging someone by the nape of their shirt. Ronan immediately recognized them as Erasmus, the shadow dealer who had threatened to assault the Ikarrians for entering the Stone Orchard.

"The fucking idiot let himself get caught," he hissed.

Zara tugged at his sleeve. "We need to go, Ronan. Tamaya is the head of the Elios guild, and not someone I want to face here."

"They wouldn't know who I am," he said.

She still watched the mercenaries with wariness. "It doesn't matter. She will question who you are, and it will put my guild under unnecessary attention."

He didn't think Zara knew she had let a crack form in her walls. Raw, genuine concern shined in her eyes. It lasted only for a breath, but he dared to wonder if the Horizon was finally seeing him in a different light, worthy of being something other than a mark.

FORTY-ONE

For once Zara didn't seek the comfort of wine or crave the splitting pain of breaking skin. Guided by the pale stars, she treaded through the lush grass and sleeping hills. As soon as she saw the red lights of the secret city, she felt her hard expression waver.

Her pacing quickened as she headed down the slope until the trees made of stone greeted her. Their branches extended toward her, eager to steal her away from the world.

There was still that lump in her chest. That thick pool of anger and self-hatred that never seemed to leave. It lingered inside her, but the more she walked, the weaker it felt. It seemed easier to carry.

Ronan Menodora was waiting for her in the clearing. As he had said he would be.

She saw him now, sitting on a stump with his head bowed, a sharp rise and fall to his back, muscles clenched underneath the dark cloth of his shirt. He looked up and she faltered.

A haunted look possessed the steel of his eyes. His dark hair was damp and stuck to the sides of his face and brow.

Her throat bobbed. "Rough night?"

Ronan slowly nodded, as if he hadn't quite heard her at first. She saw the pain he carried there, had witnessed it in the Machai Forum. An endless battle was happening in that intelligent mind.

For a moment, in the clearing, underneath the watchful eyes of the night sky, they saw one another. Broken mirrors, shards of themselves.

Zara unsheathed her twin blades. "Ready?"

Ronan barely gave a response and became a blur of midnight. The silver of his sword glistened with the tears of the stars. Her obsidian blades sang out to him. Their bodies danced, gravitated to one another. He pushed, she pulled.

Ronan's grip on his weapon trembled. Her lips quirked to the side. "Still a little shaky with the sword, archangel?"

His teeth were a flash of white. Sweat rolled down his sun-kissed face. "Bite me, Horizon."

Moon-kissed dirt twirled about their feet and legs, the stone trees their only witness. Their blades locked in a cross, and she was forced to meet his eyes. Slivers of moonlight and broken armor, remnants of battles she did not witness. Echoes of a pain that harmonized with the one pounding in her own heart.

"I can feel your ether," Ronan said. Zara pulled back but he charged after her, forcing her to face him. "I felt your power when we first fought, and I can feel it now. It's . . . familiar."

She hesitated, considering showing him more of her ether. It would only be a thread of her ability, enough for its energy to reverberate, but not enough to reveal its light. So much time had passed since Zara had seen her ether at full capacity, she wasn't sure if she had ever witnessed its true strength. Her ether was itching under her skin, and it would be a relief to release some of its pent-up strength.

Zara reached out to the void within her mind, grasping only a fraction of her ether. Whispers of red light floated over her skin, enough for the hum of its strength to bleed through the air.

Ronan's eyes widened and she used the distraction to break free. She couldn't help but feel a morbid excitement at the dangerous sheen in his eyes.

Zara circled him, the tip of her swords grazing the pale dust.

"Whatever ether you possess, I can sense it. It calls out to the void. And it's strong. Distant, but strong."

The archangel winced as if her words were a blow to his gut and his gaze darted away. He said nothing and Zara dropped the subject.

There was still so much secrecy between them. A lack of complete trust, not to mention where he came from and his unknown ether. Why did it feel so distant, as if something was holding it back? Zara knew they would eventually have to decide whether to cross that threshold. The very success of their partnership teetered on that trust.

Later. That would be another battle for later. Tonight was for them. A moment where they could just *be*.

They sparred for hours. Dawn spilled through the openings of the rocky arches above the stone trees. Sweat drenched their skin and Zara's muscles burned. She hunched over, hands on her knees, her khopesh blades forgotten in the clearing, black steel twinkling.

Ronan ran a tattooed hand through his sweaty hair, the movement dragging the hem of his shirt up and revealing his smooth stomach. Zara averted her eyes.

The knot in her chest had loosened. The weight that seemed to linger over her shoulders had temporarily left her. It was easier now that they had both left their inner turmoil behind in the clearing, had allowed their pain to scream with every clang of steel.

A realization struck her. Ronan Menodora was more than the head of the Sombra Quarter.

He was a guardian. A protector, a killer, a soldier.

A horizon of his own making.

Mercenary. Reaper. Monster.

The fyrebrand's voice had been quiet, the longest since she'd heard it. She couldn't stop herself from flinching at the sound.

The dark hall that led to her room seemed to stretch farther the longer she stared. Zara huffed out a breath. The air seemed to thin, and her hand went to her chest. Something wasn't right.

She clutched at the threshold of her room. The bed, the walls, the pottery, all blurred in the dark. The ether inside her thrashed its head, its chains wailing in her soul. Zara pressed her fingers against her temple.

The voice pressed forward. It caressed her, but only caused chills to crawl over her arms. *There, there. Remember your purpose.*

No. This is not my voice, she pleaded. *This is Raziel.*

That power lashed out, it couldn't—it couldn't breathe. Light cracked along the skin of her hands, lining the tattoos on her forearms. Flames of ruby red and deep purple swirled from her hands, untamed and chaotic.

Zara gasped as pressure exploded from her chest. She watched as her ether bruised the darkness with its dawn light, guided her deeper into the room where she slowly slid to the ground. A sigh left her lips as the last of the flames withered into nothing.

She stared at her fingers. The voice inside her head hadn't weakened. It only waited, tapping an unseen talon against the corner of her mind.

Raziel's voice—the fyrebrand's voice—snarled. *You have an assignment. You have a life to end. Do not forget who you belong to.*

Leave me alone—

The tattoo on her wrist began to burn, smoke curling from beneath the bracer. Zara hissed and ripped it off as her head beamed with pain. The tips of her nails dug into her scalp, a tormented cry peeling from her clenched teeth. The world spun, and intense nausea swirled in the pit of her stomach. Zara collapsed to the ground, falling onto her back.

The voice echoed the same words over and over again.

Mercenary. Reaper. Monster.

It was a warning, a taste of what would happen if she were to keep ignoring her assignment.

The fyrebrand's Reckoning had begun.

FORTY-TWO

Daria's ether had fully awakened. It was an odd sensation. Like her blood had begun to pulse, another presence inside her that rumbled and purred. Her power had taken its first true breath yesterday, and it desired more.

She held a light pep in her step as she tended to her obligations throughout the day. The night arrived with a dark sky speckled with stars. Daria drew herself a bath as she waited for her evening appointment with Ares. Once she had dried herself off, she slipped into loose trousers and a blouse. No bulky and showy dresses tonight. She mulled over the plan as she lathered her body with oils and creams. They were going to visit the royal library to research about the ethereal creatures and fyrebrands. Politics she could handle but put her in a room of books and notes and she would conquer.

Though it was not going to be a simple task. According to Ares, the grand bookshelves were open to royal visitors, except for a section that was heavily guarded, *to preserve the most ancient and valuable texts*, according to the High King.

Raziel had burned much of the literature on Celestrea and the Primordials, as well as on the guardian kingdoms of Valenzia and Damalis. Their histories had been purged from the Continent, except for a small stock. Scholars of the realms had protested the archangel's aim to rid the countries of all ancient texts, which drove Raziel to store some surviving tomes in his castle.

Ares thought their answers would lie within that portion of the library, and that it was best to pursue the task at night. *The less prying eyes the better*, he had said.

Daria swung her velvet cloak around her shoulders and drew up its hood. Her dark locks curled slightly after being freed of the braids.

Daria's fingers brushed the handle of her dagger tucked within her clothes. She didn't think she would have worn it again, but it felt right. Like this particular weapon belonged at her side.

When she opened the doors to the hallway, she nearly stumbled at the sight of Silas. The young vampire gave her a curious look.

Daria grasped the threshold to her room. "Oh, I'm sorry, Silas. I thought Ares would be here."

Silas's brows jumped up. "That's intriguing, he's usually off in the evenings. And where would the two of you be heading at this hour?"

She gulped, feeling perspiration along the back of her neck. Suns Above, Ares was supposed to have gotten rid of his Second for the night. Daria's fingers drummed along the wall as she fumbled for an explanation.

"I wanted to see the outer district's nightlife," she said. "I thought Ares was to take me tonight."

Silas cocked his head, running a hand under his jaw. "I'm sorry princess, he didn't inform me of your plans. The general must be running late, he was in the courtesan wing earlier."

She blinked back her surprise, fighting to keep her face neutral. There was nothing between her and Ares that prevented him from doing what he wished on his own time. Yes, he was a handsome male and she had warmed to him. But there was still so much they didn't know about one another, their friendship still young.

So, why did Silas's words sting?

Daria hoped the vampire couldn't hear the nervous flutter in her pulse, though he most likely did. "I see."

Silas watched her intently. "He goes there all the time."

When Daria didn't respond, he went on, "The castle's courtesan wing is King Matías's. Only the vampire king has access to the workers there . . . well, other than Ares. Comes to show that the general truly is the vampire king's favorite."

The princess felt her heart drop, and she hated that it did. Gods, she needed to regain some control over herself. She swallowed thickly and prepared to retreat into her room.

Just then, Ares stepped into the hallway. The torches along the limestone walls flickered at his presence, his shadows stretching long behind him. His eyes narrowed as he looked between Silas and Daria, who both clamped their mouths shut upon seeing him.

The vampire general clasped his hands behind his back, his long hair swaying at his waist. "What's happened? You look like two little gossipers."

His Second glanced at Daria and cackled. "Nothing at all, general. I hope you are feeling in *light spirits.*"

Daria took the moment to observe the vampire general. There was a light in his eyes that seemed brighter than usual. A softness in his face that would surely disappear as soon as he had to deal with his soldiers and politics again.

Ares arched a delicate brow. "I suppose I am. You are dismissed for the evening, Silas."

Whoever he had been with seemed to make him happy. Good. That was *good.*

At least that was what she told herself.

The castle's library had its own wing. Daria's heart nearly stopped at the sight of the massive arches leading from one section to the next. The marble lining of the walls and ceiling was carved with images of wings and vines. Statues of archangels stood guard along the main central path. The library was made of three stories filled with rows and rows of bookshelves and tall windows opened onto the pitch-black sea.

How in the realms were they going to find what they needed in this maze?

Ares's gaze gleamed at her shocked face. "Do you like it?" He breathed out the words, the roughness of the sound tracing a fiery line along Daria's skin.

She nibbled on her bottom lip. "It's gorgeous. Though I'm already feeling weary. Where is the guarded section of this place?"

Ares placed a hand at the small of her back and led her farther into the library. They kept to the dimly lit areas to avoid detection. Several castle staff tended to the tables that rested underneath the windows, seemingly unaware of their presence. Some horned cats strolled between the shelves, clearly the rightful owners of the space.

Daria tried not to think of Ares's hand. The same fingers that she'd seen rip a statue from the ground were so gentle against her back. She mentally shook herself. If he was involved with someone in the castle, she could not tread into those sorts of thoughts and fantasies.

Ares guided her up the stone steps to the top level. There didn't seem to be anyone on this level, but Daria wouldn't let her guard down yet.

He steered her toward the back wall. The smell of old pages and wax engulfed her senses. Daria's fingers tingled with the urge to wade through the tomes surrounding them.

"So," she whispered, glancing around. "Where are the guar—"

She nearly yelped when Ares yanked her behind a shelf. He placed a hand over her mouth just as a staff member wandered past them. The vampire stilled, his eyes going distant for a moment.

"I don't hear anyone else." Ares eventually said before he stepped away from her and continued walking. Daria clamored after him as they reached a small open area. The vampire pointed up. "To answer your question, *this* is the guarded entrance."

She skidded to a stop beside him, eyes going wide. An enormous arched doorway stood before them. The surface of the door was made of dark wood and was covered in vines and iron that weaved together. There were no handles or bars, but Daria could feel the ether strumming from it.

"Fascinating," she murmured. "Ether guards it. How are we to get inside?"

Ares drew closer to the entrance, extending a hand toward it. Leaves shuddered as a strip of vines moved. It peeled off the door's surface and curled in the air toward Ares's waiting palm. A stem sharpened like a needle and pierced his flesh.

The vampire hissed as the ether-imbued vine drank his blood. Iron groaned in response, the sound of wheels turning reverberating throughout the space as the door pushed inward. A gust of a musky scent swept out and Daria had to wrinkle her nose.

She waved a hand through the dusty air. "I didn't realize you had access to the place."

Ares glared at his wound before clenching his palm. "Only a select few can enter, remember? I am the general of Adrastea and one of the chosen few."

Daria rolled her eyes as they entered the protected section of the library. "That was a very theatrical way of putting it. *One of the chosen few*. And yet you've never visited this place before?"

He shrugged an elegant shoulder. "I lead armies, princess, I never had a reason to visit the royal library before."

Inside were another three floors filled with even more bookshelves. The walls and the ground were made of bare stone. No windows existed inside, and there were only a handful of desks and seating areas. Lanterns lined the pathways, igniting on their own as if sensing visitors.

Daria gasped. "This looks like a prison. Though the levels here are not as wide as the main library, it is still massive. We are going to be here for ages."

Ares snorted and lightly pushed her forwards. "Better get to it then, princess. I will start on one side and meet you midway."

She arched her brow. "Ares Valdemar is not going to hover over me? What will I do if a book snaps its teeth at me?"

His lips curled. It was impossible to miss the fangs. "Just don't touch the books that are chained."

Daria's jaw dropped as her vampire guard laughed and sauntered to the opposite end of the floor.

They spent the rest of the night scouring as many shelves as they could. Her eyes burned for anything that spoke of the Age of the Primordials, assuming it would bring information about either the fyrebrand or the mysterious creatures. If there was no mention of such things, Daria immediately slammed the book back into its place.

Deep growls emanated from the chained texts Ares had mentioned. They shook against their bindings like animals. Daria avoided them with a shudder. Before dawn, Ares escorted her back to her room.

A few nights later, Daria's eyes were beginning to sting as she scanned the pages of an old tome labeled, *History of the Ethereal Realm*. Though she didn't think she would find any of the details they needed, her curiosity overpowered her. Suns forbid that she could enjoy some light reading.

Hours slipped past her.

Daria lingered in the aisle, her nose in the massive book. It was fascinating to read about the hierarchy between the Primordials, deities, and archangels. Daria hadn't realized that the realm of Celestrea functioned as any mortal kingdom would.

The lesser gods were able to wield raw ether in the form of silver light but the magnitude of their power was much weaker compared to that of a Primordial so, it was deemed that the deities would serve the higher gods as servants, advisors, or common workers. They were the working class in the world of Celestrea. That fact surprised her, it was hard for her to imagine what that reality would look like.

The book, however, didn't seem to have much knowledge on how the Primordials controlled ether or how it came to be.

Daria's eyes lingered on a sentence. One that sent the hairs of her arms rising. *The only method of killing a deity is through the heart and the heart alone.*

She flipped through the wrinkled page and her breath hitched at an image. It was of a woman who looked about her age or a bit older. She had long white hair and brown skin. A warrior's armor fitted her athletic frame, a hand raised to the sky, a power that looked like the cosmos swirling in her palm. The woman's face was etched with a fierceness and anger that seemed to reverberate from the page. Daria traced a finger along her face.

"You remind me of Zara," she whispered.

Daria's eyes went to the description underneath the image: *Khaos, the Primordial of Fate and Time.*

Suddenly, she felt like she was back in Ikarria with her priestess instructor. Daria remembered learning that the goddess had been punished by the Primordials for falling in love with another god who had become Celestrea's enemy.

"What was his name again? Oh, it was Deimos, the Primordial of Dread and Terror." She flipped the pages to see if there was an image of the male god but found nothing.

The passages didn't hold any more information other than that Deimos was imprisoned within the depths of the ethereal realm and Khaos had been banished to—*somewhere.*

Daria covered a yawn with one hand and shoved the tome back on the shelf.

The book was pulled away from view and a pair of deep violet eyes stared back at her across the bookshelf. "Don't tell me you are quitting now, princess?"

She placed a hand over her heart. "How dare you, general. A soldier never quits."

He snorted. She didn't miss how his eyes sparked at the way she called him *general.*

Ares walked to the next aisle, his voice reaching for her. "Every soldier pales in comparison to you."

Daria's cheeks began to flush, and she shoved another book into its place a little too harshly. She had discovered that the vampire was a flirt, if one got over his initial silence and broodiness. *He is seeing someone in the courtesan wing, you harlot.* She brushed the thought away.

"What do you know about Khaos and Deimos?" Daria asked.

"Oh, that is a very old story. And a random question, princess."

She ambled down the aisle, seeing Ares walking along with her on his side. "I just found a passage on the Primordials, but there don't seem to be many details about what occurred."

"I think that is because the details don't necessarily matter," he replied. Ares plucked out a tome and scanned its contents. "The god Deimos represented dread and terror, and those feelings are part of the natural world, part of being mortal. The Primordial was supposed to honor his title, but even gods have flaws. He ended up becoming overwhelmed with the very values he symbolized and wanted to rule over Celestrea with them."

Daria felt a bubble of excitement learning about this. But her mind lingered on Deimos and a twinge of sympathy touched her. "Imagine having to be the god of something everyone hates or is fearful of," she muttered. "That must have been lonely. And yet, he found love with Khaos."

Ares frowned at the book he was holding and put it back. "I imagine the Primordial of Dread and Terror found peace with the one individual who saw him for him."

"Only for their love to be torn apart. I truly find that sad."

The vampire hummed in agreement. "I am sure there is more to the story, but we know what we need to know."

"Where was Khaos banished to?" she asked.

Ares shrugged. "I don't think historians ever found out. I wouldn't be surprised if there was another world that acted as a prison, a place to send the unwanted. I mean, how else would you banish a *Primordial?*"

Daria's thoughts went to the woman in the image. The cry of fury and anguish on her face. Her heart twisted for the goddess.

"Banishing Fate and Time," she whispered. "There's some irony in that."

On the fifth night, Daria made it to the top floor of the guarded section. Beyond the walls, she knew night would be sweeping the sky with its inky blue touch. Stars would be shining above the dark sea, moonlight grazing its silver hands along the surface.

The spaces between the aisles were more narrow and awkward, and the air was thick with dust. Lanterns hung above the library railings, offering dim light. She wouldn't be able to continue for much longer.

Daria was about to step into another endless row of books when ruby red text on a book's spine caught her eye. The title, *Bindings & Breakings*, glowed under the firelight. Intrigued, she picked up the heavy tome and flipped the pages. Her heart started to race.

Bindings Made by Ether, A Common Practice Originating from Celestrea.

Suns Above.

A deep velvet voice slipped down the nape of her neck. "What have you got there?"

She whirled around. Ares stood very close, an arm draped on the shelf above her. She still marveled at how she had to tip her head up to meet his gaze despite her own considerable height. That violet gaze glittered under the dim light and made something warm coil low in her abdomen.

Daria felt her lips thin and took a step away from him, her back meeting the shelves. "I think this may be something worth looking into."

She was about to continue searching through the pages when Ares stopped her. "Not here," he whispered. "You never know who may be watching. Take it with you and I will reconvene with you in the morning."

His warning prickled the hairs on her arms. She hitched the tome under her arm, her eyes catching the two books in his hand. "It looks like you made some discoveries as well?"

He lifted one to the light. "This book is based on the legends of Celestrea and all ethereal beings. I took a glance, and it seems we may be able to learn something about the creatures the others encountered." Ares switched the tomes and lifted the second. "And this one contains the ancient teachings of ether-wielding. I thought it may be useful to you."

Daria stared at the large book. Her chest tightened and her ether purred. The gesture was . . . kind. More than kind. Ares had thought of her when he found it. She was certainly feeling *something*.

The realization was staggering, the words flew out of her mouth. "Dammit."

Ares began to chuckle. The sound was silk, flame and temptation. She could listen to it again and again.

Daria looked his way. His sensual mouth was shadowed by the dim light, deep violet hues rippled down his waist length hair.

"What?" She asked.

Her bodyguard met her gaze and those lips lilted. "I think that is the first time I've heard you swear, princess."

Daria breathed out a laugh. The light in his eyes shined brighter. "That was hardly a curse word, but do you see how bad of an influence you are?"

Something wicked flashed across Ares's gaze as his voice dropped. "You might already be a little corrupted, princess. In the best way. I am curious to see what other rebellion lies beneath that royal exterior."

Daria could feel the meaning of it settling over her chest. She was sure his vampire senses could hear the stuttering of her heartbeat. How those words unnerved her, but she too would have liked to know what she was capable of.

Suddenly, as she found her bearings, her back straightened. Her voice turned clipped. "You shouldn't speak to me that way."

Ares's expression fell. "Apologies, princess. I shouldn't have overstepped."

She waved a hand and rushed to add. "No, it's not that. It's— well—Silas told me you visit the courtesan suites. You have every right to do as you wish, I simply do not want to wander farther down this path if your eyes are set elsewhere." Daria couldn't meet his gaze, her face growing warm.

Gods. It was practically an admittance of her attraction to him.

Ares blinked as if he too did not know what to say.

Then he cursed under his breath. "Silas and his fucking mouth. No, princess, it is not what you think."

She shook her head. "It is fine—"

Ares gently took the book from her hand and stacked it with the two he held. His eyes softened, a gentle touch to his lips. "Let me explain everything to you tomorrow. You will understand, I promise."

Daria relented, moreso in desperation to flee from the situation. He led her back to her room and handed her the books. It was what she wanted anyway. She preferred to drown her thoughts with literature.

What she realized though was how, on their way back from the library, she hadn't once clasped her hands across her abdomen.

Daria tried to eat a late meal, but her appetite was disrupted by the excitement of the tomes she was going to devour. The pages were splayed out before her as she chewed on tough pieces of bread.

There was much history on how the ether-laced ink bindings came to be. There were endless ways to use it. Many of the deities who practiced in concoctions had found ways to bind ether within the ink, the ability to chain great power from its wielder. She shuddered at the thought of being unable to tap into her flames.

Time bled deeper into the night, till her room's fireplace dimmed to nothing but embers, but Daria was still awake, unable to look away from the tome. Her fingers trembled, the words before her blurred behind the sudden swell of tears.

She had found it. The passages she had spent all night searching for. She had found how to break the ether-laced tattoos—how to get rid of a fyrebrand.

And her heart broke with it.

Daria pressed a hand to her mouth. The sob that lurched up her throat was immediate. Her eyes scanned the page again and again. There had to be more. There had to—no, the page ended. Whoever the *damn* author was had scribbled the last end of the paragraph as if in a hurry. Dark dots wrinkled the ends of the page.

As the truth settled in Daria's heart, she couldn't fight back the flood of tears. For there were few options for the removal of a fyrebrand—to unbind any ether-laced ink: the creator had to break it either by their own will or with their death—unless the bearer of the tattoo ended their life first.

The alternative was by the ether of a Primordial.

Daria wanted to save her sister. So, why was this so difficult to accomplish?

High King Raziel would have to give up the fyrebrand himself. Or he would have to die. Both options were impossible. The alternative even more so.

There were no Primordials left.

FORTY-THREE

Ronan trudged through the deserted neighborhood of Soleira's outskirts. An ache seared across his tattooed knuckles, blood still caked between his fingers. While he had been distracted with the happenings in the Estrella Territories, Sombra Quarter business hadn't stopped. Orion and his forces had discovered a potential traitor within the leading shadow dealers—a wolf shifter who was spotted trying to get in contact with the castle. The male didn't believe his business was safe through the shadow markets and stated he was simply trying to go legitimate.

Ronan didn't think the High King still had spies infiltrating the markets, since he was already going after the Sombra Quarter through the hunting season. But that didn't seem to stop those within Ronan's ranks from betraying him.

He couldn't let the offense go unchecked, couldn't let others see him as a weak leader. The archangel had made a personal visit to the shifter's business front, charging through the male's shop. The shifter had inevitably transformed into his animal form. It had been some time since Ronan had fought a wolf, but he had grappled with the beast and thrown him against the shop's shelves. Ronan had slashed a knife across the shifter's throat.

The archangel felt like a shadow of his old warrior self—a male who would cut down his foes in the battlefield with no remorse.

Blood still glistened under the moonlight, a loud reminder of the death he had caused. He rubbed at his skin, growling under his breath. "I should've brought a fucking rag."

Ronan entered the abandoned temple to the statue of Aspidis and stopped in front of the sculpture, looking up to the stars. Ronan felt like the serpent Primordial. Always silently roaring at the night sky, never to be heard.

He sighed. "That bastard better not be late."

As if summoned, Ares charged into the abandoned temple, the princess of Ikarria thankfully nowhere in sight. Ronan knew the general would do his duty in steering her clear from this place. The less risk of being identified outside Soleira's castle, the better.

He eyed the vampire warily. "No bloodroot tonight? It must be bad."

The slight wrinkle between Ares's brows had the archangel genuinely concerned. Whatever news he brought, it was enough to unnerve the ever-stoic war general.

"It's not good, Ronan." Ares took out two books, shoved one into his hands and pointed at one of the marked pages. "Are those the creatures you saw?"

It was a sketched depiction of mortals with glowing eyes. There were variations of the creatures, some with horns and others with the metal-like teeth Zara had noticed. Ronan read the description beneath the drawing. "Yes, it's them."

Ares's lips thinned. "I thought so. Fuck, Ronan. Those things are *specters*. Souls of ancient, ethereal warriors—cousin to the wraiths, so to speak—and underlings of the Primordial realm. They can evolve into their *true* forms, and for them to do so they must feed off the essence of their host's soul."

Ronan felt the blood drain from his face. "What do you mean by true forms?"

"It didn't say. If they are the souls of old celestial warriors, then I assume there are multiple types or races of these creatures. I don't believe the specters have ever stepped foot into the mortal world before."

Ronan cursed. "They're from Celestrea? That shouldn't be possible. The gates have long been destroyed."

The vampire pointed at another marked page in the book. Ronan froze at the sight of the three ethereal beings. Somehow, they were just as terrifying on paper. Their crowns, weapons, and eerily unique faces. His eyes gravitated to the skeletal warrior with the scythe, the one who had almost taken Zara from him.

Ares leaned in, his voice sharp and low. "You mentioned there were rumors of the Three Sun Gods' return. Well, these are not the Primordials. They are called the Spirits of the Midnight Sun."

Ronan's brows furrowed. "What are they?"

The vampire looked even paler under the moonlight. "Did you ever wonder what would happen after the connection to the Primordial realm was removed? That there might've been consequences to the removal of ethereal power from our mortal soil?"

Ronan growled in frustration. Of course he had. Valenzia and Damalis had guarded the Gates to the land of the gods for thousands of years. From what he learned, no one knew what would truly happen if the Primordials were removed.

"They are the end of the world." Ares breathed out. "They bring the three phases of the beginning of the end: water, fire and darkness. They manipulate the atmosphere to reflect these stages."

Ronan's blood went cold. It had been hot this season, even though they were treading close to Autumn, but he remembered how it had begun to rain when the Spirits arrived in the city of Adira. Only when he and the guild managed to escape had it suddenly stopped.

"Oh gods." He ran a hand over his jaw. "How are the specters involved in all this?"

Ares released a heavy breath. "The specters serve the Spirits, and they all serve a Primordial."

Ronan could've sworn the world tilted on its axis. "That doesn't make sense. How? If they are the end of all life, it would mean they are part of the ether's natural order, but how can they serve a Primordial if the gods are trapped behind the destroyed Gates?"

"Unfortunately, there is no answer for that," Ares said grimly.

The gods and goddesses were neither benevolent nor malicious. They simply *were*—as far as Ronan knew. However the War of the Skies was the result of the inner turmoil between the gods and deities, and they had ended up involving mortals in their own petty squabbles. It proved the Primordials were susceptible to flaws. He wouldn't be surprised if one of their own had betrayed their kind.

Ronan ran a hand over his face, gripping at his hair. "What does this all mean? The War, whatever strife occurred between the Primordials, must be connected to this somehow. Either the Spirits appeared of their own accord as their duty to the natural order of ether, or someone—a deity most likely—summoned them and the specters. I am inclined to believe in the latter."

"Why?" Ares asked.

He rubbed the back of his neck. "Because the gods and goddesses have already dragged their battles into our world. The Primordials who were bound to love and support us for all eternity are susceptible to making mistakes, so much so that their own deities turned on them and one another. Which could very well mean the presence of these creatures is the doing of some angry deity. All that is happening cannot be a coincidence, that I can be sure of."

"Fucking Suns Above."

A painful silence descended between them as they mulled over what had been revealed. Every word had fallen with such weight. It reminded Ronan of the quiet before a storm, the brewing of a battle.

Gods, this was becoming much bigger than deciding to control the Sombra Quarter. What was he getting himself into?

"And the fyrebrands?" He asked.

Ares hesitated, his wary gaze meeting Ronan's. As he explained what the princess of Ikarria had discovered, Ronan felt himself fall to his knees. All he saw were those green eyes and wicked smile. The answer was there. It was within his reach, and not at the same time.

His hand drifted to the ether-laced tattoo band on his bicep. He had willingly placed these bindings upon himself, but *she* had not. And he had failed her.

No. He had promised. Vowed to help Zara Santos. It did not matter if those old books said otherwise, damn whatever shit was hurled his way.

Ronan would find a way.

His gaze lifted to meet the general—his friend. "Ares, I'm going to need your help."

FORTY-FOUR

Zara knew they had reached the eastern border of the Estrella Territories when the grass began to fade into sand. Evening light crested over the dry hills. Loose dirt rose within the blades of grass. Every inhale meant sucking in harsh air.

She rolled her shoulders, slipping the waterskin into her leather bag. Hot wind hissed at her ears as she squinted against the flecks of dirt. The back of her thighs burned as she trudged up the hill, the weight of her twin blades snug across her back.

Zara reached the summit, joining Hakim and Ronan, and lifted a hand to shield her face from the burning sun. Sitting amid the hills were the remnants of a city. Even from her distance, she could see the touch of Elios architecture fashioned here. Pillared buildings made of ivory limestone, with faint glimpses of statues and temples littered throughout.

"This is the only settlement we've come across from where we left off," Hakim observed. "The specters must have gone through here."

It was odd being able to call the ethereal beings by their formal names and titles. Daria and Ares had certainly outdone themselves in identifying the creatures. To think the specters were souls of ethereal warriors taking control of their hosts' mortal bodies, all while slowly feeding off the essence of the original life that existed there, made her shiver. It was truly possession—with a vile twist.

Ronan glanced at Hakim. "I almost feared that we'd lost their tracks. We can stay here for the night and see if there is anything we can find."

The head of the guild began to make his descent toward the empty city while Eshe and Axar sprinted over the hill's edge, the vampire archer keeping pace with the wolf, laughter ringing out behind her.

Zara dug the heels of her boots into the loose dirt as she slid down the slope. She was keenly aware of the archangel watching her from the summit. Since Daria and Ares had come back with information regarding the specters, he had been more reserved. He kept his distance, only meeting with her for their sparring in the grove. And when she did see him, the skin underneath his eyes was bruised with exhaustion, growing darker every time he made an appearance.

Ronan hadn't sought her presence, and she hadn't sought his. It was better that way. If all else failed, she would have to make the choice to end him. He knew this as well.

Despite it all, she felt like she was missing a friend.

The attack on the city had been recent. Ash still fluttered about the homes, blood hadn't completely dried on the walls.

They took shelter in an empty building, a fire now roaring in its center. Eshe sat on a block of stone, sharpening her arrows. The constant *shink, shink, shink* reverberated with the flickering flames.

Axar had shifted back into his human body and lounged beside Zara. He folded his arms behind his head. "Once we capture a specter, what's next?"

She stared at the fire. "We do what we do best. Interrogate it, learn from it."

He made a sound in his throat, his jaw ticking. "My favorite pastime. We must hurry—we don't have much time before your fyrebrand begins its Reckoning."

Axar shot her a worried look, and Zara held back a grunt. Her Reckoning might've started a bit sooner than anticipated. She hadn't told the others of its early symptoms—she didn't want to worry them when there was nothing they could do.

No, that wasn't true. If the mercenaries knew about her Reckoning, they may try to convince her to kill—

"You and the archangel seem to be on *friendly* terms."

Zara's breath hitched. She found Axar gazing up at her with genuine curiosity. Gods, she was tempted to deny it, but the shifter could always see right through her.

She resorted to a shrug. "We have found some common ground."

"How would Erebus feel about that?"

Zara wrinkled her nose. It had been some time since she'd seen the Hand of the High King, other than when he needed to assign the Rogue more marks. Even then, their encounters were quick and professional. He had tried to make some more advances, but she had denied him.

The desire to have casual sex with whomever, no care in the world, was beginning to fade.

Gods, she must be getting ill.

Zara released a frustrated sigh. "Erebus will never find out about Ronan. Regardless, he and I have made it clear neither of us expect a romantic relationship."

Axar sat upright and nudged her arm. Shadows were drawn over his skin, his short braids pulled back into a knot. "Well, as for the leader of the shadow markets, I don't care what you do, whether it is taking the male to bed for the thrill of it, simply befriending him or something . . . *more*. I just want you to be careful—in case you need to make that difficult decision."

Fucking Suns, it was as if he'd pulled the thoughts from her head. She could only muster a nod and a wry smile. "Do not worry, Axar. I hardly ever find myself wanting more from life."

Something like devastation flashed over her mercenary brother's eyes. He turned to the fire. The wood snapped and popped, embers exploding into the air. "We will free ourselves, Santos. I know we will."

She wanted to lean into that glow of hope, but the thorns around her heart only punctured deeper. It didn't seem that the fyrebrands could be removed. Ronan had told the guild of what had been discovered so far about the ether-laced ink. A hysterical laugh had almost escaped her. The faint dream of a life not under Raziel's thumb was nothing but an ember. A flickering, fading light.

The archangel hadn't been deterred. He was certain he would find a way. Ever since then, they hadn't spoken much.

While she was tempted to abandon the agreement with the Sombra Quarter, the guild wanted to see the mystery behind the specters through. They had gone so far down this road already.

And maybe she wasn't that tempted to leave the Sombra Quarter quite yet.

Zara was unable to remain still and rolled to her feet. "I'm going to find Hakim. I have a feeling I won't be able to sleep quite yet."

Outside, night creatures chirped and cawed. Zara heard male voices coming from the adjacent building and moved toward them. The walls were also torn down, and when she peeked in she saw Hakim and Ronan with their swords in hand.

Hakim and a *shirtless* Ronan.

"Now as you follow the pattern I showed you, let your blade do the work. Footwork and sword in tandem," Hakim instructed as he glided among the broken stone.

Ronan mirrored his movements. His skin glistened with starlit beads of sweat that trickled down the hard lines of his tanned olive skin and his tattoos. As he twisted around her eyes snagged on his back.

Angry jagged lines stemmed out from where his wings sat, so harsh she nearly flinched. Sometime in the past, Ronan's wings had been torn off him. She clenched her jaw.

She observed the two males in their methodic dance for a while until they stopped, and Hakim patted the archangel on the back. "Well done."

Ronan bowed his head, flashing his teeth in a slightly awestruck smirk. "I never thought I would get a lesson by *the* Dragonheart." Hakim chuckled and shook his head.

The sight of them like this, so carefree, titles and duties disregarded—Zara wasn't sure why but it squeezed her heart. She folded her arms, put on her usually cocky grin and strutted toward them.

"If you two are done frolicking about, you should get some rest. I will take the first night shift," she said.

Ronan frowned. "You don't have to. I will do it."

Hakim grinned and clasped a hand around his shoulder. "Don't fight the woman if you know what's good for you." He brushed past her, tossing her a wink. "Though you can keep her company if you wish. Axar will take watch after you, Santos."

Her jaw slackened as she watched the head of the guild sheathe his sword. His eyes warmed, a knowing smile on his lips. Zara was ready to glare back at the mercenary when he turned to Ronan. He pressed two fingers over his heart before moving them toward the archangel in a gentle sweep.

Ronan's expression fell at whatever gesture Hakim had made. The Horizon only smiled before leaving through a broken arch.

Zara's eyes stayed on the spot where her guild leader had last stood. "He's taken a liking to you."

Silence at first. "Does that make you happy?"

Her stomach flipped at his question, how his voice roughened. It had been so long since she felt so nervous, yet excited, it was practically foreign to her. "I suppose I don't hate it."

Ronan's lips twitched. "You have a great teacher."

The air was taut with tension. A strange awareness seemed to have risen between them. Zara wasn't sure what came over her, it may have been a desperate attempt to keep talking to him. All she knew was that she had missed the sound of his voice. She smiled.

He took a step back as if preparing to leave. She quickly unsheathed her blades and held them to the moonlight. "Hakim gifted these to me when I made my oaths and joined the guild."

Ronan paused before slowly stepping closer to her. His eyes

gleamed with interest. "I have been wanting to ask about these. Khopesh are most used in Kairos."

"Apparently, Hakim has been a longtime admirer of the jackal warriors. He had these crafted for me, thinking they would suit my fighting style. He was right, of course."

His fingers brushed the face of the obsidian steel. She was keenly aware of how close he was. Of his bare chest and torso. The faint tracks of where sweat kissed his body. Only a blade between them.

"Stunning," he murmured.

Zara felt her throat thicken and she sheathed her weapons. "This is the most that you've spoken to me in days."

Her voice came out hurt. Shit. She knew she was revealing too much of herself, but she couldn't bring herself to care. Ronan's brows pinched together.

"I'm sorry," he said. "I didn't mean for it to happen."

No witty remark. Zara almost wished he had made one of his cocky jokes. The tether between them tightened even more. Twisted.

The archangel shifted in place. "I would've thought Hakim would've given you a weapon unique to Valenzia."

She recognized his attempt to keep their conversation flowing, but his comment had her perking up. "Valenzia?"

"I remember you mentioning you were born there," he replied. "Both Valenzia and Damalis were famous for their midnight blue steel."

She frowned as a thought bloomed in her head. "I would never have known something like that about the realms. Raziel likes to remind me that my fate as a mercenary was due to Valenzia and Damalis's ignorant dedication to protecting the Gates of Celestrea and the Primordials, nothing else."

"He may be right about that." Ronan nodded, deep in thought. "The lost king of Damalis was proud, self-absorbed, and always in search of glory. And yet, he was favored by the gods. The king took the duty of leading a guardian realm to heart, ignoring the other mortal realms' beliefs. His was the first kingdom to join the battles against the deities that sought to save the realms from the absolute control of the Primordials."

Zara perked up. "And he convinced Valenzia to join forces with Damalis, to uphold their calling as guardians, yes?"

He smirked at her keen reaction. "Someone has been reading up about their history. Yes, you are correct." His expression grew thoughtful again. "During the War of the Skies, the king was defeated, all text that contained his name and the stories of his family removed from existence. He is now known as the lost king of Damalis, a worthy punishment for the man who brought turmoil to the Continent of Ribera by getting in the way of the deities. The deaths that followed his actions are on his hands."

Zara mulled over his words. To think that the course of the mortal realms' existence shifted just from the decisions of one individual. "This piece of history is the only thing that connects me to Valenzia. The sister kingdoms are gone, and I will never know more about my home realm."

He cocked his head, gazing at her. "I wouldn't say that. You are here, Zara. A part of Valenzia lives within you."

Before she could comment on what he said, Ronan turned to grab his black shirt. She stifled a gasp when she noticed the faint red splotches that decorated his body. The skin around the band of ink on his bicep also seemed irritated and red.

Zara took a step toward him. "What happened to you? Those wounds don't seem very old."

His wings slipped into the open slits of his shirt, and he quickly turned to face her. He avoided her eyes. "It's nothing, little wolf."

"It doesn't seem like nothing to me. Is that why you haven't spoken to me in a while?"

Ronan shook his head. He gave her a smile, but it looked strained and exhausted. The purple smudges beneath his eyes had almost darkened.

Her voice turned soft. "Will you at least tell me how you got the scars near your wings?"

His throat bobbed, wings ruffling. "I'm going to scout the perimeter."

Zara didn't argue with him. She knew how difficult it could be to peel open some wounds, especially the ones that were still raw after so many years.

"Right now?"

Ronan bumped her nose with his finger as he passed her. Some of that light returned to his face. "Don't worry, I will come back and keep you company." He paused before looking down at her. That vulnerability cracked through his expression again, tensing his scarred mouth. "I want to tell you all about the wounds I carry, Zara Santos. One day, if you are willing to wait—until I'm ready."

Her heart thumped against her ribs. He had done the same for her, hadn't he? Ronan, the ruthless leader of the Sombra Quarter, who had offered his own safe space within the grove for her to escape, no questions asked. Ronan, the mysterious archangel with a troubled past, who had offered his sword to help her unleash the fury that possessed her blood. Ronan, her unlikely ally, who had sworn an oath to free her.

Zara was willing to do her part. For him. "I will wait."

Starlight seemed to shimmer over his face. "Thank you."

She felt his presence leave the broken building, the space beside her immediately feeling cold and empty.

A part of her was disappointed that he hadn't stayed.

FORTY-FIVE

Ronan was an idiot. He should've—he wanted to stay behind. To sit beside her underneath the stars and listen to that rough, smokey voice. The realization snuck up on him better than any skilled opponent on the battlefield.

Except Zara was no opponent. Not to him.

The High King was seen as a savior to the mortal world. The Continent of Ribera approved of him, and Ronan might have as well if the ruling archangel hadn't gone after his shadow markets. But as he learned of the complex history between the rulers of Elios and Ikarria, how they had thrown Zara into the fray, it had kindled a fury inside him. Ronan hated seeing others trampled under higher powers. It was what drove him to try to save Zara, despite the agreement they had made. He was no stranger to failure, and he wanted to prove that he could save at least *someone*.

It was why he had avoided her after what Ares had told him. The wounds that surrounded his ether-laced tattoo ached, reminding him of what he had been trying to accomplish.

The desolated city ran beneath him like rippling gray water as he flew. Another powerful flap of his wings and he soared higher above the empty buildings. His eyes scanned every dark corner, though he sensed no movement.

A part of him was grateful for the distraction. When Zara asked him about his wings, he saw that cell once more.

The archangel soldiers had had their way with him. Ronan had killed so many of their own, it came as no surprise that he was their target.

The tortures had been manageable, something he welcomed, as it was his punishment. Until they held him down and ripped his shirt open. Ronan was prepared to take whatever they were going to deliver him. Then he felt the cold touch of a knife at the root of his wings.

Another type of fear gripped his heart. He screamed and tried to shake off the archangels, clawing away from them, but he was too weak. Always too weak.

The soldiers jeered as one grabbed Ronan's hair and yanked him back. The male's breath was hot against his ear. "*Now* he fights back. See, I knew we hadn't broken him quite yet."

Ronan squirmed but his face was slammed into the ground. The sound of his nose breaking blared in his ears. His palms scraped against the prison ground as they dragged him closer to them. A blood-curdling scream tore from his throat as the archangels began to cut through the base of his wings.

Red-tipped feathers had fluttered to the ground as he was thrown into oblivion. All the lonely nights that had followed, filled with the excruciating pain across his back.

Ronan grimaced at the memory. Maybe one day he could bring himself to share with Zara what made him the male he was today. There was no telling where this road would end, but no matter how stained the path was, he would ensure her freedom. It was a vow that seared through his blood and heart.

Ronan wasn't sure how long he had been flying. He reached the surrounding hills and observed the various paths that provided access to the abandoned city.

There was a narrow road that diverted from the main path. It crept between two hills, bending out of his eyesight. Wildflowers bowed to him as he landed before the forked road. Ronan bent to one knee, fingers trailing over the faint prints that trampled the thin grass: tracks made by bare feet, small shoes and large boots.

His hand froze above the ground. All the footprints continued north out of the city's territory except for a group that had taken the diverted path. Ronan followed the road. He found torches discarded in the bushes, their ends blackened, ash sprinkling the dirt. A campfire rested at the bend, a thin trail of smoke that still curled from the wood.

The specters were not as rabid as he thought. They were able to build a fire. Seeing as the creatures were old warriors from Celestrea, he shouldn't be surprised.

Something glinted from beneath the burnt wood, catching his eye. He dug out a pin. Moonlight winked against the silver-white symbol of Elios, three suns between a pair of wings. He studied it more closely, letting the moonlight shine on it. Ronan cursed under his breath, blood draining from his face—he recognized it from his time in the High Throne's prisons.

"I must be losing my damn mind—this cannot be real," he muttered as he observed the emblem's texture. "What is astral ore doing here?"

The mineral came from Celestrea. Only upper-class deities would have access to this.

He frowned and let out a frustrated breath.

Fucking Suns Above.

Flickering light caught his eye, and he looked up. From the campsite he could see the guild's fire and a narrow path leading straight toward them.

Ronan's hand flew to the pommel of his sword as a howl ripped through the stars. The world dropped below him, his wings thrusting him in the air.

There was a wild, savage beat to his heart.

Zara.

The first specter appeared from the shadows. Zara had been perched along the broken rooftop, the others asleep below her. She had been searching the night sky, her eyes wandering to the same spot where Ronan had disappeared.

She should've noticed how the night creatures went silent. How the stars themselves seemed to stop shining. How goosebumps erupted over her skin. Every muscle in her body tensed at the sound of running feet. She whipped her head around, but the streets were dipped in such thick darkness it even strained her sharp eyesight.

Zara's breath hitched when a pair of cerulean blue eyes appeared in the dark street below. Then another, and another. An entire herd of ethereal monsters stared back at her for a moment, the pull of a bowstring being drawn back, back, back.

Then they charged. They were eerily quiet except for their feet pounding the ground.

Zara leapt to her feet, swords in hand. She whistled a bird call and within seconds the mercenaries were at the ready. Axar shifted into his wolf form, Hakim in tow. The gray wolf ran out into the open street, hairs bristling. Eshe scaled the building to stand beside Zara, an arrow already nocked on her bow.

A lone specter blew past the group. Her hair flew wildly, a hungry smile wide on her face. Zara shuddered at the sight. Eshe fired an arrow, piercing the woman before she could reach Axar.

The archer cocked her head. "I suppose I shouldn't have done that. We were supposed to catch one."

Zara sniffed the air and sighed in relief, her tense muscles loosening just slightly. "There's no scent of rain. The Spirits are not here."

A spark of flame hissed to life as Eshe lit the tip of an arrow. The archer lifted her ivory bow and released the string. It was a shooting star, arching over the darkened road. The amber light bled over the dirt path, revealing scores of specters. Some had their jaws hanging open, others had mottled hair. Elves and humans alike. Zara couldn't tell which were vampires, if there were any.

"Shit," Zara breathed.

Axar drove his fangs into a specter and smashed it against the ground. Hakim swung his war hammer as the horde finally reached the end of the road.

Zara roused her ether. The power in her blood purred with every pounding heartbeat, vibrated against her burning muscles. Battle was in the air, and she let it fill her lungs. The energy inside her was restless, a beast yearning to claw at the stars. Untapped strength within her grasp, but she couldn't reach it.

Not that she would be able to wield it even if she could.

No one must witness her power. It was only the mercenaries among the streets with her, but if the specters were intelligent creatures, word could spread of a light-wielding elf. Not to mention that Ronan was within distance, wherever he was. And she wasn't ready to reveal her powers to him. Not yet.

Instead, Zara would feed her blades tonight. She skewered a specter and, with the unseen strength of her ether, flung him upward, letting Axar snatch him in his jaws. Hakim twisted around, shoving a pair of specters toward her. They had been too distracted clawing for him and failed to react in time before she slit them from neck to abdomen.

Zara lashed out with her blood-drenched khopesh blades, splattering the ground. No sooner had she struck down a group of possessed mortals than another cluster of specters were ravaging their way to her. The other mercenaries were far behind her now, held back by the other creatures.

An array of arrows rained down on the path in front of her, pinning many of the unnatural beasts to the bloodied dirt. Grateful that Eshe was their defense, Zara slashed through a human's throat and slipped into the fray.

Zara fought and fought, nothing but cerulean eyes surrounding her. She dodged razor sharp teeth that seemed longer than they had been before. Even their skin had changed. A possessed elf grabbed her shoulders, and she noticed the patches of scales that peeled from beneath its mortal skin. Another specter, in the body of a human pushing toward her, had horns peeking from her head.

It seemed that Ares and Daria's findings were true. The ethereal warriors were well on their way to transforming into their true forms. Zara couldn't imagine what their final state would look like.

An elf's teeth were poised for her neck, but she drove a knee into his stomach. He staggered back and she cut him down. Zara cried out as she dug her blades into more bodies, pushing her way through the horde. Her boots splashed in puddles of blood. The scent of peeled flesh burned hot through her nostrils.

Nails dug into her armor, unable to pierce through the plates. Yet. She wasn't naive enough to think that the scales clasped to her body were impenetrable.

Her muscles whined with every swing. The roaring in her ears grew so loud she couldn't hear the monsters grappling for her anymore. Every time she blinked the world blurred. But she could still see the guild, her warrior family, as they slew their opponents. But there were too many. The Ikarrian Horizons were powerful, stronger than most mercenaries, but this enemy was new to them. There was still so much they needed to learn about their attackers.

It wouldn't be long before her guild would be driven back, and if that were to happen then chances of survival would be slim. Zara sucked in a deep breath as she found her resolve. She did not care to hide her power anymore tonight.

So, she unleashed it.

Red light rippled around her arms and legs as the ether sent her flying to one side of the road, her obsidian blades already wrenching through flesh. Warm red liquid sprayed her face. Innards spilled with every jab and twist, her ether giving her the power her tired body lacked.

Zara dug her heels into the dirt. Red and purple light flared brighter about her body. Though it didn't burn, she could feel the warm press of its power. She briefly wondered how it would be to wield the light, if it even could be used as a weapon.

Later. That was a matter for another time.

Her power felt different, senses sharpened unlike anything she had experienced before. Another layer of strength folded over her existing one. The surge of energy sent her across the street, from one side to the other, leaving a crisscross of red light in her wake as she slashed through every specter.

The world around her disappeared. All she saw was her next opponent and her weapons driving through them. She flew across the ground, feeling every tendril of energy dig into her body. It was intoxicating, this rush of power.

More. More. More.

Zara didn't feel the burning ache within her bones at first. How quickly her amplified ether was draining her. Red smoke rose from her skin, and she stumbled at the sudden drop of her power.

Her knees threatened to buckle as panic grappled her chest. The specters crowded her, swallowing every inch of the street behind them. Their hands slashed at her leathers. She weakly stabbed those who nearly bit her flesh.

Shit.

The air was beginning to thin. She lacked the mobility and energy to use her ether. A specter lunged for her face just as Ronan dropped from the sky and drove his sword through the creature.

His powerful wings shoved the others away from her. "Did you need assistance, little wolf?"

Zara had to admit she was quite relieved to see him. "Make yourself useful, archangel."

He grinned and dove into the fight.

Ronan moved like a panther, diving between the folds of darkness with impressive agility. A song of midnight and war. The training they'd had in the Stone Orchard had paid off. His sword was a flash of silver light, a beacon within the chaos.

Zara's ether was a whisper in her bones. She decided to preserve it and fell into step beside him. Her movements mirrored his own as they slashed their way through the horde. Bodies began to litter the city road. To think only a few mercenaries and an archangel had managed to render so much carnage.

They still needed to capture one of the specters. She kept track of her kills, her cloak now heavy with blood. A male specter leapt from the shadows, teeth aimed for her throat. Ronan shouted in warning but the other creatures pressed forward, shoving him farther away from her.

Stars blasted across her vision as the male grappled her to the ground, her swords falling from her grip. She tried to summon ether to force the creature off, but the specter smashed his head against hers.

The world spun but she could still see its cerulean eyes focused on hers. *"Fascinating. I didn't think we'd see a Daughter of the Dawn."*

Zara felt her blood turn to ice. The creature's voice was male but made with a myriad of high and low tones.

She struggled against him, gasping for breath. "Who are you?"

It sniffed her. *"I feel the ether. It won't be long now."*

Zara rammed her knee against the creature, but it refused to budge. The specter smiled before it clamped its teeth around her side. A bone chilling scream peeled from her lips. The bite was so strong, it pierced through her leathers.

A wall of gray soared over her. Axar ripped the specter off her, holding it between his fangs. Zara slowly went to her feet and pressed a hand against her side, her head swimming. She couldn't focus on the wreckage that surrounded her or whether her guild and Ronan were fine. Her eyes were stuck on the specter. Hakim reached them and went to help Zara, but she shook her head.

"Did you hear what it said?"

Axar's wolf gave her a questioning look. She growled and pointed at the creature between his teeth. "It—*he* spoke to me!"

Hakim sounded distant. "What in the gods' name are you talking about, Santos?"

The creature bucked and mewled against Axar's grasp. She felt a prickling heat at her wrist. The fyrebrand. Had it finally driven her mad? Surely, she hadn't imagined the voice.

The specter laughed. *"Blessed of the Ether, your souls are owed to the everlasting Sun."*

Hakim cursed. "What did it say?"

FORTY-SIX

E she dragged the specter away. Its hands and feet were tied with ropes like a caught pig. A leather strap was wrapped around its mouth to prevent future bites.

Zara blinked against the bright light as Axar shifted into his human body. His voice sounded far away, even though he stood a few feet away from her. "They knew we were here. This was a deliberate attack."

The ground swayed beneath her feet. Zara forced herself to stay still and looked to the sky. Were there two moons?

Hakim rumbled, "It spoke in tongues. It was a language I did not recognize. Zara, did you say you understood it?"

Every sound fell to a low hum. Zara tasted metal on her tongue as the insides of her stomach tumbled. Something wet seeped from where her hand pressed against the wound. She looked down, her vision blurring, and she could no longer ignore the blood that stained her palm.

"Zara, did you hear—shit."

Strong arms swept her up. Hakim. His large, familiar frame sent a wave of genuine warmth that cracked a jagged line deep inside her chest. Zara didn't know she had been craving touch. Something wet pricked at the corner of her eyes.

The head of the guild cursed. "Shit, little warrior. I need you to keep your eyes open."

Axar rushed over from . . . somewhere. "Fucking Suns. Can you hear me, Santos? *Santos?*"

She made a sound between a groan and a whimper. A burn began to ignite at her side. A deep drumming of wings made the air tremble. The energy behind it—the *anger*—Zara could taste it on her tongue.

"What happened?"

Ronan's voice cut through her mental haze for a moment like a blade. A spasm shot up her side and she bucked in Hakim's arms with a scream.

She was sinking underwater, she was sure of it. The world drifted farther and farther away. Her eyelids fluttered as she tried to cling to what Hakim was saying. "The creature we captured bit Zara, but it doesn't seem to be a regular bite."

Instantly, the scent of jasmine closed in. She felt fingers hover over her skin. "Fuck, it managed to puncture through her armor. Hold on, little wolf. This is going to hurt."

Zara could only feel who she assumed was Ronan lightly tugging at the armor pieces around her side, her eyes squeezed shut. Every jerk and pull felt like a thousand burning ants skittering from the gash, leaving a pulsating fire in their wake. Ronan murmured soothing words with every cry she gave and he slowly peeled away her wet shirt, underneath which loose skin lifted from the wound.

Zara cried out, the sound rough and pleading. Hakim's grip tightened with every tear of her throat. She blinked through the blurring vision. There was a rumble from where Ronan stood. "It's poison. You can see a trail of foam within the wound." His voice was low and urgent.

"We are not far from Kairos's borders." Eshe rushed out." The mercenary temple is east of here, closer than any other establishment. Take her there, the Horizons of Kairos will have stored medicine and tonics."

Axar sounded strained. "Will they have what she needs? Can he arrive in time?"

"There are no other options, pup. The archangel is the fastest out of all of us. He is what she needs."

Ronan folded Zara's armor back over her wound and slid his hands underneath her. "Give her to me. *Now.*"

Hakim hesitated, his grasp around her tightening. His voice cracked, and she could sense his worry for her. "Please, take care of her."

In the brief silence that followed Zara could only imagine the quiet communication that passed between the two males. Then, the feel of the archangel's body against her was almost a balm to the pain that racked through her.

Ronan was already moving. "We will meet you back at the Stone Orchard. Orion will know where to keep our captive."

A gust of wind rushed through her hair as Ronan took to the sky. Another scream tore through her lips at the sudden movement. It felt like the fire from the wound was beginning to spread. She still couldn't bring herself to open her eyes.

"It burns," she moaned.

Ronan cursed under his breath, tucking her closer to his chest. Perhaps almost too tight. "You better stay awake, Horizon."

Sweat dampened her brow, trickling into her eyes. Or were they tears? She couldn't tell. Zara forced her eyes open.

Ronan's powerful black wings beat against the night sky, moonlight rimmed the dark hair that fell over his brow, his stormy gray eyes on her and only her.

What a beautiful winged male.

Her gaze fell to the scar on his mouth. "You are stunning, Menodora."

Ronan chuckled in surprise, the sound genuine yet tight with tension. "The poison must be making you delirious. You never compliment me."

Zara almost smiled until another rush of heated pain lanced through her. A groan peeled through her gritted teeth.

He kept his voice light, his grimace betraying him. "Don't fucking die, or I will kill you myself."

"Like I would let you have the honor."

Another chuckle. He continued to speak to her, forced her to listen to him. She didn't know how much time passed as she fought the urge to fall asleep. Blood still seeped from her wound, staining Ronan's leathers as well.

"I need you," he said. Wind yanked on her hair as he dove through the streams of moonlight. "There is no one else I would rather conquer enemies with than you, Horizon."

Her body shook and she tipped her head back. She moved her lips but wasn't sure whether she spoke. Ronan's voice was soothing, like dark silk wrapping around her. It lulled her even though she wanted to keep listening to him.

All the stars gleamed above. Watching her as she slowly drifted into the void.

The only thing she heard was his voice. Deep and panicked. Far and distant.

"Zara . . . Zara!"

The world came back in shards, broken and cloudy. They were still in the air.

Ronan careened through the stars, so fast that Zara was forced to look straight ahead. Two golden spires rose from beyond the hill. They flew over rows of enormous pillars and a pool of water leading to a temple made of sandstone and jade.

The mercenary temple of Kairos. It had to be.

Darkness started to fold over her eyes before Ronan's face appeared once more. Tension bracketed his jaw and a cold fury burned through his steel eyes. "Stay. Awake."

Ronan soared through the massive entryway and into the large temple, more columns lining the unlit corridor. Zara's vision swam once again, and she was unable to see where he was headed. She felt Ronan land and tried to force her eyes to focus.

He kicked down a door. "Is anyone here?"

There was no response. Ronan was like a storm, wild and rampant as he walked through whatever chamber they entered. Only when handling her did he slow and soften his touch, placing her on what felt like a bed.

The burning returned with a vengeance. Muscles spasmed and sweat drenched her skin. Zara arched her back as another cry ripped from deep within her chest.

"Fuck," she rasped.

There was the sound of cupboards being opened and appliances thrown. Ronan cursed as he searched the room for something. Only after several, painful moments did his footsteps return.

He brushed a strand of hair from her face. "I'll be right back."

Zara whimpered against his touch. *Don't leave*, she wanted to say.

Ronan sucked in a breath. There was a pause before she felt his lips brush against her brow. He tore away from her, disappearing deeper within the temple.

She opened her eyes to a golden ceiling. It wasn't long before it began to spin. Zara could've sworn stars appeared above her. The air vibrated, humming through her essence, as ribbons of raw ether materialized above her.

Oh gods, I am going mad.

The ether danced and spun. In the space between its shimmering light, Zara saw an image. Trees. Glowing silver blossoms filled the branches while the trunks were rooted in tall grass. The groves floated underneath a sea of stars. A tear slipped down from the corner of her eyes. She had seen this place before—in a dream.

Was she going to die?

Something entered the room. It had been awhile since she'd felt it, but the force of its presence sent a visceral familiarity through her. Zara turned her head to the side to find a thick, dark figure standing in front of the doorway.

Piercing eyes. Gleaming fangs.

The black wolf had appeared *again*. This time Zara couldn't stay silent. The words broke from her dried lips. "Why are you here?"

The wolf's tail flicked from side to side. It bowed its large head, eyes on her. The animal took a step forward. Zara's heart thumped as another wave of her ether soared through her body. It collided with the poison and sent another assault of pain to her side.

She blinked through the pain, the wolf now gone, someone else in its place. There were more than one. Five figures, she counted. They were dressed in armor—dark leathers lined with ivory and bronze. Zara drew in a sharp breath. The mercenary guild of Kairos stood before her, hoods drawn over their faces.

The Horizon at the front crouched on the floor, balancing their weight on their heels, as they tilted their head to peer at her. The movement revealed the face of a male with golden brown skin, a subtle dusting of hair that shadowed his jawline. His dark eyes gleamed like the night. There was something animalistic in the way he moved as he tilted his head even more to survey her. The other mercenaries stood behind him like silent wraiths, watching and waiting.

The air swooshed as a gentle weight landed on her bed. Ronan leaned over her in a protective crouch, black wings arching high. His hair was damp and curled over his brow, nearly touching his eyes. His arm was outstretched in a fighting position, her dagger in his hand.

Ronan bared his teeth as he stared at the mercenaries. Zara forced herself to look back at the guild and noticed the male was holding something in his hands.

Cupped between his palms was a pile of loose dirt, a golden flower poking up from it. It glinted brightly, as if he held the sun in his hands. Another tormented cry released from Zara's lips.

Ronan trembled above her, his grip on the dagger tightened.

He nodded to the flower. "Will that save her?"

The Horizon said nothing as he slowly placed the plant on the ground. He brought his cupped palm to his lips and pretended to drink. His eyes slid to Zara, and he winked.

The mercenary then retreated into the darkness along with the others. If her senses hadn't been weakened, she would've been able to feel their presence leave the premises of the temple.

Ronan flew to the golden flower and disappeared from Zara's sight. She listened as more distant sounds of clattering pots and crackling fire reached her. Eventually he returned and brought the rim of a cup to her lips.

"Drink," he said.

It was the smell of the sky and honey. The liquid trickled down her parched throat, spreading through her chest in a warm wave.

Zara felt herself tumble back into the abyss, the type of darkness that soothed and protected. The archangel before her drifted from view.

His fingers went to her face, brushing her damp cheeks. "I have you, Zara." The words reached for her, aiming for her heart as she fell unconscious.

"I can't lose you too."

FORTY-SEVEN

The courtesan wing was quiet. There were little to no guards within the limestone halls. Daria fiddled with her fingers in front of her abdomen as she followed Ares.

This sector of the castle held a more lavish sheen. Olive trees decorated the walkway, and the scent of rose oil permeated the air. Expensive rugs fashioned in the Adrastean colors were sprawled about the passageways. King Matías certainly took care of his courtesans.

Ares must've sensed her apprehension. He grabbed her hand and squeezed it. "Trust me."

Daria said nothing as he let go and approached one of the last doors in the hall. "You asked me why I serve King Matías. This is my reason." His large hand landed on the bronze door handle. "She's been wanting to meet you, to see the cause of all this excitement within the castle." There was warmth in his voice.

Her confusion was momentarily washed away by the splash of warm light as they entered the room. Thin white curtains drifted with the breeze coming in from the open window. Cream-colored furniture lined the walls, delicate iron handles on every drawer. A big bed sat in the center of the furthest wall, its sheets a soft olive-green, a matching veil draped over the four-post bed.

A woman sat upright on the bed, leaning against the headboard.

She had long dark hair and ivory skin. Then Daria met a pair of familiar violet eyes.

Understanding dawned on her as Ares gestured toward the gorgeous vampire. "This is my mother, Morana."

Ares's mother.

She was his reason for serving in the vampire army. A slew of questions whirled in Daria's mind.

He pulled two chairs beside the bed and gestured for her to sit. Daria couldn't help but admire the likeness between mother and son. They looked so similar it should have been immediately obvious they were related. Morana's hair held the same deep purple sheen as the general's, her face crafted with an elegance that stole Daria's breath. Sharp eyes, full of genuine curiosity and warmth, and full lips the color of blush blossoms.

Daria found herself smiling. "It is lovely to meet you."

Morana tilted her head, eyes shining. "It is an *honor*, princess. I hope my son has not been too much of a nuisance."

Daria glanced at Ares with a smile as he settled in his seat. "He's tolerable."

"How very kind of you." There was a faint curl to his mouth, his attention sliding back to his mother with an affectionate glare. "Of both of you."

Morana shrugged. "I hardly ever leave the wing, so I only hear how scary Ares is from his soldiers. Some things never change I suppose, he's always been too serious."

Daria felt the weight of his dagger—his gift—on her person. "Ares is not all that frightening. I found him to be quite irritating at first." That got her a roll of the eyes from said vampire. "But you may be pleased to know that your son can be very sweet when he wants to be."

His mother beamed at that, reaching over to place a delicate hand over Ares's. "Good. Being a general for Adrastea may be a difficult position, my son, but do not forget how I raised you to be."

Ares gave a small bow of his head. Daria was still teeming with questions, and she scooted to the edge of her seat. "Pardon me,

Morana, but I didn't realize you lived here in the castle as well. Nor did I know of you, to be completely honest."

The vampire shot a look at her son. "You didn't tell her about me?"

Ares looked like he had been caught doing something he wasn't supposed to. "We both know why I don't share details of our lives so openly."

"Well." Morana gestured toward Daria. "Bringing the princess here means you trust her, so why don't you explain."

Daria waited as her vampire guard faced her. She was struck speechless to find vulnerability in his gaze, the look of a male opening a piece of himself and offering it raw and bleeding to her.

"Not many in the castle know Morana is my mother," he said. "I intended it to be that way. I don't want to put her in harm's way if someone tries to hurt me through her. King Matías knows, of course— as does Silas. My Second figured it out on his own, so for him to allow you to think otherwise angered me."

Daria considered that. "To give Silas some credit, perhaps he was just trying to keep your secret."

Ares scoffed. "My Second is not that kind of male, princess, I can assure you. Anyway, my mother has worked and lived as our king's courtesan for years. Matías took us off the streets of Adrastea when I was young, and we have served him since."

"I've told Ares many times that he should leave this place, make himself a new life—" Morana started.

"You know I'm not leaving you here alone, mother." He murmured.

Daria's heart clenched. Though she was grateful that their fates had turned, leaving poverty behind, it seemed there was something she was missing.

Morana coughed, a rattle in her chest. Ares's expression turned solemn. "How are you feeling today?"

The vampire sighed. "The same as before. Steady."

Daria noticed a slight tremor in her hands and the rasp of her breaths. Ares leaned over to the nightstand and pulled on a drawer. From her angle she shouldn't have been able to see what was inside, but she still caught sight of dozens of vials.

"I will make another visit next month and bring more," he said.

His mother gave him an unsure look. "Will you be able to?"

"What do you mean?"

She tapped a slender finger against the sheets, lips thinning. "Matías mentioned the vampire's forces were going to be preoccupied during the coming weeks."

Ares cocked his head. "I haven't heard of anything. I know the final celebration of the Summit will be hosted within a fortnight. Perhaps that is what the king meant."

Daria couldn't believe it. The time she had spent in Soleira—and with the vampire guard—had been so eventful that she had almost forgotten the Summit was ending. She fought back the sense of failure for not having found out more about the Council. For not having accomplished more.

Morana looked to be deep in thought for a moment. Her shaky hands folded over her lap. "I suppose you're right."

They continued to converse for another hour. Ares's mother asked the princess questions regarding her childhood and life, and Daria was happy to share the little adventures she'd had in Ikarria. As she chatted with Morana, Ares simply watched her, drinking in every word, something unreadable in his eyes. There were fleeting moments when Daria could feel her cheeks flush and she fought the urge to chide him for staring, but she was grateful to see Ares without any of that coldness he normally had within the castle halls.

Ares Valdemar was no general in that moment—simply a son and a friend.

The Summit would end soon and Daria would have to return to Ikarria. Her companionship with the general would come to an end, they'd eventually have to say their farewells.

Her chest tightened.

They returned to the training ground that afternoon.

Daria's muscles quaked with exhaustion as the last fumes of her ether settled beneath her skin. Moisture clung to her ether-worn flesh, and she could've sworn she saw steam rise from her body.

Ares straightened. "You haven't said a word since we left the courtesan wing."

Daria lowered herself to the ground, extending her legs on the wet stone. "I'm sorry, I've been lost in thought."

Ares plopped himself beside her. They gazed at the ocean, watching the spike-tailed seabirds dive in and out of the water. She chewed on her lip for a few seconds.

"Ask me your question, princess. I know you have one." Ares smirked.

Daria rolled her eyes. "I was wondering . . . What about your father? You haven't mentioned him."

Ares's lips thinned. "That is only because there is nothing much to tell. I know that he was someone of wealth and that his death left us stranded. My mother never talks about him, though I suspect she loved him very much."

Daria nodded. "Well, I enjoyed speaking with your mother. Thank you for introducing me."

"I am happy to have been able to share this part of my life with you. I wish I could do more for her."

His voice had gone grim, and Daria turned to see that the gleam in his eyes had dimmed.

"You said something about not wanting to leave your mother here alone. You're the Adrastean general. Are you not free to go as you please?" Daria asked softly.

Her guard sighed. "My mother and I have always been poor. When I was a child, she would often work long nights. She never told me what she did, but I could smell the thick perfumes on her skin, how she would try to cover up the other scents. I never judged her for it—she did what she had to for our survival. Though she was always kind and loving towards me, I knew she wasn't happy."

Ares's jaw tightened. "I gave all my blood and tears to my duty and ascended in rank, so we could live under a working roof with endless access to food, so that my mother could sleep in a proper bed with castle staff at her beck and call. I feel as though part of my effort fell through when King Matías found a certain *interest* in her. She leads the same life as before, only with prettier dresses and a nicer home—and she can't get out. I can't help but feel that it's my fault, that I didn't save her."

Daria thought of a younger Ares. A boy, hardly a man, forced into the position to provide for his family. Her heart ached for that young vampire. It also mourned for Morana, knowing that she was unhappy, stuck here, yet still did all she could for her son.

"It's *not* your fault, Ares. You've worked hard to be where you are today. You did all you could," she whispered.

He nodded slowly. "I will always be indebted to my mother. It is the reason why I serve—even more so now that she has fallen ill."

"I suspected something was wrong," Daria said. "I saw the vials. It may sound ignorant of me, but I didn't realize vampires could get sick."

His lips twisted into a smirk. "I thought you knew everything, princess."

Daria put on a haughty look. "Never in my life have I said those words, vampire."

Ares chuckled. The sound fell into a sigh, and suddenly she saw how tired he really was. A son who didn't truly take care of himself. His efforts designed to support the single significant figure in his life.

"There is a certain disease that is rare amongst my kind called the Red Blight. Historians and healers don't truly know its origin; however they discovered that if a vampire drinks from several blood sources of different races, then their own blood is prone to poisoning itself. It is why my kind tends to keep to either elves or humans. In theory, their blood is the purest and most compatible with ours."

Daria's jaw dropped. "Your own blood could become contaminated over time."

His sensual lips curved. "Aren't the Fates fickle things? The one thing that gives us life can also give us death. My mother only ever drank from blood centers. But we couldn't afford quality sources. I suspect the cheaper items they gave us may have caused the disease to awaken in her."

Another wave of understanding dawned on her. "That's why you looked so unnerved when we first came across the blood banks. And why you work with Ronan. He provides you with medicine."

Ares nodded. "All of this is done without my king's knowledge. He owns my soul, and I keep serving him as payment for getting me and my mother off the streets. He would never let us leave."

She recalled how distant he became when others would bow to him or give him praise. How his lips would twist in disgust anytime politics were brought forth. It shouldn't have come as a surprise. Within these halls, he was honored for the atrocities he had committed to gain the vampire king's favor just so he could take care of his mother. It was all a means to an end.

Daria slipped a ring from her finger. It was a band of obsidian, a trinket she had worn for as long as she remembered.

She offered it to Ares who gave her a startled look. "For you. As a token of our friendship and a thank you for being my personal guard this entire time."

His brow furrowed, gaze jumping to her. "What?"

Daria leaned forward, lips twisting with amusement. "It is my gift to you. Now you will have a keepsake that is unique to Ikarria. It's pure obsidian, you know, straight from the draconic realm. To remind you that I'll always be on your side."

Tension bracketed his mouth for a moment. Ares stared at the ring, his expression softening. He looked up at her then, and the purple in his eyes deepened. Maybe even glistened.

"No one has ever gifted me anything like this before. Thank you, princess."

FORTY-EIGHT

Day and night bled together. No dreams or nightmares came for her. The few times Zara rose from the depths of the void, she'd feel a tender touch on her brow or the rough fabric of a blanket being tucked under her chin.

Light peeled through the slits of her eyes as she opened them and tried to focus on where she was. Gold lined cream-colored walls. A carved-out window sat to her right, revealing a clear blue sky. The heat of the sun was comfortable and dried the sweat that had dampened the bedsheets.

Her eyes went to *him*, as if something was drawing her to his presence. The archangel sat at the edge of her bed. His boots were planted on the ground, head bowed, wings folded neatly behind him. Sunlight kissed his midnight hair and the breadth of his shoulders. Faint lines etched the space between his brows and mouth.

Beautiful and tortured.

Ronan's eyes slid to her. There was a subtle tightening of his jaw that morphed into the loosening of his shoulders before he leaned forward and pressed his fingers over her slick brow. Zara was silent as he continued to check her temperature and pulse. The feel of his skin scraping against hers—it shouldn't have brought her the awareness it did.

The rest of the world hated her, but he looked at her like she was the light of the sky and the glow of the night.

Ronan cupped her face, his thumb sweeping over her cheek, his eyes searching hers. "How are you feeling?"

She wasn't sure he realized how affectionate he was being, and a part of her melted at his touch. His voice sounded rough, as if he hadn't spoken for some time. Zara swallowed through her dry throat and managed to force out the words. "Much better. I don't feel like I'm burning from the inside anymore."

Ronan released a steady breath. "Fuck, Zara."

She looked down and noticed that she was no longer wearing her armor. She still wore her black clothing but felt gauze plastered to her wound. Ronan had tended to her—had saved her life.

He helped her sit upright, every muscle aching with the movement. The sensitive skin at her wound pulled, making her wince at the slight sting. The archangel twisted around and brought a small cup of water to her lips.

Water trickled down her cracked throat. He watched her drink every drop. "You scared me."

Her heart skipped a few beats. "Thank you for helping me."

No sarcastic remarks. He clenched his teeth. "The sound of your screams—I don't ever want to hear that again."

She swallowed the last of the drink, desperate to change the atmosphere between them. It was too vulnerable, too raw. "How long has it been?"

"Two days."

Zara cursed. "Shit. We need to head back to the Stone Orchard. What if Raziel summoned the Rogue? What if the other mercenaries are looking for my guild?"

His fingers wrapped around her jaw and gently made her meet his eyes. "You're alive and well. That is all that matters. If anything happened, I am sure the others handled it."

She swallowed, pulling away from him. "I recall seeing the guild of Kairos in the temple."

"Those mercenaries saved you. I had been tearing this place apart looking for medicine but couldn't find anything."

"Well, the mercenary temples are hardly in use nowadays, other than the one in Elios," she explained. Ronan took her empty cup and pulled on the bed sheets as she spoke, covering any part of her legs that fell exposed. "I saw the Kairos mercenaries that day in Adira—those figures on the rooftops before the Spirits appeared. They assisted us against the specters."

Ronan blinked. "I don't know why they're helping us. I'm sure they've gathered who I am. If they know that the Ikarrian guild is working with the Sombra Quarter, then why haven't they attacked or reported us? Do they not want to gain Raziel's favor?"

Zara remembered Eshe's words on how the Kairos mercenaries hadn't been seen in the Elios temple since the other guilds had arrived. "I don't think they care about the hunt. If they did, they would've attacked when we were at our most vulnerable. Any other guild would've acted."

He sighed. "Well, we are lucky then."

Zara was careful to avoid looking at the fyrebrand, currently bare for the world to see. She fought the urge to cover it. "Now I owe you for saving me, archangel. I guess we're stuck with each other. Since when did our paths become so entwined?"

Stars seemed to dance in that silver gaze. "I am not sure, but I would tread that road over and over again if it led me to you."

Zara lowered her eyes, unsure what to say. The archangel was kind, perhaps too kind. Ronan had always teased her, carried a flirtatious demeanor, but he couldn't possibly care about her any more than that. If he did then he was a fool, the risks were too great for such naivety.

Yet, the sincerity in his voice was undeniable.

A warm sensation bloomed across her cheeks—was she *blushing*?

She hesitated. "There are so many unknown forces fighting against us. So much that we don't understand."

Ronan gave her a soft look. "Everything will be fine because you and I will face it together. I am honored to have a warrior such as yourself by my side."

"I am no warrior. I told you this."

"One day you will see what I see."

Gods, her lungs were tightening. All the belief that this male had in her, it was something she couldn't bring herself to acknowledge. For all she saw in her own reflection was a battered, unworthy soul.

Ronan cocked his head, his eyes searching. "Why don't you freshen up while I prepare something to eat. We can plot and scheme later."

Zara nodded and slowly swung her legs to the side of the bed. The floor was cool beneath her bare feet, made of squared stone painted in pale blue, red and orange. She stood up and took one step, legs wobbling. Zara tried to tap into her ether, but it drifted farther from her touch.

Ronan's arm slipped underneath her own and she grabbed onto it. His wing extended behind her the moment her hand curled around his bicep. The movement seemed so natural, it took her by surprise. She could smell the jasmine from his skin as she leaned into him. A sigh escaped her at their closeness, how *safe* he made her feel.

The mercenary temple of Kairos stood along the edges of the desert and the grassy plains of the Continent. She could see the dunes outside the arched windows as they walked; the capital of this realm was somewhere beyond the golden sands.

When they entered the hallway, hot air blew through Zara's hair. A slight gasp escaped her lips as she looked up at the high ceiling. This ruin was much larger than the ones in Ikarria and Elios. Pillars carved into the shape of jackal shifters lined the limestone path. The statues wore the Kairos armor—circular breastplates, armored wrap skirts, and golden headdresses. Each held their own spear.

Cracked pottery with short date palm leaves decorated the floor along with unlit lanterns. It took her a moment for her eyes to adjust, but she noticed the colored carvings along the walls. Kairos's own stories laid bare.

"I know." Ronan's breath was next to her ear. "This place is magnificent. While you were sleeping, I may have gone exploring."

She choked on a half laugh. "You went exploring?"

There was a smile in his voice. "Well, what else was I supposed to do? I had some time. My companion wasn't much *company*."

She snorted as he led her into another hall. The smell of citrus and wildflowers swarmed her senses as they went down a few steps to a pool. Its water was a blue-green, the surface filled with lily pads and lotus flowers. Surrounding it was more shrubbery and small palm trees. Pillars held up a ceiling made of carved openings shaped into suns, allowing the daylight to pour in.

"Fucking Suns, this place is beautiful," Zara whispered. "I joined the wrong guild."

Ronan chuckled, helping her to the water. "Are you able to wash on your own?"

Zara eyed the pool. "I should be fine. Is this sanitary?"

"Yes. I found running water in the adjacent room. It filters the pool in here. I bathed earlier before you woke up."

She looked at him then. His dark hair was still damp, curled and clinging to the sculpted planes of his face. The silver of his eyes seemed a misty gray today.

He began to smirk. "You can bathe with me next time."

Zara scoffed and lightly pushed him away, earning her another chuckle. She imagined what it would be like to see him remove his clothes and step into the pool. To feel his naked body against hers, every muscle and scar lining up to her own. For him to press her against the smooth stone, her leg sliding up and around his waist. All for his aching cock to enter her—the thought ignited a yearning within her, and she stifled a groan.

It had been too damn long since Zara had felt that reprieve.

Ronan left to tend to the food while she stripped and waded into the water. It was colder than she'd liked but, *gods*, it felt good.

Dirt and dried blood wedged in the creases of her skin faded into the pool. Zara tipped her head back, hair spreading out on the water's surface, sunlight bathing her cheeks. Rivulets of water fell over the swell of her breasts like beads of crystalline jade.

The pains of her body slowly subsided, only to welcome the

onslaught of memories of what happened two days ago. She heard clanging steel and shredded flesh in her head. Saw the red light of her ether as well as cerulean blue eyes. The specter had *spoken* to her. She could still hear its myriad of voices.

Daughter of the Dawn, it had called her.

She remembered how confused Hakim and the others had been. They hadn't understood the specter. Only she had.

The realization prickled her skin, the water suddenly colder than before.

FORTY-NINE

Ronan spent the two days trying not to think about the sight of Zara's blood on his hands or how her screams had pierced through his chest. Most of that time, he was at her side, afraid to wander too far for too long. But the silence and solitude forced him to face the jagged pieces of his mind.

His lips trembled as he tried to focus on the brewing pot in front of him. There had hardly been anything in the ruin, but he had found a sack of broth, small bundles of coriander leaves and some onions all laid out. The food was too fresh, and Ronan had a hunch that the Kairos guild had left them a parting gift.

Ronan swallowed thickly before a shaky breath left him. He sifted through those memories, held every image of his family against his heart. There had been a red burning sky that day. His lungs had filled with smoke, eyes stinging with tears. He had seen so many warriors fall. So many questions had scourged his mind. *How could it have happened?*

Ronan should have seen it coming. He should've known the moment he had failed to protect the friend he cared for. Ronan would never forget the disgusting feeling of betrayal, how it had violated his soul as he found that same person in a battle against his family.

Those eyes had seared through him, full of rage and anguish.

"You were blessed with a destiny, but I *needed* you, Ronan. Now look at what happened."

Ronan had felt the defeat, the tired ache in his heart and a regret so profound it choked him. "I'm so sorry."

He'd had to raise his blades against someone he had loved. But he didn't realize how weak he was until his power betrayed him too. The ether he had been blessed with moved of its own accord, devouring everything in its path. Ronan had been too inexperienced with that part of himself, he couldn't tame it. There was nothing he could do but scream as his power attacked his family.

The world he had come to know became nothing but ash and dust. Ronan had fallen to his knees, unable to look away from the destruction he had caused. The one he had called a friend merely watched him, and then left him alone with the pieces of his soul.

It had all been Ronan's fault. All of it. He had been given a calling, a fate that was to be revered. And he had been too weak, too selfish to uphold it.

What a fool.

Ronan's breathing was hard as his gaze went back to the pot. He controlled his breaths until his erratic heartbeat had slowed. He stirred the contents, rolling his shoulders.

The skin around his ink band was still sensitive, an array of new scars would be collected along the expanse of his arm. His ether had been calling out to him, it cried to be reunited—he felt it in his soul, the gaping hole that was left behind when he locked away his power. He had sent for the ink artist who created his tattoo, but his shadow dealers reported the male had passed away.

Ronan had been trying to free it himself in recent weeks. Ares beside him, holding and observing him as he attempted to force his ether out of the bind. How it had burned and lashed against his body, ruining the skin around the tattoo. All to no avail, no matter how hard Ronan summoned it.

It wasn't long before that familiar scent of lavender entered the chamber. His wings slackened at her presence. He hadn't realized how tense he had been holding himself.

Zara approached and stole a peek over his shoulder. Her green eyes went wide with delight. "That smells delicious."

He hummed in agreement, stirring the pot. "Thank the Suns, because I am no chef."

She chuckled. The sound radiated like daylight, a warmth he wanted to bask in if he could. Zara limped away to sit underneath an open window. Old pillows and blankets were piled into a makeshift lounge seating. She had put her form-fitting shirt and trousers back on after bathing. His eyes lingered on the array of tattoos along her arms.

Ronan went to sit with her, bringing their meal with him. Zara took a sip of the broth and beamed. "Gods, this is good."

He smirked. "Something must be wrong—you've been nice for quite some time now." She scowled at him, and he laughed. "There she is. Balance is restored."

Zara rolled her eyes and went back to eating, a smile dancing on her lips. They ate in silence as hot desert wind swept into the chamber.

The mercenary looked around the room. "I have always wanted to visit Kairos. This is the closest I've ever been."

He propped up his bent leg on the sill and leaned against the ledge of the window. "Did you not have the chance to travel here?"

Zara shrugged. "We never really had an opportunity, especially us mercenaries."

"But you are also the Ikarrian king's daughter. Does that not mean something?"

Her gaze lowered. "I suppose. My pater has been more protective than anything in the last few years, and with Ikarria refusing fealty . . . I think he worried it would put us in danger if we ventured to the other realms."

Ronan took another sip of his broth. The liquid warmed his insides and filled his belly. "I suppose I can't comment on that, as I isolated myself from the world."

Something in her expression softened. "You haven't said much about your past, only that you took over the existing Sombra Quarter many years ago. What made you take on the shadow markets?"

His stomach twisted as the memories threatened to resurface. *No.*

He focused on the woman in front of him, finding his voice. "Fourteen years ago, I lost my family—my mother, father and younger brother. Even though I had Orion beside me, I felt alone for a long time, suffered at the hands of corrupt leaders and powers. I witnessed the cruelty of the world, knew that there were many others still experiencing hardships post-War. And I kept having this need for penance. Mostly everyone I loved was dead except for me. So I felt like . . ."

"Like you needed to prove that you being alive meant something," Zara finished for him, and it tightened something in his chest.

"Yes," he breathed. "So, to answer your question, I envisioned a place where runaways, refugees, anyone seeking a new beginning could have a place they called home. The Sombra Quarter had many resources and it thrived in the underbelly of the Continent. I started as a mere shadow dealer, but didn't stay in that position for long. I was eager to make the organization my own."

Her lips twitched as she finished her meal. "I would've loved to have seen you take on the Sombra Quarter leaders. You're a better swordsman now, but I can assure you it was hard to watch at first."

Ronan flicked her nose. "Yes, make fun of me. Count your days, Horizon. Though I suppose that is why I forgot my bladework. I dedicated myself to being leader of the shadow markets, locking myself away from the outside world, except when it came to Sombra business. I didn't have much need for a sword."

Zara nodded, discarding her bowl. She pulled her knees up to her chest, crossing her arms over them. It was a relief to see the paleness in her face had lessened. "The people of the Stone Orchard are not aware of everything that is happening within the outside world, but they trust in your leadership." She rested her head against the wall. "I think you underestimate just how powerful your influence is. How much you've made a difference."

Ronan stared at her a bit longer than he should've. "Thank you, Zara."

Her name rolled so easily from his lips. A taste he was beginning to crave. He held her gaze and couldn't look away. How the light speared through the green of her eyes, gold dusting her cheekbones.

He saw the nicks and pricks that scarred her skin. Despite her relaxed demeanor, there was a harshness in her gaze that never seemed to leave.

This courageous woman. In the time he had gotten to know her, people had spat on her name and cursed her for what she'd done. What she'd been ordered to do. And he could see it, there behind every witty remark, every look of disgust, every roll of the eye—pain lingered.

A ruthless beauty.

He placed his bowl down. "I admire you. You took a chance by working with me, a shadow dealer. It goes against every mercenary's need to survive, and yet you did it. You and your guild deserve so much more than what you've been dealt."

She paused as her face slowly fell. "It's terrifying," she whispered.

"To do something you yearn for, something that may be good for you, to fight for what your heart desires," he replied. "It always is."

There was another beat of silence. The drapes fluttered, brushing against the wooden furniture. His eyes lowered to her tattoos again. The detailing was intricate, the ink not too heavy on her skin. The leaves and images of skulls, suns, and moons were of some importance to the Horizon, he was sure.

"Your artwork is beautiful," he said.

Her face beamed with pride. "Eshe did them."

His brows flew up. "The archer surprises me every day."

Zara chuckled and stretched out her legs. She sighed. "There is something that is bothering me. The specter . . . spoke to me. I was the only one who could understand it."

Every fiber in his being stilled. Even the ether in his soul went abnormally quiet, as if trying to listen.

Ronan's voice went low. "What?"

"Is this something I should worry about?"

He ran a hand through his hair. "There are some ancient languages that are passed down by birth. Whoever is born of that bloodline does not have to formally learn the language, they will just *know* it."

Her face blanched. "What does that mean? Do you think I am *related* to those creatures?"

Ronan waved a hand. "No. At least I don't think so. Many species can speak the same language."

She groaned. "You're right."

He smiled. "Say that again. I like it."

"Fuck you."

"I like that even better."

Zara threw a pillow his way, a faint smile gracing her lips. The sight didn't last long. He would need to try again.

Worry etched over her expression once more. "There's something else, it's been happening for a while now. I keep seeing this . . . wolf."

"What do you mean?"

Her eyes flipped to the open window, her hands fidgeting as she searched for the words. "It's like a spirit, but I know it's real. An actual wolf appears to me whenever I am in need. Though it doesn't do much, it just watches me."

Ronan stared at her. It reminded him of someone very dear to him . . .

He leaned toward her. "Next time you see it, try summoning your ether. It might cause a reaction from the wolf, and maybe you can understand more of this apparition."

She exhaled through her nostrils and nodded. They stayed in silence for a while, listening to the desert wind brushing through the curtains. Stray specks of sand skittered across the tiled floor. Zara spoke again. "So, when are we going to head back?"

"In the morning. You barely woke up a few hours ago, allow yourself a day to recuperate and we will return to the battlefield tomorrow."

She smirked. "I didn't realize we were going to war."

"Where the High Throne and Council are concerned, there is always a war. No matter how silent." His hand flew up to the pockets of his leathers, cursing under his breath. "I also have something to share." Ronan lifted the pin he discovered and showed it to her. "I found this in a campsite among the hills of the city where we were attacked. It is made of astral ore, which is available *only* in Celestrea."

Her eyes went wide. "What do you think that means?"

"The emblem is that of Elios and, from what I know, only deities of wealth or nobility would have access to something like this. While there are other cities in the realm, as the attacks started near Soleira, I suspect that it is someone from the capital."

Zara's lips thinned. "That certainly complicates things. Does that mean that our culprit could be someone from the castle?"

Ronan shook his head. "Not necessarily. It could very well be a random deity citizen living in the capital seeking some sort of revenge."

"How is that related to the specters and the Spirits? From what you told me, Ares found that they signify the end of the world."

He grunted in frustration. "I don't know, but I suspect that someone is pulling on their strings. I am not convinced that the ethereal creatures came to this world of their own accord. If a deity is truly behind this, then the High Throne will eventually have to deal with it, especially the Council. If it is one of their own kind creating this chaos, they will need to exact punishment."

"All the more reason for us to leave at first light. These are all still theories—we will continue as we originally planned. As you mentioned, the High Throne is bound to discover what is happening in the Estrella Territories. We will make our own discoveries for your shadow markets before then."

Ronan put the trinket away, nodding. "You're right."

She smirked. "Say that again."

He rolled his eyes but couldn't fight the grin on his face. They settled into a comfortable silence and spent the remainder of the day meandering around the Kairos temple and its outdoor courtyards. Their bare feet touched the sun-kissed sands as they basked in the warmth of the sky.

Zara dipped her toes into the shallow pools, spread out her arms and tipped her head back. Daylight grazed her deep olive skin, golden teeth nipping at the column of her throat. Ronan should've looked away, but he was captivated.

Captivated by *her.*

FIFTY

They left the Kairos temple at the first streak of dawn. Zara was much more alert this time to admire the rush of light breaking across the morning sky. How the stars peeled away with every drift of the painted clouds. She was reminded again of how quickly archangels could fly.

Ronan had said little to nothing since he'd scooped her into his arms. She couldn't bring herself to speak to him either. His arms were folded around her, the pads of his fingers digging into her back. The position caused her face to be near his, her lips to brush his neck. Every glance, every touch of their bodies, threatened to burst through the awareness between them that hadn't seemed to fade with the beginning of a new day.

They stopped to rest while Zara prepared the small meals they had packed. He'd force her to stretch and walk for her body to continue healing. Her wound was still tender to the touch, but her strength had been returning in waves.

It had only been a day of traveling, and she could already see the faint ivory of Soleira's buildings, the sea shimmering beyond. Zara rested her head against the crook of Ronan's neck. Their closeness had awakened a primal need in her that she could no longer deny. To feel his body against hers. Even if simply being held by him in the sky. Her gaze moved from the beauty of the world to the beauty that was before her.

Zara traced the scar on Ronan's mouth with her finger. "How did you get this?"

His breath hitched, arms tightening around her. At first, she thought he wasn't going to answer her.

"Someone I cared about once did this to me. They needed help, and I failed them. It led to a fight, and they raised a knife against me."

Her heart almost broke at the sorrow in his tone. She didn't ask for details, though she was curious to learn more. His lips slowly parted as she continued to explore the shape of his mouth with her fingertips.

Ronan growled under his breath. "You keep doing that and I will have to find a place to land." He turned his face to her abruptly, their breaths mingling against the sunset breeze. "And claim those lips of yours."

Zara's stomach dipped. A languid heat bloomed, spreading low in her abdomen. She could give into it. Her teeth would tug on that bottom lip. He'd take her finger into his mouth. Maybe she could brush her lips against his neck as he flew deeper into the sky—his fingers could dig into her skin, scraping down her backside—

The sudden need to protect herself washed over her. Survival instincts slammed walls over her heart and the needs of the flesh.

She cleared her throat, a rough half-chuckle breaking through. "That would be dangerous."

Gods. She was a mercenary, a Horizon. She had fought many battles, but this was one that she didn't trust herself to wage.

Ronan smirked. "One day, Santos."

It was a promise, one she wanted to echo but couldn't. Yet, there was no denying the amount of peace she'd felt recently. The archangel had done that for her. Helped her in a way she couldn't comprehend.

Zara planted a chaste kiss on his cheek. Ronan blinked, looking at her with wide eyes, his cocky expression gone in an instant, and she laughed.

Truly laughed. The sound held the roughness of rusted steel, but it was real. Her heart lifted, taking the weight from her shoulders with it. Ronan's brows pinched slightly, gray eyes searching her face, his expression melting into something like awe.

The decision found her easily. For the first time in gods knew how long, Zara Santos would choose where her blades would fall. Let the Reckoning consume her till she was nothing but a memory.

The newfound truth settled within her as she leaned farther into the hold of the archangel.

Around midnight, they arrived at the Stone Orchard. The air cooled as Ronan dove through the cavern openings into the secret city. His wings remained outstretched as he slowly descended toward the ground. His heart hadn't stopped racing since Zara had touched his scar.

Feeling her skin trail over his own had nearly sent him to the edge. If she had wanted to, he would've found a secluded area to properly press his lips against hers. To worship her the way she deserved.

How he wanted to continue holding her.

And that kiss. How simple and kind it was and had nearly ended all coherent thought for him. Ronan could've stared at her the whole flight. She had fallen asleep not long after that, the effects of the antidote still running through her. Had drifted into unconsciousness in his arms, lit by the golden ribbons of the sun.

The night watch must've sent word to Orion, for he was already waiting for them. His brother's gray wings were a welcome sight as he reached them halfway in the air. "Thank the gods. I was ready to go search for you."

Ronan offered him a weak smile. "You know I will always return."

Dark smudges smeared the skin under Orion's eyes. Gods, he looked as tired as Ronan felt. The reckless bastard would have forgotten all responsibility to the Stone Orchard to hunt him down. How Ronan had managed to find such loyalty in this friendship was something he would always cherish.

Orion looked at Zara, still asleep in Ronan's arms. "I can take her."

Ronan brought her closer to his own chest. "No."

The reaction was so natural he didn't think twice of it. Orion's expression shifted to something akin to confusion, eyes darting from him to Zara and back. Ronan couldn't bring himself to care.

He had surpassed all reasoning at this point.

They soared to the ground, landing in the middle of the grove. The carved trees arched over them, shaping shadows with the fallen moonlight.

Zara stirred in his arms. "Did we make it?"

He dipped his head low, nose nearly grazing hers. "Yes."

The Ikarrian guild emerged from the darkness, their faces flushed with relief upon seeing her. Ronan helped Zara to her feet. She staggered a step before regaining her footing and fell into Eshe's and Axar's open arms.

He watched her, how that smile returned to her beautiful face. He was becoming addicted to the sight.

Ronan's gaze shifted beyond them to find Hakim looking at her with genuine warmth and love. The brawny Horizon met Ronan's gaze. *Thank you*, he mouthed.

Ronan could only nod. A lump formed in his throat at the sight of the reunited guild. He turned to leave, his steps soundless as he waded between the stone trees.

Orion met his stride. "What are you doing, brother? You know you can't—"

"Don't," Ronan growled. He glanced away, jaw clenching. "I know."

He said the words, but they didn't sound convincing. Not to himself and neither to his brother.

Orion sighed. As if in pity.

FIFTY-ONE

Ronan was informed that the mercenaries had helped Orion in guarding their new prisoner. His brother had kept the specter in one of the chambers within the Sombra Quarter's grand hall's prison as they waited for Ronan and Zara to return.

"And here I thought I was the only one getting attached to the mercenaries," Ronan said coyly.

Orion folded his arms, lips twisting. "I think my relationship with the Horizons is slightly different compared to yours."

They stood in the hall to the chamber, waiting for the guild to arrive. The walls were thick, no one would've been able to hear the specter thrashing against its chains from outside.

Ronan feigned ignorance. "I don't know what you mean."

His brother scoffed. "I see the way you look at Santos."

Ronan ran a hand through his hair, wings rustling. "I don't need your input on the matter. I already know what you're going to say, anyway."

Orion leaned against the door. "No, you don't. I was being over-protective last night. I do still fear what could happen to you if you venture farther on this path. But . . . "

Ronan's lips thinned as he waited. "I swear to the gods, Orion, you better spit it out."

His brother's golden brown eyes gleamed. "You look happy, brother. Like life has found its way back to you."

Ronan hadn't expected that. He hadn't expected any of this. His feelings toward Zara Santos were a clash of steel and storm. A burning hunger he needed to feed. A thirst he had to quench. All of that and more.

And yet . . .

He looked away. "She doesn't know me."

Orion knew what he meant. "Will you tell her?"

Ronan didn't respond for a few moments.

"Is she worth it?" Orion asked softly. The question was not unkind. His brother had always been one to seek difficult truths.

Ronan didn't hesitate this time. "Yes."

Silence. "Then you know what you must do."

Footsteps neared from the other side of the hall. Zara and Axar emerged from the flickering amber light of the stone wall's torches, the other two Horizons behind them.

Axar clasped Orion's forearm in greeting with a wild grin. "Gold or silver marks?" he asked.

His brother mirrored the smile and Ronan almost stumbled back at the sight. "Gold, you prick. I do not bet cheaply."

Ronan raised a brow, but before he could ask, Zara waved a hand toward the two males. "Apparently, they made a bet. Axar chooses not to tell me what it is."

The shifter slipped an arm around her shoulders and tucked her close to him. "Do not worry, dear sister, I gambled on you."

She rolled her eyes, lips twisting in annoyance. "That doesn't please me, Axar."

"It should. Orion barely took his chances on Ronan."

Ronan gave his brother an offended look, and the archangel laughed. Orion shrugged. "I prefer to make winning bets but you'll do."

Axar snickered but Zara rammed her elbow at his ribs. The shifter grunted and wrapped his arms around his torso while she sauntered into the prison chamber with a flick of her hair.

Ronan could only grin at the sight of her fire.

Ronan's nose wrinkled at the smell of sweat and soiled clothes. Chains bound the specter to the floor and walls. Its head lifted at the sound of the two archangels and the guild entering, its cerulean eyes glowing brighter, tracking their movements.

A table made of stone sat at the center of the chamber, an array of sharpened tools and blades carefully lined atop it. Ronan didn't miss how Zara's gaze lingered on it. It was a dark gleam, one he had witnessed before.

When she approached the specter, the creature strained against the shackles. An animalistic snarl ripped through its teeth. Its mouth opened, pools of saliva dripped from its lips.

"Daughter of the Dawn. You live."

Ronan felt the blood drain from his face as the words reached him. They curved and rolled over the tongue. A language that was old and familiar.

He shared a glance with Orion who looked as bewildered as him. His brother wouldn't have understood it, but he would've recognized the sound of the language.

Zara sneered. "You should've tried harder."

The initial shock quickly waned. Ronan's fingers slipped a thin blade from his belt and pointed it at the creature.

"You speak," he said through clenched teeth.

Zara's jaw slackened. "Can you understand it too?"

Ronan nodded slowly. She marched to his side and cocked her head at the specter. "You're not surprised, are you? You knew we would be able to speak with you."

The specter chuckled. The sound was like winter winds. *"Of course, I knew. I can sense your power. Who you both are. The essence that runs through you."*

Ronan's blood turned frigid, but Zara pressed forward. "Who we are?"

The specter fell silent. Ronan felt as if the floor shifted beneath his feet. He shoved away what the creature had insinuated and folded his arms. He pointed with his dagger to where Zara now stalked toward the stone table.

"Do not tempt her," Ronan rumbled. "The woman favors the blade."

Zara lifted a hooked weapon, a strip of silver reflected on her cheekbones as she admired it. Her voice turned dark. "I do like shiny things."

There was hardly time for a breath before a flash of light hissed across the air. The specter lurched against the wall, screaming, the hilt of a dagger protruding from its abdomen. Zara was still holding the hooked blade with one hand while the other hovered above the table, where another dagger had been sitting. She had thrown it so quickly that not even he had caught the movement.

Orion cursed and tossed a gold mark to Axar. His brother met Ronan's inquisitive gaze and shrugged. "We bet who would make the first cut."

Suns spare him.

Zara's green eyes blazed. Her arms were tense at her sides, two short knives now in her hands. She slowly raised her chin. The movement was slow, a promise of wrath and ruin.

The Rogue and Horizon, hand in hand.

Ronan took one step closer while the others took two steps back.

Zara bared her teeth. "I am more than happy to play this game. You follow the Spirits of the Midnight Sun. How did you come to this world?"

"*There are many of us,*" the creature hissed. "*We are never alone. And together we feast, feast, feast. This mortal plane is ripe with souls to taste.*"

A slash of silver. The creature howled, binds clanging against the stone. Ronan prowled behind Zara, wings flared and gaze hard on the specter.

"That wasn't an answer," he said.

Zara lashed out with swift movements echoed by the sound of ripped fabric and skin. The creature cried out and she laughed. The sound empty and dry.

The archangel's eyes slid to hers. She paused—hesitated—as if seeking his reaction to this raw version of her. The dagger was still in his hand as he began to smirk.

Like lightning, Ronan thrust the steel into the specter's chest. Power purred underneath his skin as he dragged the weapon along the length of the creature's shoulder. Blood splattered to the ground. Mutilated screams of many voices bled through his ears, threatening to send ice down his spine, but he braced against them.

Zara watched him with dark intrigue. He stepped back from the specter, bloodied weapon in hand.

"My blade is your blade," he whispered.

She blinked, raw emotion reflected in her eyes, and he knew she understood. He accepted her as she was. As she would for him.

The specter was still screaming. *We are from the forgotten realm. Awoken by words of ether. We follow the one who made the call.*

Ronan and Zara shared a glance. The mercenary disregarded the knives she had been holding, and he placed the hooked blade she had initially admired into her palm.

She grazed the weapon along the specter's throat. The creature's eyes glowed brighter, lips peeled back into a snarl.

"Who made the call?" she asked.

"The Fallen. The one who saved our Creator. Together, they will satisfy their desire for retribution. And it will be done by the sacrifice of the ether-born."

The Fallen . . . Ronan flipped the word in his head with the language the creature spoke. The purr and growl of it rolled over his mind. Somewhere in the depths of his thoughts, something tapped at a memory. But he couldn't see it.

"The ether-born," Ronan repeated the words softly. He glared at the specter. "What do you mean by that?"

Those gem-like eyes darkened and shifted between them. *"Like you. Like her."*

Ronan took a step forward. "Enough riddles," he growled.

"What is your purpose here?" Zara hissed. She pressed the curve of the weapon deeper against its neck. A line of red trickled down, joining the pool at their feet.

The specter gave her a bloodless smile. *"The Spirits serve them as we serve the Spirits. We do not sleep or eat. We tread this Continent, searching for those of the ether-born, while we take the bodies of those who are not."*

"Your true form," she said. "What will happen to the body you possess?"

"I can still hear the elf who owned this flesh and blood. How he screams and yearns for release. For death. It is only a matter of time before I am made whole."

Ronan's stomach clenched while Zara snarled. The creature laughed, thrashing its body side to side.

"This is the beginning of the end. The Spirits have been awakened. It seems you knew that much, so ask me your true question. You want to know why you can understand me."

Zara took a step back, bumping against Ronan's chest. Her eyes darkened as she tightened her grip around the weapon.

"I was bound to get there," she gritted out.

"Funny elf. We come from a common place, you and I. A dormant instinct of yours has finally awakened now that the Spirits have risen. What I find most entertaining is that the archangel at your side knows the origin of the language that I speak, but hasn't said anything."

The world came to a halt. The dripping of blood silenced. Ronan couldn't tame the roaring in his ears. He felt Zara go still against him.

Her voice turned lethally quiet. "What?"

The specter laughed, the blue light of its eyes blinding. *"The stories don't say who he was, how he looked. How deep his failures went."*

Zara tensed.

"It is a language that belongs to the ether-born. I speak the original tongue of the gods, from the broken realm of Celestrea. As does the archangel."

Ronan's chest cracked as Zara took a step away from him.

"He is the long-lost king of Damalis."

FIFTY-TWO

Zara's heart sank. Her legs began to feel heavy as her senses seemed to dull. The truth—the fucking truth about the archangel—had been before her all this time.

She wasn't sure how she hadn't seen it. From the first moment she met him, she had known there was something different. Something *ethereal* about him. From the way he fought to the way he spoke. How others gravitated to his authority.

Ronan Menodora was the king of Damalis. The forgotten realm that had been destroyed alongside its sister kingdom of Valenzia.

So many questions raided her thoughts. She didn't know where to begin.

Ronan yanked the short blade from the stone table and slashed it across the specter's throat. The sound of icy laughter was cut short, and its head plopped onto the wet ground.

He slowly straightened and dropped the weapon. There was a rumble in his chest. "I am no king."

The snap of ether was a welcomed rush through her body. She slammed Ronan against the wall.

The dagger from her thigh strap was pressed against his throat. "Explain yourself."

Orion shouted and rushed toward them, but Axar twisted around to hold him off and protect her back. The wolf inside growled through his human teeth.

"Not another step farther," he gritted out. "I don't want to fight you, Orion."

Zara didn't have to look to know that Hakim and Eshe had their weapons poised against the archangel. Orion was outnumbered, but she wouldn't put it past him to try and fight till his dying breath to save Ronan.

She wasn't going to kill him. Yet. Her previous decision to spare him was muddled by the lack of truth.

Ronan never took his eyes off her. "When the War of the Skies began, my father turned the crown to me, but he was the true king for Damalis. He may have known that his life was going to end, putting me in his stead, but I have never been a worthy ruler to my realm. I have not returned to my homeland in decades."

Hurt pierced Zara's chest, managing to penetrate the gilded thorns around her heart. She didn't truly know the male before her. She didn't trust herself to speak, and he didn't seem willing to stay silent. Like he had been wanting to loosen the chains within him.

His throat moved against her dagger. "Alongside the people of Valenzia, I was charged to protect the Gates of Celestrea during the War, but I failed. I failed my realm and the Continent. No text knows my name. My story has been ripped from every page of every book the High King destroyed. I am the son of the late King Elijah and Queen Miriam. I am what the Continent named me, the lost king of Damalis."

The back of her eyes burned, though nothing betrayed the cold expression on her face. Zara's grip on the dagger trembled. "Does the High King know who you are? Is that why he sent us after you?"

The silver stars in his eyes dimmed. They were broken shards of moonlight as he looked at her like she was his last hope.

"No," he responded. "As far as we know, he thinks I died or ran away."

Anger flickered through her veins. "Were you really planning on helping us remove the fyrebrand?"

His gaze flashed then. "I meant every word I promised you."

She laughed that empty sound. "How can I believe you? You withheld the truth from me!"

Zara pressed against the dagger, a bead of red rising from where it pricked his skin. Still, Ronan did not move. "Why did you not tell me?"

She tried to ignore how her voice cracked, how sharply her chest rose. Ronan didn't miss it, he never did. His expression crumpled. "The truth is that I am a king by title, but I have done nothing to deserve it. It was my destiny to oversee the Gates and rule Damalis. All these years I never acknowledged my birthright, I removed all pieces of who I was. The ether I was born with, I sealed it away through a tattoo of my own." He pointed at his exposed arms, at the band of ink around his left bicep.

Her eyes widened slightly. To remove one's ether was equivalent to lacerating half of your heart and offering it to the Fates. "You willingly cut off that part of yourself?"

He looked at her, a plea there. "I know I waited too long to tell you, but I didn't hide who I truly am."

"Liar," she whispered.

Ronan's face fell. "No, Zara—"

She pushed off him and walked backward toward her guild. She kept her dagger raised as Axar flanked her, his own weapon at the ready.

"We are leaving," she said. "Our deal is broken. You can handle the Spirits on your own."

Ronan took a step forward, his tattooed hand reaching for her. "Little wolf, please. I want to tell you—"

"Do not call me that," Zara hissed. "I will spare you this one time, to honor whatever *partnership* we had. Next time you won't be so fortunate. Watch yourself, archangel."

She turned from the prison chamber. The mercenaries said nothing as they followed. She tried and failed to leave the thought of Ronan Menodora with the fading light, flickering torches and weathered stone.

FIFTY-THREE

Anger refused to leave her, but Zara clung to it rather than face the stings of heartache. She allowed her frustration to simmer through her blood, snapping every tendril of ether in her being to attention. Her power quaked within the depths of her consciousness. It tossed and turned, the strength of it feeling *more* than ever before.

The week since leaving the Stone Orchard passed in bloodshed. More assignments poured in from the High Throne, sending the guild to many corners of the capital. Zara couldn't bring herself to think about who those marks worked for or the repercussions their deaths would bring to the Sombra Quarter.

Hakim and the others had tried to speak to her. Zara suspected it was to discuss what happened with Ronan, but she refused to talk about it.

She needed time. Time she didn't have.

Zara gazed at the red-orange light that filled the sky from the Elios temple's balcony. No matter how much she tried not to think about him, Ronan still haunted her thoughts. He had seen her in all her bloody glory and hadn't run—he had placed his own scarred hands in hers and walked that red-stained path beside her.

He'd promised to help her, even as he withheld the truth of who he truly was. The lost king of Damalis. She racked her brain trying to think of the guardian realm's history but came up short.

With Ronan's true identity revealed, she suddenly felt her defensive instincts bleed through her veins. It was second nature to shield herself against the unknown. Especially when it came in the form of piercing gray eyes and black wings.

Time. Zara needed time but, within the clash of emotions that filled her head and heart, she knew she still wanted to help him. There was unfinished business between her and the head of the Sombra Quarter.

Stupid, naive girl. The fyrebrand echoed.

Aye, that is me.

A gust of wind blew through her hair, tousling the cloak around her legs. Wings of snow and ice unfurled before her, blocking out the dusk sky. Erebus landed on the balcony. The Elios symbol glistened on his armor breastplate, and the sight of it made her stomach churn.

"I thought I'd find you here," he said. "It's been some time since we've properly spoken."

Erebus had been visiting the temple less and less, though it was quite nice to see a friendly face now.

Zara squinted at the Hand of the King. "It doesn't help that every time I see you you're passing along orders for Raziel."

Hurt flashed in that cool gaze. "I guess I deserved that."

She pinched the bridge of her nose. "I'm sorry. Exhaustion must be wearing on me."

He sat on the balcony's ledge beside her. "No, you're right. I could've made more of an effort to visit you outside of mercenary work."

"You have a duty to uphold. As we all do." She looked at him sidelong. "Erebus . . . What do you know about the lost kingdom of Damalis?"

The ocean breeze ran its fingers through the length of Erebus's white hair. A shadow flickered across his face, his eyes shimmering like water. "Why the sudden curiosity?"

Zara returned her gaze to the golden sky. "You know I am from Valenzia. Damalis is my sister realm. I've always been curious."

The half-lie slipped through her lips so easily. She couldn't bring herself to talk about Ronan and the Stone Orchard to Erebus. The power to change everything was at her fingertips. The forces of Elios could be unleashed upon the refugees of the hidden city, and the Sombra Quarter would finally be ended. Raziel would bestow his *gift* to the Ikarrian guild.

The thought of Ronan in chains before the High King sent a sickening sensation through her abdomen.

Coward.

Aye, that is me.

Erebus was silent for a while, and she couldn't bring herself to look at him. "Damalis was the first realm to hear about the civil war within Celestrea. They knew trouble was brewing within the ethereal lands, that the rebelling deities wished to separate the mortal world from the Primordials, to ensure that the Continent's ether was not taken for granted by the gods," The archangel murmured. "Yet, Damalis still chose the Primordials over mortality. They chose *duty* over their neighboring kingdoms. When the guardian realm unleashed their forces to protect the Gates of Celestrea, so did Valenzia. It can be argued that *they* started the War of the Skies by involving the rest of the Continent."

She thought of Ronan's words, how he had mentioned his failures. "And Valenzia didn't object to any of this?"

Erebus scoffed. "The sister realms were given the honor of protecting the Gates, they were too blinded by loyalty. All the deaths that could've been avoided . . ."

Zara fought the urge to shudder at the mention of her homeland. There was so much she didn't know about the guardian realms—what it had even meant to be a guardian.

She pressed two fingers against her temple.

They stayed in silence for what felt like hours. The sun bled the last of its light as it descended over the sea.

Erebus raised a hand, tracing a finger along her cheek. "It's been some time since you and I have *distracted* ourselves."

Zara smiled at him. "I have to thank you, Erebus. You've been there since my first night as the Rogue. And you became a friend, probably the only one outside the guild and my family."

Erebus balked at that. "Finally, you admit it. *Friend*. What an honor."

She spat out a laugh and lightly shoved him. "You mean more to me than you'll ever know, but I think our *distractions* can stop now. I've recently started to realize that I want something more than the life I used to lead."

As the words left her lips, she felt the truth of it. The confidence that came with admitting something so vulnerable. Zara had not said it for Ronan or anyone else. It was for *her*.

Zara had been filling the voids of her heart through fights, drinks, and sex. There was no shame in it, she had always known what she was doing. It was her journey, her path to navigate the aches in her soul. But perhaps it was now time to move on.

Erebus gave her a soft smile. He ran a hand through her hair and leaned in to press a kiss on her forehead. "I must say it comes as a bit of a surprise, but I'm happy for you, Zara. You deserve it." His wings rustled as he got to his feet and extended a hand to her. "We must be off."

She knew it was coming. Raziel would always search for her. It was a truth she could no longer run away from. What would he gain if she petitioned for her freedom?

The dream of living without the fyrebrand had dissipated.

Zara was prepared to accept whatever was coming her way.

Erebus jerked his chin. "We should start walking if we are to make it to the castle in time."

She stifled a chuckle. "Why don't we fly there?"

His eyes went wide, placing his hands at his waist. "Zara Santos is asking to be flown somewhere? I don't know how many times I have asked you to let me carry you from one place to another. Gods know how much time we could've saved all those years."

Zara almost cringed, feeling as if she had been caught doing something she wasn't supposed to. If she mentioned that another archangel had forced her to overcome her anxiety of flying, it would open the conversation about Ronan.

It was not something she wanted to risk.

"I wouldn't mind trying it out," she said, though it sounded more like a question.

Erebus's eyes narrowed slightly, giving her a curious look, but the archangel gathered her in his arms. As they soared over white pillars and marble statues, she wished that the arms wrapped around her were someone else's.

"What is your progress with the head of the Sombra Quarter?"

King Raziel did not shout the question, but she still felt it boom within the private courtyard. She dipped one knee to the ground, her head bowed. The hood of her cloak fell over her face. All she could see were the shadows of the trees around the courtyard stretching farther along the dirt.

Zara's voice was low. "We have yet to find them."

"Stand before your king."

Slowly, she rose to her feet. The humiliation couldn't touch her as the void inside swallowed the remnants of what made her Zara Santos. Only the Rogue and a jaded will to survive remained.

Raziel's golden brown wings shined like armor. His wine-red hair flowed in the breeze. It had been a few months since she last saw him, and the sight now appalled her more than ever before. Every instinct inside her roared to back away.

He sauntered across the courtyard, eyes pinned on her. "I find that hard to believe, Rogue. I know you, and you never miss your mark."

Zara sank deeper into her mental abyss. Allowed her ether to sink even farther. "The Sombra Quarter is vast. We have hunted down plenty of their supporters and eliminated all the names you have given us."

Raziel's lips twisted in disgust. "The fyrebrand has sickened you,

I felt its signal. The Reckoning has begun, though you do not seem to care."

Shit. The ether inside her rumbled, outstretched a claw through the void. She prayed to the Suns that Raziel could not sense that too. It was a battle to keep her breathing even.

When she didn't respond, the High King began to shake his head, the movement slow and mocking.

"Ah, my Rogue," he cooed. "Have you reached your end? Did I push you to the point of no return? Have I *broken* you?"

The voice that responded in her head was not one she could so easily recognize. It was not the fyrebrand's—but her own.

No.

Raziel grinned. He moved closer. "You do not get to die on me, Rogue. What are you hiding from me?"

She inhaled slowly, fighting to keep her face neutral. "I hide nothing."

He cocked his head, lips curling into a smirk. "If you do not finish what you were set out to do, then the rest of your guild will suffer the same fate as you."

Blood drained from her face. The waves from the nearby shore stopped their crashing. The birds in the sky halted their singing.

She blinked. A crack in the cold mask she had always donned. "You can't do that."

The High King stopped in front of her and tipped her chin up with a delicate finger. "I can do whatever I please, Rogue. The truth you are hiding will be pried out of you when you least expect it. Now, finish your task or you will witness the demise of the guild of Ikarria."

PART IV

RAGE OF THE SUNS

FIFTY-FOUR

Blood tracked Zara Santos's cheeks like tears, the red droplets rubies that glistened underneath the dying sunlight.

The thundering crowd didn't reach her ears. Neither did the smell of piss and alcohol. She was nothing but the heartbeat of pain, the endless throbbing at the corner of her eyes and mouth. A bruising that tainted her sun-kissed olive skin.

It had been in these bleeding moments that a pleasant silence found her.

Now, it was torturous.

A sneer split Zara's lips as the world slowly returned to her. Her knuckles were bruised, but there were no gashes on her face. No cuts on her mouth nor the corner of her eyes.

You will witness the demise of the guild of Ikarria.

Her grip tightened around the collar of her opponent. Bone crunched underneath her fist. The crowd roared through her bloodstream.

There was no mercy from her tonight. No longer did she let the opponents attack her so she could feel the pain. No. Zara threw the fighter across the ring, blood smearing the ground.

You will witness the demise of the guild of Ikarria.

She stalked toward the other fighter. The poor fool tried to scramble to their feet before she launched at them. Her knees slammed on the ivory stone, cracking underneath her power. She clenched her teeth, breathing erratically. Her fists landed, one after the other. Blood and bone.

The High Throne had always been a threat to those she cared about, but now it had made a promise of death. How many years of the hunting season could she take after that? She hated Raziel; how could she continue to serve him? Was she capable of sending innocent people from the Stone Orchard to their deaths?

Could she kill the male she had begun to care about?

The war in her heart pained her.

She was tired. So tired.

How far she had fallen.

How she yearned to rise.

Zara didn't know where else to go. No, that was a lie. There was nowhere else she wanted to be. The moonlight guided her. Ether sang to her body, its melody thrummed through her blood with every step.

The night guards still allowed her to pass through the entrance to the Stone Orchard. She didn't question it. Dust curled around her boots as if rushing to greet her. She walked among the stone trees, her fingers trailing over the smooth trunks.

The blood and sweat had been cleaned from her body, but the bruises on her knuckles remained. As the clearing emerged, she thought of all the nights Ronan had sparred with her. How those simple moments had saved her from her own destruction.

Wings of midnight descended upon the clearing, and her heart raced. Ronan landed with a thud and stalked toward her. His eyes were bright, long legs eating the space between them.

"Zara," he breathed. "Are you alright?"

Those were the first words he said.

The last time they had seen one another, she had threatened him. Had put a knife to his throat. But his first words were to ask if she was fine.

Ronan lifted his hands as if to touch her but stopped. He searched her gaze, glancing down over her body. He slowly took in Zara's hands under the moonlight. His thumb brushed over the bruising and redness of her knuckles. Thunder flashed over his eyes.

His voice roughened. "You returned to the Siren's Song."

She grimaced against the dull pain that still thumped along her muscles. "At least I am sober."

Whatever Ronan saw on her face caused his expression to darken. "What happened?"

Zara had to lift her chin to meet his eyes as he towered over her, and she was quickly reminded of who he was. *The king of Damalis.* Ronan had become an ally—a friend—and she feared he would fall back to being a stranger.

No. It was more than that. Zara was afraid she was becoming weak.

Was she not supposed to keep those thorns around her heart? Had she not fought every damning year of her damning life to maintain the walls around her soul?

In the beginning, they had only used one another for a common purpose, but somehow along the way those lines had become muddled. Tainted and blurred by their hearts. There was still so much she didn't know or understand. Yet, she had still found her way back to this place. To him.

She laughed and tore her hands from his grasp. "You happened."

His lips parted. "Zara."

She shook her head. How her name fell from his lips. It was a prayer to the Suns.

The skin between his brows pinched slightly. "I've made many mistakes in my past life, and I waited too long to tell you." His eyes fluttered shut for a beat before meeting her gaze once more. "The War was not Damalis's fault. We involved the mortal kingdoms because we were trying to *prevent* the deities and Primordials' battles from entering the Continent. But, even though the War may not have started because of me or my kingdom, how it ended may as well have been our fault."

The words came out sharper than Zara intended, the emotions inside her fighting for air. "While I am upset that you withheld these truths from me, I also can't blame you for keeping such secrets. You were working with mercenaries assigned to *kill* you. I would've done the same if I were in your position." She sucked in a breath. "There is so much I do not know about you, Ronan."

He searched her face, lips parting. "And I want to tell you all of it."

Zara's breathing went shallow. The air seemed to have left her, and only the gentle beams of moonlight remained. She stood in that pool of night, holding his gaze. "I wasn't expecting someone like you to enter my life, and now I am risking *everything* dear to me."

His black wings rose higher, casting a veil of darkness around them. Shadows embraced the planes of his cheekbones, and the storm in his eyes brewed harsher.

"And do you think I was expecting someone like you? You sauntered into my life with all your blades and armor—and that wicked mouth. All that brilliant ruthlessness that makes you *you* wreaked havoc in my sad, shit life." Ronan tipped his head back, exposing his inked throat, and scoffed. "Gods, you were even sent to kill me!"

He took a step forward, she took a step back.

"This was not supposed to happen, we were not supposed to *care* about each other. It was not part of the deal," she growled.

His smirk was a flash of white. "How dangerous it is to have something worth protecting. Let's be honest, you and I like to take risks."

The deepness of his voice reverberated through her body. Zara couldn't look away from him, not as her back met a stone tree. He followed. The archangel slowly lowered his gaze to meet hers. His breathing was as uneven as hers, as if they had been sparring on the battlefield and he now held her at knifepoint.

For a heartbeat, his expression turned serious. His voice a shade softer. "I was the one who first sought you, but in the midst of my own chaos and despair it was you who found me instead."

Zara felt the shudder of his ether against hers. Even though it was bound and unseen, she could sense the warm press of his power. It coasted over her skin like lips that aimed to worship. Her back arched against the sensation, her body brushing against his.

"I welcomed your storm just as you welcomed mine," she breathed. "The pieces of my heart are in your hands."

Ronan's gray eyes darkened, a dangerous hunger pooling there. His gaze dropped to her mouth. "You honor me, but it is you, Horizon, you who has full power over me."

The words were a deep rumble, and the sound went straight to her core. A strangled breath escaped her lips. And that snapped whatever restraint the archangel had.

"*Fuck.*"

They moved as one and the force of their lips and bodies crashing against each other knocked them back. Her body slammed against the stone, his arms sliding around her and pulling her close. Ronan cradled the back of her head as he slanted his mouth over hers. He was as desperate for her as she was for him.

Zara explored the breadth of his chest, every muscle clenching underneath her touch. She plunged her fingers into his hair; her grip tightened as his teeth tugged on her lip.

"You promised to help me," she said against his mouth. There was a bite to her words, even as she ran her tongue along the seam of his lips.

The silver stars in Ronan's eyes stilled. He lifted her, his broad hands on the curve of her ass as he pressed her farther against the stone tree. Her legs wrapped around his waist, his body now lined up with hers. The feel of his massive body, the confidence and power she felt from him had wetness pooling between her legs.

His lips trailed down the length of her neck. "I meant every word. I have not stopped looking for a way to free you."

He dragged his tongue up the column of her throat and her fingers dug into his back. A moan escaped her, the sound making him shudder. Ronan kissed her again. His hips drove forward and the feel of his hard cock straining against his fighting leathers had her arching her back. An unbridled heat surged through her.

More. She wanted more.

Wanted *him*.

All reasoning left her. She didn't want to consider the many obstacles facing them. The hunting season. Raziel's threat. The Spirits and the specters. Each kiss, every touch conquered every battle in her mind. And she succumbed to it—to him.

Ronan's lips returned to her neck. His wings flared as his teeth dug into her. Not hard enough to break skin, but every delicious sting of pain was followed by a burning stroke of his tongue that sent her blood buzzing, dragging desperate whimpers out of her.

His voice rumbled. "That wicked mouth of yours, I wonder what other little sounds you can make."

Zara rolled her hips, trying to ease the tension at her core. His hold around her tightened, a groan tumbling from the back of his throat.

"More," she moaned.

Ronan cursed under his breath. Their lips clashed once again, full of teeth and desperation. He slowly helped her legs down and wedged his thigh between hers. She continued to rotate her hips, finding the right angle of pleasure. There were too many clothes and not enough skin.

Still, she rubbed herself against his thigh. Moans poured from her lips, and he swallowed every sound.

"Are you going to finish yourself on my leg?" His smooth, dark voice summoned another whimper from her.

Their control broke even more as they battled to unfasten each other's leathers. Her hands went to his waistband and loosened the belt. She pressed her palms along his muscled skin, fingertips grazing the fine hairs that angled down—

The fyrebrand hissed through her head, shattering the haze of her lust. *You will witness the demise of the guild of Ikarria.*

Everything she felt before coming here, every flicker of chaos returned to her with a vengeance. It echoed Raziel's threat to her. Her stomach tumbled and spots fluttered about her vision. A pounding grew in the back of her head.

Stop, please.

You will never be free of me, it sneered. *Not even in death.*

The decisions she had to make. Gods, she was too weak for this. The back of her eyes burned, though no tears fell.

"We can't do this," she breathed.

Ronan immediately stopped. His eyes flicked up to hers as he slowly pulled back. There was still little to no space between them, but it was enough for her to miss how his body felt against hers.

The archangel let his wings drape behind him and onto the dusty ground. "I'm sorry."

Zara shook her head, fighting the rising pain in her head. Her hands went to the sides of his face. "No, it's not you. It's—"

The fyrebrand. The fyrebrand is killing me.

The words were at the tip of her tongue, but she couldn't say anything as the Reckoning assaulted her senses again. Her vision blurred and it felt as if the air in her lungs was being squeezed out.

Zara scrambled away from him, her heart ramming against her ribs. "I can't," she gasped.

Ronan reached for her. "Zara, what's wrong?"

She struggled to her feet, turning to leave the grove. The hunger for him inside her—every fiery tendril of it—had been stamped out. "Don't touch me."

"Wait, Zara." He grabbed her hand, tugging her forward so she met the glistening silver in his eyes. "I'm sorry for not telling you who I was. There is so much I want to say, and I want to answer all your questions. Please, meet me at the Machai Forum tomorrow night. We can talk for as long as you like."

She was shaking her head. His words were muffled but she fought to hold on to them as she battled the Reckoning inside. All she saw in her head was Raziel, his threat hanging above her like a sword.

Ronan stared at her as if he was trying to see the pain lashing at her thoughts. "I will be there, waiting for you."

Zara wanted to walk back into his arms. Wanted to feel his lips against hers, lose herself in his embrace.

The fear for her guild—and for *him*—overpowered what she craved for herself. Her hand slipped away from his, and she turned her back on the archangel once again.

FIFTY-FIVE

Firebirds streaked through the dawn. Their indigo tails ignited into thin flames, making them look like shooting stars. Zara was enraptured by the sight, unable to leave the temple's balcony once again. There was no other place she could find solace within the mercenary ruin. The hood of her cloak was drawn back so she could feel the cool breath of the young sky.

She had not slept since she'd returned from the Stone Orchard. The feel of Ronan's lips against her own hadn't waned. It burned through every coherent thought. Her fingers went to her mouth, remembering the sting of his tongue and teeth. How he sounded against her flesh, as if pleading for more. Just like she had.

"Santos."

That voice, so deep it could cause the seas to shudder, but this time it did not seek to reprimand. Instead, it sounded concerned. For her.

Hakim drew up beside her and leaned against the railing. "The Reckoning has started for you, hasn't it?"

Zara shut her eyes. She dug her hands into the limestone railing, shards of rock falling into the grassland below.

She bowed her head. "How could you tell?"

"I know you, little warrior. You may think yourself a monster, but your heart is selfless. I've seen how pale and distant you've become. I had my suspicions."

The skin between her brows pinched as the words slipped from her lips with much more ease than she ever anticipated. "Hakim, the fyrebrand speaks to me. It has been speaking to me for as long as I can remember. At first, it happened sporadically, but now it is constant. And it sounds like Raziel. He'll tell me horrible things about myself. Always reminding me of the atrocities I committed."

His eyes widened slightly, though his voice remained kind. "Ether is a strange essence. It created all that we know. It may *feel* like it is alive, but it is not sentient. You have fed into your anger and self-hatred for so long that they manifested into the thing you feared the most."

Zara opened her mouth to speak but paused. All this time, the fyrebrand—Raziel's voice—that spewed every poisonous word . . . had all been in her head. The feelings were still real, the unseen gashes in her heart evidence of that.

Her lips trembled. "Every resentful thing I've heard all these years was my own voice under the guise of the High King—"

Hakim hugged her, so suddenly that she was frozen in his grasp. He didn't let go as he said, "I'm so sorry that you've been suffering through this alone. I'm sorry you didn't feel safe enough to confide in us—in me. I wish I had known, and yet I understand your reasoning."

Slowly, Zara wrapped her arms around him. Her mentor. Her teacher. And in more ways than one, her pater. Yet, she felt her heart mourn for the little girl she had been, how her younger self had been tormented by something of her own creation.

The fyrebrand had fallen silent. She wasn't sure if its presence was still there, but she couldn't bring herself to care.

They stood like that for several heartbeats. Apologies and for-giveness echoed in their embrace. Eventually, Hakim took a step back, his large hand lightly resting on her shoulder. "The Reckoning. Why did you not tell us?"

She dragged her eyes to meet his. "I didn't plan on keeping it a secret. Raziel threatened all of you. He extended his ether's power so that you will undergo the Reckoning too if I do not finish what I originally set out to do."

Hakim nodded. He seemed to peer into her soul, witnessing every fracture in the hard exterior that shielded her heart. Something cracked in his expression. "You cannot kill him, Zara. You cannot kill Ronan."

She reared back. "How can you say that? It is your life on the line as well."

The head of the guild folded his arms and looked to the sky. "The High King doesn't give a shit about any of us, Santos. He cares about his kingdom—at our expense. His rule has been a threat to us for as long as we can remember. Do you truly think he would let you go that easily, even if you did kill the Sombra leader? Why would he go through all the effort of creating the Rogue, only to let her go?"

Zara recalled Raziel's words, how Ikarria meant little to nothing and he could've *rained the bowels of war* on the realm. She still did not understand what he'd meant by that.

Hakim met her gaze. "You care about the archangel."

Something burned through her cheeks. It was a terrible mix of embarrassment and shame.

The corner of his lips tilted up. "I'm happy to see you like this. It's the start of you doing something for yourself."

She scowled. "Why are you acting like this? None of this is okay. I do not have the luxury of doing what I want, pursuing what I desire. It will only open the door to pain."

Hakim's golden earrings shined as the dawn rose higher. His expression softened with the growing light. "We have allowed Raziel's rule to suffocate everything out of our lives. We have killed to survive and survived to kill. None of our hands are clean. I am simply content that one of our own managed to find something precious for themselves. For that to be you—I think you are the most deserving of it."

He twisted around to rest his side against the railing. His large arm brushed against hers affectionately. "I know that the others will agree when I say that these threats do not really matter anymore. Raziel has made his intentions clear for years, and I'd rather fight for a chance to see you and Axar be free than continue the way things have been."

An icy dread filled Zara's stomach. "I can't lose any of you."

Hakim smiled warmly. "Little warrior, we are Horizons. We rise and fall like the sun, but we never die."

Zara's eyes watered as they stared out at the world bathed in gold and blue. They had served a higher power for so long. While working for Ikarria hadn't been as torturous, they still catered to the High Throne. Many years had passed, and it had become easy to get lost following rules and seeking to please those who would rather see them fall.

And so the guild of Ikarria would take up arms against the High Throne. This realization terrified her, but she couldn't deny the thrill that ran with it.

Zara Santos was a Horizon, after all.

"If we succeed—if we free ourselves from our fyrebrands and find who summoned the Spirits, then Ikarria will be in danger."

Hakim continued to stare ahead. "After all that has happened, I believe we are beyond that. And I think our king has been aware of such a possibility for some time."

Silence for a breath. The firebirds cawed, the sound of the waterfalls running down the peak upon which the temple sat thundering in the near distance.

"So, we continue as planned." Zara gave the head of the guild a sidelong glance. "Befriend a criminal, fight ethereal beasts, and commit treason against the High Throne?"

"Sounds like an adventure," Hakim said, eyes gleaming.

"I want to do this, but I also cannot deny that I'm scared."

"It is time to unleash yourself and press through it. Let yourself feel that fire, Zara, that drive to desire more for yourself. You will make this world your own with that kind of power."

The Ikarrian guild entered the temple's foyer, preparing to return to the Stone Orchard. Eshe tied the leather strings of her weaponry belt around her waist as she walked. Axar strode with swagger and a mischievous smile on his lips. He tossed Zara a wink.

Hakim had been right. They were more than willing to finish what they had started. There was an unresolved mystery regarding the Spirits and a long-overdue confrontation with the High King. Zara wasn't sure how they would manage this, but the Horizons of Ikarria never strayed from a challenge.

Her spine stiffened upon seeing the shining white armor and cloaks. The mercenaries of the Elios guild were lingering in the dining hall. Tamaya's eyes landed on her, and the scar on her cheek seemed harsher than before.

Her lips twisted into a sneer. "Where are the Horizons of Ikarria heading to now?"

Hakim shot her a stern look, keeping to Zara's side. "Easy, Tamaya."

Axar shoved his hands in his pockets. "We are making headway on our hunting season, much more than what the guild of Elios has accomplished, I'm sure."

He flashed a cocky grin which earned a hiss from an Elios vampire. Zara wanted to roll her eyes. Leave it to the arrogant wolf shifter to farther agitate the mercenary.

Tamaya tracked them as they continued to walk past. "You disappear for weeks at a time. The Kairos guild has made more appearances than all of you." She cocked her head, red wings rustling. "What do you know that we don't, Ikarrians?"

Zara spun a pair of daggers in her hands before sheathing them at her thighs. Her lips curled as she growled out. "I don't see how that is any of your concern."

Gods, she was no better than Axar.

The head of the Elios guild tilted her head up, surveying her. But before any of them could speak, the doors of the temple blasted open. The Adrastean mercenaries stumbled in from the young daylight. Sweat drenched their tunics, their wine-red cloaks torn. Dried blood splattered their bronze armor. Zara's nose wrinkled at the most prominent scent.

Fear.

It was so thick that the other Horizons—including those of Elios—went to their weapons. But it was Hakim who swept over and caught the leader of the Adrastean guild, Warrick, before he crashed to the ground.

There were tears in the elf's eyes. "They took one of our own."

The Horizons shifted in place. It wasn't until one of the Adrastean mercenaries choked out a sob that Zara noticed one was missing. There had been five of them in the guild, but only four had entered the temple.

Warrick clutched Hakim. "They took one of our own. Monsters we have never seen before."

Zara felt the color drain from her face. She fought to keep her expression as neutral as possible. Axar dared to share a glance with her.

"They came like wraiths. Floating and singing. They had a horde of the undead—*fuck*—gods know what we saw! We fought them overnight within the Estrella Territories." Tears left clear tracks along the Horizon's dirt-smeared face. "They took Cyrus. Captured him and dragged him away. The monsters took others along with him."

He gasped for breath, nearly screaming the words. "Fuck, they took him from us!"

The rest of the Adrasteans either bowed their heads or gritted their teeth in sorrow. Zara's heart wrenched at the sight. The bond among Horizons was something as strong as being forged by ether. To lose one would be to lose a piece of one's heart.

Zara finally processed what Warrick had said. *Oh gods*. One of the Horizons had been taken by the Spirits.

Hakim held on to the male, a solemn expression on his face. "I'm sorry, Warrick, but you'll have to tell us more. Where exactly did you encounter these creatures?"

The mercenary clenched his teeth, his hand going to a wound at his shoulder. "We were on a hunt and ran into them. They were on the hillsides leading to the outer district."

Shit.

Hakim's eyes narrowed. He looked at Zara and the others, a

silent command there. They needed to inform Ronan. They had been wrong, believed that the Spirits and specters were making way out of the realm's borders.

The ethereal creatures were making their way *into* the capital.

Someone had brought the Spirits and specters into this world, and it seemed their summoner was now calling them home. Zara mulled over their next steps, feeling Tamaya's burning stare at her back the entire time.

FIFTY-SIX

The smell of liquor tickled Zara's throat, but the temptation to blur her thoughts had begun to wane, drifting away with the Elios winds, rolling back to the Ikarrian mountains. It was her choice and she felt a new sense of power in that.

The Ikarrian guild had returned to the Stone Orchard while Zara visited the Machai Forum. The archangel was where he said he would be. He stood within the market, a pillar of broken darkness. The night bowed to him, and the moon revered him.

Ronan had been staring at the fire dancers in the Forum's center when she approached him. His tight expression was on the flames but, as his eyes slid to hers, a softness cascaded over it. His shoulders loosened and a slow breath left his lips.

As if seeing her had given him air.

Zara wasn't sure if she was worthy of such a response, but she also couldn't deny how his presence drew her in. It was warmth, affection, and comfort. It felt like . . .

"You came," he said.

For a breath, her mind conjured an image. She could see the archangel under a sky of dusk and dawn, surrounded by the stars and suns, a crown of light and flame on his head. And what a sight it was.

Her heart pounded, echoing every word through her blood. "For you."

Ronan's throat bobbed. He extended an inked hand to the road that led to the Siren's Song, his eyes not once leaving hers. "Shall we?"

Zara followed him to the tavern. Her eyes gravitated to the fighting ring, and while its excitement still resonated through her bones—most likely forever as battle was her air—she didn't see the ring the same as before. It was no longer a way for her to receive pain as penance. She'd find the courage and strength to redefine what the fighting ring meant.

Much to her surprise, Ronan led her to the office on the top floor. The place where they first properly interacted, where she discovered his role within the Sombra Quarter. There were no archangels guarding the doors, she knew Orion would be with her guild by now.

When Zara entered the office, she halted. Remnants of their first fight still lingered in the space. The broken stone archway of the window they had crashed through and the cracked wooden desk. Lying on the floor, at the foot of the windows, was a blanket.

It was made of cotton and had a tassel fringe, lined with red, orange, and white. An artisanal design, she realized. One that she vaguely recognized as Valenzian. Decorative pillows of dark contrasting colors were placed thoughtfully about, including a platter of flatbread and a bottle of wine. There was a flutter in her chest.

"This looks romantic." What was she saying?

Ronan chuckled, the sound like music. "We are on the brink of battle, on the cusp of solving a mystery, all while drinking wine sharing our deepest, darkest truths. That seems to suit us."

Zara snorted and arched her brow. "We hardly know what this *us* is."

He smirked, eyes twinkling. "And I am looking forward to figuring it out with you."

She fought her own smile as she settled on the blanket. The archangel beat her to the wine, lightly swatting her hand away so he could serve her. Zara took a sip and relished the gentle sweep of berries that trickled down her throat. It was light in terms of the alcohol she was used to drowning her sorrows in.

"How is the Sombra Quarter?" She was mildly surprised by the question that came out.

He seemed shocked as well. "The shadow dealers have a responsibility in securing the safety of their businesses. While some of the trade businesses have fallen, I managed to take precautions with others. We can manage so long as the hunting season ends soon."

Zara inclined her head. "If we succeed, then there may no longer be a hunting season."

His expression sobered as he took a swig of the wine. "Where would you like me to start?"

The beginning. The end. All of it. The words were on the tip of her tongue.

"How did the lost king of Damalis become a criminal to the High Throne?"

Ronan chewed on a piece of flatbread. "The Stone Orchard is a front. In a way."

Intrigue lit her face. Her nails clinked against her glass. "You're going to have to pour me another glass before you continue."

Amusement touched his mouth as he did. The night markets and public feasts happening on the streets exploded with cheering and clapping. From where they sat, the boisterous noise was a comfortable hum.

Ronan sighed. "I was taken prisoner after the War of the Skies. My realm was already in shambles then, and when I escaped from the High Throne I feared the worst. But by some miracle, my kingdom still lived. The Continent believed Damalis had been destroyed, and there was no record of any survivors. So we kept it that way. By then, I had to find some means of support for an entire population. I heard about the shadow markets and their growing popularity. I saw an opportunity and I took it."

Her eyes widened. "Damalis still lives." She breathed out.

He nodded, a flicker of pride there. "We still live."

Raziel hadn't cared enough about his opponents' realms to consider the possibility of survivors attempting to rebuild their kingdom. Ronan had seen an advantage in that.

"How did you escape Elios's prisons?"

A fondness grew over his gaze. "Ares Valdemar."

She wanted to slap a palm to her face. Of course the broody vampire general was in on it. He had been serving alongside Ronan when it came to the shadow markets. She had sensed there was history between the males.

"I understand why you wanted to go after the missing towns. If the Sombra Quarter's businesses are disrupted, then you wouldn't be able to financially support your kingdom."

She could only imagine the broken realm, its people surviving off whatever supply came through from the shadow markets. A land of ash and ruin. All while their king wrestled with the forces of the Sombra Quarter, avoiding the High King.

Her eyes gravitated to him. "What did you mean when you said you'd failed your realm?"

Ronan's face paled slightly. He leaned back against the wall. "I chose my destiny, to take over the throne and to lead the guardians of Damalis. There was unrest within Celestrea, and while deities have never been strangers to our mortal world, it was the first time they arrived with armies. The ether I was born with gave me the responsibility to save everyone. To stop the War from happening."

He hesitated, flinching at whatever flashed before his eyes. "But I couldn't. I lost my family and, at the same time, my kingdom. I was so disgusted with myself that I couldn't look at my power again. I began to *despise* it. So I found an ink artist who worked in ether and had them bind my power. That was fourteen years ago."

"Can I see it again?" Zara didn't know what overcame her. She wanted to blame it on the wine, but it had hardly inhibited her senses.

Ronan took a steady breath and nodded. Whatever surge of courage that had found her had her crawling to his side. His steel eyes sharpened as he watched her.

She leaned over him and looked over his ink-covered arms before her gaze landed on the thick band around his left bicep.

"It's different from the fyrebrand, but it serves its purpose." He murmured.

Zara dragged the tip of her nail along the tattoo, watching as chills skittered across his skin. She had been branded with ether-laced ink by force, and he had done so willingly.

"To lose your power is a great loss. Do you regret it?"

It may have been due to the closeness of their bodies, but she could hear Ronan swallow. "I do."

Zara turned to face him, tempted to trace that scar on his mouth. Something made her hesitate so she pulled back slightly, gesturing to his lips. "And that? Did that happen during the War?"

His hand went to her lower back, holding her there as if he didn't want her to retreat any farther. But she saw how the silver stars in his eyes broke. "It did."

She brushed the dark locks that fell on either side of his brow, and Ronan closed his eyes at the touch. "And why is it at times you cannot stand the sight of fire?"

He opened his eyes, his chest rising and falling beneath her. "It was how my family was killed. They were burned by the power of flames. I—I was forced to watch. Couldn't do anything to save them. Sometimes, I can still hear their screams at the crack of fire." His voice came out strangled.

Her heart twisted. She couldn't fathom going through something like that. How he managed to keep persevering while helping his kingdom survive. It spoke to his true strength. He may have believed himself unworthy of being king, but he was more of a ruler than she had ever seen.

"When was the last time you visited Damalis?"

He winced. "Too long. Years. I've always sent Orion there on my behalf."

That was something Zara could understand, not being ready to face the harm you've endured and done. Ronan had shared so much, laid out his wounds at her feet. And she would do the same.

Zara took a deep breath and told him of the fyrebrand's voice, how it had haunted and tortured her for so long. How her own self-hatred was so strong she had created the enemy in her head.

"Not that this sort of thing would occur to everyone who struggles with the depths of their thoughts," she clarified. "But it happened to me. Ether is truly a mystery."

"Shit. I saw you frowning at the fyrebrand a few times, some kind of darkness coming over you, but I thought it was calling you back for an assignment." Ronan reached for her wrist. His thumb brushed over the bracer. "May I?"

She could only nod as he loosened the leather, letting it fall to the blanket. He leaned closer and raised her arm between them. The black tracing of the Elios symbol blended within the other inked designs.

His finger followed the patterns, bites of ember in his wake. Zara bit her bottom lip, fighting to keep herself still. Ronan stopped at the fyrebrand. Something flashed over his stormy eyes.

"I hate that he has a hold on you like this," he whispered.

The mercenary looked up at him, saw the strain on his face, but he spoke before she could. "There is so much more I want to say, I could spend the entire night speaking with you."

The corners of her lips curved up. They were unveiling the broken pieces of their souls. Bit by bit. But it was enough for tonight. Her heart and soul were too tired.

She met his own weary gaze. "Do you wish to retrieve your power?"

Ronan's eyes seemed to glow under the dark as he nodded. Zara gave him a wicked grin. "If we survive this, if we manage to break the fyrebrands through Raziel, then I will help you free your ether."

The archangel brushed his lips against her brow. She stilled at the touch and felt his words graze her skin. "Thank you, Zara."

She leaned toward him, allowing her body to rest against his.

This. She could allow herself this.

Ronan couldn't take his eyes off her. This mercenary, who had been sent to kill him, was sending him to his knees.

Zara stayed in his arms as they continued to speak business. She told him of the Adrastean guild and their encounter with the specters.

He was glad he had informed Ares that they suspected a deity was behind the attacks.

During the time since he had last seen her, Ronan had been a wreck, sickened by guilt. He'd kept himself busy with Sombra Quarter affairs, seeking for ways to confront the specters' attacks on his own. When Zara had returned, Ronan knew he would do everything in his power to make it worth her sacrifice. Though, he knew that this act of rebellion against the High King meant more to Zara than he could imagine. The elf was finally regaining her free will.

They walked through the Machai Forum, keeping to the shadows. He followed her as she admired the night markets and street shows at a distance. As they slowly approached the fire dancers, Zara gravitated to his side. She didn't touch him, but the action had tightened his chest.

Ronan couldn't stop thinking about their kiss. The moment he had touched her lips, he knew he would never stop craving her. He glanced at Zara now and watched the way the fire's light embraced her. It gilded her high cheekbones, grazing the curve of her jaw. Shadows flickered at every brush of her lashes, and her green eyes seemed a molten jade.

Suddenly, he pulled her into the space between two buildings. She protested at first but went quiet at whatever she saw on his face. Ronan's chest rose and fell sharply, his hands cupped her face. He wanted to burn each of her features into his memory.

Whatever was to happen beyond this, Ronan wanted to capture every bleeding moment with her.

Zara's skin was soft. He ran a hand down her arm, could feel the hardened touch of her muscles.

He had failed so much already, but she was allowing this—whatever this was between them—and he would make it worth it.

Their bodies were flushed against each other. With his other hand, he slowly sank his fingers into her hair. He curled his grip and tilted her head back. Zara gasped and his cock twitched at the sound.

Her nails scraped the skin along his neck. Ronan pulled her closer and inhaled the gentle wave of lavender. Zara's lips parted and he brushed his mouth over hers. It wasn't a kiss, but it felt more sinful, more agonizing this way. A silent yearning that echoed between their breaths.

They held each other. Tightly. Unwilling to allow the realms of the Continent and the forsaken will of the Fates to tear them apart from this moment.

He skimmed his lips along the curve of her ear. Nibbled it. "You're a temptation. A forbidden gift." She sighed at the rumble of his voice. Ronan's mouth drifted to the curve of her jaw. "The things I want to do to you. How I want to take my time with you."

Zara tilted her hips toward him and gasped as she moved against his body. She was so ready for him. Fuck. His cock had become so hard at the thought.

She went to his waistband but paused, waiting for permission. He growled against her mouth and thrust himself into her waiting hand. "Touch me, Santos."

Zara bit on her bottom lip as she cupped him over his trousers and began to work him over.

"I want to feel you inside me," she whispered.

Fucking Suns Above.

Ronan coasted back to her lips, explored the delicate lines of her mouth as his fingers drifted down to her waist—

Fire burst from the Forum's square. The fire dancers sent bigger flames into the air. Spectators clapped, but it was all drowned out in Ronan's ears and he flinched at the bright light.

Shit. Shit. Shit.

He didn't realize he had closed his eyes until hands landed on either side of his face. He felt the rough calluses of her palms and he slowly opened his eyes to the beautiful Horizon before him.

Zara's voice was soft yet firm. "Ronan Menodora, you are *safe.*"

Her focus was on him and solely on him. Ronan didn't remember the last time anyone had cared for him like that.

He still saw the flames of his tortured memory, but didn't shy away. Zara's touch grounded him, a tether to this broken world.

More fire ether erupted from the fire dancers. Again and again.

His teeth clicked as he forced himself to face the pain. He was too tired to keep running from it.

The screams echoed in his bones. Ronan saw his family within the tongues of blue and orange-red fire. Their piercing cries. He saw his father, the crown he bore melting within the flames. Everything had been ripped away from him that day.

There was so much more to this. His sins that had started the War of the Skies were not something he could easily ignore.

Zara's voice broke through his haze. "Respect the memories and let them brush past you as you take the mantle and forge a new path. A healed one."

The words sank deep into him, touched the far corners of his heart he hadn't acknowledged for years.

For now, this was more than enough. Ronan could face the flames.

He lifted his gaze and looked toward the fire dancers. Their figures still twirled in the fiery light, twisting and turning. Music drummed against their ether.

Peace.

Peace found him unexpectedly. Ronan felt the weight slowly lift from his shoulders. It shifted and softened as he held the most stunning woman he had ever met in his arms.

As soon as it occurred, Zara doubled over. She gasped for breath, hand clutching her chest. Ronan moved without hesitation even though his heart was racing. His arms wrapped around her and held her up.

"Zara, speak to me." He growled.

She pressed a hand to her temple and gritted her teeth. "Gods, this can't happen right now."

His confusion was forgotten when he felt eyes on them. Zara followed his gaze across the street and stiffened.

Beyond the ribbons of fire, amid the blur of dancing and cheering, was an archangel. Her wings were red like the bleeding sunlight and a scar ran down her face. He immediately recognized the silver armor and blinding white cloak. It was as if they had gone back in time, seeing the archangel in the same place as a few weeks ago.

The Elios mercenary watched them with such fury it made Ronan take a step, nudging Zara behind him. It was too late. His mercenary was already pushing him away, reaching for the twin blades at her back as she stepped into the amber light.

Zara's voice was twisted with panic and desperation. *"Tamaya, don't."*

FIFTY-SEVEN

Tamaya had seen them—had seen *him*. Zara couldn't see any of the other Elios mercenaries, but there was the strong possibility they were hiding within the Machai Forum. At first, she wasn't sure if the archangel would've known who Ronan was, but the flare of realization in Tamaya's eyes spiked fear through her heart.

Those large red wings unfurled as the archangel burst into the sky and flew toward them. Zara fought through the Reckoning's symptoms and leapt from the ground, the echoes of her power cracking the cobblestone beneath her boots. She collided with the mercenary midair and they both crashed to the ground. The crowd and street performers screamed and scattered about the Machai Forum.

Zara slashed her blades side to side, meeting every one of Tamaya's attacks. The archangel was a force made from the skies and the wind. Her hateful glare remained steady behind the whirlwind of her sword. The dancing steel was so blinding that Zara found herself taking a step back.

A cruel smile spread across the elf's lips. "A worthy opponent. We should've fought sooner."

Tamaya snarled. "Enough, Rogue. I knew the Ikarrian guild couldn't be trusted. My mercenaries and I have killed so many of the shadow dealers, spilled so much blood. I thought surely my guild would reap the High King's reward, until I noticed that the Ikarrians were purposely not hunting. From that moment, I knew something was amiss."

They prowled around each other in a circle. Zara's body thrummed with an ache for battle. She held on to that blood thirst, feeling her ether trickle through her veins.

The archangel grinned. "After what I saw in the Elios temple I decided to follow you, and what good fortune that brought me. I find you fondling an archangel who I suspect is part of the Sombra Quarter. You are a *traitor*."

A war cry peeled from Zara. She knew it was a foolish mistake, a slip on the hold of her riling emotions. She charged Tamaya who met her with brute strength. Zara felt the ground slip from beneath her as the Reckoning raged against her senses again. Her vision fluttered, head splitting with pain. She cried out as she tried to hold the archangel at bay.

Tamaya's grin grew wider. "You don't look so good, Horizon. Am I right in assuming that *he* is the head of the shadow markets and you haven't had the balls to follow through on your assignment? I wonder how Raziel would feel to know his precious Rogue is bedding the enemy."

Zara felt like the air was being squeezed out of her lungs. They had come too far to be brought down by an angry, bitter mercenary. She knew that her actions were letting the archangel know just how much power that threat had. Zara felt the rush of night-kissed wind behind her, and her heart lurched.

"I hear someone's been looking for me?"

Ronan.

Tamaya's hungry gaze slid toward him before she kicked Zara square in the chest. Pain ricocheted to her back as she fell. Her hands slipped against the slick ground, slicing her palms. She watched as Ronan guided Tamaya farther down the street. His mouth was a twisted sneer and by Tamaya's thunderous gaze, she figured he was baiting her.

His movements were fast as he lunged and retreated. He was

leading the archangel farther away from her, to buy her some time. Zara struggled to her feet. The Reckoning clung onto her, causing her fingers to shake and loosen their grip on the khopesh blades.

Gods, she couldn't move. Her head tipped back as she fought for breath. She could hear Ronan calling out her name. Zara made the mistake of meeting his eyes, wide with concern.

The splitting moment between them was enough for Tamaya to move. Ronan cried out as the mercenary slashed a blade across his side. Blood flew from her silver sword—and the Reckoning quieted. All the pain the fyrebrand had unleashed on Zara stopped the moment Tamaya injured Ronan. The realization sent a shudder through her, but she forced the dread away.

Red misted across her vision, power snapping awake. Ether obeyed her call, swirling through her bloodstream. It fed her hunger to draw blood. Zara curled her fingers around the pommels of her blades.

The ground beneath her boots cracked with a loud boom as she took hold of the ether to soar across the street, red light flaring about her legs. She rammed into Tamaya with her shoulders. The strength echoed through her, the impact sending the archangel flying into a nearby wall.

Ronan swayed in place, a hand at his side. His eyes widened at the plumes of dust from where the mercenary had crashed. "Remind me to never piss you off again."

Zara scoffed, planting herself in front of him. "You've gotten a taste of it already, haven't you?"

"I have the scar to prove it," he grumbled.

Blood-red wings rose from the clouds before a very angry archangel stepped onto the street. She clenched her teeth and raised her sword. "Step aside, Horizon. I won't hesitate to cut through you to get to him."

Ronan snarled, but Zara lifted her twin blades. "Tamaya, there is more at stake than just the hunting season. Think of the attack on the Adrastean guild. Those creatures they saw, we have come across them as well. It is what my guild has been trying to understand, why we haven't been hunting."

The archangel searched her gaze, breathing heavily through her nostrils. "Lies!"

Zara's eyes went to the white cloak flowing behind the archangel. Though stained with dust, the Elios emblem still flared like steel against the light. She slowly lowered her blades. "You don't believe in the hunting season either."

Zara knew the words hit their mark with how Tamaya's wings flared. "Please, Tamaya, I am begging you. I know we have always been at odds, but I did not ask to be the Rogue. I did not seek to be in Raziel's spotlight, and it has never done me any favors. We are trying to end this—all of this. Have you not heard the rumors of the Three Sun Gods returning? The creatures we saw are not of this world. Someone is controlling them. This is greater than all of us. Ask the Adrastean mercenaries again about what they saw. They will tell you."

Tamaya didn't seem to breathe. Her hardened gaze jumped from her to Ronan and back. "What you are doing is foolish, Rogue. It will be your undoing."

"It may be so, but I am tired of sacrificing myself for a purpose that doesn't care for me."

The mercenary blinked. Several painful heartbeats passed before the archangel scoffed, wiping saliva from her lips. "You are bound to doom us all, and I will not allow harm to come to my mercenaries."

Zara watched as the Horizon disappeared into the night, her heart pounding against her ribs. Tamaya's parting words had caused her stomach to tighten. They hadn't made the Horizon's intention clear, but there was little she could do.

She hoped their act of rebellion would be worthwhile.

FIFTY-EIGHT

Ronan wandered about the Stone Orchard, savoring the sight of life in the city. Of refugees who had become residents and made this place a sanctuary. Passersby who recognized him as the leader of the Sombra Quarter bowed their heads. He'd never asked them to behave so, as if greeting a royal. Ironic as most of them, if not all, didn't know that he was the true king of Damalis.

Zara was with the Ikarrian guild, preparing for battle against the oncoming specters. He would join them soon. According to the Adrastean guild there was no indication as to how many specters were making their way to the outskirts of Soleira, but it didn't sound like the Spirits were with them. That somehow concerned him even more.

They hadn't seen the Spirits since the attack on Adira. He only hoped that Ares would be able to find something on the deity behind all of this.

Ronan ran a hand through his hair, gritting his teeth. Gods. There was still so much they didn't understand.

Orion appeared on the main road, another male archangel beside him. His brother was tying up his messy hair into a knot while the other adjusted his breeches. The male spotted Ronan and gave him a firm nod before brushing past Orion and tossing him a sly look.

His brother joined him on the main path and Ronan noticed a

light bruise peeking from underneath his collar. It wasn't difficult to guess what his brother had been up to. Ronan smirked and Orion shoved him away with a grin.

They walked in comfortable silence for a while, passing through the markets and shops. Ronan admired the colors that adorned the stalls and greeted the shopkeepers before moving on.

"We are on the cusp of a battle."

Orion knew what he was referring to. "When do we leave?"

Ronan admired a trinket from a stall and placed it back down. "That is what I wanted to speak to you about. You are not coming with me."

As expected, his brother whirled around to face him. His gray wings shot up as if preparing to fight. "Do not start with me, Ronan. Not right now, when everything is about to get good."

Ronan grasped the archangel's shoulder. "If something were to happen to me, I need someone I can trust to take my place. To take control of the Sombra Quarter and continue the work we've been doing."

"Stop," Orion hissed. "Stop making it sound like you're not coming back."

Ronan leaned forward and held his gaze. "Brother, I ask that you do this for me. If I do not return, take my place or assign someone else to lead the shadow markets. I trust you."

Orion's brows pinched together, pain etched over his face. "I can't lose you again."

His chest tightened, as well as his grip on his brother's shoulder. "You never did."

Orion searched his eyes, his voice coming out in a ragged whisper. "And what of Damalis?"

Ronan thought of his home realm, a pang in his heart. He thought of palm trees and white sands, the smell of jasmine weaving through the sky. It had been too long since he'd last visited.

"That is another thing. When I leave with the guild, I need you to go home. Warn them, prepare them. Soon enough, the High Throne may become aware of our realm's existence."

Orion's jaw clenched. "So be it."

"Thank you." Ronan gave him a half-smile. "I love you, brother."

Orion rolled his eyes and forced him into a hug. "I love you too," he grumbled.

Later, Ronan reached the stone trees. The space was cool even as the last of the sunlight poured through the cavern ceiling. His eyes roamed from branch to branch, remembering all the nights he had spent here. Every tear he had shed, every scream he'd unleashed.

It felt different. The clearing before him had witnessed many of his agonies and now his sanctuary seemed to have served its purpose.

As he left the grove, he couldn't help but feel the trees were bidding him farewell.

FIFTY-NINE

I t felt like the eve of a storm. Sunset splashed over the damp cobblestone. Moisture clung to Daria Calderón's cloak, droplets crowning her head. She could've sworn there was the smell of rain in the air.

As soon as Daria and Ares had received word that a deity was suspected of summoning the ethereal creatures, they had begun to concoct a plan. After a week of preparation, she had called for Zara, who was now currently walking beside her.

The streets of the capital's inner district were overflowing with citizens and tourists going about their day. The scowl on her sister's face was enough to send bystanders scurrying in the other direction. Daria had to admit she was impressed by it.

Zara had informed her that the Spirits and specters were capturing *normal* mortals, and that they were looking for the ether-born—whatever that meant. The Ikarrian guild was preparing to attack the oncoming specters. The thought of such creatures making way to the capital sent chills down her spine.

"There is other news I must share with you," Zara said, her brow furrowing. "It involves Ronan, but I cannot speak of it here. Once all this is over, I will. Just remember to avoid the outer district tonight."

Daria looped her arm around her sister's. "Don't worry. We have the final Summit's celebration tonight, remember?"

Her sister smirked. "Except you won't really be attending the festivity."

Daria smiled. "No, while the castle is busy with the final celebration, and you are off slaughtering monsters, I will search the royal offices to see if a deity from the castle is behind this. If I can't find any proof, we can assume it is a deity citizen within the capital."

Zara whistled as if impressed. "I'm not surprised you were the one to come up with this plan. I would've been shocked if it had been our broody vampire."

Daria stifled a chuckle and glanced over her shoulder. "He's not *that* broody."

Ares walked several yards behind them. His hands were shoved in his pockets, his long cloak drifting in the occasional breeze. His hair flowed around his face, showcasing that dangerously sharp jawline. Those violet eyes went straight to her, as if he could feel her gaze.

"He's protective of you," Zara observed.

The princess made a face. "I'm quite positive that is the purpose of his duty."

Her sister rolled her eyes. "You've always been so oblivious. I am sure it is more than that."

"And I'm quite sure the vampire is listening to us right now."

The mercenary smiled, a sinister look flashing over her eyes. "Good. I want him to hear my threat. If he fails to protect you, I will rip his spine out."

"Dear gods."

Zara leaned in, voice dropping to a whisper. "It's interesting that the general has managed to live two lifestyles for as long as he has."

Daria frowned, sensing her sister's tone. "Do you doubt Ares's intentions?"

"I always doubt, sister, though that is not what I meant. I am simply wondering what the general would do if he ever had to choose between his loyalty to his king or his association with the Sombra Quarter?"

Daria had nothing to say to that. The question of Ares's true allegiance had indeed crossed her mind, though she had never voiced it. While her sister may not have been aware of the situation regarding his mother, she still had a point. Ares only seemed to work with Ronan out of some emotional debt.

Daria had to admit that a part of her was afraid of the answer.

Silence fell between the sisters as they continued to wander the streets. Daria forced herself to admire the shops, noting the tradesmen hauling carts and wagons while families strolled into temples and other businesses. Anything to distract from the sudden turn of her thoughts.

Zara leaned into her. "Something is bothering you."

Daria felt a rush run up her cheeks. She fought to keep her hands loose at her sides. "I used to question my value to our family. Our pater is king, and manages to rule a realm while remaining active in our lives. And you, my dear sister, have given so much of yourself to secure our safety. Everyone has a purpose. What about me? Am I solely a little princess who wears pretty dresses, tends to her education and doesn't amount to anything more? What good am I to this family if I don't practice my skills, if I don't explore more of who I am? I am beginning to believe that I *do* have something to offer."

Her gaze coasted about the capital's bustling central plaza. "I know it sounds silly, especially because you and Pater have suffered during your livelihoods, and it may be easier to say that I should simply enjoy the goodness life has given me. And I am grateful, so utterly grateful. But I wish to contribute, make a positive impact, for my family—and if possible, for my kingdom."

The words poured out of her heart. It was the most she had ever expressed of her inner desires to her sister. She didn't notice that the torches lining the street were burning brighter.

It was silent for too long. Daria risked a glance and found Zara staring at her. Her sister's green eyes seemed to shine. "There is nothing wrong with wishing to do more with your life. Your heart is pure, sister of mine, and how beautiful that is. You owe it to yourself to discover more of who you are and what your place is within this life."

Zara's lips broke into a warm smile. A smile Daria had not seen in a long time. "And there is nothing wrong for a woman to enjoy wearing pretty dresses, nor to want to fight for something more. Fierceness and bravery do not always have to come in the form of blades and armor, and boldness does not always have to come in fiery retorts and flares of anger. Strength is shown in many ways."

Daria felt the ether in her veins begin to sing. She had done her part in Elios, clawed her way through the damning politics. And she would continue to fight whatever battles came her way.

For her kingdom. For her family. For herself.

There was something she had left unturned in the Soleira castle. Another final mystery she needed to unravel.

The nape of her neck tickled, and she turned to find Ares watching her. His violet eyes gleamed, a soft curl to his lips. The way he looked at her made her feel like she had the strength of a thousand warriors.

Emboldened, Daria's grasp tightened around her sister's arm. She turned her gaze to the street ahead. "You always know what to say, Zara. If you'll let me, there's something I'd like to say to you."

"Here we go." She could hear the teasing in her sister's voice.

Daria stopped them in the middle of the plaza. Her heart raced against her chest. "You've been avoiding our pater. I know you were ignoring my messages to meet and I understand why, but not once since we've reconnected have you asked for him. He also wanted to see you."

Zara stayed silent, the energy about her presence muted. When her body stiffened, Daria knew that her sister had noticed their pater in the crowd. Within the blur of passersby, the king of Ikarria stood. Waiting for them. He wore no fancy clothes nor his obsidian crown— solely a pater seeking his daughters.

Zara cursed under her breath. "So, my innocent sister ambushed me."

Daria felt a twinge of guilt. She squeezed her sister's arm. "Please don't be mad. The Ikarrian advisors sent Pater messages about some unrest in our realm, so it has been decided that he will leave the Summit early."

It certainly wasn't ideal, but there had been no protests from the High King. She supposed they could thank the Suns that Raziel hadn't pushed farther for Ikarria to join the Aligned Realms—if anything, he seemed more than pleased to be rid of the Ikarrian king—and Daria would still be escorted back home when it was time to depart.

She nudged Zara. "He wanted to see you at least once before he returned home. You are welcome to walk away, I just thought . . . I don't know. I suppose I wanted to try to bring the family together . . . like before."

Zara's eyes widened, the skin on her face paled. "No, you did good Daria, thank you. I should've spoken to him long ago."

Daria squeezed Zara's arm once more before letting go. The princess stepped away, the mercenary giving her sister one last look before facing their pater.

Daria turned toward the castle, a vampire at her heels.

There was a roaring in Zara's ears. She took one step toward the draconic king, her legs beginning to feel numb. It suddenly felt like she was back in the Ikarrian mercenary temple, her pater bidding her farewell before she ventured to her first hunting season. The onslaught of emotions she had felt in that moment came hurtling back to her.

The ugly, twisted feeling of resentment toward her king. The male who had saved her from the burning fields of Valenzia. The pater who had failed to keep her away from the games of politics and corruption.

Her jaw tightened as she faced Idris, the throng of people around them falling into a myriad of colors.

He looked tired and worn out, the fire in his amber-brown eyes not as bright as before. But his face lifted slightly at the sight of her. "My storm."

Zara stopped mid-stride. Her fingers curled into fists but her voice was softer than expected. "Pater."

The king of Ikarria offered her a small smile. "How are you faring?"

His question cracked a fissure in her chest, opening the wounds of her fate. "How am I *faring?*"

Zara felt the fyrebrand's weight on her wrist, the ache that had built every year. All the blood she had shed, the lives she had ended to appease the treaty that these kings had created.

Her pater winced. "I have heard this hunting season has revolved around the Sombra Quarter. I've seen the kills other guilds have made in the streets."

"But you've always known how gruesome the hunts are. You have seen battlefields, the War of the Skies itself. You knew exactly what you were sending me to."

Sparks of flame rose in his eyes before lowering. "I know I failed you, my storm, but I did not *willingly* throw you to the High Throne. I took you in, a survivor of their opponents, and *they* did not like it." He pointed to the domed castle behind him. "I argued with Raziel countless times to ensure your life was spared and that Ikarria remained safe. At first, the Council wanted to *kill* you—this was the compromise."

She growled to herself, pressing the heels of her palms against her eyes. "My feelings are tangled, Pater. In the beginning, I understood the cost that came with the treaty and I was eager to do my part. But everything changed after my first hunt." She lowered her hands, her gaze fell along with them. "As the years passed, it became harder to face you. I know it's not completely fair but I was . . . disappointed."

Zara met his tortured gaze. "I love you, and I am so grateful for you. You gave me a home and a family. I just—" The swell of emotions clenched so tightly in her chest she almost couldn't breathe. And the voice, the words of her younger self escaped through her clenched teeth. "I just wish it didn't have to come at such a great cost."

Zara sounded small. A child reaching to her parent.

Idris closed in, his hands extended toward her, preparing to take her into his arms. But the mercenary was quick, her body moving away before she could process what she was doing.

She wasn't . . . she wasn't ready to hear his apologies.

The Ikarrian king froze. A flood of regret, guilt, sadness and understanding filled his gaze. Idris Calderón must've known that he would not be forgiven so easily, that it would take more than an embrace and words to wash away the pain she'd felt most of her life.

"My storm," he whispered. "I love you."

Those words brought a burning sensation in the back of her eyes. Zara looked up at the sky, gathering herself. White clouds floated within the orange-blue light. The smell of sweets and candles surrounded them.

The king spoke again. "You're right." She met her pater's gaze as he continued, "I did fail you, and I think I've always felt that since I took you in. The decisions that were made should *not* have come at the expense of your heart and wellbeing."

Idris took another hesitant step toward her. The sunset gleamed against his white braids and the tattoo along his face. For a moment, Zara saw the draconic king in his full might. Just as when she first met him, in shining steel and bloody glory.

"You have every right to be upset with me, resent me, hate me— anything and everything you feel, Zara, is valid. I should've done better. But know this," he gave her a sad smile, "I haven't stopped fighting for you, and I will continue to do so until my body joins the soil in the ground."

She couldn't find the words, her throat clogged with the weight of her life's burdens. Zara knew he meant it. Gods, she knew her pater loved her, but the ache inside her refused to lessen.

His amber-brown eyes warmed and he gently placed a palm over her cheek. "My beautiful daughter, my promise to you hasn't waned. There is no rush for you to move past this and to be on good terms with me. Take the time you need and know that I will always be here for you. By the ethereal skies, I will protect you with my every breath."

The first vow he had made to her. Zara felt his warmth and affection. She felt weak for not being able to push past this.

One day, they would be able to heal together.

Zara gave him a weak smile as she prepared to take a step back. "Thank you, pater."

She drifted away into the moving crowd, as if she hadn't been standing in front of the Ikarrian king at all.

Later that evening, Ares was called to meet with the vampire king. Daria managed to steal some time to herself in the training ground while she waited. The skin of her palms had begun to tear from gripping the dagger's pommel. Once she returned to Ikarria, she would demand formal instruction. Perhaps Hakim could even teach her.

Eventually, Ares charged into the courtyard with a thunderous look. She jumped to her feet. "What's wrong?"

His violet gaze jerked to hers. "Nothing. I—I have to lead another roust this evening. I'm sorry, it looks like I won't be able to train with you."

Daria narrowed her eyes. She wasn't sure how she could tell, it may have been the subtle tightening of his jaw or how his fingers twitched at his sides, but she knew there was more. "Tell me, Ares."

He went to the weaponry rack along the walls. "King Matías made some . . . threats."

"Explain."

"It's really nothing, princess. It's not the first time he's done this, especially when he doesn't get what he wants."

Fire growled in her veins at that. She watched him pick off several knives from the wall and sheathe them along his waist. The sight of the steel teeth strapped to his body sent nerves through her. It was the first time she'd seen him wear that much weaponry.

The conversation with Zara hadn't left her. Seeing him now, like this—she knew she needed to say the words. "What are you doing?"

He unsheathed a sword, examining the blade. "What do you mean?"

"I mean, what are you *doing*, Ares? You are about to lead a vampire roust during the hunting season. Haven't the citizens had enough of this tyrannic behavior?"

Ares shoved the weapon back into its sheath. "My king commanded it. I do not *wish* to do it."

She could see the raw guilt on his face and knew he meant it. But it wasn't enough, and the realization cracked her heart. "Who do you serve? Your vampire king or yourself?"

Ares flinched. "I do not have the luxury of choice, princess," he rumbled.

Daria gritted her teeth. "Zara and the Ikarrian guild are currently risking their lives to fight for themselves, for what they believe."

Ares prowled toward her, but she refused to move. "I told you why I serve."

"For your mother's safety, I know," she said, softly. "I've seen how much you loathe the politics here. The wealthy adore you, but you *hate* them. In the beginning it may have been a means to survive to stay here, but you are not alone anymore. Is there no way to help your mother escape as well? Wouldn't she want to leave this place?"

His expression was unreadable. "My mother often hides her true feelings behind her smiles and laughs. But no, she isn't happy here."

"Then perhaps Ronan can help you. He has the Sombra Quarter, surely he can do something."

Ares shook his head. "You don't understand, princess. The vampire king and I made a deal when he removed me from the streets of Adrastea. If I trained to become strong enough—*murderous* enough—to be his general then he would protect me and my mother. Now, I am his *favorite*, and if we were to flee, Matías would raze the Continent to the ground to find us. He is a proud male, one that is kept in check by Raziel's rule. It is the reason why Ronan and I never pursued that option."

Daria felt the war behind his words. The rumble of a merciless, yet trapped, soldier. She had only seen Ares, the bodyguard. She had not seen the general of war in true form.

Something in her chest deflated. "You will always serve them, won't you? The vampire king and the High Throne."

Ares's hardened expression fell slightly. "I can still support Ronan and his cause. I can still support your sister . . . I can still support *you*."

She felt her eyes dampen. "That is not sustainable, Ares, and you know it. How long can you play a double life before you get caught? What will happen to you then? Your mother?"

His lips curled to the brink of a snarl. His violet eyes seemed to glow. "I am doing everything in my power to prevent such things from happening. It is better this way than the guaranteed wrath we would experience if we were to run away."

"There is always a risk, Ares. Whether you stay here or leave with the Sombra Quarter."

It was silent on the training ground. Sea winds caused loose pebbles to skitter across the stone floor. The smell of citrus and cooked meat grew thick. Ares's cloak snapped with the breeze.

It was a fraction but Daria saw it—the vampire's expression cracked. "What if I *am* afraid?"

She blinked. The general clamped his mouth shut and glanced away, his throat bobbing, like he needed a moment to collect himself.

Daria sighed. "It sounds like you made your choice. If you wish to continue the life you've lived, then have it your way. Know that it will eventually bring us on opposite sides of the battlefield, whether among politics or in bloodshed."

The skin between Ares's brows pinched. "It doesn't have to, though. Please, try to understand my position, princess."

She stepped away from him, suddenly growing very tired. "But I do. I guess time will tell, won't it? You may escort me to my rooms. I know you must leave for the vampire roust," she said stiffly.

Ares didn't respond and followed her out of the training ground.

As they passed through the castle's main courtyard, halfway to her private quarters, a small patrol of vampire soldiers marched toward them. They were escorting someone, Daria realized. She then saw King Matías within the cluster of bronze armor and red cloaks and, at his arm, was Morana.

Ares stiffened at her side, stopping in his tracks. His eyes were pinned on his mother who didn't look his way. She wore a blood red gown that made her pale skin glow. Her chin was held high, a slender hand splayed across the vampire king's arm.

The world seemed to slow as Matías's gaze slid to his war general. His lips curved into a wicked grin and Daria's stomach dropped.

Whatever disagreement had transpired between the males, this was Ares's punishment.

Her bodyguard growled. It reverberated through her blood and bones, enough to crack the ground beneath her feet.

"Fucking bastard."

As soon as he had escorted Daria back to her rooms, Ares left without a word.

SIXTY

Zara sauntered along a white, flat rooftop. The Machai Forum was silent tonight. It was odd not hearing the constant barrage of music and drunken laughter. No street shows lit its center, no market stalls lined the dirt road.

After her visit with Daria, the mercenary had spent the remainder of the evening watching members of the Sombra Quarter escort residents out of the Machai Forum before the specters arrived. Ronan had arranged for several of the shadow dealers to use their warehouses and other businesses as a place to house the temporary refugees. He even went as far as preparing to offer them a place within the Stone Orchard. That option was reserved for those who might lose their homes or place of work after tonight. Zara hoped it wouldn't come to that, but she had been itching for a fight and wouldn't mind breaking a wall or two.

The last of the escorted parties left the Forum, their thin line of wagons and carts fading into the night. The other Horizons of Ikarria prowled along the other rooftops, weapons glinting against their scaled armor. With the moon shining brightly behind them and their hoods drawn, they truly resembled reapers of Death.

You will fail.

Her fingers curled into fists. She hadn't heard the fyrebrand in so long, especially not since Hakim had told her that it was her own worst creation.

You have no power over me. You have no power over me. She repeated the words over and over.

Zara had thought that since she had become aware of the fyrebrand's origin that she wouldn't have to face it anymore—that it was gone. Its presence now crouched in the back of her thoughts. The sensation was so prominent, so shocking—so *familiar*—that she flinched.

Do you think you can be rid of me that easily? You have been feeding your fears and anger all these years and now suddenly you wish for control? How naive.

She shut her eyes. It was both fascinating and terrifying how her own emotions had grown to have a voice. How the ether echoed her truest thoughts back to her.

Silence. In the dark corners of her mind, Zara faced the direction of the voice. Nothing. But she felt it. Like a coiled beast, ready to strike. She pointed a finger into the nothingness. *I have allowed you to torture me long enough. You will learn to obey me.*

The fyrebrand shrank away, tossing a scoff before slinking back into the darkness. She felt the pressure eddy from her head and sighed.

Her eyes opened to see Ronan flying to a nearby rooftop, his black wings gathering the stars. To think no one else knew that the long-lost king of Damalis stood among them. But he was no king tonight. He was a rebel, a criminal to the High Throne, and a warrior of the heart.

He looked her way and offered a close-lipped smile. Something in Zara's chest squeezed.

The Elios guild had gone silent since their altercation with Tamaya. The mercenaries of Adrastea were still in mourning, and she hadn't seen those of Kairos since she'd been injured. The Horizons were scattered and divided, and there was little they could do about it.

"Are you ready?" Axar drew up beside her, fingers tapping against the pommel of the sword strapped to his side.

Zara kept her eyes on the outskirts of the Machai Forum, her body stiff with tension. The hills loomed in the distance as they waited for the specters to appear out of the darkness. "No matter how close we are to solving the mystery behind those creatures, I feel like the true answer is standing before us but we are not seeing it."

Axar must have known what she meant. His voice was firm, though she caught the underlying wave of unease. "I think we've managed well with what we had."

They looked at Hakim and Eshe who were walking down the empty street. Their mentors had unsheathed their weapons, and seemed to be deep in conversation. The head of the guild met their gazes, the dark gray, scaled armor making him look more beast than man.

Hakim called out to them. "We tread the path of silver and red."

Axar and Zara bowed their heads. "We are the Horizon."

Time dragged as they waited. The air didn't hum with unnatural energy. No cerulean blue eyes glowed within the night. Zara pressed her body against the wall of a building, eyeing the empty streets. Perhaps the horde had veered onto a different path. No, that couldn't be. She had memorized the map of Elios and the Continent down to every traced line. If the specters were coming from the East, it would be difficult to miss them. They would have to pass through the Machai Forum to reach the capital.

Her thoughts halted when she felt a droplet of water on the tip of her nose. She felt another and another, until it turned into a downpour. The shifting in the air's energy was practically tangible.

"The Spirits," she breathed.

They were here. They had to be.

Zara unsheathed her khopesh, the obsidian steel shadows at the palms of her hands. She peeked around the corner to see a swarm of glowing blue eyes appear in the darkness. She could hear their running feet, pounding the ground before their animalistic movements took shape. The way they ran—as if the ethereal souls were still getting accustomed to the bodies they possessed.

A surge of energy rumbled through her bones. In the depths of her soul, she felt a crack in the void. A break in her mental walls. Zara felt the breath of power, one she had never experienced before. It pressed against the surface. She felt its weight, tried to reach for it, but it remained unmoved.

The shudder of ether was enough for her lips to spread into a wild grin. Zara stepped into the open street, Axar emerging from his post as well. He gave her a smirk as they prepared to meet the onslaught.

The creatures poured into the Machai Forum. From what Zara could tell, there were hundreds of them. Her knuckles tightened around her blades. She and Axar braced, ready to charge.

"Not so fast, little ones."

Hakim and Eshe appeared on the main road, joining them. The head of the Ikarrian guild prowled through the beams of moonlight, his war hammer grinning in his hand. He placed a hand on Axar's shoulder and nudged him a step back.

"We will take care of the specters' first line of attack. You two can handle any who manage to get past us."

Eshe cackled, her alabaster bow already in hand. "I think it is time the students witness the full might of their mentors."

Axar snorted. "We have seen you fight plenty of times. You only want to flaunt your skills."

Zara smacked the back of the shifter's head. He yelped and threw her a glare.

Their mentors awaited in the center of the Machai Forum, surrounded by old pillared buildings, as a swarm of specters came rushing toward them. Eshe was the first to move, firing off an array of arrows. Handfuls of the possessed people fell to the ground, their cries ringing through the Forum. The vampire moved so quickly, Zara almost didn't notice the foam on some of the creatures' wounds. It seemed Eshe had been tinkering with more poisons. Bile formed in Zara's stomach.

Specters pushed through the archer's attacks and Hakim charged them, swinging his war hammer. His large body was a battering ram itself, plowing through the field of creatures. The Horizon pivoted, using his beastly weapon alongside a long dagger in his other hand. Blood spurted with every swing of his arms.

Eshe strapped her bow to her back and unsheathed a sword. She was a wind of dark silver as she darted between the specters, each falling at her feet with gashes across their throats. She flanked Hakim, taking down the creatures that he missed. Using her vampire strength, Eshe leapt into the air and over Hakim's head, landing on the shoulders of a specter and beheading it before moving onto the next.

The creatures managed to grapple Hakim to the ground, piling on top of him. Zara's heart lurched in fear and she was about to run toward him, when—

The specters wailed as Hakim's weapons punctured through their ribs and torsos from underneath. He emerged from the carnage, body dripping with his opponents' blood. The *Dragonheart* spread his arms and roared to the night sky as he stood victorious among the remains of those who sought to kill him.

Zara grinned, in awe—she wasn't sure how he'd managed it. Axar's jaw was almost on the ground. A human had bested a horde of ethereal creatures. Hakim must have been blessed with the strength of the Suns.

Axar suddenly grabbed her arm, steering her attention away. His nostrils were flared as he scanned the dark alleys and corners of the buildings around them.

"There are more," he rumbled. "Specters are moving behind the shops and businesses. They are coming this way."

Zara raised her twin blades. "I don't see the Spirits or our suspected deity."

"What if our enemy is not a deity?" The shifter narrowed his eyes on her. "What if we have it all wrong?"

Her lips twisted into a sneer. "I don't pray to the Suns often, but I do hope what you're saying is not true."

Specters rose in waves between the alleys. Some clawed their way up the walls to the rooftops. Seeing human bodies, now imbued with strange godlike strength, puncturing the limestone with their bare hands chilled Zara's blood.

She saw a flash of wings before Ronan dove for the horde, disappearing within the buildings. Zara turned back to the specters just as they reached her. Teeth grazed her arms and legs but her blades cut them down before they could make purchase. The mercenaries had padded their armor with extra layers of leather to prevent the creatures' poisonous bites.

Guts spilled onto the dirt and nearly caused her to slip. The smell of broken flesh stained the air. Once Zara had cleared her section of the street, she summoned her ether. Its strength propelled her forward, bright tendrils fading along with her movements. Axar was behind her, having shifted into his wolf form as they tried to head toward Hakim and Eshe. The specters were persistent, eating up more ground as the mercenaries tried to clear the path.

Eshe cried out as a specter managed to rake their claws against her chest. Zara's body trembled at the sound, Axar's wolf howling in response. They were still too far to reach her, the archer slowly being overwhelmed by the never-ending specters.

Hakim plowed through the Forum's center, trying to get to her.

Gods, if anything happened to Eshe. If Zara was to lose one of her own, the world would know her grief. There would be no corner of the Continent where they could avoid her.

Two spears of silver light plummeted from the sky, landing in the center of the Machai Forum. The ground cracked on impact, killing nearby specters by the force of its presence. White mist curled from the ground as two figures rose. Before Zara could see who they were, they cut through the horde. A sea of red flew from their movements, obliterating strings of specters. They closed in on Eshe and removed the creatures before they could harm the vampire.

The figures stopped, their rippling aura and strength wading off to reveal who they were.

Zara sucked in a sharp breath. Hadeon and Nadira stood in the Machai Forum.

Two deities of the Council. The fucking *Council* had saved them.

Their swords were lit with white flames. Not a drop of gore touched their gleaming armor. They didn't look spent after using all that energy. Surviving specters around them retreated.

Nadira's head jerked to the side, ethereal eyes landing on Zara. Zara gasped when the deity appeared before her in a cloud of ether. The deity surveyed her and pursed her lips, as if unimpressed.

"Well, it seems the Ikarrian guild has been busy," Nadira said. "You're welcome, by the way."

Zara's throat bobbed. "How did you know we would be here?"

The deity looked insulted. She placed a hand on her waist, her pulled-up hair flicking to the side. "The Estrella Territories are provinces of Elios. Did you really think we wouldn't find out what was happening on our lands? But I am surprised to find that *your* guild was aware of these beings."

Zara's mind was reeling. It shouldn't have come as a shock to see that the Council knew about the specters. Rumors had been spreading for so long that the news would have eventually reached the High Throne. Even Ronan had known this.

Fucking Suns. Zara hoped the archangel was keeping out of sight of the deities.

She sighed. "It is a long story, but we came across these *things* during our hunts. We couldn't stand by and do nothing." Zara pointed her bloodied blade at the Council member. "Something else you should know is that we suspect one of your own—a deity from the capital, is behind these creatures."

Nadira's eyes widened. "That is quite an accusation."

"We found evidence of astral ore among some wreckage these

beasts caused. It led us to believe that a deity from Soleira is leading them." Zara couldn't reveal that the guild was tracking the ethereal creatures on purpose and why.

The deity's face twisted into a sneer. "I hope you're wrong, Rogue. We cannot risk another uprising ending how the War did."

A specter—in the body of a vampire male—sprung out from between two buildings and ran toward them. Hakim swung his war hammer, crushing its head on the ground. The stone floor was splattered with blood, tendrils of blue smoke curling from it.

Nadira watched with a gleam of interest as the mercenary joined Zara's side. "I suppose I should thank you Ikarrians for acting of your own accord. No doubt Raziel will want to hear what transpired here."

Hakim bowed his head. "We are grateful for your help, Lady Nadira. Though it seems we are not quite finished here yet. The others are keeping the specters at bay for now, but there are too many."

"Specters?" Nadira repeated softly. She turned to face the Machai Forum's center, where Hadeon and the other mercenaries were still battling the creatures. "Yes, it seems we will be overwhelmed soon."

Zara couldn't see Ronan but she was sure he was close, cutting down any stray possessed mortals. She felt his gaze on her—by some unexplainable force in the ether she knew the archangel was keeping guard over her.

The deity pointed toward an open road across the way that connected to the plaza where a band of specters had peeled away from the main group to make their way toward the inner district. "As you can see, they are already using their heads and creating a diversion. Hadeon and I cannot be in two places at once."

Zara's heart pounded against her ribs. The ether in her veins crouched as if waiting—*begging*—to be used in the fight.

The head of the guild growled. "Change of plans: Zara drives the runaway creatures out of the city while the rest of the guild takes care of those here with the Council members. Does that sound like a feasible plan, Nadira?"

Nadira kept her gaze on the battle. "I suppose that will do. So long as the Rogue can handle it *alone*."

"Such little faith," Zara mumbled. She exchanged a look with Hakim. She heard his unsaid message: *Keep the archangel away from here.*

Zara gave him a wicked grin, and he smiled back, amused. "Go hunt, little warrior."

By the will of her mind, she careened over the buildings, jumping from one rooftop to the other. Thanks to the invisible force of her ether propelling her forward, Zara soon gained ground on the specters. Her eyes narrowed as she observed them from above.

These ones looked different from the type she'd encountered before. The horns on their heads had grown larger and came in different forms—curled, jagged, or straight. There was even one that possessed the form of a human male while flaunting a spiked tail, scales beneath his torn clothes.

"What in the blazing Suns," Zara murmured. "Just how many different kinds of specters are there?"

Ronan had yet to appear, perhaps he would meet her farther out. It was better that way.

Zara sprinted across a next rooftop. She jumped, the air whistling beneath her boots. Pain surged up her leg and she cried out as a horned specter clung to her. The possessed woman had dug her claws into the openings between Zara's leathers.

The force of their collision had them rolling onto the next rooftop. The creature straddled Zara, reaching for her neck. The specter's grip was too strong, and black dots scattered across her vision. She didn't know where her khopesh landed, couldn't feel her blades near her. Her pounding heart quickened the tighter the grasp around her neck became.

The world exploded in splinters of darkness and light as the weight of the specter was flung off her. Zara pushed herself up to see Ronan dragging the specter into the air, the creature already impaled by his sword.

Ronan stilled in the sky, letting the lifeless body slide down his lowered blade and fall several hundred of meters to the ground. The moon beamed behind the leader of the Sombra Quarter, igniting him with the glow of the stars for all to see.

Ronan met her gaze from above.

A cold fear pierced Zara. The battle was not far behind them. The Council would be able to see an archangel flying in the air.

He soared toward her and helped her up with his callused hands, running them over her hair and face.

Her lips trembled. "The deities. They might see—"

"It doesn't matter," he said, his gray eyes soft.

That cold fear turned into a truth that blazed through her heart. The archangel had risked his identity to save her.

His scarred lips turned into a dark smile. He gestured to the specters still running through the district. "Shall we hunt together this time?"

The mercenary and the archangel raised their weapons under the night. They dove into the streets, and the cry of monsters followed.

SIXTY-ONE

As the night deepened, the more bloodied Zara's fighting leathers became. She and Ronan hunted down the specters, luring them away from Soleira. One by one, they created a trail of bodies that led to the Estrella Territories.

"*Daughter of the Dawn,*" a specter with metal teeth hissed. "*Your soul is owed to us.*"

Her grip tightened around the collar of the creature's tunic. Zara drove her sword deep in its gut, hearing the squelch of flesh. The specter reared its head back and howled.

Zara peeled her lips back. "Fuck. You."

Another specter, one Ronan had been grappling for what felt like hours, shouted from the archangel's grasp. "*The Midnight Sun will cover the world with its light, a light that only brings death. Neither one of you will be able to hide from our Creator.*"

Ronan ripped its head from its shoulders, throwing its remains to the side. His lips twisted in disgust. "No more of these riddles and threats. We've been hearing them all night."

The last creature fell at Zara's feet, blood slushing on the starlit grass. She blinked through the sweat to see petals glowing like pale moonlight. They filled the rolling hills, a replica of the sky above. Zara sheathed her blades, fingers trembling. The last of her strength had bled through her muscles, her body whined with every step.

Ronan had been beside her the entire time. Anytime one of them drifted away during the fight, the other would follow. They never left each other's blindsides unprotected. There had been too many enemies tonight.

"You look like shit." Ronan's voice was ragged, despite that wicked smile. Sweat, dirt, and blood smeared his skin.

She couldn't fight the smirk on her lips. "At least I'm not that out of breath. I thought our sparring had been appropriate training for you."

Ronan winced. When that cocky grin slipped, Zara knew something was wrong. He groaned, barely uttering her name before he fell to the ground. His wings of night stretched across the plush grass. With the shining blossoms surrounding him, he looked like he had fallen straight from Celestrea.

Zara's heart nearly leapt out of her chest and she crashed to her knees beside him. "*Ronan?*"

Her voice twisted in a way it never had before.

He grimaced. "I'm fine. Fighting all those bastards took more out of me than I thought. I only need to rest."

Deep gashes covered the skin on his arms. The specters had managed to pierce through his leathers. Zara could've scoffed. "Look at these wounds. You are *not* fine. How come you are not healing?"

Ronan breathed through clenched teeth. "It is most likely due to my locked ether. We've been in combat most of the night without stopping. My body hasn't had time to catch up."

Zara mumbled a slew of curse words as she slung his arm around her shoulders and heaved them to their feet. Ronan tried to help her, attempting to push himself up. His weight nearly toppled her over as he swung his face toward her, closer than he normally would. She felt his breath against her nose.

"Are you alright?" He whispered.

She tried to angle her face away from him. The sudden openness he bore was too much. "I'm fine."

A rumble sounded in his sweat-trickled throat. "Adira is not too far from here. We can rest there for a bit."

They limped to the abandoned city. Its white walls were now beginning to be overrun with vines and weeds. Glowing flowers protruded from the cracks, streaming the ground and rooftops.

It hadn't been that long for wildlife to claim the place, the very ground ridden with natural ether. She still couldn't comprehend how powerful it was.

Zara's lips parted. "It's beautiful."

Ronan grunted, pulling her back to reality and tightening her chest. Right. They trudged over to a small villa. Its broken walls were decorated with the glowing blossoms, lighting their way in the dark. Wild greenery stretched along the brick and limestone.

Inside was a bed, the cracked ceiling above it open to the stars. The room had been mostly claimed by the wildflowers and shrubbery. Zara guided the archangel onto the bed. He lowered himself with a hiss.

"I'm going to remove your clothes," she said, quietly.

"It's about time, Horizon." Ronan tried to smirk before it ended in another wince.

Zara sighed, a grim smile on her face. "At least your humor hasn't waned."

She helped him remove the fighting leathers and sweat-drenched clothing from his chest. Her fingers brushed over his sun-kissed skin, the tattoos that blessed his body. Ronan bowed his head, thick hair falling over his eyes. He made a sound, as if her touch was comforting.

Zara's face heated. Her fingers curled, and she considered running them through the black waves of his hair. Instead, she rummaged through the drawers to find the cleanest linen she could find. Ronan temporarily stood while she draped it over the bed before he sank back down on the fabric.

After checking his wounds, Zara clicked her tongue in disappointment. "They seem to be healing but the process is too slow. I'm going to scout our surroundings, maybe I can find some natural herbs that'll help."

She retreated a step, but he grabbed her. His large hand practically swallowed her own. Gentle and rough.

Those gray eyes lifted to hers. "Stay."

Zara felt a lump in her throat. There was that raw vulnerability again. And she was a coward. She took a step back, her fingers slipping from his.

She forced the words from her throat. "I will be back soon."

Zara walked out, trying to stop herself from running.

Behind the villa was a garden. Zara looked around, amazed at the overflowing plants, vines and greenery, before she decided to follow the pleasing sound of rushing water. She pushed through the shrubbery toward a stream. It was a streak of blue-silver, curving along the edge of the city. Not an herb in sight—not that she would've recognized any anyway. It looked like the archangel would have to suffer his injuries naturally.

Zara didn't think twice before unlacing her fighting leathers. Armor dropped from her aching body. Water nipped her skin and she sighed as she waded deeper, to her waist. Zara plunged under the surface, allowing her rampant thoughts to drown in the cold water.

The guild would have managed to fight off the remaining specters by now with the Council's help, and would be waiting for her at the rendezvous point. Ronan would have to tend to his shadow dealers and the citizens they'd helped evacuate. She didn't want to contemplate on how the Council's rescue would affect their efforts.

Zara emerged from the water. Her hair fell over her breasts, long enough to cover her nipples. She continued to scrub the grime and blood from her body, the residue of the battle swept away with the current.

Eventually—begrudgingly—she stepped out of the river and slipped on her long shirt. She didn't don her trousers or leathers, holding them in her arms.

Someone cleared their throat from behind her. "Were you not going to tell me there was a stream?"

Ronan stood at the edge of the wild shrubbery. His voice was light, but his gaze was sharp. The way he stared. He hadn't looked down at her body, but she felt his gaze everywhere.

Zara was acutely aware of how her shirt had pushed up along her thighs. She tried to make her voice more clipped though it sounded more like a question. "Eventually."

The corner of his lips twitched. He strode toward the riverbank, shrugging the rest of his clothes off. Zara tried not to stare as he slipped off his trousers, the muscles that perfectly lined his thick thighs. Not to mention the view from behind . . .

Lust rushed through her. An unfamiliar warmth threatened to melt through the thorns over her heart. And it was terrifying.

His gaze slid to her and she quickly averted her eyes. "I'll leave you to it," she muttered.

Zara had barely made it a few steps back to the garden when Ronan called out. "Don't go. Stay . . . please."

SIXTY-TWO

Zara glanced back at the archangel. Under the glow of the surrounding blooms she saw the faint bob of his throat.

"I would like to clean my wounds, but I may need some help," he said. "If it's alright with you."

She looked at the cuts and burns that looked less harsh than before, faint bruises mottling his skin. "You're relentless, aren't you?"

"Desperate, actually," he breathed.

Zara tried to ignore the rush of emotions that came from those words. In that rough, deep voice. It was unsettling and not something she was accustomed to. She dropped her clothes and padded toward him. He tracked her movements, his gaze dragging up along her muscled legs. Zara couldn't deny she liked his attention on her.

"I do not want to get wet," she said, plopping herself on a slab of rock that sat in the water at the edge of the stream.

Ronan's lips twitched in amusement. "That's no fun."

Zara scowled when she caught the innuendo. She beckoned him to her with a finger. "Come."

He smirked and pushed through the water. When he reached her, she made a circling motion with her hand. "I will help with your wings."

From where she sat, she was angled slightly above him. Ronan had to tip his chin up to meet her eyes. There was only mischief in his expression. "It's the least you could do after I tended to you."

Zara rolled her eyes. "Fucking Suns."

He chuckled and turned around, careful not to hit her with his wings. Up close, they were magnificent. Each feather held a faint glimmer, like the cosmos streaking through the darkness. Her fingers brushed over them and she could've sworn a slight iridescence of red-orange colors shimmered under her touch, so faint she'd almost missed it. It was odd, and yet stunningly beautiful.

Ronan shuddered against her touch.

"Sorry," she mumbled.

He shook his head, his voice deeper. "Not your fault."

Zara bent down and cupped water with her palms, pouring it over the dirt that had gathered between the feathers. She brushed through every single one, hearing the soft hitch of Ronan's breath. He continued to wash his body, as if in an attempt to ignore how her cleaning his wings was affecting him. The small sounds he made, the low grunts and sighs . . . she wanted to hear more.

Heat curled low in her abdomen. A small ache blossomed between her legs and she rubbed her thighs together.

They worked in silence, listening to each other's breaths. Hearing the unsaid pleas and yearning while the night creatures howled and sang. The area smelled of damp grass and fresh air.

"I'm sorry," Ronan said.

Zara paused. "What do you mean?"

"I'm sorry that I have been unable to fulfill my end of our original agreement. I was supposed to help free you."

Yes, the fyrebrand was still on her skin. Yes, Raziel still had a hold on her life. It had been many years—her whole fucking life—of being aware of that heavy reality. The sorrow and hatred had weighed so much on her, but she had been willing to carry it. Had allowed her body to scar and bleed to hold that burden.

Ronan had . . . inspired her. He was imperfect and damaged. Had avoided his true identity for so long. Still, he was gentler than she ever was. He was simply *good*. A pure warrior of heart. Zara had shown herself to him, the truest and ugliest parts, and he had not cowered. It was in moments like that, bit by bit, that she desired *more* for herself. Whatever that meant—it was for her to define.

A soft smile touched her lips. "You already have."

The muscles of his back tightened. "It's not enough. I am not giving up."

She wasn't sure what to say to that. A small smile touched her lips as she stroked a hand between his wings. Ronan outright shuddered.

"You wicked woman," he said through clenched teeth.

Zara chuckled, the sound rough. "I thought you archangels didn't have weaknesses."

If she was being honest, she wanted to see him unravel. To hear the sounds he would make before they returned to their bleak reality. Sounds caused by *her* touch.

Zara traced two fingers along the root of a wing, eyeing the angry scar that ran beneath it. She pushed away the thought of Ronan having his wings ripped off him. The screams that must have torn through him. Helpless and alone. Her chest tightened to the point of pain.

Ronan lifted his head to the stars. A whimper escaped him.

He spun to face her, water whipping against the night sky in glittering gems. He grabbed the flesh of her thighs, his gaze a silver fire.

"Two can play that game, Santos."

Ronan's hands went to the back of her knees, gently guiding her legs deeper into the water, the apex of her thighs now closer to his reach. Her shirt was long enough to cover her, but she felt exposed to him.

The archangel raised one of her legs above the stream's surface. He brought his mouth to the inside of her thigh, his lips grazing up her leg. Ronan didn't fully touch her, didn't kiss her. He only teased, every feathery light brush of his lips causing her lower abdomen to twist tighter and tighter.

His eyes never left hers. "Is this your weakness?"

Zara released a shaky breath. "No."

"No?" Ronan lowered even more and she felt the light, damp touch of his tongue, the nick of his teeth, as he continued farther up to the place where she ached for him. Water sluiced down his wings as he rose higher. "How about this?" His words caressed her skin, even closer now.

Zara was tempted to throw her legs over his shoulders and let the archangel devour her. But this intensity was overwhelming, and she couldn't keep up with her roaring thoughts and emotions. Ronan pulled back slightly, making the decision for her.

He smirked as he turned away to finish cleaning himself. "Perhaps you've met your match, Horizon."

Several minutes later, they made their way to the villa. Ronan paused at the room's threshold. He only wore his trousers, which hung low on his waist, the rest of his clothes in his hands.

Zara halted as well, her eyes on the bed. The awareness between them hadn't waned. She felt that languid heat settle even lower. It was agonizing. She dropped her fighting leathers. "Technically, you are still my mark."

Ronan was silent for a heartbeat. A painstakingly long heartbeat. "I know."

Her breathing turned shallow. "There is so much against us."

He exhaled the words. "I know."

She turned to him. Ronan's lips were parted as he fought to steady himself. "However you want me," he whispered. "I will gladly take what you give me."

A mercenary and an archangel had been at opposite sides of a battlefield. Now they were facing a different sort of war. One that was more dangerous, more thrilling, with the potential of being the most beautiful.

Zara never thought something like this would ever come to be, but here she was.

Shrouded by the starlit blossoms, they took each other in. Another painful breath, one that had the power to sweep them into oblivion.

They unleashed themselves.

At first there was nothing but teeth and tongue. A heady rush that was all-consuming. There was only them, the outside world long forgotten as they became lost in every touch.

Ronan kissed her like he had been deprived of air. Zara could hear his heart race, wild and brutal like him. All she felt was his hot skin against hers, their bodies mirroring one another like they did on the battlefield. She pushed and he pulled.

How his lips burned her—she wanted to be scarred.

Her fingers lightly traced along the muscles at his lower abdomen.

Ronan stiffened, growling the words against her mouth. "Tell me what you want, Horizon."

Her arms went around his neck. He curled over her as she licked the pale scar on his lips. "All of you," she whispered. "I want everything."

"Suns Above," he groaned.

Ronan kissed a trail down the column of her throat as he swept his large hands down her hips, yanking the hem of her shirt up so he could reach around her backside. The scrape of his calluses tingled on her skin and she fought back a shudder. Ronan's hands went under her clothes and to her breasts, and he brushed a thumb across her nipple. She arched into him, seeking—begging for more.

"You like that, don't you?" Ronan helped her remove her shirt and then bent to drag his tongue over the tightened bud. "Let me hear how much you like it."

Between her legs, she could feel his swelling cock. A whimper clawed up her throat. When his teeth scraped her skin, Zara moaned. The sound seemed to unravel Ronan, and he swept her off her feet. Her legs immediately wrapped around him and she was thrown back to the night they first kissed in the grove.

They were finishing what they'd started.

Ronan placed her on the bed, in the center of the glowing petals, and went to kiss her once more, tongue diving between her lips.

Zara couldn't wait any longer. She slid her hand beneath his waistband and stroked her fingers down his length. *Gods*, his size. The ache between her legs intensified. He ground into her, pressing his thick cock against her palm. Zara pumped him and spread the growing bead of liquid along his tip.

His teeth nipped at the curve of her ear. "You savage woman."

She chuckled, the sound wicked and sultry. Unlike the cold nothingness of when she hunted.

"I want to taste you," Ronan whispered along her neck.

Zara's legs parted for him, almost of their own accord. But she wanted this. Wanted him. He gave her a hungry look, one that awakened something primal within her too. She watched as the starlight danced over the ink that decorated him. The designs that defined him.

Ronan pulled back and removed his trousers. Her tongue swept over her lips at the sight of his hard cock, thick and beautiful. Veins lined the length and it looked smooth to the touch. Fucking Suns, she wanted to put her mouth around it. It was only then that she realized she was naked before him. Her legs were spread open, her nipples peaked and her mouth parted.

Ronan stared at her like she was a treasure from the skies, his eyes burning like dusted starlight. "You are stunning, Zara Santos. My ruthless beauty."

Ronan tugged her to the bed's edge and pushed her thighs open even more, her sex bare for him to take. He went down to his knees, wings flaring above him. A growl rumbled in his chest as he planted a kiss above her core. Heat spread with blazing wings, her body quivering with need.

A sharp breath left her when he dragged his tongue down her center. His fingers lightly dug into her flesh, holding her in place as he continued to lick her up and down. Then he closed his mouth around her clit and sucked.

Zara hissed. "Gods."

She was sure she had been sent soaring to the stars. No one had ever given her such a sensation, and she understood that it was because of *him*.

Ronan feasted with teeth and tongue. He dragged her closer and closer to the peak of bliss only to bring her down again. His silver eyes flipped up, watching as she grasped at her breasts and bucked her hips. It was too much. Such beautiful torture that she had to touch herself.

The corner of his lips curved. He plunged his tongue inside her, making her arch her back. A pathetic whimper left Zara's lips as she tried to fuck herself with his mouth.

He chuckled and drew back long enough to slide two thick fingers inside her. Fuck. How he stretched her was enough to have her eyes rolling back. It was everything, and yet not enough.

Ronan thrust his fingers steadily, pace quickening with every plunge. Each stroke sent a fire through her. "Look how wet you are," he murmured. He pulled out and sucked her wetness off each finger. "All for me."

The absence of him inside her—it was too much. She reached for him just as he reached for her. Their mouths met, tongues sliding over one another. Her fingers fisted his hair as she drove her hips forward to slide up and down against his cock.

Ronan shuddered. "Gods, Zara. I need you. I fucking need you."

She rolled him onto his back before moving down to settle between his legs. Zara was panting, as if she too needed him to breathe. "My turn."

Her tongue ran up his thick length. Suns, he tasted perfect. Ronan grunted as her lips swept over his broad tip. His deep voice raked her skin. "Take me, Horizon. Please."

So she did. Her eyes met his as she took every inch into her mouth. When he hit the back of her throat she gagged. Saliva dripped down her chin as she muffled a curse. Zara wrapped a hand around him before withdrawing her lips.

"I love the way your cock tastes in my mouth," she said, licking up his length.

Ronan's chest was moving heavily, as if he were restraining every part of him from lunging toward her. She pumped him and wrapped her lips around his tip again.

Zara held on to his large thighs as she sucked him, swallowing him greedily. He filled her mouth so well. She withdrew again and gazed up at the archangel with a drunken stare. "I want you inside me."

Ronan sat up to take her face in his hands. There was that gentleness, that rawness that always seemed to test her own vulnerability. His thumbs swept over her cheeks. "Are you sure?"

Zara nodded and brushed her mouth over his. "This is what I want."

"I take the tonic."

"So do I. I want you, now."

Those silver eyes turned molten, with a touch of something she wasn't sure she wanted to see. He twisted them around so she was flat on her back. Ronan kissed her on the lips—again and again and again.

He gently nudged her thighs open and she complied. She felt the thick tip of his cock press at her entrance, and she spread her legs even wider. Ronan held her gaze as he slid in. He paused at the slight grimace of pain that flickered across her face. He retreated and entered, inch by inch.

Zara couldn't comprehend just how good it felt. How good *he* felt. Because it was only him, she realized, that caused her to feel this way. Every stroke of burning pleasure was something they only could offer one another—it was only them in this damning world.

Ronan panted heavily as he leaned over her, bracing his arms on either side. His lips met hers as he made a final thrust, slamming into her. Zara cried out against his mouth just as he moaned. "*Fuck.*"

"Please," she breathed.

It was desperation. Desperation and obsession. Her legs trembled around him. He began to move his hips, plunging his cock farther into her. Zara groaned, sinking her nails into his back. Ronan quickened his pace. Faster and faster. A steady, forceful rhythm that had her tightening around him.

Ronan slid a hand under one of her knees, lifting it slightly to fuck her deeper. The sound of skin slapping against skin, the sound of their ragged breathing, echoed in the room. More. More. More.

"The sounds you make," he growled. "I can't get enough."

He brought his fingers back down to her clit and Zara's fingers drifted over his ass, digging into his skin. He growled, unleashing himself even more as he pounded into her. She screamed and sobbed, begging and begging.

Ronan's wings were spread out on either side of him, the moonlight crowning him.

A criminal. A warrior. A king.

He gritted his teeth. "I know, darling. I know."

Her orgasm spiraled through her, an eruption that sent her dizzy. Ronan moaned in her ear as he climaxed. His body curled over hers as she took every drop from his cock.

Their pants filled the room. Steady and rhythmic. He brushed his lips over her brow. "You are perfect."

Zara licked that scar one more time. "I know."

He laughed and tugged on her lower lip with his teeth.

They held each other, unwilling to let go of this moment. When he did pull out, the loss of him inside her was not something she was ready for, even as she felt his release spill out of her.

Ronan left the room to retrieve a clean rag. That hunger had never left his eyes. "Look at the mess I made of you."

She sighed as he cleaned her, as he planted kisses along her legs and stomach. Eventually, they collapsed back onto the bed. Ronan pulled her into his arms, a black wing draped over them.

No words needed to be said. This moment they had stolen for themselves was how it was meant to be.

Their hands drifted to each other, fingers interlocking.

They slept as the stars guarded them.

SIXTY-THREE

It was still dark when Zara woke, still cocooned in Ronan's embrace. Even though his wing shielded her from the world, she could see the stars beyond the broken ceiling.

The soft breathing at her neck told her he was still asleep. His tattooed arm hung around her, and she wanted to wiggle deeper into his embrace.

But this moment couldn't last. They would have to leave. She would have to don her armor and face Raziel soon enough. There was still the concern of the Council's involvement in the Machai Forum, and how the High King would react to this whole ordeal. Fucking Suns, the sudden rise of her thoughts caused a dull throb to pulsate at her temple.

Zara slowly slipped out from Ronan's hold. She glanced over at him, surprised that he hadn't moved yet. He must have been so exhausted.

Never would she have believed she'd end up sleeping with one of her marks. No, what happened between them wasn't just sex. There was something powerful that connected them.

She was almost afraid to admit it, but when she had touched him—had kissed him, it was as if she had been consumed by the light of the suns and stars.

Ronan was more than a mere mark, just as he was more than a friend. Zara rubbed a hand across her chest. Gods, she was ruined.

Once her feet hit the cool ground, she slipped on her shirt and wandered outside and through the ruined city. It was a dire attempt to distract her thoughts, but the pain in her head didn't stop. Zara returned to their temporary room some time later. She had barely caught sight of Ronan's figure as he was pulling up his trousers when the muscles in her legs spasmed.

A splintering pain seared through her mind and she leaned against the threshold, heaving for breath. There, in the back of her mind, a familiar voice slithered into focus. Zara gritted her teeth. *No. I had gotten rid of you.*

The fyrebrand hummed. *How many times do I have to say that you will never be rid of me? Your weakness and self-hatred persist, even when you think otherwise. I remind you of your realities.*

"No," she groaned. Her footing slipped, and she was about to fall to her knees when large arms swept around her waist.

"Zara." That voice. Deep and smooth. Strong and gentle.

Did you forget? You're dying. You haven't killed him, so you will suffer.

"Get away from me," she snarled. Her hands lashed out, hitting a solid chest.

"Zara."

Unless you finish what you started. What you truly started.

A scream peeled from her lips. She bent over, clinging her arm to her chest. The fyrebrand burned and burned and burned. Pain rippled through her body, pounding at every thread of muscle. Unseen claws raked through her mind, images of all those she killed flashing before her eyes.

The blood. Oh, gods, there was so much of it. It drenched her fingers, dribbled down her arms, splattering on her feet. Faces of the lives she ended. Faces of their loved ones who spat and cursed her name.

Stop. Stop. Stop.

"Zara!" A voice reached for her, wrenching her away from the torture.

The world snapped back into focus for a moment before her vision blurred again, smearing the image of the beautiful male in front of her.

Ronan searched her face with a wild, panicked look. "What in the fucking Suns is happening to you?"

His breathing had become more erratic, a hand slipping to where she clutched her wrist. When his fingers found the tattoo, his expression fell. "The Reckoning. It's hurting you."

Fear lanced through her, just as painfully as the fyrebrand punishing her. "Get away!"

Zara tried to crawl away, but didn't get far. She slapped a palm against the wall and clawed her way up to her feet.

Ronan slowly rose with her, his eyes never leaving hers as he eased closer. "It is the ether. You haven't completed your assignment. I saw it happen before, in the Machai Forum. When the archangel hurt me, the pain left you."

He reached for a dagger that had been discarded with their clothes and forced the blade into her hand. Zara shook her head, her body growing weaker with every passing second.

Suns, *please* no. She had been fighting this fate for so long.

"Stop," she mumbled weakly. The back of her eyes began to burn. Flashes of pain erupted throughout her body. "Don't, Ronan."

The archangel went to his knees before her, his wings draping over his back. Ronan's fingers curled over her own as he pressed the tip of the blade over his heart.

He tipped his chin up, baring his neck. "Do it, Zara. Relieve the pain."

Zara whimpered through the lashes against her heart. Her very soul. "No. No. No."

The corners of his scarred lips lifted slightly. "It's okay. This is how I can free you. There will always be someone else who can take over what I've been doing. My destiny has no more value than yours."

Ronan pressed more weight against her grip, the pointed steel digging through the inked lines on his skin. She saw the stars in his eyes, an image unveiling before her: beams of moonlight and a land filled with jungle and ocean. And power. It rippled like fire, but it was no average flame. It burned bright, a blood-red orange that twisted with the last light of the sun.

Ronan claimed there was no destiny for him, but she was witnessing it. And it sang to her.

His gaze drank her in as if he too was seeing something in her own eyes. Until a groan seeped from his lips.

The pain lessened in that moment. Zara latched onto that reprieve and shoved Ronan away from her, throwing the dagger into the darkness.

She shouted. "Why would you do that? You don't have to sacrifice yourself!"

Ire flashed over his eyes. "If I wish to put a blade in my heart so you may know peace, then I will do it."

The stinging returned to the back of her eyes. He closed in on her then. Though his body didn't touch hers, she felt like she was burning.

The storm in his gray eyes suddenly banked, and she could see a crack of sorrow within it. His hands went to her cheeks. He had done this often the night before. Like he couldn't keep himself away from her. Like she was a carefully crafted jewel that could draw blood.

Ronan's voice was calm. "You have a heart of war, darkness, and heartache. You have been made into a weapon, killed parts of yourself so others may live—so *you* may live. You face the hatred of the world, without ever licking your wounds. It may be selfish of me, but I want you to see you lead a life of your choosing."

Her legs wobbled and he slowly took them both to the floor in the bed of wildflowers. Zara's lips trembled. "Please, always continue to fight, Ronan. You have been beaten but you were never broken, despite what you believe. The pain that shines in your eyes, it is familiar, but I have never met anyone stronger."

The skin between Ronan's pinched as if his next words almost pained him. "The scars you bear, my Horizon, I quite like them. Let me bear them with you."

A shaky breath escaped her. The thoughts that had warred in her head just moments ago returned with a vengeance. "I joined your cause to revolt against the High King. Though now that the time to face Raziel has come, I don't know if I am strong enough."

Ronan ran a hand through her hair. The other was still held on her cheek, holding her close enough for their noses to touch. "You may have believed you had to fight these battles alone. I know you have the strength to do it, but you do not have to. Let me be your blade. The world trembles beneath your feet, Zara Santos. And I will stand by your side as you become its reckoning."

Ronan Menodora. Her friend. The male who had seen the jagged pieces of her soul and shared his own.

They were reflections of one another, yet so different.

They were strong in their own individuality and had blazed their own paths. But together, they could be more.

The burning in the back of Zara's eyes finally broke. Whatever tether that had strained to keep her intact all this time finally loosened, and wet tears streamed down her face.

Zara tried to look away. "I never cry."

Ronan's fingers caught the gleaming beads on her cheeks. "Tears fall with a purpose. They represent the strength you have been holding as you bare it to the silence that will not judge but listen. It will witness the power you have been carrying, the burden you have been shouldering, and will strengthen you even more."

Her eyes welled. "Even someone like me?"

His brow touched hers. "Especially someone as divine as you."

Zara felt the broken shards of her heart put themselves back together. Silent tears continued to run as Ronan's wings folded around her.

SIXTY-FOUR

The final festivity of the Summit was larger than ever. Several parties and banquets filled the castle courtyards and gardens. Performers and musicians were scattered about, entertaining the guests. The celebrations had stretched as far as the inner districts, though open only to the wealthy.

Daria spent the first half of the feast in the company of diplomats. She had taken note of opportunities for Ikarria to advance its business with several regions of the Continent. The diplomats and royal officials guzzled down one drink after the next. Every glass given to her, she'd spit the contents back into the cup, and she watched as those around her began to fall drunk.

The less sharp eyes on her the better.

She cast a gaze around the courtyard. King Matías strolled about with two of his courtesans at his side. Her brows furrowed as she realized the High King was not present. Odd.

"Princess Daria, a moment of your time?"

The voice was feminine and sultry. Daria halted and turned to see Kamari, the queen of Kairos, standing before her. Thin chains of gold dangled through her obsidian black hair. The strands reached her shoulders and looked silky to the touch. There was not much information about the royal, not even what ether she possessed. Rumor had it she was some sort of shifter.

Daria gaped at the queen of the sands. "Of course, Your Highness. I only wish I had more opportunities to speak with you during the Summit."

Kamari waved a hand. "I had plenty of time to become acquainted with your pater, the king. I only came to say that I heard of what you did for the outer district here. For a royal to commit an act of kindness for people they do not rule over is something I greatly respect. So, thank you for being a better example than the rest of us."

Daria was flustered. Her hands were tempted to cross over her abdomen, but she found the will to keep them at her sides. The princess of Ikarria bowed. "I appreciate your words, Your Highness."

The queen gave her a gentle nod. "You and the royals of Ikarria are always welcome to Kairos. We will see each other again, princess."

Kamari drifted into the crowd without another word, leaving Daria dumbfounded. The scent of roses and sea tickled her skin.

A voice purred in her ear. "Would you care for a dance?"

Daria turned around and met Ares's intense gaze. She gave a small, curt nod before the vampire took her hand and waist, sweeping her along the ivory dance floor. It would be so easy to lose herself in this trance where his scent filled her lungs and his presence consumed her thoughts.

Daria hadn't spoken to Ares since their argument at the training grounds. She had been at a loss for what to say with how the conversation was handled. Nor had she particularly *felt* like speaking to him.

Except she did. She liked talking to him.

Ares watched her. His expression seemed blank but she knew better. The general of war tried to hide how his lips thinned or how the skin between his brows creased as he waited for her to speak.

Daria gave him a dry look. "Don't pout, general. You and I have a job to tend to, no?"

Ares looked at her with . . . something like regret. Like he had something to say but thought better of it.

He glanced around, steering her to the edge of the crowd. "Right.

Explore the royal offices to see if one of the deities within the castle summoned the specters."

She frowned. "Even if we try to cut down the possible suspects, there is still the question as to *how* and *why* the creatures are being released into our world."

The vampire sighed. "One problem at a time. Let's be quick and get this over with."

They ended their dance with a bow and curtsy and managed to slip out of the festivity and into the halls. Statues of archangels loomed over them, only the soft flicker of amber light to guide them. Many of the diplomats met and stored formal records within those rooms. If the High Throne had received any reports on the ethereal creatures, then they would be there.

Ares spun to face a door. "This is the chamber where many of Elios's advisors meet. Anything regarding the Estrella Territories will be in the back of this room, where the main offices are located. I will guard the door while you go exploring."

She rolled her eyes. "I'm hardly exploring."

He pulled the door open for her. "What if there is nothing to find?"

Ahead of her, the office chamber was doused in darkness. She opened her palm and exhaled a slow breath. Through the depths of her mind, she reached out to her ether and lit every candle and lantern in the room. "Then I will have to pray to the Suns that my sister can manage on her own."

There hadn't been any news in Soleira of attacks or creatures raiding the outskirts. Daria could only hope that was a good sign.

Ares stared at what she'd done for a moment before pulling the door behind him and leaving it cracked open. "Be careful."

Daria shook off whatever fluttering sensation she felt by his words. It was certainly not the time to mull over the conflicting emotions surrounding the general.

Desks and long tables filled the chamber. She walked down the center path toward the main offices that Ares had indicated.

Dread sank down her abdomen. By the Suns, how in the gods'

names was she supposed to search this place? There were piles and piles of parchment and books—Daria was mildly appalled by the mess. This was not like when she'd been in the library. She didn't have the time to explore every cover and page.

Her nails drummed the wooden surfaces as she paced the office. Her eyes scanned the various books and notes. If there was any vital information, it wouldn't be lying about for just anyone to read. Daria went to try the main desks but the drawers were locked.

Daria certainly didn't have the strength of a vampire, though she *did* have ether. It purred within her and its strength flowed out as she yanked on the handle, wood snapping from its lock. She supposed it was a good thing that she would be leaving to Ikarria soon. It would be difficult to hide the fact that someone had been in here.

A voice echoed from outside the room. "Ares, is that you?"

The blood drained from her face. Her fingers shook as she tried to shove the broken drawer back in its place. "Dammit."

She held on to her gown and sprinted toward the door. The moment she opened it, the world spun and—

All she felt was him.

That salty taste of the ocean mixed with the rose. A floral scent that melted into something sensual and tempting as Ares pressed her against a nearby statue. His hand wrapped around her waist and the feel of his fingers burned through the fabrics of her gown.

He towered over her, one hand placed on the stone above her head. Ares's long hair drifted forward, hiding them from the world—and the voice that was drawing near.

But Daria couldn't think about that. Couldn't think about anything. Not as those violet eyes pierced right through her, his long eyelashes lowering as he tilted his head, the bridge of his nose caressing her cheek. She couldn't move, couldn't speak. Her heart was pounding so loudly as she fought the urge to lean forward.

"Excuse me for this," he breathed.

Air lodged in her throat when Ares brushed his lips against hers. The touch was feathery light but it sent her blood rushing. His eyes went half-lidded as he lingered above her mouth.

"Ares, I thought that was you—oh." The voice. Daria recognized it.

Her general met her eyes once more before pulling back. The sudden absence of his body against hers was like being doused in cold water. Daria placed her fingers over her lips, heat in her cheeks.

She didn't have to feign embarrassment as she turned to see Silas gaping at them. The general's Second's wide eyes jumped between them before his lips curled. "Ares, you are a rebel aren't you? I knew something was happening between you two, but I kept my thoughts to myself. Matías is going to be extremely entertained by this."

Ares took a step in front of Daria. He stared down at Silas with a coldness that hadn't been there before. "Our king doesn't need to know."

Silas snickered. "I don't think he will even care, to be brutally honest with you. In fact, I am here on his behalf; he demands your presence."

The general growled. "Now?"

Whatever teasing light existed in his Second's eyes flickered out. His voice went low and stern. "*Now.*"

Daria felt her stomach churn. They hadn't achieved anything tonight. She had been so confident they could find something worthwhile. Something to aid her sister and the archangel. Ares glanced at her with the same troubled look she probably had.

Silas grinned. "I can escort her."

She couldn't explain why, but the sensation she felt from the vampire's tone—she took a step back. Ares noticed, and something flashed over his eyes. He fully placed his body in front of hers.

Before he could respond, another voice entered the hall. "That won't be necessary."

Daria froze at the sound. It had been some time since she'd heard that soft lilt. She looked around Ares to find the deity, Maira, standing in the middle of the passageway.

Her silky black hair was combed to one side, a soft green gown melded to her body. The deity offered them a smile. "I'll escort the princess back. I've been meaning to catch up with Daria."

Silas blinked, as if he couldn't believe someone like Maira would want to speak with someone like *her*. Daria didn't give it a second thought as she went to stand by the deity.

Ares's face remained cold as his gaze slid to Maira as if assessing a threat.

She gave Ares what she hoped was a reassuring look, her voice light. "I will see you later."

Silas nudged the general along and, as soon as the two vampires were out of earshot, Daria exhaled. "Thank you for your assistance."

She clamped her mouth shut when she noticed Maira watching her with an unreadable expression. Silver light thinned in the deity's eyes and a trickle of fear entered Daria's blood.

"Maira?"

The deity looked at the door that she and Ares had been in front of. Daria couldn't stop the sickening sensation that burned her stomach. Maira was no fool. She would have figured that they were intruding on Elios's private business. *Oh gods.*

"Try Matías's office."

The world came to a screeching halt. Daria's fingers trembled as she clenched her gown. "Excuse me?"

Maira folded her arms in front of her, her gaze stern. Daria couldn't determine whether the deity was upset or not. "I suggest looking in the vampire king's office. Trust me. You will know it when you see it."

Whatever *it* was, it was enough to pique the princess's interest. But Daria couldn't stop herself from speaking out. "Why should I trust you?"

The deity smiled. She looked so much like her terrifying twin sister, it was a wonder that Nadira dared shame her in public. "You may have thought no one paid much attention to you, but I have. I noticed your interest in our politics, your questions about deities and the Council. It's brought me to believe that . . . perhaps we can help each other."

Daria was floored. "I don't understand."

Maira looked over her shoulder and began to push Daria farther down the hall. "We do not have time before someone else comes.

Matías's office is at the end of this hall, it has a window that faces the sea. I cannot explain it to you now—you will have to see it for yourself. You are brilliant, princess of Ikarria. I trust that you will be able to manage."

A flurry of questions bolted through Daria's brain, so quick she was surprised she was still standing. She was about to turn around when the deity grabbed her arm. "Consider it payment of a debt. You helped me before, and now I have helped you."

Daria met her ether-touched eyes. "Thank you."

Maira's lips thinned. "Do not forget me, princess. And know that not all of us deities want this *new world*."

SIXTY-FIVE

Daria didn't understand how the vampire king fit into all this.

She stood in his office, the sea watching her from the open shutters like a beast waiting for its prey. The room smelled faintly of citrus and copper. Leather-bound notes were now scattered about Matías's desk. She had found them on shelves and in drawers and had tossed them onto the wooden surface. Her fingers were full of cuts after rifling through pages for what felt like hours.

She couldn't linger any longer, but for Maira to point toward the vampire king's office . . . Daria couldn't waste this potential lead.

Gods, none of it made sense.

The notes were hardly helpful. Many of them were about dull yet vital topics such as finances, shipment schedules, even soldier rotations—

Her eyes snagged on a set of numbers. Many of them were standard records of the patrols throughout Elios. She could see Ares's signature at the bottom. His penmanship was elegant, not unlike himself.

The following page was blank—save for one entry. Nearly three-thousand vampire soldiers were scheduled to depart from

Elios the next day. Daria narrowed her gaze, running the pad of her finger along the destination.

Her heart began to race. *Ikarria.*

No.

She looked to see if it had been signed by Ares, but it hadn't. That didn't stop the pain that lanced through her chest. He had to know. Gods, he was the general of *war*.

It had never made sense why Elios would go through the trouble of inviting Ikarria to the Summit after all these years. A hysterical laugh left her lips and she clamped a hand over her mouth.

Fools. Her family had been tricked. Her chest tightened, the air punched out of her lungs.

A sound echoed from the hall and Daria fell into a crouch behind the desk. It sounded like something clattering on stone. She realized it hadn't come from outside the room, but from *behind* her.

A bookshelf sat beside the window. Daria inched forward and pressed her fingers against its edge. Another sound echoed from behind it.

"Suns Above, this has to be a joke," she muttered.

Daria dug her fingernails behind the bookshelf and pulled on what was apparently a makeshift door. When it creaked open, a soft breath of sea wind exhaled on her face. Stairs led into a dark abyss.

A blossom of flame appeared on her palm. "I have a feeling this is what Maira was referring to."

She glanced over her shoulder. Ares had not come looking for her, though from what she had just discovered about the vampire soldiers and Ikarria—she couldn't bring herself to think about it yet.

Daria looked back into the darkness. The shadows seemed to pulsate, beckoning her down. Her hand gravitated to the dagger between the folds of her dress, pressed against her ribs. This was why she had left the safety of her home, no? For answers to questions she didn't quite know herself. There had been concern about the relationship between Elios and Adrastea. She had been right to suspect something was amiss.

The princess of Ikarria took her first step into the dark void.

The sea was on the other side of the wall. Daria could feel the rhythmic thrash of the waves against the stone. She suspected the stairs were leading her away from the castle and toward the waters. Every step caused more sweat to trickle down her back.

Time seemed to drag down there, she wasn't sure how long she had been walking.

The air was beginning to thin, but her flame hadn't winked out. When Daria noticed a curve of the staircase, she immediately closed her palm, darkness swallowing her. She blinked, willing her eyesight to sharpen. Though hardly enough to see clearly in the dark, it was manageable and she began to move again.

Daria heard something and pressed her back against the curving wall. It sounded like . . . feet pattering on the stone floor. Her hand went to her dagger. Whatever was on the other side, it was whispering something. Words she didn't understand. It sounded like there was only one of them.

Once Daria's hand met its handle, she slowly took a peek around—

Cerulean blue eyes met hers. They belonged to a woman who looked younger than her. Her dark hair was wet and matted against her head. Dirt and blood smeared her brown skin.

Icy cold fear bled through Daria. This had to be one of the—

The specter screeched and bared her sharpened teeth. She lunged for her and Daria's body moved of its own accord. She fell into step, remembering all of Ares's teachings. Her movements were clumsy and hardly quick as she dodged the creature, but Daria hadn't considered how difficult it would be to fight on a staircase.

The creature slammed into her, and Daria's knee scraped the wall as she stopped herself from tumbling down the steps. The specter leapt again. Daria screamed, thrusting out the dagger as Ares had shown her. From the depths of her being, that power that always purred within her blood crouched and lunged. Fire sparked to life, running along the length of her arm and over the face of her dagger.

The specter cried out as Daria pierced her with the fiery weapon. Her hands clawed at Daria's face, but the princess of Ikarria held on, the flames burning the creature from within.

When those blue eyes dimmed, Daria dropped the body and sagged against the wall. She bit down on her lips, holding back her scream of shock until she tasted blood. The smell of burnt flesh reached her nostrils and she gagged. Daria doubled over and retched.

Her fingers trembled as she tried to clean herself.

Killed. She—she had killed someone. The knowledge sent another painful twist to her abdomen and she puked once again. Daria braced herself against the cold wall, breathing through her nostrils as she tried to regain control.

She ran her bloodied blade across the folds of her dress, still keeping it in hand. A cold sweat began to bead upon her brow. The specters were *here*, within the castle. Her teeth had started to chatter, a nauseating anxiety threatening her insides. That wild flare of ether had shocked her. It had drained so much of her energy. She needed more practice.

Her ears caught voices speaking. The tunnel seemed to have crumbled in some parts so pale moonlight now seeped through the openings of the wall, enough to light her way. She walked a bit farther until she came across what looked like a foyer of some sort. More passages with stone-arched ceilings like the one she came from opened out from where she stood. Catacombs, she realized. Daria had been aware of such architectural designs in most castles of the Continent. Although, she had thought the High King had closed off most of the underground passageways to prevent any forms of rebellion.

Shadows moved along the walls and she followed the voices. Her ether bristled, causing the hairs on her arms to rise. The energy down here felt malignant, like unseen talons were grazing the stone walls.

A male's voice echoed in the tunnels. "The reaping has been successful thus far. We expect more to be collected within the coming year."

Another—a female—spat out a curse. "I grow impatient with

this. We need more control over them, one is already slinking around these halls."

Daria suspected the *one* the voices were speaking of was the specter she had killed. The possessed woman's face flashed in her mind. Those bright cerulean blue eyes that looked like jewels. More frightening than the ethereal silver glow of the deities'. Bile curled in her stomach and she begged the Suns not to be sick here.

She crouched underneath an arched window and peeked into what looked like an underground courtyard. An opening above allowed more columns of moonlight to shine through.

Figures were gathered around a stone table, vines and roots crawling along its surface.

No, they weren't just figures. Each had those ethereal eyes that only deities had.

The Council of Deities. Only three sat in the clearing—Arwan, Saija, and Lucian. Daria threw a hand over her mouth before a gasp could escape her. What were they doing here? She recognized the woman who was speaking as Saija.

The male, Arwan, responded. "You know we do not have that power. Only *he* does."

"And the captured ether-born? Are they safe?"

"Of course. He ensured they were hidden far away. No one will find them."

The ether-born. Daria had heard that term from Zara after she had told her of the specter's capture, though neither of them knew what it meant.

There was a vibration in the air. The energy hummed, whirling about the room with an ether-laced wind. Daria crouched even lower as a presence descended from the opening.

"There he is," Lucian drawled.

A third voice replied, one that sent ice through Daria's veins. "I'm sorry to keep you waiting. Warriors were needed tonight."

Daria took another peek. She had to see for herself. Her eyes widened, the blood draining from her face. *It couldn't be*—

The deity, Arwan, sniffed the air. "Someone's here."

Daria slipped from the archway, keeping low as she darted back up the staircase. Adrenaline pumped through her veins. There was hardly any sound behind her, but she couldn't bring herself to look back.

Run. Run. Run.

Her legs burned as she charged up the stairs. There was so much more at stake than what they'd believed. There were even more questions. But none of that mattered yet.

All she could think about was Zara. Her sister needed to know. The door to Matías's office appeared ahead. Daria ran through the opening. She had to warn her sister—

Pain exploded at the back of her head and the princess fell into darkness.

SIXTY-SIX

Dawn had risen. Morning light seeped through the sky. Zara Santos felt the ache in her chest lessen, the tears long dried from her face. It was as though she had been born anew.

Zara stepped over a thin row of collapsed brick and stone. The guild would be waiting for her in the abandoned Primordial temple in Soleira's outer district. During their initial planning, Ronan had told her that he and Ares had been meeting at the site for years and that it was safe. Since it was an old, uninhabited neighborhood, she understood the advantages of such a place.

Ronan. He would be on the far side of Soleira by now, preparing to meet with the shadow dealers. The citizens they helped evacuate would have been long-time supporters of the Sombra Quarter. It was only right for him to tend to his forces and people right now even though she wished he were here beside her.

She didn't know how long she had cried in his arms the previous night, but Ronan held her through every tear. Soothing her and whispering words of warmth and support. If only she could have stayed longer, her cheeks pressed against his chest.

Zara approached the abandoned temple. It was quiet. Too quiet. She unsheathed her weapons and entered the building. A soft layer of dirt covered the brown tiles. Broken pillars greeted her and opened into a courtyard. She didn't see the Primordial Aspidis's statue at its center, nor did she notice how the sky had begun to bleed a light red.

Not as her blood turned to ice.

The Ikarrian guild—*her* guild—were on their knees, hands bound. Deities stood behind them, swords pointed at their backs. Silver fire licked the steel of their blades, making them into sconces. Zara's eyes widened. She recognized them as members of the Council. There was no sign of Nadira or Hadeon. Their faces were shrouded in the shadows and light of their flames, hiding their expressions from her view. But the ruling body of deities were all *warriors* in their star-white armor.

An archangel with brown wings stretching to the dawn-kissed sky flew into the courtyard from behind them. Flickers of red blurred the corners of her vision. Zara steadied her breath, fighting that flare of panic as High King Raziel landed in front of the guild. No alabaster crown sat upon his wine-red hair, but there was a cold fury in his eyes.

While seeing the Council present had startled her, she had not forgotten the High King's threat.

Raziel tilted his chin. "You look surprised, Rogue."

She had to stop herself from raising her blades too suddenly. "Your Highness, what is the meaning of this?"

The High King sighed. "Do not play me for a fool. You were supposed to end the Sombra Quarter. You disobeyed my orders."

She dared to take a step, glancing at the guild behind the archangel. Hakim, Eshe, and Axar had been beaten. Brutally. Their bodies were covered in wounds, blood pooling where they kneeled. They had fought the deities, had managed to stay alive against the ethereal race, but had eventually been defeated. If it had just been Elios's archangel soldiers against the guild, then they wouldn't have stood a chance.

Zara needed to tread carefully. A dreadful thought crept into her mind. Maybe he'd always assumed that she wouldn't go through her assignment and had planned to punish her all along.

Guilt engulfed her. Suffocated her. Her guild had been here, facing the powers of Elios, while she was with Ronan . . .

Color drained from her face. Her legs began to feel numb. "Your

Highness, you must be aware of the greater enemies that stalk your lands. My mercenaries and I have seen creatures of Celestrea *possessing* your citizens. Specters—ethereal warriors—who obey the command of beings called the Spirits of the Midnight Sun."

It was all she could think to do, to tell him everything. The image of her guild bound and bleeding on the ground was burned into her mind even as she didn't take her eyes off the High King. "It sounds outrageous, but I am sure members of your Council, Nadira and Hadeon, informed you of the attack in the outer district. They witnessed those creatures while *we* helped your citizens to safety."

It took everything to prevent panic from slipping into her voice. The only comfort she had was knowing the Summit would have formally ended by now, which meant her sister would be on her way home. Thank the Suns.

Raziel's gaze sharpened. "*We?* As in you, your guild, and a certain archangel?"

Bile formed in the back of her throat. Ronan *had* been seen after all. But if he had been recognized, that meant . . .

The sound of a woman laughing echoed in the Primordial temple. It was dark and vicious and caused Zara to grind her teeth. Nadira stepped out from behind her, followed by Hadeon, and tilted her head to the side, silver glowing eyes peering at her.

Nadira grinned. "The look on your face is precious, Rogue. Let me just say that I could recognize the lost king of Damalis from anywhere. After we handled those specters, Hadeon and I waited to see where your guild would head off. Once we saw them come here, we decided to attack. The High King thought it was time to enact your punishment."

Zara's legs threatened to buckle, but the hatred on Raziel's face forced her to stay standing.

"I didn't think Ronan had survived all these years to be honest," he murmured. "I assume he is involved with the Sombra Quarter, then?"

Hadeon's voice rumbled. "Does it really matter—fraternizing with any enemy of the High Throne is *treason*."

Zara paled, meeting the large deity's gaze. He stared her down, a quiet rage etched on his face. He shoved Nadira forward who snarled at him before strutting over to the other gods behind the bound mercenaries.

Zara forced herself to speak, addressing the High King. "Is the matter of your citizens being possessed by otherworldly beings not important to you? You have ethereal warriors taking over mortals' bodies. Not to mention the Spirits of the Midnight Sun, who are the *literal* end of this world. They are not your common enemy, Raziel, for they are made of absolute power. I've *seen* them."

It was a dire attempt to drag the High King's attention away from the guild's involvement with Ronan.

Raziel's eyes widened. "So the Spirits made an appearance to you. That's intriguing. They're quite picky in who they reveal themselves to. Usually, any who lay eyes upon them do not survive."

Zara felt as if claws had captured her heart and punctured it. A sickening taste of metal formed over her tongue. "You've known about these creatures all this time. Did you summon the Spirits?"

He looked amused, lips pursing. "That requires a more complicated answer."

"I—I don't understand. Why would you allow this to happen?"

His hands were in his pockets as he began to pace in front of her. There was a sharpness in his eyes and she knew he was waiting to strike. "That requires another long, difficult explanation. You will understand in due time, my Rogue. First, we must discuss your betrayal."

His golden wings flapped a powerful sweep of air that stung her eyes. "I had higher expectations for you, daughter of Ikarria."

Zara's grip trembled around the pommels of her blades. She was ready to throw down her weapons, fall to her knees and beg for mercy. For the guild, she would.

Hakim's voice stopped her. "*Santos.*"

The head of the Ikarrian guild narrowed his eyes, pinning her in place. There was a message there, one she knew all too well—and she hated it. Zara began to shake her head but Hakim growled only two words, forcing them between his bloodied teeth. "*Little warrior.*"

It was all he needed to say. To remind her of who she was and where she came from. She was not to give up yet.

The deity behind Hakim swung the flaming sword and struck his back with the handle. Hakim grunted but did not fall. The other mercenaries snarled and struggled against their bindings. Axar's boots slid against the tiles as if preparing to launch himself at the deity. The rest of the Council brought their swords closer to their necks, holding them in place.

Zara couldn't help but take another step, her gaze clashing with the High King. "Please. Let them go."

Raziel's expression smoothened. It was difficult to decipher what emotion warred behind that mask. "Do you know the reason I favored you? Why I chose to make you my personal assassin?"

Throughout the years Zara and her family had believed it was due to her Valenzian lineage. In the depths of her heart, she had known that was untrue. She might've already suspected his reason.

He seemed pleased by her silence. "A power was birthed inside you. Strength beyond comparison, strong enough to rip the seams of this mortal world. I sensed it in that battlefield all those years ago. But Idris found you before I could, and I knew I needed to find a way to keep you close. Your power was bound to unfold and I wanted to witness it. For years, there was hardly anything ethereal about you and I began to wonder if I'd had it all wrong."

He paused as if he could see the air leaving Zara's lungs. The corner of his lips lifted. "So I thought I'd try to . . . push that monstrous power awake. I made you into the Rogue. Ether thrives heavily on emotion, so I had you kill and kill and kill. Eventually, our world began to hate you and darkness fell over you, thickening over the years. It was only a matter of time before that ether of yours was unleashed."

Zara lost feeling in her legs. Raziel prowled closer but still kept his distance. "Do you know where all the marks I assigned you came from?"

The world seemed to still.

A satisfied smirk appeared on his lips. "What, did you really think you were killing *evil* men and women this entire time? All these years, the Rogue brutally hunted down runaways and war criminals—all traitors to the High Throne. Of course there was the occasional rapist and murderer, but overall they were hardly violent. But they all had one thing in common—they were all Valenzian." He tapped a finger against his lips. "In fact, I think some were some distant relatives of yours. Your first mark of this season, an elf, I believe—he had a human girl with him—didn't he seem familiar to you?

Raziel's face twisted into a cruel grin. "You brought me your uncle's head, Zara. How tragic."

Mercenary. Reaper. Monster.

Zara didn't realize she had sunk to the ground. Her guild was crying out to her, though she couldn't focus on what they were saying.

See? This is what you truly are. Raziel's voice echoed in her head. The fyrebrand's voice.

All those lives she had ended. Her fingers dug into the leathers of her legs, so deeply it hurt. How could she have been so blind? The cries for mercy. The spews of hatred. There were moments when she had paused, even for a breath, and wondered why she was hunting them. Zara was dimly aware of her shuddering breaths and trembling body.

Until a fury rose within her, swallowing everything else. She gripped onto the fyrebrand's presence, so tight that the binds of her mind were on the verge of snapping. The voice thrashed, screaming and shouting. It burned in the core of her thoughts, ashes withering and drifting away into nothingness.

And it was Zara's voice that responded, reaching every dark corner of her mind and soul.

Enough.

The ground trembled beneath her feet. She thrust a hand into the void, where she had always felt that rumble of power resembling a coiled beast, and tugged on the chains.

No longer will I hide.

Light cracked along her forearms like broken glass, and ether erupted from it in the colors of the dawn. Zara was on her feet, arms alight with unnatural flames of purple and red. She raised her blades and faced the High King.

Raziel smiled. "I wasn't wrong after all. You *have* been hiding something from me."

Zara screamed, the flames roaring with her. That familiar flare of power surged through her body as she flew across the courtyard. Raziel opened his arms as if ready to embrace her, and she realized her mistake.

Someone yanked her back midair, arms wrapping around her, suffocating all her fiery ether. Air was slammed out of her lungs as she was pinned to the ground. The impact caused her flames to wither out. Zara gritted her teeth and managed to look over her shoulder.

Nadira grinned. "Not so fast."

Zara kicked her legs out. Her hands scratched at the tiles. "Fuck you."

Raziel laughed again. "So angry, my Rogue. It is no wonder that your power feels so *otherworldly*."

"I am not yours," she spat out.

Nadira dug the heel of her boot against her back. The strength of the deity's ether flowed with the movement, forcing Zara deeper into the ground. Cracks exploded from beneath her. She cried out, gasping for air.

The deity grabbed her hair. "Watch."

She didn't realize Raziel had moved. He kept his golden eyes on Zara as he walked behind her guild, the corners of his lips curled. Wicked and full of bloodlust.

Raziel stopped behind Hakim and slid a dagger out from his leathers. He forced the mercenary's head back and pressed the short blade against his neck. Zara strained against Nadira, her breathing growing frantic, her cries muffled and desperate.

No no no. *Not him*. Not the male who had taught her, who had raised her. Who had *loved* her despite her imperfections and endless darkness.

Ether thrashed inside her, smashing through her mental barriers. Blinding light exploded around her. It was untamed, difficult to manage, but Zara didn't think twice. She twisted herself free from Nadira's grasp and charged toward them.

Raziel's wings snapped out. That cold, ruthless gaze wavered as he watched the fiery Horizon coming for him. The flames of the dawn reared back as Zara prepared to let them loose on the High King.

Nadira collided with her again, this time with the force of the deity's silver flames. The strength of it was unlike anything Zara had felt before. It swept her off her feet. Her chin rammed against the ground and she felt blood seep between her lips. Again, her ether winked out.

No no no.

Panic seized her as Nadira laughed and forced her to look. Her eyes went to the wicked dagger in Raziel's hand. "Stop, please—"

Hakim didn't move. Not even as Eshe and Axar fought against their own binds. His attention was on her, eyes glossed over with a sheen of admiration. "I am proud of you, Santos."

Tears burned behind Zara's eyes. "*Don't.*"

The corners of his lips turned up, his own eyes glistening. A softness she hardly ever saw. "I love you, daughter."

Her mentor, a second pater.

"Close your eyes." He murmured.

But she couldn't.

And then, a slash of Raziel's dagger—

Zara's mouth opened into a scream. A sound that didn't reach her ears as the chaos around her fell into a deathly silence. As her heart was cleaved in two. Ripped through and forever seared.

She could only continue screaming as blood fell from Hakim's throat. As the life dimmed in his eyes. Zara wasn't sure if she was shouting for Hakim or cursing Raziel. The archangel smiled wider and wider. He let Hakim's body slip from his grasp, and the leader of Ikarrian guild slowly fell to the cold ground.

Raziel raised his bloodied blade. "The punishment for disobeying me."

He moved toward Eshe. *Eshe.* Zara clawed the ground, her fingernails breaking, blood bubbling. The power inside her whined, already too weak to rise again.

She couldn't—couldn't breathe.

The High King yanked on Eshe's hair as Axar became frantic.

Ether flared as he tried to shift into his wolf. The deity behind him drove his silver-flamed sword into the shifter's side, stopping the transformation. Axar toppled to the ground, his power curling from his skin like thin steam.

Axar was breathing heavily through his nostrils, panicked eyes on Eshe as the High King raised the dagger once more.

"Fight." He croaked. "*Fight.*"

No one would come to the Ikarrian guild's aid. Eshe's lips moved and Zara managed to catch the words: *My pup.*

Another slash of Raziel's blade.

Another chasm opening in her heart.

More blood fell and Eshe slumped to the ground. Axar's screams ripped through the sky, causing the remaining stars to flee behind the rising sun. The sound raked claws down her soul.

The ground beneath her trembled even more. Angrier. New cracks formed, reaching the Primordial statue in the courtyard. None of it seemed to faze Raziel as he slowly looked at Zara.

The High King's voice was eerily calm. "You did this."

No. Zara sobbed. She hadn't meant for this to happen. If only she had just followed orders. If only she hadn't clung onto some reckless, selfish goal to rebel against a fucking realm. If only she hadn't fallen in—

Raziel held her gaze as he strode toward Axar.

No more. Please.

Zara's muscles burned in agony as she tried to move. She couldn't gain footing with the deity pinning her to the ground. Axar strained against his binds, trying to slide away from the High King.

Raziel reached him and kicked him in the stomach. He traced a finger along Axar's jaw before tipping his chin up. "I think a shifter would do nicely in my ranks," he observed. "Well, I suppose that depends on our dear Zara."

The High King arched a brow at her. "Bring me the head of the Sombra Quarter in one week, and I will allow the wolf to live. If not, then he will join the rest of the Ikarrian guild."

Zara went rigid, tasting salt and blood in her mouth. Raziel's last offer. She would rather waste away in the ether if she could not save Axar.

The deities began to drag her warrior brother away from the courtyard. He shouted through his own tears. "Don't you dare, Zara! Just run!"

Raziel smirked. "Let's strike a new deal. Complete your final assignment and agree to serve me and only me. You will no longer be considered Ikarrian as you will fight at my side. I will help nurture that power of yours. You simply cannot comprehend what rests inside you and what we can do together. Agree to this and I will let your friend live."

He didn't allow her to respond. His wings lifted him into the sky, the deities disappearing after him. Nadira stepped off her and left without a second glance.

The world went quiet.

Zara didn't wait. Her torn fingers slipped against the tiles as she crawled over to Hakim and Eshe. Their blood met her first. She choked on a sob as she waded through the red that stained her skin. Slowly, she managed to pull herself over to Hakim's body.

No heart pounded against his chest. No longer would she experience his warmth, his kindness, his love. Hakim Salvador was gone.

An agonized cry broke from her lips as she curled between the bodies of her two mentors. The Ikarrian guild was no more.

She had failed.

She had been broken.

Fiery light, shards of stars and suns, roared into the dawn.

SIXTY-SEVEN

Something was wrong.

Ronan Menodora flew as fast as he could. There was a whispery touch of agony in his chest. When he'd felt it, surrounded by his shadow dealers, he hadn't hesitated to take to the sky. The wind now hissed at his ears, urging him to go, go, go.

For so long he had hidden himself from the world. Had tried to ignore the weight that came with his name.

No longer.

He had allowed his enemies too much control, and now he would take it back.

Ronan was going after them. Those who had destroyed his homeland and imprisoned him. Who had defiled his people and sought to remove his name from history. Those who had shoved weapons into Zara's hand and forced her to cut off her own innocence. Who had tossed her into the dark waters and watched to see how she would survive.

And gods, she had.

The woman who had risen from the pits held no softness. She was hardened and jaded, had taken it upon herself to roughen whatever gentleness remained in her soul. The monsters had grown cocky and did not see what they had created.

Ronan knew Zara did not need him. She had served, only to be used.

No longer.

Yes, she would fight, and he would be beside her. He would help hold her arms so she could continue holding the blades.

As she unleashed the monster they had made.

There was one final task he had to do first. One that not even Zara was aware of. Ronan banked lower as the mercenary ruin of Elios emerged, bathed in morning light.

Zara Santos fell apart.

The red and purple flames shined like starlit gems and droplets of sunlight. A final stretch of power that had arrived too late. She couldn't hold back another mournful wail. Her power screamed with her, spiraling and lashing at the sky.

Zara held on to them. Hakim and Eshe. Her guild, who had been more than just family. By her will, the flames did not burn them. She bowed over Hakim's too-still chest, her hand wrapped around Eshe's. As if holding onto them would bring their souls back, as if it would stop the bleeding of her ether-laced soul.

Her power fell in one swoop. It sank back into her, diving deep into her center, the weight of it had her gasping for breath.

The ether had left her. Left her to the void, and only anger remained. It rose from within, clawing its way out of the depths. "I did everything they asked!"

Zara's screams met silence. "I did what they wanted!"

A hysterical sob escaped her. She did not know who she was speaking to. It may have been to the High King, the Council, or the godsforsaken Suns who had abandoned her. Who had fucking spurned her. "I did what they asked of me and this—*this*—is what they do in return?"

Zara wailed to the sky. "I did *all* that was asked of me. I killed for you. I suffered for you. I became this way because you spoke of promises and futures—but they were nothing but empty and meaningless words. And yet, I believed in them. Deep down, I knew your words were false, but I continued to believe. It felt like the only choice I had. And I know—"

She ran her blood-soaked fingers through her hair, fisting her scalp. And the tears still ran. "I know I wasn't the only one who suffered. I know, I know, I know. But you destroyed me, crushed whatever heart I had left, for I no longer remember how I was before all this. What is there left of me?"

Zara slowly bowed over the bodies of her fallen mercenaries again. "It should've been me! They did not deserve this. I caused this. *My family.*"

She rocked in place. The same words wept from her lips. "My family, my family, my family."

The very world she had been forced to serve had turned its back on her. It was the end of the guild of Ikarria. Hakim and Eshe now walked the path of silver and red until it led them to the skies. Leaving her behind.

Zara Santos, mercenary of Ikarria and Rogue to the High Throne.

It was her own end.

The fall of the Horizon.

SIXTY-EIGHT

When Ronan arrived at the temple, the first thing he noticed was the blood. Every muscle and vein in his body stopped. There was so much of it. At first he feared it was Zara's, but then he found her, sitting in a pool of red. In her arms were—

His heart fell. For he knew the Horizons of Ikarria were gone.

From the lingering smell of pure ether, like crackling embers and winter winds, he knew it was a powerful foe that had been present. It didn't seem as though Zara had noticed him entering. How long had she been here?

He slowly approached her. "Zara."

Tendrils of bleeding sunlight and purple flames erupted, sending him across the courtyard. He crashed against a pillar, clouds of dust billowing around him. Ronan groaned at the pressure that pinned him against the stone. The ethereal fires caressed him, tongues of fiery light kissing his cheeks. They didn't burn him, but he could feel the vibrations of their strength.

Ronan could only stare at the wondrous colors surrounding him.

Zara emerged from the rippling ether. Her eyes glowed red, nearly swallowing all the jade green. His lips parted at the sight.

A ruthless beauty.

He recognized this power. Felt it from deep within the caverns of his soul—and suddenly he understood why his ether would react to Zara's presence.

An ancient power was born this dawn.

Ronan felt the cold kiss of steel press against his neck. No fear could be found within him, though. Not as he saw that she lacked her light. That wicked glint was no more. He felt whatever hope had managed to remain inside her shatter, the pieces sifting through his scarred fingers.

"Axar." Her voice was rough and ragged. "The High King . . . the Council . . . they know everything, and they have Axar."

Ronan quickly put the pieces together of what occurred here. So, the High Throne was behind the possessions and the ethereal attacks. He didn't understand why they would do such a thing, after fighting in a War for control of the mortal world. There had to be more to it.

His hands slowly covered hers and lowered the dagger. The ethereal flames still roared around them as Ronan pressed his brow against hers and held her in the midst of the burning sunrise.

"How long can you summon your ether for?"

Zara blinked, the confusion evident on her face. "Not for long. It'll flicker out again soon."

Ronan placed his hands over her shoulders, meeting her gaze. "Use your ether on me."

Her eyes widened. "What?"

In the depths of his soul, he felt a faint rumble. Ronan knew what needed to be done. "We will finish what we started, and we will save Axar. But I need you to unleash yourself."

Zara snarled and returned the dagger to his neck. She gritted her teeth. "Raziel still wants you."

"Trust me." Ronan thought he could feel something trickle from where the blade touched his skin. But before he could utter another word, she did what he asked. Waves of her power surged into him. The flames blinded him, pummeling through his essence.

His own power, neglected and alone, began to stir. It yanked on its chains as Zara's power attacked it in torrents.

Ronan screamed, falling to his knees before his mercenary.

Her face was emotionless. A coldness he did not recognize. His heart yearned for her, but he could do nothing as Zara Santos continued to send her power through him.

Just as the beast of power inside him was on the verge of exhaling its first breath, his mercenary lifted her dagger and lunged at him.

SIXTY-NINE

Daria was jostled awake. Her eyes snapped open to sunlight pouring through an open window. She stared at the sky. The ocean air wasn't as strong now. Instead, it smelled more of woodland. Daria was lying on her back, her hand sliding over cushions and polished wood beneath her. Her body was rocking side to side, and she groaned at the pain pulsating in the back of her head.

She was in a carriage. The events of last night—last night? Gods. She wasn't sure how long she had been unconscious. Dread sank through her bones. Someone had kidnapped her. From outside, she could hear a deep roll of thunder.

Not thunder. *Hooves.* And the echo of steel against steel and the gentle chatter of men and women.

"Ares, you haven't left the carriage's side since we left."

Daria froze. Something in her chest cracked at the sound of his name. He was here. She could only imagine who the other voices belonged to. Ares snarled at whoever had spoken without giving a response.

Slowly, she pulled herself up and looked out the window. That sense of dread thickened to the point of suffocating her. There were rows and rows of gleaming bronze and wine-red cloaks.

The Adrastean army.

"Daria."

His voice didn't purr. It was quiet, softer than she'd ever heard it. And it only infuriated her. Daria curled her lips and dragged her gaze to Ares, who was riding a black horse beside the carriage. He looked terrifyingly beautiful. His chest was covered by a deep bronze breastplate, black roses etched along the sides. A long deep red cloak was draped over his shoulder, hanging along his horse's thigh.

Daria stared at him. She wasn't sure what her expression looked like, but it was enough to cause his face to pale even more. "It seems you have chosen your side," she said quietly.

Ares edged closer. "Daria, I'm so sorry. I didn't know it would come to this."

Daria shook her head, silencing him. A silent rage coursed through her. "I went to your vampire king's office. I saw the order for three-thousand soldiers to head for Ikarria."

He flinched. "I didn't—please, allow me to explain. I want to help you."

"How do you expect me to believe anything you say? You are the general of war. You must've known Adrastea planned to raid my home."

"Believe me, none of us knew this was the plan." Ares growled out the words.

Just as she was about to spew out a retort, she heard a horse galloping toward the carriage. "General!"

Ares's face changed at the sound of his Second's voice. His expression smoothened and the light in his violet eyes darkened. She might have been impressed with how quick and easy it was for him to change expressions if she weren't so angry.

Silas yanked on his reins as he neared. "We will be crossing the Ikarrian border. The elven king's forces have already gathered. We must send our first unit to distract them as we continue onto the capital."

Daria's heart plummeted. Would her pater be on the front lines with the main battalion, or would he stay within the capital?

Silas's eyes slid to hers and he smiled. The sight, so unlike the quiet soldier she had become acquainted with. Chills ran down her arms. From the start, something about him had always unnerved her.

"It looks like the princess is awake," he drawled. "I must have hit your head too hard, love. You've been out for nearly a full day. My apologies, Your Highness."

Daria's stomach churned. It explained why they were already so far inland, the sea nowhere in sight.

Silas chuckled as he reached for her. "I hope I didn't leave a mark."

Ares snarled, grabbing Silas's armored collar. "I've already warned you. You are *not* to touch the princess."

His Second grinned like an adolescent who wasn't taking his reprimand seriously. "Come now, Ares. You had your fun with her—you can't honestly be that protective of her."

Ares hissed and flashed his fangs. "Disobey me again and I will rip your throat out, *Second*. Even Matías commanded that no one lay a finger on her, including me. Remember your fucking place."

He shoved Silas away and his Second made an animalistic snarl with his teeth, all amusement gone, before he ushered his horse forward.

Ares watched the vampire go, his jaw clenching. "That one is becoming too reckless." He glanced at her and that cold expression softened a fraction. "I will do everything to make sure you are safe, Daria. I know that things between us are not—"

"Stop talking," she snapped. "You wish for me to be safe? How about my kingdom? What does Adrastea even want with Ikarria?"

He searched her gaze. "When Adrastea partnered with Elios, Matías was promised more control over land and resources. Apparently, Raziel had his eyes on Ikarria for some time. Both rulers managed to find common ground."

"You claim you didn't know of this plan until it was too late. So, your king does not even trust *you*."

Ares's lips thinned. "The kings do not confide in anyone."

She glared daggers at him. "It doesn't matter now, does it? The truth remains: you are to attack my home."

"Daria."

522 ○ JESSICA J. AYALA

She turned away from the window and rested on her side. He fell silent, but she could still hear the soft nicker of his horse. The ache in her chest deepened the longer they traveled.

Her eyes fell onto a bag resting at the foot of her seat. Daria reached out a hand and fumbled with its contents. Her fingers landed on the pommel of her dagger. Heart racing, she slipped it out and admired it under the light. She had been so distracted when she came to, she hadn't even realized it was missing.

Ares had saved it for her. Her anger returning tenfold, she sheathed it on her person. Her eyes gravitated back to the bag and she saw the book he had found on the ancient teachings of ether-wielding, as well as all her notes on the Council.

Daria wished the ache in her chest would disappear.

She twisted to lay on her back, staring at the ceiling of the carriage. Her thoughts wandered to what she had discovered in the catacombs beneath Soleira's castle. *Who* she had seen there.

The ache quickly turned to a gnawing pit in her stomach.

She didn't get to warn her sister.

They reached the Ikarrian forest at nightfall about a week later, and they finally let her out of the carriage. Dae Asari, Ikarria's capital, was beyond those trees, she could already see the twinkling torchlights. She was so close to home.

Within the past week, Daria had planned to flee, but with scores of vampires that always surrounded her, she knew she wouldn't get far. They wanted her alive, for whatever reason. The vampires even went as far as having her dress in a black gown.

It was form-fitting, with a slit along the thigh and a deep plunge between her breasts. She had never worn something so revealing, but the mere fact they had dressed her for this occasion was insulting.

"I've always wanted to see Ikarria."

Ares's voice yanked her from her thoughts. She hadn't spoken a single word to him since their last conversation.

Though, he always made sure she ate and slept.

How kind, she thought dryly. *I need energy to face the fall of my realm after all.*

The general stared at the torchlights ahead. "Never did I think it would be like this."

She had nothing to say to that. Her eyes drifted to the battalion of vampires preparing to attack. One thing she came to understand was that Ares knew how to conquer. He knew the Adrastean army couldn't overcome the elemental elves of Ikarria alone and without some form of surprise. His first unit of vampires were currently fighting Ikarria's main forces farther back, distracting them as Ares and select soldiers crept toward the capital.

Daria could smell it now. The smoke. She could only imagine the elves summoning their flames and water, manipulating the ground and wind in their favor. Whether her pater was there among his soldiers or in the capital, she couldn't know.

"Do you truly believe you will be able to sneak into the capital?" she asked.

Ares jerked at the sound of her voice. He gave her a sidelong glance. "No. I know King Idris will have forces waiting for us."

Her eyes snagged onto the Watcher, the largest tree in Ikarria.

When they neared the capital, some of the vampires whistled at the sight of the imposing and ancient watchtower. The thought of those soldiers claiming the Watcher sent her blood boiling.

Ares pointed at a soldier. "Stay put and watch the princess. Wait until we've reached the castle, and then you may join us."

The vampire snarled, as if disappointed he couldn't storm the Ikarrian stronghold himself, but nodded. Silas went to stand beside Ares, smirking. "The soldiers of Adrastea will lay siege to the city. Where will you be, general?"

Ares was silent at first. Daria didn't want to look his way, but couldn't help herself when his voice turned to ice. "I will be at the castle. The elven king is mine."

Whatever control she had held all this time finally cracked. "Please don't do this."

The battalion of vampires moved at Ares's command and prowled through the trees. He watched her with an unreadable expression. The silence even more painful than an answer. He nudged his horse into a walk.

"*Ares.*"

The general of war—whom she'd so naively believed her friend—kept walking, sinking into the darkness.

"*Ares!*"

The soldiers disappeared within the ancient trees. The vampire pulled her back when she tried to go after them.

Daria could only wait. She didn't know how much time had passed before large columns of smoke rose into the sky.

And the screams started.

After what felt like hours, the vampire pushed her to start walking. She cast a look around the trees, the noise of the distant battles the only sound she could hear. Her ether had been waiting for this moment. She still had little control of the fires in her blood, but she didn't care much for restraint right now.

Ares didn't order for her to be chained, and she knew he had done it on purpose. He probably didn't think there was anything she could do for Ikarria.

Anger caused the flames to hiss across her skin. She conjured a blade of fire in her hand. It shocked the vampire enough to give her an opportunity to slash his throat. He grabbed at his neck and snarled through the gush of blood. Daria sucked in a breath as she plunged the makeshift blade into the soldier's heart.

As he died, her flames withered out. Daria had only seen a few Ikarrian soldiers mold their elemental-ether into shapes in the past. She hadn't realized how taxing on the mind it was to have to think of an image and hold it while using the ether.

She cried out as another truth sank into her chest. Daria had killed once again.

Her palms grew sweaty, knees quaking. Daria gritted her teeth as she breathed through the horror of what she had done. She curled her fingers into fists and sprinted toward the capital. Wind yanked on her hair, the air thick with smoke and ash. Her lungs cried out when she finally reached the city. She skidded to a stop, her heart falling.

The streets were filled with bodies. Blood and flames had claimed the streets and buildings. Ikarrian and Adrastean soldiers still fought, elemental ether lashing out at the vampires. Citizens were tearing through the battlefield, running away from the carnage. Some held their loved ones in their arms as they cried out for help. For anyone to save them.

So this was a taste of war.

Suns, save them.

No gods would hear her pleas though.

Daria felt the pounding of her heartbeat against her ribs as she leapt into the fray. Ikarrian soldiers commanded whips of water and sharp gusts of wind to collide against several vampires. They recognized her immediately.

An elven soldier shouted to his comrades, an order laced through his coarse voice. "There's the princess! Protect her!"

She could hardly pay the elves any heed as she charged toward the castle. Torrents of flames soared across the air, devouring the vampires with their fiery teeth. Rocks shot through the sky as the ground sank and swallowed up some of the Adrastean forces. Her pater's soldiers cleared the way for her, blocking any of the vampires from reaching for her. There was little she could do, but she had to try. She had to find out what Ares was planning.

Soot smeared her cheeks by the time she got to the royal courtyard. Battles were taking place within and without the Watcher but she forced herself to keep running, fighting the tears that welled in her eyes.

She ran toward the obsidian doors to the throne room and froze. Many of the court members still lived, vampires holding them at sword point. But it was the sight of the Ikarrian soldiers with their hands up, slowly going to their knees, that had her trembling.

Silas appeared from the crowd with a bloodied grin. "Just in time, princess."

He extended a hand, commanding her to walk. Her legs felt numb as she waded through the cluster of advisors and court members. They stared at her with horror and anguish—she felt their desperation press against her. Daria had never felt so powerless.

Blood dripped down the steps of the draconic throne.

And her pater—

The Ikarrian king was on his knees at the top of the dais, five vampires holding him back. Ares stood before him, in front of the obsidian throne. The general was heaving for breath, face twisted in pain. His armor had been pierced and ripped through. His left arm hung loosely at his side, the fabric shredded to reveal burned skin. The war general of Adrastea had battled her pater, and somehow won.

The king of Ikarria roared a sound worthy of a dragon. Flames erupted from between his teeth, dousing the throne room in bright red light.

Ares spoke through clenched teeth. "It is done. Ikarria has surrendered."

SEVENTY

Daria ran toward her pater. She knew it was pointless but she didn't care. She had already been separated from her sister—gods knew where Zara was—and the sight of her pater at the mercy of the vampires snapped whatever resolve she had left.

Someone grabbed her from behind and she crashed onto her knees before the king.

Idris's eyes went wide with fear. "Firelight."

Tears began to fall. "Pater."

He searched her eyes. "Zara?"

She merely shook her head.

Something cracked in his eyes as he leaned toward her. "I need you to listen to me." He murmured urgently. "All this time I have been trying to find them, reading every book and traveling to the far corners of our realm. They must return. We *need* them."

Daria looked at him as if he were mad. "Who? Find who?"

The vampires began to haul him to his feet but her pater yanked against them, making them stumble. "The *dragons*," he hissed. "Find the dragons."

Ares's voice echoed in the throne room. "Idris of Ikarria has broken the treaty with Elios and the Aligned Realms. Your kingdom's mercenary guild colluded with an enemy of the Continent." Daria's breath hitched. His expression cracked ever so slightly before he turned and waved a hand to his soldiers. "Escort the king to Soleira. He is to be imprisoned by the will of the High Throne."

Daria's body shook. *The Ikarrian guild*. What had happened?

Her pater clenched his teeth. Despite the chaos they were in, the love he had for her shined in his eyes as they started to drag him away. Idris looked at Ares. His gaze lingered on him longer than necessary before the vampires began to pull him away.

"It's meant to be you." The king of Ikarria cried out to her. "It was always meant to be you!"

What did he mean? She was hardly a warrior; what could she possibly do?

"*Pater!*" Tears flowed down Daria's her cheeks as she watched her pater being taken away. Ikarria had just lost its king.

The books, she realized. Daria had wondered why her pater had been reading so profusely the past year. She even remembered the random excursions he took with his soldiers. Gods, he had been searching for the dragons that entire time.

The ultimate weapon against their enemies.

She turned to face Ares. Shame burned her cheeks as she felt the eyes of her pater's court on her.

The skin on his arm had peeled off and hung loose, while his raw flesh bubbled in some places. The longer he waited to have it properly healed, the more those burns would scar. He would forever bear the mark of a dragon's fire.

Ares looked her over silently.

"My wounds are not the kind you would be able to see." Daria hissed.

He flinched, so quick that the others wouldn't have noticed, before that cold expression returned.

In Ares's hand was her pater's crown, the black spires dull in the torchlight. He lifted it with one hand for all to see. "By order of the High Throne, the realm of Ikarria is now under the rule of Adrastea."

The vampires in the hall cheered. Her stomach twisted, bile

threatened to choke her. Daria glanced hopelessly at the Ikarrian court who cried out in protest and fear.

"As Idris Calderón is no longer fit to be king, Ikarria will need a new ruler. But the throne of the draconic realm cannot be occupied by an outsider," Ares said. He slowly turned to her. "Only those of Ikarrian blood may be crowned."

Daria shuddered as murmurs stirred around the throne room. Something flickered over the coldness of Ares's face. Something tortured. "By the will of the High Throne, under the united rule of Elios and Adrastea, Daria Calderón is crowned acting queen of Ikarria."

He placed the crown over her head. The weight of it was lighter than she expected, but the sensation she had always imagined she would feel wasn't there. The honor that was supposed to come with this moment—stolen.

Anger unfurled inside her. She spat at the floor by Ares's feet. "I will take back what is mine."

The soldier behind her shoved her to the ground. Her knees slammed against the marble. "Stay down, Your Highness," he mocked.

Daria didn't have the chance to blink before Ares moved. She felt the spray of something wet splatter over her dress.

Ares stood beside her, holding the head of the soldier in the palm of his hand. The vampire's body slowly slid down the dais, his chest punctured through, neck torn apart.

The general's gaze coasted over the rest of the vampires before he let the head slip from his hand, and it rolled down the throne's steps. "If any one of you touches her, you will meet the same fate."

The vampires bristled at the words but said nothing. It was only Silas who looked pleased at the bloodshed. He folded his arms. "There is King's Matías's favorite."

Daria's heart thumped wildly. She wasn't sure if she felt disgust or astonishment. Perhaps the latter.

Then the world fell silent. She recognized it as she dragged her gaze to the obsidian throne. It began to whisper. Speaking to her, reaching for her. Daria couldn't—her hands clenched—she couldn't decipher it.

The voices—there were so many—spoke a language that was not her own. A rumble echoed beneath her feet. No one could hear or feel the presence. Only she.

Daria Calderón stared at the throne of Ikarria. Her heart echoed with the roars she heard. She would play this game. She would entertain those who had ravaged her home.

Her black dress glided over the marble floor as she turned to face the vampires and her beaten court. She inhaled deeply and sat on the throne. A vow seared through her heart and into the fires bestowed upon her. Flames lit every torch as they flared to the high ceilings.

Some soldiers shouted in fear, while others raised their weapons. Ares watched her attentively, something igniting in his eyes. There was a different sort of pain anytime she looked his way, but she could not afford to dwell on it.

The dragons. She would find them and bring them home. It was a simple truth that burned within her soul.

Queen Daria Calderón would see her kingdom unfurl its wings, unsheathe its talons and reveal its teeth.

The Continent of Ribera would remember the flames that were born within this realm.

Ikarria would rise again.

SEVENTY-ONE

The Elios coliseum loomed before Zara. After a torturous week, she had been instructed to head here. To think it would all come down to this place, where she'd had to bare her bloodied soul to her family. It was laughable.

The sky turned gray, hiding the setting sunlight. It was too silent for her liking. Not that it mattered. He was expecting her. Ever since she had taken Hakim and Eshe's bodies to be burned at the mercenary temple, this moment was all she could think about. She had hoped to be able to find the other guilds, to tell them what occurred, but they were nowhere to be found.

Many things held little importance to her now. All she could see was her mercenary family's death. All she could see was red.

Her knuckles tightened around the rope in her hands and she yanked on it. Ronan jerked forward, stumbling beside her. He spat a wad of blood and groaned. His skin was bruised with a small array of cuts all over his body. One of his wings even looked bent.

Zara looked at him sidelong. "Poor head of the Sombra Quarter."

Ronan swallowed and kept his gaze downcast. He hadn't even looked at her all this time. Especially not after what she had planned. Good. It was better that way.

They entered the arena. Elios guards—archangels—were posted

throughout the seats of the coliseum. She couldn't tell if they recognized the male she was dragging in. Her focus was on Axar who was kneeling on the execution platform.

The same stage where she had killed the elven male. She briefly wondered how innocent that prisoner had been. If he was simply fighting for a better life, and she had ended it before he even had a chance.

All the lives that rested on her callused palms. They would haunt her for the rest of her days.

Raziel stood beside Axar, wings spread like rays of bronze. He also wore his alabaster crown and gleaming armor. For a moment, she was almost flattered. The High King had made so much effort for her arrival.

That cold mask she had always worn as the Rogue slid over her face. It used to click with a cold familiarity, but now she was repulsed by it. Zara stepped behind Ronan and kicked him in the back. The archangel fell on his knees, wings splayed out awkwardly.

Those silver eyes glared at her. "Stop it Horizon, don't do this"

Zara ignored him and stared at the High King. Her hood was drawn over her head, hiding her cold fury. She spread her arms and allowed her voice to drip with that dry, ruthless humor Raziel was familiar with. "Behold, the leader of the shadow markets."

Raziel slowly cocked his head, observing the archangel. His golden eyes flared with recognition. "So you do live, son of Elijah and Miriam."

Ronan stiffened, and she tried to ignore how her stomach twisted at his reaction. He flipped his hair off his face, breathing heavily through his anger. "Fuck you, Raziel. I beat you once before, I will gladly do so again."

That piqued her curiosity. The High King laughed. "When did you win? From what I recall, I've always emerged victorious, and you were either in chains or running away." His eyes slid to Zara, then. "Rogue, you and I have so much to catch up on. You've brought me a great prize indeed."

"No." Ronan struggled to his feet, his hands tied in front of him. "Please, Zara. I beg you."

Her lips curled into a snarl. "Quiet."

Zara swept out a leg, knocking him off his feet. She pounced on him, unhitched a dagger, and let it hover above his collarbone. Her cold gaze met his. "I care for nothing. Not anymore."

Something in his expression shifted. No, something in his expression *broke* at her words.

She slowly stood and turned to face Raziel. He looked amused at the altercation, but she only growled at him. "I did what you asked. Now let Axar go."

Zara was closer to the execution platform now. Axar stared at her with wide eyes. A gag had been shoved in his mouth, and she could see how damaged his body was. They had beaten him, badly. Fury simmered through her veins. He tried to say something, the words coming out muffled, but she returned her focus to Raziel.

She bent to one knee and bowed her head. "All my life I have served you. I tried to believe otherwise, but the truth is that I am not of any realm. If it means the safety of those I care for, then I will yield to you, High King Raziel."

There was a sharp breeze as Raziel flew toward her. "I am pleased to see you've come to your senses." He landed and extended a pale hand. "I imagine that fyrebrand has been hurting you for quite some time. Let me relieve the pain, as now you will be mine."

She rose to her feet and extended her arm. The High King unlaced the bracer and froze, the leather piece falling to the dirt with a light thud. Yet, it seemed to be the loudest sound in the arena.

Raziel blinked. Once. Twice. Anger and disbelief cracked through the casual demeanor he always wore as he stared at the bare patch of skin among her intricate tattoos.

Zara began to smile, tendrils of red smoke rising from her body. "The fyrebrand is gone. You no longer have power over me."

His brows furrowed. "*How?*"

Zara would never forget that godsforsaken morning in the temple. She had unleashed her ether on Ronan, felt the rush of power collide with an unseen wall. Zara had pushed farther into the void, the barrier beginning to break, and the answers that had been there all along had floated through her mind.

Ether-laced bindings can be broken by their creator's will or death. The alternative is by the ether of a—

Zara had understood Ronan's intention. So she had attacked him, had allowed all her rage to bleed through her ether.

Ronan had welcomed it, despite the excruciating pain. As her power burned through him, he screamed and screamed. It was something she never wanted to do again. As that unseen wall grew weaker, Ronan's eyes began to glow. Her own power had thinned, and he snatched her wrist. The way he had moved—animalistic and lethal.

His own energy sank its teeth into her. How potent the weight of it was. She had tipped her head back as it spread like wildfire and shattered the fyrebrand.

Now, Zara smiled at the High King. At the male who had toyed with her life. "I understand why you were so obsessed with my ether." Raziel's face paled as red and purple flames flickered along her skin. Her hair lifted with its force. "It is because I have the power of a Primordial."

Daria and Ares had discovered the answer all that time ago. They simply thought it was impossible.

Until Ronan had seen the force of her ether and recognized it—because it was like his own.

A wave of dawn flames exploded from her hands. It collided against Raziel, sending him careening into the stands. Zara didn't have to turn to know that Ronan had broken from his binds with ease. That he'd spun to his feet, pressing his back against hers. That he would have been flashing his teeth in a wicked grin before unleashing the ether he had reunited with.

Spears of light, a powerful blend of the deepest blue and blood-red orange, similar to the colors of her ether, struck the arena. Ronan blasted soldiers into sprays of blood, striking down the wall of the coliseum like a crack of lightning.

Yes, the mercenary and the archangel had saved each other.

Freed one another from their own binds.

A crack formed along the wall, the ground rumbling as the stone peeled away. Rocks tumbled, forming enormous clouds of dust. His ether had done that, had completely broken down a part of the coliseum.

Ronan leaned back to speak to her. "I didn't realize you were such a good little actress."

Zara smirked. She knew if she had arrived without him, Raziel would have killed Axar. They had to *sell* the act, making it look believable. "You are not so bad yourself. Pretending your wing was broken was a touch of genius."

Elios soldiers began to soar down the arena. Zara leapt in cracks of light, snapping in and out of existence from one place to the next, slashing and evading any archangel that approached her as she got closer to the execution platform. She was keenly aware of Ronan attacking the rest of the soldiers, trying to give her time to free Axar.

When she snapped off her brother's binds and removed the gag, he slumped against her, pressing his face into the crook of her neck. "I told you not to come for me."

Axar's voice was so rough. Torn. He had been screaming for gods knew how long. Her body trembled with rage as she helped him to his feet. "I won't lose you too."

An archangel dove toward them. Zara pushed Axar out of the way just as the soldier slammed into her, sending them both rolling across the arena. The massive clouds of dust that Ronan's destruction had created still thickened the air. She could see the glint of the soldier's armor coming closer to her.

He raised his sword, ready to strike her down, when wings appeared between them.

Red wings.

Tamaya of the Elios guild stood before her, holding the soldier off with her own blade. Zara froze at the sight of the mercenary who had attacked her in the Machai Forum now protecting her. The archangel glanced at her, still with that usual glare. "You better make this worth it, Santos."

Zara nodded, snapping out of her stupor, and pushed herself to her feet. She couldn't comprehend what she was seeing. The guilds would never have intervened on High Throne business unless they believed in her cause. The only explanation that made sense was that Ronan had something to do with this. And if Tamaya was here, then that must have meant—

Sounds of steel and ether echoed from outside the broken wall of the coliseum. She saw the rippling cloaks of white and red as the mercenaries of the Continent emerged from the clouds. The guilds of Adrastea and Elios—even Kairos—unleashed themselves upon the High King's forces.

Something in her chest lifted at the sight, the corners of her eyes pricked with tears. Ronan landed before her, his expression solemn. "You told me of his dream."

His. Hakim's. All the mercenaries united once more. To bare their silver teeth against a common enemy.

If only he could see this.

Ronan had done this. Zara felt her throat thicken with emotion. There had been little to no time to understand everything she was feeling. Especially when it came to the beautiful archangel standing before her.

But this. She was grateful for this.

"Thank you," she whispered.

Ronan gave a slight bow of his head. "Take Raziel down. I will fight with the others."

Ether flared from her body at the name. Without a second glance, light sent her soaring across the arena. More soldiers came at her in an attempt to block her from the High King, who was fending off other mercenaries. She danced with her flames, driving her blades through armor and bone.

When the last soldier fell, there was an opening. She launched into the air, colliding with the High King, and they crashed onto the execution platform.

Raziel rolled to his feet and swung his sword to the side. "You may have figured out what your ether is, but you do not know its lineage."

Zara growled. "I know all I need to."

"Come now, Rogue. You are thinking too small. I can help you."

She roared, letting a column of her ether charge at him. Raziel dodged the attack, hovering above the ground.

He smirked. "Sloppy."

Their blades clashed again and again. Zara had never seen how much of a fighter the High King could be. He met every strike and counterstrike. She was mindful of her ether, how little control she had over it, its strength coming out in spurts.

Raziel was still grinning, like the fight invigorated him. "It is admirable what you've done so far. Too bad it is all in vain."

Zara tried not to listen as she drowned herself in their battle. The High King crossed his sword with hers, blocking it, and leaned in. "As we speak, Ikarria is being taken by the Adrastean army."

Her grip faltered and he took the opportunity to push forward, causing her to stumble a few steps back. Raziel's face darkened. "The Adrastean guild may have betrayed the High Throne, but they are not the kingdom's armies. Why do you think you haven't seen any other vampire in this arena? Ikarria will no longer be an independent realm. It is now *mine*—just as you will be."

No.

Not her home.

Daria. Idris. Her family. They had left Elios. She had believed they were safe.

The High King pursed his lips. "How sad. You've already lost so much, Zara."

A pained cry escaped her lips. No longer would this male have such a hold over her. Her fyrebrand had been destroyed, but it was still not enough. She needed to end it all.

Her dawn light roared into the air, it ripped through the seams of the world, and she latched onto its strength. The colored flames surged her forward and she clashed with Raziel's blades, appearing only inches in front of him.

The High King jerked forward a moment. He parted his lips, looking at her as if in question before glancing down between them. Both of her blades were wedged deep within his torso.

Zara's lips curled as her power burned brighter and angrier. "You say this was my fault."

Ether engulfed her body, following the length of the blades. Raziel breathed heavily through his nose as his death neared. As Zara leaned in.

"No," she whispered. "This was *your* doing. I am the monster you created."

Flames roared, barricading them from the outside world. Raziel could no longer bite back his guttural cries of pain as Zara's strength began to burn him.

"You have broken me," she seethed. "But I will be remade."

Death had followed her, had prowled beside her, a loyal beast. All her life she had been commanded when to raise her blades and at whom.

But this death—this death was at her will. She poured all her anger, her hurt, her fear into her ether.

Raziel managed to latch on to her arm. His eyes went to the seats surrounding them, and she followed his gaze. Between the tongues of fiery light she could see the Council standing throughout the coliseum, their glowing eyes on them.

"It seems my use has worn out," he choked out.

Zara looked back at him then, but Raziel only offered her a wicked grin. The archangel tried to push against her even as he burned. She released a war cry as her ether cracked the execution platform beneath their feet. The flames swallowed them both, and the High King roared.

She watched as her ether devoured him. His flesh peeled off bone as he thrashed in her grasp.

It wasn't enough.

Tears streaked down her face and the ethereal fire spiraled out, lashing out toward the coliseum stands. Within the heartbeat of her fires, she could feel Hakim and Eshe. Their presence surrounded her, offering their strength and love.

Hakim's voice was clear, as if he stood right next to her. "You are *more*."

Warmth gathered over her shoulders as her mind conjured the image of Eshe holding her. "Show him, little warrior, show him who you are."

Zara cried out, a sound that wrenched her heart. Her power was all-consuming, devouring the ground and sky. Until the High King was nothing but ash at her fingertips.

She wouldn't have seen the Horizons looking down and watching as the three suns between a pair of wings faded from their wrists. As the realization settled—they had been freed.

Slowly, her ether sank back into her. Raziel's remains fluttered in the air. Somehow, the alabaster crown survived and lay discarded among the debris.

The coliseum was silent. Everyone had stopped their fight to see the end of the High King. She had done it, she had avenged Hakim and Eshe.

There was no swelling sense of victory, only an emptiness that terrified her even more.

Zara looked up. Many of the seats and stone walls of the coliseum were damaged, but the Council remained. As if they were waiting.

She suddenly remembered Raziel's last words.

A familiar figure appeared.

Zara sighed in relief. "Where have you been?"

The white-winged archangel walked through the broken pieces of the execution platform and plucked the alabaster crown from the ground.

Zara could only watch as he placed the crown on his head.

Erebus looked at her, the skin between his brows pinching slightly. As if what was about to happen pained him.

"I'm sorry, Zara."

SEVENTY-TWO

Zara did not recognize the male standing in front of her. The Hand of the King was not the same archangel she had spent time with all these years. The air hummed like there was another presence that shadowed him.

Her body trembled, her bones ached. She had overdone it with her ether, and there was little she would be able to do if the deities decided to attack.

Ronan landed beside her, his fingers brushing against her arm. "Are you alright?"

Erebus staggered back. His eyes went wide. "Ronan?"

Ronan stiffened, a ragged breath leaving his lips when he turned. He pushed himself in front of Zara. "Erebus."

The Hand of the High King blinked as if he couldn't believe what he was seeing. "But you're—you're dead."

"I can assure you that I am not."

What in the *fucking* Suns?

Erebus released a sharp breath, and Zara could've sworn he almost sounded relieved. Even though he was at a distance, the archangel reached out a hand, but stopped. "How did you survive? Where have you been all this time?"

Ronan took a step toward him, his face etched in anguish. "I don't think that really matters right now. What have you *done?*"

Erebus, the only ally Zara thought she had in Elios, began to sneer. "I am finishing what I started all those years ago."

"The specters," Ronan murmured. "That was you. You summoned them."

Erebus scoffed and stepped over the ashes of the High King. "I did more than that. I created *everything* you see before you. The High Throne and the Council were my doing. During the War of the Skies, the rebelling deities and I had . . . a common goal."

Zara watched the archangel, her legs weakening. "What common goal?"

Erebus tapped the crown on his head. "I told you that the Primordials were selfish creatures. They fed on the natural ether of our mortal world—it gave them power, and they kept it to themselves. So, for us to obtain a world without the gods, I had to make a deal."

Ronan snarled. "Those were all lies and you know it. The Primordials maintained balance in our mortal world. We need them just as much as they need us."

White wings snapped out. "I see your ideals haven't changed. The Primordials have wronged us—they have wronged *me.*"

Ronan flinched, his hands curling at his sides. "I know you have suffered, Erebus. I told you to wait for me, I was going to help you—"

"You said you and I were going to change things between us and the gods. I waited and waited, but that change never came. *You* failed me." Erebus's expression smoothened. "So I had to go another way. To a power that even the Primordials shied away from, had gone so far as to banish her."

"You didn't. Tell me you didn't."

Erebus's eyes brightened. He unsheathed his sword as he stalked toward him. "I made a deal with the very Primordial who was once loved by the Three Sun Gods, the goddess who is despised and feared by all."

She was once revered and now hated . . . Zara recognized the story. It was not often shared, but it was common knowledge that there had been a betrayal amongst the gods. They'd had their own conflict when the mortal world was still young.

A sickening sensation twisted in her stomach.

Ronan's face went pale. "Khaos, the Primordial of Fate and Time. You bound yourself to her."

"We found a likeness in each other," Erebus said, pale smoke curling from his skin. "She has her own vengeful desires against the Primordials, and I am her blade. Khaos gave me access to an army, and I was blessed with a strength that surpasses that of a deity."

A blast of light sent Ronan rolling across the ground. Zara shouted and tried to move but her knees gave out. Gods, her body was failing her.

Erebus strode toward Ronan, curling his lips in disgust. "While you were hiding in the slums, I climbed toward power. One day, I will be remade into a Primordial."

Ronan spat out blood as he slowly got to his feet. "That is impossible."

"Of course, because you are the *chosen* one. You were given that birthright. Not me."

"That is not what I meant," Ronan seethed.

Erebus shrugged. "Nothing is impossible, I believe you said that to me once."

It was no wonder how the rebelling deities had managed to defeat Celestrea. They'd had the backing of a *Primordial*. Not just any god—but the goddess of Fate and Time, one of the first ethereal beings to exist, who had woven the cosmos and had once stood beside the Three Sun Gods.

Zara couldn't even fathom how Erebus managed to contact such a creature. She felt a deep sense of dread. There was something darker, crueler happening within the Continent.

Zara struggled toward them, falling to her hands and knees. "How does removing the Primordials from our world help Khaos?"

Erebus's gaze slid to her. "You were never one to know your histories, my dear Zara. The Primordials imprisoned her lover Deimos when he grew angry at the mortal world for not worshiping him and amplified their own dread and terror. He sought to punish them, but the other gods and goddesses stopped him. As a repercussion, Khaos created the Spirits of the Midnight Sun. She is Fate, and she designed the end of the world."

He prowled toward her, wings rustling. "When the Gates collapsed, nature ran its course and they were summoned. They act by their own will, but they heed the call of their Creator. When the Spirits arrived, they came to me, whom they call the Fallen, to uphold my Primordial's end of the bargain. They are preparing my armies of specters. Ethereal warriors are claiming mortal souls as we speak, while the Spirits hunt down those who are ether-born."

Ronan groaned from somewhere behind her, but Zara didn't dare look back. Understanding dawned on her. "You mean those who hold an ethereal bloodline."

He grinned. "Exactly. Deities have been wandering this world for thousands of years—of course they birthed children. Those descendants are a . . . power source to my goddess. She needs their ether to return to the mortal world. The Spirits have been reaping the ether-born—they call them their *children*—so that Khaos may return."

"What does Khaos plan to do exactly? Where is she?"

Erebus crouched before her, ignoring her questions. "Raziel's offer to have you at his side was at my request. I was the one who sensed your potential. The High King was a part of our rebellion all those years ago, and he played his role as tyrant well. He was a means to an end. A beautiful distraction for the Continent while I served the Primordial. And he really seemed *fascinated* by you, Zara."

She had been so blind, played like a fool. For so long she had believed Raziel was her enemy, when her true villain had been beside her all those years. Every time he smiled at her, every time he walked about the mercenary temple with her, every time he *slept* with her.

"You lied to me," she whispered, something in her heart shattering all over. "All this time."

Something like regret flashed over Erebus's face and he cupped her chin. "Be at my side, Zara. You and I can create our own world. One we'll have *true* power over."

She shuddered. "What happened to you?"

The shine in his blue eyes seemed to still. "I suppose you can ask the archangel you've been working with about that."

Ronan suddenly collided against him with a blast of his ether, shoving him away. *"Don't touch her."*

Erebus staggered back and wiped at his mouth, silver light crackling along his white wings. He watched as Ronan helped her to her feet, as he held her face in his hands.

Erebus's eyes jumped between them before settling on Zara. Something pulled at his expression. "I see now." He glared at Ronan. "I hope you won't fail her as you did me."

"I'm sorry," Ronan breathed, pain etched along his face as he clutched a hand to his chest. "I did fail you when you needed me. But you have already punished me, Erebus. You fought me, brought deities to my home *knowing* how it would affect my Primordial power. You knew I had little control over it and you still forced me into a battle." He winced, fighting for air. "My ether killed—*I* killed my family."

Blood drained from Zara's face, her heart shattering into pieces. His family? Her gaze went to the scar on Ronan's mouth. Erebus had done that to him.

"You had it all!" Erebus roared. "You were destined to have the power of a Primordial—while I had *lost* everything. I did what I had to do to get my retribution."

Ronan cried out in anguish, reliving the pains of his past, receiving its lashings. "I loved you like a brother."

Erebus's eyes seemed to glisten. "I did too. But it is too late. I *will* finish what I started."

The sky darkened above them. Zara felt cold droplets splat on her cheeks. Her heart pounded even louder as the rain began to fall.

Erebus raised his arms, and a voice echoed in the coliseum.

"Where are my children?"

The Spirits of the Midnight Sun stepped through the veil, materializing on either side of Erebus. The mummified woman placed her hands on Erebus's shoulders, her milky eyes scanning the bloodshed before them. The other two Spirits unsheathed their weapons, and the skeletal warrior with the scythe faced Zara.

Zara stumbled into Ronan, fear latching onto every limb and bone in her body.

Erebus spoke as if addressing the world. "I am the High King. The Horizons of the Continent are traitors to the throne. Ronan, the lost king of Damalis, lives. He and Zara Santos are to be captured and brought to me."

The Spirits charged them. Ronan summoned a wall of his ether, it rose like a wave of dusk light, blocking them. He faced Zara. "Take Axar and run. The mercenaries and I will hold their forces long enough for you to escape."

She hissed. "I will not."

"Your ether is tired and we cannot win against the deities and the Spirits. Not right now. Once we've held them off long enough, I will follow you."

She breathed through her nostrils. "Where do we go?"

"My home. My *true* home."

Damalis.

Zara wasn't sure why he had told her to flee to a broken realm, but anything was better than in Elios. She could only nod before diving into the arena. Ronan's ether roared behind her, the coliseum flashing in brilliant colors.

Erebus shouted after her, but she ran and ran. The mercenaries picked soldiers off, clearing a path for her. Axar had shifted into his wolf form and barreled toward her. His snout nudged at her side, flinging her onto his back.

"Run, Axar." Her hands gripped his fur as he sprinted out of the coliseum and into the inner district of Soleira. "To Damalis."

SEVENTY-THREE

The outer district was long behind them. They didn't have to fight their way through the capital—word had yet to spread of what happened in the coliseum. Zara wasn't sure what would come of it.

The Spirits and the specters had been unleashed. She wondered if the ethereal beasts would consume all of Elios, but she doubted it. Erebus had had the power to do so for some time and hadn't. He was dragging out his plan, solidifying his control of the Continent through supposed alliances with the other realms.

Eventually, the Continent would know of the new king who had taken Raziel's throne.

And Ikarria.

Her home had been overthrown. She had wanted to tear through the woodlands toward it, but Axar convinced her otherwise. They were in no position to lead an attack against armies of vampires. Zara hated it. Hated *them*.

All of those who had brought their civil war with the Primordials into the mortal world. The deities did not care what their battles wrought. They were willing to drag every mortal into their affairs, all to banish the gods and have their power for themselves.

They had first gone to the mercenary temple of Elios. Zara had barreled through the stables to Río. After all she had lost, she was not going to leave her warhorse behind. Seeing Hakim and Eshe's horses waiting in their stalls had her heart aching.

The grief would never leave, she knew, but it pierced through her then. She wasn't sure how long she stood there until Axar stepped in. He whispered something before setting their guild's horses free. They would no longer have to bear the burden of riding with the mercenaries.

Zara kept atop Río as Axar sprinted beside them. They blazed through the Estrella Territories, hardly stopping. The High Throne would send soldiers after them soon enough, and they needed to put as much distance between them as possible.

Days bled together—Zara wasn't sure how many had passed.

She sat in front of a fire, Río ambling close by. She stared at his yellow pelt, kissed by the starlight, as he grazed the strips of grass. They were now within the northern parts of the Ikarrian forest. Seeing the ancient trees gave her some comfort, a sense of home, until she remembered the danger her sister and pater were in.

She gazed at the massive branches and could've sworn she saw her guild within those leaves.

Axar sat beside her. He had hardly left her side, as if afraid to take his eyes off her. She found herself feeling the same way. A sense of paranoia had grown since leaving Elios, like the darkness of the night could steal him away from her any moment.

Under the solace of the stars was when their heartache would find them.

"This region looks more jungle than forest," Zara observed.

Axar had been staring at the flames. He hadn't spoken much since she'd freed him. She hadn't asked what happened during his time as a prisoner. Zara didn't trust what she would do if she knew.

"It is because we are reaching Damalis's borders," he responded.

His voice was rough and cracked. The light in his hazel eyes had dimmed and the skin on his face had sunken. The sight of her brother like that caused her chest to constrict. Axar was in pain. They both were.

She inhaled the scent of burning wood and damp grass. "We have never gone this far. There was hardly a reason to, there is no civilization beyond this point."

"Except there is. A kingdom still lives. I am curious as to how Ronan managed to maintain his realm all this time."

The thought of the archangel sent a confusing rush of emotions through her. He had still not arrived. She didn't want to acknowledge the fear that brought her.

Axar nudged her arm. "He will find us."

Zara lowered her gaze. "I do not know how I feel."

Among the grief, there was a thick sense of guilt. She had been with the archangel, writhing with him in bed, feeling pleasure and even happiness, while her guild was in danger. They had needed her, and she hadn't been there.

The back of her eyes burned. She knew it wasn't Ronan's fault, but that torment still resided inside her.

Her eyes found the empty space among her tattoos where the fyrebrand had once been. She still couldn't fathom that she no longer held the ether-laced tattoo—it was all she had known for most of her life. No longer would she have to feel its burn, no longer would she have to serve a corrupted king.

Though, it felt as if she had finished one battle only to be thrown into another one.

"Time."

Zara looked up to see Axar gazing at the Ikarrian trees. There was a faint sheen of silver lining his eyes. She wondered if he could see their guild within the leaves too.

"In time," he whispered. "You will understand and make peace with what you feel."

She looked back at the campfire. Wood cracked and spat embers into the air. Horned owls sang out with the nighthawks. Leaves rustled and branches stretched.

"What happened back in the coliseum? I have never seen such power from you, Zara."

Zara felt Axar's curious gaze on her. She took a deep breath. "After Raziel took you, my ether had a sudden *awakening*, I suppose. Ronan recognized it as the power of a Primordial."

The shifter gaped at her. "If that is the case, then wouldn't you have always been able to remove the fyrebrand from yourself?"

She shook her head. "Though mine wasn't an ether-binding tattoo like the one he bore, Ronan suspected the fyrebrand still affected my power's growth. My ether was nevertheless getting stronger but, since my ink had already been placed, I wouldn't have been able to remove the fyrebrand myself. I needed another's power."

Zara remembered the conversation she'd had with the archangel after she had broken his ether-binding tattoo. Ronan had then released his power onto her. The energy of his ether was untamed, vast and surreal in ways her mind couldn't comprehend. It had left them both gasping for air, crackling stars flickering over their bodies.

"And Ronan was the answer," she whispered, finally looking at Axar. "Once I freed him, he freed me."

Axar stared at her with a touch of awe. "And you freed the Horizons."

Her throat bobbed.

"Hakim would be so proud of you."

She leaned into him. "We made oaths, you and I. We are in this together."

"We are stars made by the Suns."

The words he had said when they first joined the guild. They wrapped around her with warmth and comfort. Zara's gaze went back to the trees, to the lights shining above them.

It was then that she recalled Hakim's words. *We are Horizons. We rise and fall like the sun, but we never die.*

Zara was starting to understand. For even when their bodies became dust and starlight, souls weaving into the veils of the world, their memory would live.

Hakim and Eshe would live on, beyond the horizons of the world.

The edge of the Ikarrian forest opened onto a valley of destroyed land. Nature seemed to have healed some of the terrain where patches of grass and wildflowers grew from the ground. Thin strips of water coursed through the valley. Mist curled all over the land, a glimpse of what looked to be broken towers appearing farther in the distance. Discarded helmets and breastplates were scattered along mounds of dirt, waiting for their owners' return. Evidence of destruction still lingered.

"Gods," Axar breathed. "*Damalis's border. This probably happened during the War of the Skies.*"

They continued deeper into the desolated city, unable to see what awaited beyond it through the mist. They came across buildings with white stucco walls and red clay roof tiles, some still preserved, some in shambles. She could only imagine what this place had looked like before the War.

How far did the destruction go? Ronan was ruling over nothing.

Axar tilted his head. A rumble in his throat. "*Something is coming.*"

Zara snapped Río's reins. "Run. Who knows how far Elios's forces have traveled. We cannot risk being caught."

They ran, stumbling over rocks and terrain and almost colliding with buildings and fountains as the mist held the town's remains hostage. When they reached the city's border, the mist lifted slightly to reveal a jungle. Her lips parted at the sight of vines and canopies. Zara didn't know there were trees bigger than those of the draconic realm.

Where in the gods' name were they?

There was the sound of beating wings. In her mind, all she saw was Raziel. It was ridiculous. She knew he was dead, and yet it didn't stop her from urging Río to run faster, her heart pounding in her ribs. He galloped between thick trees, leaping over roots. He managed to slide his powerful body down a slope as Axar flanked them. Sunlight streaked through his fur making him into a shard of steel. Desperation and fear caused them to claw mindlessly through the wilderness.

As they fled, Zara caught flickers of blue in her peripherals. Her heart raced as chaneques appeared on either side of them. The water sprites morphed into their humanoid shapes as they kept pace.

Axar looked stunned. "*I didn't think we'd see them again.*"

A chaneque floated closer to Zara, and she recognized it as the same elemental who had interacted with her before. The creature brushed a hand against her cheeks, a sweep of sadness with a twinge of hope along with it.

Zara's heart pulled, feeling the drumming of Río's hooves beneath her. "Can you help us?"

The chaneque made a chirping sound and dove ahead of her. The other water sprites followed, a swarm of blue orbs and reflecting light. Zara held on to the reins, flanking the group of chaneques. They soared between thick trunks and plants. She didn't care where they were headed, so long as they could get farther away from whoever was coming toward them.

The water sprites suddenly dispersed into the wilderness, except for the one Zara knew. The chaneque drifted past her, giving her one last touch on her cheek before disappearing in the leaves.

Zara felt a pang of loss. "Wait!"

Río threw back his head, rising onto his hind legs. Zara's hand flew to her dagger but stopped when she saw what stood in front of them.

Piercing eyes. Gleaming fangs.

The black wolf watched them among the jungle's trees and greenery. Axar skidded to stop beside them. His hairs bristled as he growled a warning, but the wolf did not move.

She kept her eyes on the beast. "You see it too?"

"*Do you mean the wolf? Yes, Zara. I can fucking see it.*"

A brittle laugh escaped her. "Good. I've been seeing this one for quite some time now. Thought I was going crazy."

The wolf swung its head to the side and turned, taking a few steps into the jungle. It glanced back at them, swinging its head again in the same direction. Bright eyes landed on her, and it was only then that Zara noticed an iridescence of blue and green around the wolf's black mane. It oddly reminded her of feathers.

"I think it wants us to follow," Axar said.

Zara hesitated. Time and time again this wolf had visited her and done nothing. Now it felt like it wanted to help. Her grip tightened on the reins. "So be it."

The wolf leapt over roots and darted between vines, guiding them deeper into the realm of Damalis. It climbed up a slight slope, disappearing within a thick line of plants. Zara slid off Río to lead him upward.

Axar shifted into his human body, fighting to catch his breath. "I wonder where it is taking us."

As they pushed up the slope, there was a ripple in the air. The sky seemed brighter, the air cleaner. Energy thrummed in her veins. There was something different to this place. Nothing like the wasteland that had greeted them before. This was not the Damalis that the Continent knew of.

Zara had nearly reached the top when an arrow whistled by, slamming into the wood beside her head. She only had time to unsheathe her dagger when she met the jaws of a giant jaguar.

She stumbled back into Axar. "Shit!"

Río shrieked at the jaguar, which was the size of a horse. The beast snarled, revealing large fangs. Atop it was a woman with elven ears. She wore a mask that covered the lower half of her face, depicting a skinless human jaw and teeth. Her curly hair was the color of sand, her skin a golden brown.

The woman's green eyes gleamed with suspicion as she pointed a spear toward them. "Who are you?"

Her accent held the same melodic roll as Ronan's. Zara recognized it now as a Damalisan.

She wasn't sure what had happened to the wolf they were following, but she couldn't take her eyes off the warrior atop the jaguar. The elf's weapon was made of midnight blue steel. Zara's jaw slackened.

The guardian realms were known for their unique bladework. The mercenary's grip on her dagger threatened to falter.

But she raised her blade, Axar tensing beside her. Ether whispered about his skin as he prepared to shift once more.

Wings thumped above them—behind them. Ronan slammed into the ground. His wings unfurled as he slowly straightened. Zara exhaled, relieved to see him, even tempted to take a step toward him. Her eyes scanned his body to see no grave wounds, but he did look exhausted.

His gaze landed on her first, running along her body as if he were doing the same. After a moment, he raised a hand to the warrior. The elf's eyes widened and she lowered her weapon.

The archangel gestured to her with a small yet exhausted smile. "Don't mind her, she is a warrior of Damalis."

Axar cursed under his breath. "Fucking Suns."

Zara couldn't move. She returned her gaze to the woman and jaguar as she spoke to Ronan. "Where have you been?"

He stalked toward her. "Soldiers followed us through the Estrella Territories, but I managed to lose them at the mists."

The archangel stopped at her side, but she didn't look his way. He towered over her, the presence of his powerful body tempting her to lower her guard. "You are safe. I promise," he whispered.

Zara steadied her breath as she slowly slid her gaze to meet his. The light in his silver eyes softened a fraction. "There is something I haven't had the chance to tell you. Follow me."

He walked past the warrior on the jaguar, pushing through the last line of plants and trees. She left Río with Axar, who kept a wary eye on the woman.

"As you know, Damalis still lives. In the years following the end of the War of the Skies, survivors came together to rebuild," Ronan said. He glanced over his shoulder. "Many from Valenzia as well."

Zara's breath caught, wondering where he was going with this.

The archangel went on, "In a way, the lands became one. The people of two realms joined together to restore the might of the guardian realms."

She jumped back when she realized they were standing along the edges of a cliff.

He gestured to the open expanse. "What you see before you is the rise of both Damalis and Valenzia."

Her lips parted. Mountains and more jungle filled the scenery in front of them, going on and on. It took her breath away. If she squinted she thought she could see small signs of civilization, of *life*.

A calmness swept over Ronan's face, his eyes softening the longer he gazed at the beauty before him. "Welcome to my home. To *our* home."

The true Damalis, the guardian realm.

And Valenzia. The kingdom of her birth was there as well.

Beyond the rolling greenery, she could see the Jade Sea, on the other side of which the remains of the Gates of Celestrea would be.

Ether hummed through her heart. It called out to the ground and sky, and the world seemed to respond in turn. Welcoming her.

Zara understood that her battles were not yet over. And how it thrilled her.

Her anger was ancient. Birthed by the abuse of false crowns and false gods. It became embedded in her blood, sinking deep within the crevices of her very being. The past was not her fault, but she had suffered from it anyway. And her present was her remaking. She was reborn, scarred by the tears and pain of those before her and her own, and she would rise. Those who had conquered these lands would be overthrown.

They would learn to fear her.

Zara Santos was *more*.

EPILOGUE

I n the realm of the forgotten, there was still life.

The sky, a never-ending twilight, hadn't changed, but the lands and its kingdoms had. Shards of the battles that had led to this realm's doom still lingered.

The fallen warrior beasts remained untouched. Their ether had gone, bleeding back into the celestial ground, their bodies turned to stone. Much of the destruction lay where the Gates had once stood. The veil never to be opened again.

And yet, there was still life.

A black wolf prowled between the tall blades of grass. It kept its nose low, sniffing at the mist of ancient powers that pulsated through the dirt. The wolf followed the rivers that sliced through the endless land until it met the mouth of a temple.

It leapt up the slabs of stone and into the entrance where shadows awaited. Silver flames sparked to life along the torches, revealing dark stone and vines.

The wolf stood at the threshold of a long chamber. It didn't dare tread inside, its presence was more than enough.

A creature sat on the throne, his body a dark hide and shadow, a face of bone.

His empty eyes began to glow silver, fingers curled around the arms of the throne. He inhaled deeply, feeling every tendril of energy that made his home. The colored feathers rippled, brushing against the decorated daggers that made his crown. Bones and teeth that hung around his neck swayed.

The Primordial of Death opened his jaws, ready to receive the setting stars, the fading souls that bled across the veil.

"Finally," Mikatán breathed. "The powers of a Primordial have been born."

ACKNOWLEDGEMENTS

I am so grateful to this book and its characters. I had drafted this beauty during some challenging times and at the end of the day when I was emotionally drained with a heavy heart, I found comfort when I returned to this world. It is incredible how our passions bring us peace and I am thankful to be able to do what I do.

Thank you to my loving parents, my mama and papa. Thank you for your constant support in all my endeavors. Both of you have been there for me in the toughest of times and I am so grateful to have you in my life. Los quiero mucho.

Thank you to my siblings, especially to Emily. My little brat, I love you. Thank you for always being a phone call away, day or night. For always cheering me on and helping me get back on my feet when I needed it the most.

Now to my editor and dear friend, Jen. You have been there from the beginning! Ever since we connected on Bookstagram, you have been my rock. To think we both shared each other's goals to become an author and editor—now look where we are! I thank the suns and stars every day that I met you. I am so thankful for you. You are incredible and deserve all the happiness and more.

Thank you to my twin flame, Dani. I cannot express enough how you light up my world. You are the best hype woman a gal could ask for, thank you for all your love and cheers. My poptart, my Dani phantom. THE DELULU IS THE SOLULU!

Thank you to mi amor, Nouha. Thank you for always checking in on me and all the talking sessions we've had. You are such a light in my life and I cannot wait to squeeze you. I am so grateful for you and I am SO proud of you.

To my loving friend, Reme. I don't think you realize how impactful your friendship has been for me. From us eating cheeseburgers and fries in the study rooms to traveling abroad together, I am so grateful for you. You lift me up when I am down and I am so lucky to have someone like you in my life. You're a badass and I cannot wait to see how you take over the world. I admire you.

Thank you to my author colleagues: Nicole, Liz, Max, Chiara, and Imani. Thank you for being such wonderful companions in the author space and for taking the time to read an early copy of *Fall of the Horizon*. You inspire me and I'm cheering you on in all your endeavors!

To my Beta readers—Dani, Caroline, Heidi, Shelby, and Max—thank you for being one of the first to read the rough draft of this book. Bless your hearts for reading this book when it was in its roughest stage. Your support means everything and I couldn't be here without your help.

A big shout out to the ARC team! I thank you all for being part of the journey and dedicating your time to read *Fall of the Horizon*. I couldn't do this without you.

Another massive thank you to Bookstagram and all my other colleagues in the best corner of the internet. This community is truly amazing and it has changed my life for the better.

And to you, the reader. I can't thank you enough for giving this book and myself a chance. I hope you were able to connect with this story and its characters in whatever shape and form that means to you. I couldn't be here without you either. Thank you, I hope we cross paths once again. Take care!

Much love, Jess.

MEET THE AUTHOR

 Jessica is a graduate of the University of California, Irvine and received her Master's Degree in Business Administration in 2022. Jessica has always been passionate about writing and has often found herself creating stories ever since childhood. When not writing, she can be found weightlifting, watching anime, playing video games, or wandering around a bookstore. She currently resides in Southern California, most likely listening to Epic music in search of creative inspiration.

www.jessicajayala.com

Instagram: @authorjessicajayala
TikTok: @authorjessicajayala